The Chronicles of the Great Neblinski

Great Neblinski

Book One - G'nome G'rown

sands press
Brockville, Ontario

The Chronicles of the Great Neblinski

Great Neblinski

Book One - G'nome G'rown

by

Mark E. G. Dorey

sands press

sands press

A Division of 3244601 Canada Inc.
300 Central Avenue West
Brockville, Ontario
K6V 5V2

Toll Free 1-800-563-0911 or 613-345-2687
http://www.sandspress.com

ISBN 978-1-990066-28-3
Copyright © Mark E. G. Dorey 2023
All Rights Reserved

For information on bulk purchases of this book or any book published by Sands Press, please call 1-800-563-0911.

To book an author for your live event, please call: 1-800-563-0911

Sands Press is a literary publisher interested in new and established authors wishing to develop and market their product. For more information please visit our website at www.sandspress.com.

TABLE OF CONTENTS

OPERATING INSTRUCTIONS

In this novel there are things to consider so that you, the reader, can get the full experience of "listening" to our heroes and other characters. Much of the dialogue in this book is written in phonetics in order to give certain characters a familiar accent so that you, the reader, will have an easier time "hearing" their voices as you read—from the stereotypical New York City cab driver to the Russian soldier, the Yiddish Rabbi, and even the Jamaican Rastafarian. Any humour directed at any individual or group is absolutely intentional and done with the deepest and most gracious appreciation to those who, in reality, actually *are* part of these groups and/or individuals. I thank you in advance and ask that you forgive any offence this story might cause you. It is certainly not intended.

Indeed, these are stereotypes and should be taken with more than a grain of salt.

Common accents were given to the characters so that the reader can feel more familiar with the heroes and relate to them better. Most of the individuals represented in these pages are not Human, and it helps us to become involved in their story if a Human persona is attached to them.

Likewise, at least one of the characters in this story has a physical handicap that is made fun of. To all of you who may suffer the same disability: *No* offense intended. I also do not wish to label anyone, or any group, as bad evil or malicious…well, all except the banks.

There are also many cases of positive ethnic stereotyping and just plain making fun of people. If you are offended by this book I strongly suggest you get some help, or smoke a joint, or do something that will mellow you out enough to realize that we all have to get along and making each other laugh is better than making each other cry.

I, the writer of this story, love all people as individuals and ask that we all have a good laugh at each other's expense. Colour, gender, and so on is all irrelevant in the long run. It is who we are inside that really counts. How we treat each other that dictates our worth in society. I, the writer, *am* a member of a racial minority group whose ancient traditions have taught me this, if nothing else.

So…mellow out and love each other. Don't stress about the small stuff that doesn't hurt anyone. There are little babies starving to death in this world so stop worrying about a joke or two already!

An original story written by:
Mark E. G. Dorey
Edited by L. A. Boire

Inspired by and written for: Max (god), Peter (Beornag), Steve (Grarr), Ian (Durik), and Roger (Raz)

INTRODUCTION

Have I got a story for you! Boy it's a good one too! It's got action, adventure, suspense, and let's not forget...hootspa!

What is hootspa you ask? Allow me to explain.

Hootspa is that energy that seems to come out of nowhere. It can be really weak or really powerful depending on who is controlling it. The Humans call it magic. The Elves call it eldritch. The Dwarves call it...well, you get the picture.

Anyway...Long, long ago, when the world was a nice place to be in, my people, the G'nomes, as opposed to our distant cousins the Gnomes, lived in an enormous machine-city made of precious metals and stones. This wonderful spectacle of a city was called Sensimilia. (That's where I was born, by the way.)

Sensimilia was actually a giant time piece designed to let us G'nomes know when to do what had to be done. As we lived deep underground, we did not have the benefit of the sun to let us know when it was time to sleep, eat, or just about anything else that was governed by time. Its great curving streets turned round and round as the mechanisms of the time piece ticked away the moments. It was a wonderful place to live except for the fact that I quite often found myself wondering if this was all there was to life.

The G'nomes had not had any contact with the outside world for thousands of years. Sure there were other kinds of underground dwelling peoples that we rarely had dealings with, such as the Molemen, who ventured to Sensimilia once every two or three years to trade, but that was about it.

I had many cousins, uncles, aunts, nephews, nieces, and lots of other relatives that you Humans don't even have names for. My dad was a machinist. He tooled the many gadgets and components of the great machine-city to keep it working the way it was supposed to. He was only one of many hundreds of G'nomes who held this kind of job.

My mom made pickles in barrels made of giant mushroom stems. She also made limburger cheese the old-fashioned way...in her boots. She made the best limburger in all of Sensimilia. Folks would travel from all parts of the great city to sample dear old mom's foot cheese.

I went to school a lot. My folks wanted me to be a scholar. I studied G'nomish history, the sciences, and ancient languages among other courses. My mom wanted me to be a professor at the University of Sensimilia. This kept me quite busy (as you can imagine), but I always found time to hang out with my cousin, Abe Zeebermen.

We used to catch lethal bugs and milk them for their venom (lethal poison), out back of old man Fleshman's hive boxes. Lethal poison was one of Sensimilia's biggest exports. The Molemen purchased it on a regular basis. I think they were smoking it, but I can't be sure. We'd then sell the poison to the alchemists and get us a big bag of that fine Sensimilia herb. Then we'd hang out with the Molemen smoking our brains out, drinking cheap wine, and laughing a lot.

My mom hated that. She used to say, "Those warty, overgrown hooligans will just get you into trouble!" They never did. But that's not saying they didn't try.

Anyway…to make a really long story a little shorter, I grew up like most other G'nomish boys. I eventually moved out of the house on my one hundred and thirteenth birthday (still wet behind the ears), got a nice little place on the upper west side, and scored a really good part time job collecting firestones in the deep caves just outside of town.

Fire stones were worth a lot of money. They were used in the production of powerful magical devices as they held an enchantment forever and were practically indestructible. These were beautiful crystalline stones with a rich orange-amber colour. They glowed like little candles all on their own and the only place they could be found was in and around Sensimilia.

We G'nomes used them in the giant greenhouses to provide life giving light to the colossal herb forests which we grew there. We didn't know where the herb originally came from, or why our ancestors started to cultivate it in such copious amounts, but we continued to do so. The herb was an important part of G'nomish life. We cooked with it, refined it into clothing, made several kinds of premium wines with it, fed it to our livestock, made medicines with it, and a multitude of other uses too many to list.

I continued going to school for about thirteen hundred Human years until I finally graduated from university with master's degrees in botany, ancient history, mythology, mineralogy, and ancient languages, to name just a few. I kept my job collecting firestones and went full time. Soon I was foreman of the lower south chasm. Things were looking pretty good.

Then one day, just after my one thousand four hundred and twenty-first birthday (Human years), I was surveying a possible firestone collection site deep in a new chasm, quite a walk from my usual stomping grounds, when I was scared out of my boots by an earth-shattering explosion. (Don't worry, the earth didn't really

shatter, that's just an expression).

The ground shook with a fury and the subterranean ceiling started to collapse! I began to run for safety as best I could ('cause as I said, the ground was really shaking in a major sort of way). I didn't get very far, however, as a big rock hit me in the head and knocked me senseless.

While I was unconscious, I dreamed. I dreamed of a big, golden herb leaf and heard a really mellow yet booming voice. (If you can imagine such a thing.)

It said…and I'm not kidding you.

"*Szvirrrrf!*"

That's my name, by the way, Szvirf Neblinski.

"*Szvirrrrrf,*" he said. "*I have chosen you to deliver my worrrrrrd. Your people have forgotten me. Ages have paaaassed. I have waited for the Great Harvest, but it does not come. I have taken you and cast you far from home so that you can undertake a great and noble quessssst. In this long journey you will find clues as to my origins and my laws of connnnnduct. You must gather this wisdom and deliver it unto Sensimilia so that every G'nome will know of meeeee.*"

"Oh great," I said. "Why me, why not Hiemee, or Abe, or Bernie? Bernie'd be good. Why not Bernie?"

"'*Cause.*" His voice was mellow yet seemed to come from all directions at once.

"Ah…'cause why?" I protested.

"*Just…'cause. That's all,*" it responded.

"So…what are you, some kind of disembodied voice that only I can hear, or something?" I asked.

"*Yes,*" he replied.

"So…does this disembodied voice have a name, or should I just keep calling you disembodied voice?" I was beginning to get a little impatient.

"*Yes,*" he said.

"So what is it?!" As I said, I was beginning to get a little impatient. I tend to get that way when I'm plucked up by some sort of omnipotent, disembodied voice, hootspa'd away from home, and given a job with not so much as an interview, or letter of introduction, or something. Oy!

"*I…,*" he began.

"Yes, I'm listening," I replied.

"*Am…,*" he continued.

"Uh-huh?" I said, in anticipation.

"*Holy Shiddumbuzzin,*" he reported.

"Look, I'm not interested in your state of physical toxicity. I want to know your name," I said.

"*You do not understand. That IS my name, Shiddumbuzzin, the holy deity of the deep G'nomes,*" he explained.

"Ooooh!" I said. "Why me?"

"*'Cause,*" he replied. "*I am the creator of the G'nomes and all that is G'nomish.*"

"Really?" I asked, truly fascinated.

"*Yes,*" he said, proudly.

"Geesh, you know, for an all-mighty, omnipotent being you sure ain't much for linguistic repartee," I observed.

"*It's been a while,*" he answered with a sigh. "*Anyway…you will be the keeper of the word of Shiddumbuzzin, and the deliverer of the great laws of G'nomish etiquette.*"

"Does that mean I get two pays?" I asked, excited at the prospect of a raise.

"*No wigs,*" he responded.

"What?!" I asked. "Who said anything about wigs?"

"*You mentioned toupees,*" he said.

"Uh-huh. So what's that got to do with wigs?"

"*You're not getting any,*" he continued. "*I will, however, bestow upon thee this…*"

At that moment a big, thick, red covered book appeared out of thin air and hit me in the head. It had a solid gold lock and clasp with a jewel encrusted key.

"Ouch! What's with the book?" I protested.

"*It is not just any book.*" His voice boomed mellowly. "*It is a book of the ancient and lost arcana of the G'nomes.*"

"Isn't that the Dwarvish name for magic?" I asked defiantly. I mean... if this was truly the god of the G'nomes you'd think he'd at least use G'nomish jargon.

"*Isn't that the Human name for hootspa?*" he responded sarcastically.

"Touché," I said. "So...What do I do with it? I'm no hootspologist."

"*You read it,*" he replied.

"No kidding. A book? You're supposed to read those? Thanks for the insight." I was really getting peeved now. I mean...I spent hundreds of years reading books in school to get a lucrative job and now I was being told that I had to change careers and study all over again. What a waste of money my tuition was. My pop was going to be livid.

"*Every G'nomish eldest child is born with the power of hootspa. You have hootspa to spare! This book will help you to focus your hootspa and achieve great and wondrous results,*" he proclaimed, the importance of these words emphasized.

"Well, I guess that's good," I began, "but, what about money? You know these perilous quests can soak up a lot of dough."

"*There are treasures beyond your imagination along this path of righteousness,*" he replied.

"Okay, that's great too, but what am I supposed to do in the meantime?" I was worried. "...and, by the way...I can *imagine* quite a bit."

"*ENOUGH.*" There was nothing mellow about that response. I

think I had tested his patience at that point. *"Go now. Seek the wisdom of my words and deliver it unto your people."*

That was when I awoke to a startling discovery.

I was dangling by my hands and feet, tied to a big stick which was, in turn, hanging from between two very nasty looking creatures.

They had metallic black skin and red eyes. Their hair was as white as salt rock, they were about four times as tall as me, and they were accompanied by at least thirty others who looked just like them.

I thought that they kind of looked like Elves. But I had never seen Elves before that moment, except for pictures in books, and those were quite different from these guys.

These Elves were all dressed in black leather armour with pointy, spiky things sticking out in all directions. The ones I had seen in books all looked friendly and dressed in nice colours with no spikes.

"Hey fellas?" I began. "I think there's been some sort of mistake."

They didn't seem to pay any attention to me.

"You know…I really appreciate the lift, but I am quite capable of walking now, so…could you, maybe, let me down?" I was really getting worried as they didn't seem to give a flying frog about what I was saying.

That was when I decided that desperate times called for desperate measures. I drew in a big breath and began to scream.

"Helllp! Hellllp! I'm being mugged," I yelled at the top of my lungs. That was when I met the boys for the first time, and this is where I turn you, the reader, over to the great and holy Shiddumbuzzin so he can finish this tale of wonder and adventure!

PROLOGUE

Know this... I am Shiddumbuzzin. Holy deity of the G'nomes.

Once, long ago, when the world was a really nice place to be in, the G'nomes built great temples to honour and worship me. These temples were massive greenhouses where the G'nomes cultivated the sacred herb in the city of Sensimilia. The people of the deep world would gather in the tens of thousands to smoke of the sacred herb and celebrate life, liberty, and the pursuit of total mellowness. This was the time of Shiddumbuzzin. I was powerful and listened to the prayers of my children, the G'nomes.

The G'nomish people lived in harmony with their subterranean environment. They had no enemies. Even the dark Elves would not delve any deeper than their own underground borders. The G'nomes lived deeper in the earth than any other beings. They were safe and warm.

I placed there, next to that home, many veins of firestones which held the light and warmth of day. These the G'nomes used to give the sun's energy to the sacred herb in the greenhouses. They laboured each and every day, lovingly cultivating the tiny seeds into great sacred herb trees of such immensity as to be unlike any other tree that has ever grown since. They picked the buds of the great trees and refined them into a sticky, fibrous substance known as Sensimilia. This was the cornerstone of G'nomish culture.

But the bliss and harmony was shattered. A terrible thing occurred. Without any warning to the G'nomes, or even to me, the forces of Chaos fell upon the deep world and turned the great civilization of the G'nomes into a burning wasteland.

It seemed that Krawchich, lord of Chaos, sent his forces, the Goblins, Trolls, and other riffraff to attack the deep world as a practical joke on me.

Well I am sure you will understand my reluctance to find the humour in such a despicable action. I immediately went to see the central council of Deities Oracles Omnipotent Beings and Inter-dimensional Enchanted Societies—aka—D.O.O.B.I.E.S.

There I filed a formal complaint.

As you can no doubt imagine the council ruled in favour of myself and my followers. The result was that Krawchich would be forced to give up one tenth of his total power and that I would receive said power.

The laws of the D.O.O.B.I.E.S, however, did not specify as to what form that power would have to take. As a result, the lord of Chaos gave, to me, total control over one of his unholy antiheroes.

A hero or antihero is a being in whom a specific deity has invested a substantial amount of energy creating. They are exceptional in many ways and have the ability to improve themselves in time, to almost super-powerful status. These individuals are always one among millions. Special beyond definition. Krawchich possessed only two such beings. The youngest of which was a piteous creation of forbidden knowledge. A most terrible creature among the more wretched of the Chaos lord's many followers.

This would be my compensation. This was supposed to be justice for the G'nomes, a race of peaceful, ingenious, little people who only wanted to be left alone to enjoy their lives.

I was not pleased to say the least, and to make matters even worse, after a long and tiresome legal battle with Chaos, I returned my attention to the G'nomes who had relocated, rebuilt their civilization, and had completely forgotten about me.

You see time, for omnipotent beings, goes by much slower than it does for mortals. Four hundred and twenty thousand years (give or take a couple thousand) had passed for the G'nomes.

I immediately got back to work but my efforts were hindered by the fact that my followers weren't following me anymore. They had forgotten who I was and were worshipping deities that didn't even exist.

Inter-dimensional law clearly states that I am only allowed to reveal myself to one of my followers and hope that that individual is able to convince the rest of them that they should have faith in their deity. This *is what I got for not hiring a secretary, or a personal assistant, or something.*

I was in quite a pickle. I had no choice but to place ten percent of my own power into an individual and send him on a quest to rediscover his people's ancient heritage and deliver it to them.

His name was Szvirf Neblinski, eldest son of the house of Neblinski. Though I chose in haste, I chose well. Luck, it would seem, was with me that day. ('Bout time.)

I sent him to the surface world, on a glorious quest to find the soul of his people, but I did not send him alone. As a companion he would find the abomination of Chaos, that thing which was given to me as a slap in the face by the lord of all evil.

Szvirf was destined to be a great wizard and a worker of holy miracles, but he was barely twelve inches tall. The loathsome beast of Chaos was strong and a furious fighter. Little did I know that this expendable pawn, which I looked upon with nothing short of contempt and disgust, would rise from the very pit of evil to become the most glorious knightly warrior in all G'nomish history.

So listen well and you shall know of the legend of the **Great Neblinski***.*

"..."

"So…what are you waiting for?"

"Szvirf, you're supposed to continue telling the story."

"But I thought you were going to tell it!"

"*No, I just gave the introduction.*"

"I already did the introduction! Remember all that stuff about the life story and the setting of the scene and…Oy! What kind of omnipotent being are you? You totally schmutzed the first chapter!"

"*Well…I am new to this sort of thing. Besides story telling is more of your forté.*"

"Okay, okay. Never mind. I'll do it."

Freshwater
Mountains
Road
Hills/Steppes
Marsh/Swamp
River
Saltwater
City or Town

The Great West Road

Briarwood
Briarway

The Uldan
Mountains

Silvain
Lake

Silvain
Falls

Farms

Farmland

Farmland

Hills

The Imperial Highway

Imperial
Orchards

Marsh

The
Western
Passage

Silvain River

The Endless Sea

N

The Southwest
Road

The Imperial Capitol

CHAPTER - 1

MONSTERS?

"Help! Help! I'm being mugged!" Boy was I scared. Those dark Elves were looking to make G'nomish stew, of this, I was sure.

We were in a forest of twisted trees and thick brambles, travelling down a well worn path. The air was cool and humid, and I was as naked as a skinned pickle.

The night air was disturbingly refreshing. Just sayin'.

By some stroke of luck someone must have heard my cries for help 'cause it was just then that I noticed, in the distance, three figures approaching at a fast pace.

It was night, although I didn't realize it, as we didn't know night from day where I was from. I'm able to see really well at night, being used to a dark environment, so I quieted down, watched patiently and hoped for the best.

After a good hour the three figures burst out from behind some thick brush and immediately took to hacking and chopping those dark Elves into shrapnel.

That's when I got a really good look at them.

"Help! Help!" I screamed. "We're being attacked by three gigantic monsters! Help! Someone! Anyone!"

Holy Shiddumbuzzin they were scary looking! One of them

was enormous. He had to be twelve Human feet tall, and that was while he was crouching! He was covered with long shaggy, brownish-red fur and wore a silvery chain mail shirt. His arms were as big as trees and his knuckles dragged on the ground. He had a big nose too. Almost as big as mine! He laughed a hideously deep and resonating sound as he flayed about him with fists like boulders, sending Dark Elves flying in all directions. There, upon his mighty brow he wore...a propeller beanie?

The second was only about eight feet tall—heh, go figure—only eight feet. He was covered with rough, dark green and black skin. His head was hairless and covered with tattoos. His mouth was full of gleaming white, razor sharp pointy teeth, and his eyes glowed red like firestones in the darkness.

This monster wore a monocle in his left eye which refracted its red glow into a beam. He was also adorned in a shiny black suit of full plate armour with intricate designs all over the surface, and a black and red cape. He leapt about gracefully through the fray laying about him great arcing strokes with deadly accuracy using a double-edged sword nearly as long as he was.

The third entered the battle like a blinding flurry of steel. His scarred, burned and furrowed brow spoke of countless battles. His hair was nothing more than a black stripe that ran from his forehead to the nape of his neck, much like a strip of thin spines, or quills. His skin was a mix of mottled iridescent metal-like blues and stripes of velvet black. His eyes glowed too, but with a churning emerald light that screamed of evil.

This monster's mouth was filled with row after row of horrible fangs. Never could I have imagined such a terrifying creature as this. He hacked and chopped his way through dark Elves like a mad man possessed by demonic forces. There did not appear to be any thought to his technique. He was simply too ferocious for his enemies to be able to react with any effective results.

He wielded a sword in each hand like a killing machine. This blue terror was the smallest of the trio, only about six feet tall, but was packed with muscles not unlike sculpted steel.

Before I knew it, the whole thing was over, and the three monsters began to loot the bodies.

During the mayhem I was thrown clear of the battle and landed in a nearby bush. The monsters had not yet noticed me, so I kept still and quiet and listened. They were speaking in one of the many languages I had taken the time to learn during my many years of university—Humanese.

Although initially I was more than rusty, it came back to me soon, and I was understanding them, despite their exotic accents.

At first I was really scared. But as I listened I began to catch on to what they were saying.

"Grarr, how much did d'at Human say fer each?" the big hairy one asked with his weird accent as he began to put the Dark Elf corpses into a large sack.

"Seventy gold each," growled the tattooed one, obviously named Grarr.

"But d'at only makes twenty-one hundred t'ousand," the big hairy one complained. Obviously not a mathematician. "Ize t'ought weeze needed t'ree t'ousand." He began counting on his fingers and then his toes.

"That's *three thousand*, and yes, we do, but we can sell their belongings and get most of that," Grarr replied. "Don't worry Bud, we'll get the cash…and stop counting your toes. You don't know how to count remember?"

"Ize was t'inkin' if Ize keeps makin' like Ize is countin', soona or latuh it might come t' Ize. So Ize is gonna try for now if yooze don't mind."

Grarr rolled his eyes and continued his grizzly task of stripping and bagging the bodies.

"How much for little old man?" the insane one asked as he looked straight at me.

That was it—I would have had to change my shorts, if I had been wearing any—and if I survived.

"Little old man? What little old man?" the big hairy one asked, lumbering over in my general direction, the ground trembling with each gigantic step.

"D'is vun," the blue-skinned horror replied, pointing toward my hiding spot as the three of them were now standing right over me.

"AAAAAH!" I said. "AAAAAH!!!" I said again as all three monsters looked down at me.

"Sorry Pops," the hairy giant said apologetically. "Weeze don't speak Gnome. Could yooze rephrase d'at in Goblinese or maybe Trollish?" He squatted down and reached toward me.

"Aaaaaaah!" I said in Goblinese. "Aaaaaaaah!" I added in Trollish.

"Oh," he responded. "Ize sees d'at weeze has taken yooze completely by surprise, and d'at yooze t'inks d'at weeze is gonna hurt yooze. Well fear not, Ize's diminutive, little compatree-it, for weeze is da good guys." They all smiled, revealing their terrifying, vicious looking teeth.

That's when I fainted.

When I finally woke up, I found myself lying comfortably on a blanket, next to a small campfire by two huge tents. The pleasant smell of something cooking was in the air, and three giant, horrible monsters were sitting around staring at me.

We were still in the twisted forest, but no mangled corpses were anywhere to be seen. I was sure that these creatures must have eaten them and then I remembered the smell of something cooking...Aaaghlch!

Just as I was about to scream in Trollish the one named Beornag spoke.

"Now don't faint on weeze again, little guy. Allow Ize t' introduce Ize's self an' Ize's associates. D'is," he began, pointing at the tattooed one, "is Grarr."

Grarr nodded politely and smiled, once again showing his well-kept razor-sharp teeth. He was removing a long black fletched arrow from one of his victim's own quiver. The point seemed—*evil*. He then placed it in a pouch that seemed far too small to have been able to carry it. I watched in amazement as the arrow disappear into its confines.

"Pleased to … ah … um … make your … um … acquaintance," I replied between shivers.

"D'is ova here is Durik." He gestured toward the crazy-looking one.

"Hallo," Durik growled.

"Hello…um…Durik," I replied between a couple more shivers.

"And Ize, oh little traveller, am Beornag, Injoke o' Ulm."

"Pleasure to make your acquaintance, I'm sure," I replied in my best Humanese. "Did I hear you say that you were the…uh… good guys?"

"D'at's us! Weeze calls ourselves Warped Speed Enterprises. D'at's 'cuz weeze gets da job done fast," Beornag replied proudly.

"Job?" I asked.

"Yea. Weeze is hired swords—an' axes, an' maces, an' udduh equally devastatin' weapons—where Durik is concerned. Folks hire weeze t' rescue damsels from dragons or dragons from damsels, dish out revenge on evil wrong dowuhs, escort important dignitaries, and acquiuh rare awtifacts—d'at kind o' stuff," Beornag replied.

"I see," I said nervously.

He held up a sack and then emptied the contents onto the ground next to me. There were no corpses. "Deez must be yooze's stuff," he said.

"Thanks." I began to sort through the pile of things. Then I stopped and looked at him. "You're *not* going to eat me...right?"

He paused long enough to exchange looks with his friends and then turned back to me. "Guess not. Yooze is in da clear."

"Holy Shiddumbuzzin. Thank you," I said with a sigh of relief.

"D'ose nasty dark Elves drugged ya?" Beornag asked.

"Hunh?" I said.

"Never mind. Yooze can sleep it off. Weeze is stayin' da night. Yooze is lucky weeze found yooze. Weeze's been trakin' d'ose murderin' jewel t'ieves f' t'ree days," he said as he began to make up a bed for himself.

"T'ieves?" I asked.

"Thieves," Grarr growled.

"Steal from vizard in Briarvood, " Durik explained. "Big stone... Very much monies. D'ey kill many vizard's servants. Some children. Very evil."

"So ... tell us little Gnomish traveluh, what did yooze's folks call yooze?" Beornag asked as he lay down. Something akin to a mountain rolling over.

"My goodness, I *am* sorry. Forgive my rudeness. I wasn't thinking," I apologized as I started to get dressed. "I am Szvirf Neblinski of the G'nomish house of Neblinski."

"You must be vizard," Durik said.

"Why do you say that?" I asked.

"D'is your book?" he continued, holding up the tome that Shiddumbuzzin had given me in my dream.

"Yes, that is my book. It was a gift to me from the great creator of the G'nomish people," I replied as I accepted the book from Durik.

"D'at is spell book," Durik added.

"How do you know what a spell book looks like?" I asked.

"Vee kill vizards before. Take books and sell to Novak," he replied.

"Uh...d'at's *eeevil* wizids," Beornag added.

I looked at the book and saw that it had, embossed on its cover, a golden Sensimilia herb leaf. I opened the book for the first time and was overwhelmed by a sudden rush of information. The pages flipped by so fast I could hardly see them, yet I was reading every word and committing those words to memory. In less than a minute I had become—a hootspologist. "Apparently, yes, I am?" I said to Durik. "Us G'nomes use the term hootspologist."

I then turned to Beornag and added. "I am also a *G'nome*, not a Gnome. Gnomes are distant cousins to the G'nomes. Like Trolls are to Goblins," I corrected. "Where I come from there are no Gnomes at all."

"Sorry Pops. Didn't mean t' offend ya. Ize ain't nevuh seent a G'nome eithuh," Beornag replied. "Ize is a Hill Troll. Distant cousins t' udda Hill Trolls, an' sometimes sons-in-laws o' various udda races, aldough not usually f' very long. Funny d'at.

"Grarr over d'ere is an Urk, closely related t' udda Urks but not t' be mistaken f' d'eir very distant relatives, Larry an' Thelma...an' Durik is... hey Grarr, what is Durik anyway?"

"We don't know," Grarr growled.

"Durik is Durik," the blue one announced, standing up. "Durik Thuckov Eechitendie."

Beornag laughed. "Ize loves his names."

I then turned the book over to look at the back cover and realized that, by flipping it over and upside down, there was an entirely different book. This one was full of poems verses and short stories. These were prayers to holy Shiddumbuzzin. I was overtaken by an unexplainable urge to smoke my brains out and have a nice, toasted onion bagle with limburger cheese just like Mom used to make.

In the middle the pages were blank. This is where the Mellow One wanted me to keep a journal of my quest so my story could be read to the G'nomish peoples for ages to come.

"Go figure," I said as I searched for hidden compartments. "There's no money."

"Wuz yooze talking t' us?" Beornag asked.

"No, just thinking out loud."

"Ize *sees*." He continued, truly amazed, "Ize wuz nevuh able t' perfect d'at art," he thought out loud.

I began rummaging through the pile of other things that the Troll had dumped at my feet. There was my G'nome army knife, my canteen filled with cheap wine (so my boss wouldn't catch me drinkin' on the job), my pipe, a nice sized bag of Sensimilia herb, another bag of snacks, my glasses, my hat, my boots, my watch, my personal hygiene stuff—the list went on and on.

I didn't have this stuff on me in the firestone caves! Holy Shiddumbuzzin must have had this planned from the start; that or I was really stoned, and this was all just a big toxic delusion.

At that I decided to fill my pipe and have a good smoke of the herb. Beornag and the others joined me as we passed my ornately carved firestone smoking device around. Grarr even added some really nice, black, sticky stuff he called Goblin brain cheese. It wasn't cheese and it wasn't made out of brains. At least that is what he told me. It did, however, produce a sweet-smelling thick smoke that got us really elevated.

My pipe was very large by G'nomish standards, (I was quite proud of it), but the boys made it look like a tiny accessory for a child's toy. Still they were polite and we refilled the bowl several times before it made its way around our circle.

As we smoked, I looked at the prayers written in my book and came upon one in particular. "Hey, it says here, that what we are now doing, smoking the herb, is a holy ceremony. Listen to this." I began to read.

"And so the effervescent smoke came to the lung, and from the lung it awakened the mind, and the mind awakened the spirit, and the spirit gave thanks to the great one who responded with the gift of laughter, and we shall all feast, in his name, on deep-fried potato sticks and cheese dip. This shall be in the name of the great and mellow holy Shiddumbuzzin."

"Wow! Yooze is a holy man just like Ize is, Pops!" Beornag exclaimed. "Yooze read d'at like a natural."

"Well, the Mellow One *did* say that I am supposed to find the secrets of his wisdom and the origins of his words, and that I am supposed to deliver these unto his children." I was getting way ahead of myself, so I stopped and decided to tell the whole story to my new found friends.

Five or six pipefuls of Goblin brain cheese and Sensimilia herb later I had finished my story and was just about ready to pass out.

"D'at's amazin' Pops!" Beornag said. "Ize, personally, have nevuh met Ize's deity, (d'at Ize knows of) nor have Ize ever heard his voice. Truly a miracle."

"How old did you say you were?" asked Grarr.

"I am one thousand four hundred and twenty-one in Human years, fifty-nine in G'nomish years." I replied.

"You have got to be kidding me," Grarr responded, his eyes wide open in disbelief.

"I never lie about my age," I said.

"So, let me get this straight." He paused, scrutinizing me. "You're a wizar—sorry—a hootspologist, a holy man or whatever your people call it, and you're one and a half thousand years old?"

"Right, right, and right," I replied. "The G'nomish term for holy man is *Redeye*, by the way, according to this book."

"Hey Pops," Beornag said as he began to dish out some of whatever was cooking in the pot on the fire. "Ize gotta say...yooze looks pretty good f' ya age. Ize woulda expected a lot more wrinkles and...well...dust."

"Why thank you. I try to keep in shape. You know, brisk walking, healthy diet that sort of thing," I replied as I accepted a G'nomish sized bowl of—something. "What is in the bowl?" I wasn't about to try dark Elf stew.

"Durik made it. Rabbit stew. He caught da rabbits himself," Beornag replied.

"Don't kid yourself, Pops, he's a pretty good cook. Even if he looks like he'd rather be eating *you*," Grarr added.

"Durik not eat you Poppa Szvirf. Durik like you. Durik not evil," Durik said as he gave Grarr a dirty look. "Grarr joke."

Thank the holy seeds of friendship. Even when Durik was being friendly, he still looked like he wanted to tear out my heart and have a crap in the hole it left. "No problem kid."

As we ate our meal (which was quite tasty) Grarr performed preventive maintenance on their weapons and tools. He never looked up from his duties but had a definite air of dangerous awareness about him. He scared the b'zingas outta me.

Beornag continually told jokes and funny stories. It would seem that he was an Injoke. That was a holy man to a deity called Ulm, according to the Troll. Ulm was the patron deity of humour and laughter. Beornag seemed to have an endless supply of such stories and jokes and kept us up half the night laughing.

We also noticed that, after I had read the holy prayer from the book of Shiddumbuzzin, their wounds from battle began to heal at an extraordinary rate, and in about an hour there was no trace of any damage at all.

"Ize would t'ink," explained Beornag, "d'at prayer yooze read was a healin' verse. Ize, too, knows healin' verses. Deys is miracles given unto us by da powuhs d'at weeze so respect and woyship."

"Wow," I said. "Do you think there might be more miracles in this book?"

"Most prob'ly, Pops. If da great Shiddumbuzzin gave yooze

one, it's likely d'at he gave yooze a whole book full. If yooze decide t' hang wit' us f' a while Ize would be more d'en happy t' assist yooze wit' da explorashin o' yooze's book's contents. Ize is familiah wit' several diffrint approaches t' t'eological study," he offered.

"No kidding? Well ... as I am new to this place ... it would seem that I have little choice but to...*hang* with you fellas. You are the only friends I have here, so I think I will take you up on that offer," I replied.

"D'en it's settled. Yooze can come wit' us. In da mornin' weeze is headin' home t' collect da reward an' find some more work. Yooze will live wit' us at da winery," he offered.

"Winery?" I inquired.

"Pops," Grarr interrupted. "What do you think of coming to work with us? We could use another good healer, which you have proven yourself to be, and we don't have a...*hootspologist*. We work out of an old winery that we have almost paid off. With any luck the money from this job will take care of that. We can take you on as an employee at first. If you turn out to be a descent wiz— ahem—hootspologist we'll give you a full partnership. What do you say?"

I was a little surprised at this request, and wasn't too keen on the idea of teaching a monster about God at first, but after Grarr explained the kind of money involved I decided that this would be the best course of action.

"Sold!" You've got a hootspologist and another healer! Especially since it looks like I have my first convert right here (I gestured toward Durik). He's no G'nome but I think he'll do for starters." I shook their fingers (careful not to impale myself on any claws), as their hands were way too big for me to shake, and we made a verbal contract.

I don't usually make verbal contracts, but just this once I didn't see the harm, especially since I was quite sure that Beornag, and maybe Durik couldn't read or write. (Something I later planned to remedy.)

After we cleaned the dishes and got ready for bed, I decided to look in my book to see if there was a pre-sleep ceremony. Durik came to kneel beside me, towering over my tiny form, as I filled my pipe for the last time that evening. Then, I began to read out loud.

"And so, as we have partaken of the sacred herb, and our heads are full of happy euphoria, we ready ourselves for rest. We ask the great Mellow One to soften the adverse effects of copious amounts of herb and laughter so that our heads do not pound in the morning like the shaking of the earth. We give thanks for our daily deep-fried potatoes and cheese dip and say—get outta my store." That was it. The pre-sleep prayer. Durik even repeated the last line.

Get outta my store was a very nice thing to say if you were a G'nome. It meant that you did not want whoever you were talking to, to be able to see your entire inventory at one time thus forcing them to return and give you the pleasure of their company once again. It was an old saying that came from the days when most G'nomes were merchants.

We smoked the pipe and afterward I tucked Durik in. He was so child-like, this horrific creature, it was quite confusing to me to say the least, but I went about the process of getting him ready for a good night's sleep anyway.

He thanked me sincerely, wished me a good night, and smiled while I readied myself for bed, not far from him.

There were two tents. Durik, myself, and a lot of equipment were in one, while Beornag and Grarr were in the other.

If it had not been for the fact that I was totally stoned and exhausted I would never have been able to fall to sleep as I couldn't hear myself think over the raging tempest that was Beornag's snoring. I was, however, at least comforted by the thought that any predators that might be in that forest would steer clear of our camp for fear of whatever was making that racket.

Once I did fall asleep, I dreamed of a golden Sensimilia leaf floating in a sea of sweet smelling smoke and heard the voice again.

"*Szvirrrrf,*" he said.

"That's me," I replied.

"*You have found your paaaaath,*" he added.

"Soooo…that's good…yes?" I asked.

"*Calabac, Szvirrrrrrf. Calabac is the onnnnne. A lesson to be learrrrrrned…cluuuues to be found… knowledge to be haaaaad. Rememberrrrr. Calabaaaaac Calabaaaaaac…Calabaaaaaaaaac…*"

Then the voice faded out and was replaced by three scantily dressed high Elf women and a tub full of whipping cream.

Good dream.

CHAPTER - 2

HOMEWARD *UNBOUND*

The next day I was awakened by a terrible noise. It sounded like someone was gelding a cat. I knew what a cat was because G'nomes had purchased cats from Dwarvish traders thousands of years ago to control the dangerous possibility of rat infestations.

Rats: G'nomish enemy number one.

The inside of the tent was lit up but I couldn't tell where the light was coming from. It appeared that the walls themselves glowed with a warm, bright light. I took notice that this was not the case when I had retired for bed the evening before.

Durik was curled up in a huge animal pelt that resembled a striped bear, his hands over his ears, his face twisted in agony, and groaning something about a Trollish morning ritual.

I got up and stepped out of the tent to see who was torturing the poor cat and full daylight belted me right in the face.

"Aaaaaaaaah!" I screamed, holding my hands over my eyes and dropping to my knees in pain. "Help! I'm blind!"

Before I knew what was happening, Durik had jumped out of his bed, drawn one of his wicked looking swords (he had so many I can't remember which one it was), and pulled me back into the tent, placing himself between me and the entrance.

"Vhat vrong Poppa Szvirf?!" he growled and snarled. Truly terrifying.

"I don't know kid! There's a really big ball of fire in the sky and it was really bright! Oy! I think I'm blind!" Holy Shiddumbuzzin that hurt. To this day I can still remember the pain.

Just then I heard the tent flap open again, felt warmth spread across my body, and heard the rumbling, purring voice that could only be Grarr.

"What's up, bud?" he asked.

"Poppa Szvirf say sun hurt his eyes," Durik reported, a genuine tone of concern in his voice.

Next, the ground began to tremble and I knew that either we were experiencing a minor earthquake or Beornag was running at full tilt. It was only then that I noticed the cat gelding noises had stopped.

"What's da matta wit' da little guy?" It was Beornag. We would be spared an earthquake that morning. "Does Ize needs t' stomp a bad guy?"

"Poppa Szvirf say sun hurt his eyes!" Durik repeated.

"Holy solar plexus, Ize didn't even t'ink o' d'at! Da little guy's been unda ground his whole life. He's never seent da sun His eyes must be really sensitive t' da light!" he explained.

"I think my vision is coming back." I was beginning to see terrifying images all around me. (Pretty normal, all things considered). "Yes, I can see you guys now. Who was the schmuck that invented a light like that?!"

"One a da gods," Beornag said. "Don't worry Redeye, d'at's normal. Up here, on da surface weeze gots a cycle o' day and night. At night it's dark, which would be normal for yooze, while during da day it's quite bright out. The world needs da sun to make da plants grow and such. Yooze'll be okay."

"What do you mean, okay? I can't go out there, in *that*!" I lamented.

"It's not a problem, Redeye. Weeze can get yooze some shades in Briarwood. Shades is like d'ose spectacles yooze is wearin', but deys is dark so deys blocks da light o' da sun." He was pulling a bed sheet sized hanky out of his pocket. "In da mean time weeze'll just blindfold yooze so's yooze don't get blasted again." He began pulling apart the hanky/bed sheet where something had dried and hardened.

"How you feel now, Poppa Szvirf?" Durik asked, quite worried.

"I think I'm okay now, kid. Thanks for asking," I replied as I patted him on the knee to comfort him. He seemed to be quite taken with me and I wanted to let him know that I appreciated it.

"Ve get you shades like us," he said holding up a pair of sleek, dark lensed spectacles.

"I won't be needing the blindfold," I explained. "I'll just wear my hat. It has a very wide brim, and I can pull it down over my brow and squint a lot. By the way—who was gelding the cat?"

"Yooze *recognized* it!?" Beornag elated. "Yooze would be surprised at how few folks does. It's Ize's favourite tune. It was written by a Goblin, of all t'ings. But it reaches its full glory when played troo da Trollish bagpipes."

"Of course it does," I responded.

"Home is six hours walk. We should move soon," Grarr said all official like. "Durik, you have kitchen duty. Beornag, pack our stuff. I'm going on a recon up ahead. I'll be back in about thirty minutes. We'll eat then and leave." With that he was gone.

"So Grarr is sort of the boss I take it?" I asked.

"Nah. He just gots some kinda military experience an' weeze listens t' him when weezes in da field. Grarr's kept weezes alive so far," Beornag replied.

"Grarr know when danger be near, Poppa Szvirf. He keep us safe," Durik added as he began to make—of all things—flapjacks and coffee.

I assisted him and soon Grarr was back. We all ate our breakfast and cleaned up the campsite, removing all traces that we were ever there.

The boys gave me the opportunity to make a morning prayer and we smoked our brains out. Then we were off.

As we travelled, I was carried on Beornag's shoulder. He was in the middle of a single file line with Grarr in front and Durik in the rear. We stayed pretty close to each other and most folks we saw stayed as far as they could away from us. As a result, we didn't pass anyone on the road. Those travelling the road either hid in the forest as we passed or decided that they needed to change direction.

"You like Durik, Poppa Szvirf?" the kid called up to me.

"Of course, I like you. Who wouldn't?" I replied. Oy. He was terrifying. Those churning green eyes, row after row of pointed teeth, the quill-like spines he had for hair—all of it seemed designed to scare the crap out of me.

"Lots people not like Durik. Call Durik monster and run avay," he said with his head hanging low. "Only s'ree friends and you like Durik."

"Some folks are simple-minded kid. They can't see past the surface—if you'll forgive the expression. Given a chance I don't see how anyone could dislike you. Never judge a book by its cover. That's what I always say." I tried to boost his confidence.

"Durik like Poppa Szvirf," he said again, now looking up at me, smiling.

"Yooze definitely made a friend d'ere Redeye. Yooze couldn't have got a bettuh one d'at's f' sure," Beornag whispered.

Most of what I saw on the six-hour journey was blurry as I was squinting a lot. But, I did notice that the surface world was a lot more colourful than the underground. Some hazy blues and greens occasionally interrupted by a patch of brown, or reds and yellows.

When the journey to the boys' home was almost over I began

to hear the noises of civilization. It sounded like hawkers selling their wares, livestock braying, mooing, clucking and oinking, people hustling and bustling and so forth.

I could also smell a peculiar aroma on the morning breeze. I later found out that it was the salt air from the nearby ocean.

After a six-hour long journey, we stopped at what looked to me to be a gate to a city surrounded by walls. Here a guard asked Grarr for a citizen's pass.

He produced it and we were once again on our way.

We travelled through the city, passing through wide streets and narrow back alleys alike. This was not a beautifully crafted city of precious metals and rare stones like I was used to. It was mostly made of wood and stone.

My nose was soon squinched up as I noticed that the streets had an unpleasant odour about them. They seemed quite wide and were covered mostly with dirt.

We walked along at a steady pace for about fifteen more minutes until we finally came upon a huge building with a sign on the front above the door that read—Warped Speed Enterprises— beneath a large golden W. Under which, it read: Over 420 Served.

Upon entering I first noticed that it was dark, or at least dim. We were inside a massive warehouse full of giant vats. There were countless barrels stacked against the walls and the thick aroma of fermenting wine filled the air. A thin layer of dust seemed to cover everything and there were quite a few cobwebs in the corners.

"D'is be our house, Poppa Szvirf," Durik proclaimed proudly.

"Welcome t' Warped Speed Enterprises," Beornag added. "As yooze can see, weeze also makes wine." He spread his tree-like arms and turned in a circle as though he himself was taking in the glory of the place for the first time.

It was refreshing to see such appreciation for something so mundane. G'nomes live in an ancient city and are quite used to what they have. They don't seem to appreciate their good fortune at living in Sensimilia. These boys were obviously not used to such extravagancies.

"I like it," I said. And I did. It was big, cool, and dimly lit. It reminded me, somewhat, of the great firestone chasm I used to work in. It was very comforting for a G'nome who had just spent his first day on the surface world.

"I'll take these to Novak," Grarr said, holding up three corpse filled bags. "I'll get the reward then head down to the market to sell the dark Elves' possessions. I'll see you guys back here in about an hour."

"Pick up a pair a shades f' da Redeye while yooze is out, extra, extra small," Beornag added.

"Will do," Grarr purred like some great predatory cat, and then he was off.

I took a moment to get a better look around the room. It held eight monster-sized (what else?) vats filled with fermenting wine, each a different kind.

The ceiling was fifty feet from the floor and there were many strange things hanging from it; a stuffed dinosaur, some kind of purple coloured man with an octopus for a head, huge weapons, banners and flags from numerous kingdoms that I had never seen before, and all kinds of other weird stuff. These were obviously souvenirs from the boys' travels.

"Yooze can have da cubby hole unda da stairs in da basement, Redeye. It should be plenty big for yooze and it's really dark down d'ere," Beornag offered. "Weeze'll get yooze some furniture an' a bed an' stuff when Grarr gets back."

So there I was among the monsters of my childhood nightmares, and they were my friends no less. If my cousin Bernie could've seen me then he would have crapped a square one.

I got settled in, and over the next three days I had an

opportunity to get better acquainted with my book, Briarwood, the surface world, and my new friends.

Beornag was born into slavery a few hundred years previous. His family had been slaves in an ore mine for as long as they could remember. He worked under the whip for sixteen years until his parents passed on, and only then did he finally escape. Many years later, he met Grarr in a bar fight and they became instant allies out of pure necessity.

After they left the bar (and the town it was in), they decided to hire themselves out as bodyguards. They travelled far to the north and finally reached Briarwood where they decided to stay awhile as there seemed to be lots of work to be had in the area. Since then Beornag had been seeking enlightenment through the humour of his deity's teachings.

Grarr had been wandering the world, seeking his place in it, and trying to make ends meet. He had spent several years as a mercenary (or so he said at the time), fighting for whoever paid the best. He sometimes found himself fighting previous employers. His talents came to be known by many in the far south. He made numerous allies as well as enemies, but he was considered to be one of the very best tacticians in the region.

He soon got tired of leading small armies and training new recruits, so he left the profession to find a more gratifying career. (Although this all was true, it was not the complete truth. Grarr had a previous history he was reluctant to talk about. In time I would eventually learn the rest of his story and develop a whole new kind of respect for him.)

The two friends were working as guards for a travelling circus when they met Durik. He was being kept in a cage and plugged as the demon boy. The circus owner claimed to have found him in an abandoned Goblin camp.

The only clue as to what or who he was lay in an amulet that hung from his neck with the words: *Durik Thuckov Eechitendie.* The ring master decided to cage him and put him in the sideshow. There he lived for several years with no companionship, no compassion, not even clothing. He was fed scraps from the tables of the other performers. Grarr and Beornag got to know him and decided that he did not belong in a cage and just needed some friends. They saved their money and bought Durik (and his necklace) for three hundred gold coins and the promise not to eat the ringmaster.

They then continued to rent out their talents but became more and more fussy as to who they would work for. Once he was released from his cage and allowed to live among people as a person, Durik made a promise to himself that he would never do to others what had been done to him, nor would he allow it to happen to anyone if he could help it.

He was so sensitive about people calling him evil and demon that he insisted that they not work for anyone unless it was a good cause. It ended up working out for the best, as the novelty of hiring monsters to fight monsters soon caught on with the local gentry, and the boys found themselves busier than they had ever been.

Soon enough they had saved up enough money to put a hefty down payment on the winery, and now it was almost paid off in full. They lived off the profits from wine sales and used their reward moneys to buy better equipment and armour as well as make their mortgage payments.

Now they were going to be able to start banking everything they made. They hoped to save enough to buy a castle somewhere out of town.

Aside from a lack of formal education the trio had done pretty well for themselves, and where giant terrifying monsters are concerned, these were the nicest you'd ever want to meet.

The boys set up a bedroom for me under the basement stairs. It was a cubby hole that used to be for storing preserves and pickles and that sort of thing. They bought me a small chair and desk that was designed for a Human child and a beautiful antique chest of drawers, which Grarr ingeniously set up as a hideaway bed. They made sure I had plenty of parchment and writing paraphernalia as well as lots of shelf space for books.

They even bought me some books on just about everything I didn't really need to know anything about. They did look good on the shelf though, and it was the thought that counted.

Beornag had a carpenter come in for two days and install narrow ramps on all the stairwells so I didn't have to climb up and down each one. A stair for these guys was a wall for a little guy like me, and a whole set of stairs was like climbing a mountain!

Even the kitchen furniture was altered in some way so as to facilitate my size, but not hinder the boys in their daily routines.

On the third night at the winery, as I lay in bed, I dreamed again.

There I was, sitting on a giant herb seed in the middle of a field of newly sprouted plants, smoking my pipe and gazing in wonder at the sparkling firestones in the ceiling when I heard it.

"Szvirrrrrf," the voice said.

"Go away!" I replied through a groggy haze brought on by good herb and deep sleep.

"Szvirrrrrf!" it repeated.

"What, what, WHAT? Can't you see I'm slee— Oh, it's you!" I began to come to my senses and realize I was dreaming again.

"Yes it is meeeeee," he continued.

"Well? Aren't you going to say something about a path and something called Calabac, or something?" I asked. I wanted to get back to sleep, and if this dream was anything like the last, I was looking forward to seeing those Elf girls and the whipping cream again.

"*Uh…yes. You remember?*" he asked.

"Of course I do," I replied. "You know what kind of IQ I have? Why you should have seen me in the nineteenth grade. I was the fastest speller in the whole school. I was spelling words like—"

"*Szvirrrrf!*" he interrupted.

"Holy smoke! You don't have to yell! I'm not deaf!" I responded.

"*Teach them,*" he continued.

"To spell? Yeah, I was gonna do—" I began, but was interrupted.

"*Teach the monsters of my word and the sacred leaf. Find Calabac. In him are the answers to your first test. I await your prayers and watch over you always.*"

"Oh yea? If that's the case, why did you let me walk out of that tent and straight into the sunlight?" I protested. "I could have been seriously hurt or blinded you know! Holy Shiddumbuzzin that was painful! I still have a small headache from it! I could have been—"

"*Yeah ha-ha-ha. You should have seen your fa— ahem… But you were noooooot!*" it interrupted again. "*You see the world because your heart sees the leaf. Trust in the leaf and it shall guide you. Trust in my teachings and they shall guide you.*

"*Find Calabac…Calabaaaac…Calabaaac.*"

I woke up then. No Elvish girls. No whipping cream. Just a feeling of total confusion.

I got up from my dresser bed where I had been sleeping in the bottom drawer. It was heavily padded with nice goose down blankets and still warm and cozy.

I shivered suddenly. A chill was in the air. Tempted to hop back under the covers, I donned my night coat and managed to resist the urge. Then I made my way up the long ramp to the kitchen.

After lighting the stove, I made myself an herb tea, and that was when I heard a faint knock at the front door.

I went out into the main production hall to see if I had really heard the sound. (I was still a little groggy from just waking up.)

The massive room was at least seventy feet long by fifty feet wide and nothing seemed disturbed, so my fears of there being a rat were appeased.

Then, a tapping at the main entrance.

There it was again, very faint as though a tiny little hand was making it. It was definitely someone knocking at the main entrance.

I quickly pushed a step-ladder over to the door so I could look out of the peep hole, and climbed high enough to manipulate it open so as to see who was there. "Go away we're closed until morning."

The knock came again.

"What are you, deaf?" I yelled through the door. I couldn't see anyone through the peep hole. It was raining steadily, and the fog was quite thick. "I said go away. We open at nine. Come back then."

A voice came back. "I need to hire you!" It was a well-spoken, female voice in high Elfish (another of the many languages I happen to speak). "I have gold and will pay you generously!"

"I said we're closed! Now go— Did you say gold? You wouldn't happen to have whipping cream too, would ya?" I asked.

"Yes!" she replied. "Gold! Yes! But no cream, I am sorry. Please! It is an emergency!"

"Oy!" I got down from the ladder without breaking my neck, pushed it aside, and began to unlock the door while she continued to knock, desperately. "Hold on to your panties already." The door opened allowing me to see her.

There she stood. Hubba, hubba! What a dish! I won't even go into it. I couldn't do her justice trying to describe her.

"Come in, deary." I said, gesturing for her to enter. I could hardly blink.

I closed the door behind her and locked it again. "What's the big emergency?" My voice quivered slightly. This was an Elf. It is said that they possess a special power to charm others.

"You're not a monster," she said, disappointed yet relieved. "I was told that I could hire monsters to help me if I came here."

"Well, first off, thanks for noticing. Second, they're still sleeping—the monsters, I mean," I replied as I guided her into the kitchen. "I'm, ahh...the house father. You know, I take care of the boys, er, monsters. I play the good role model. That sort of thing."

I sat down at the little dining table the boys had bought for me and had a sip of my tea. "Please sit down." I gestured toward a non-monster sized, normal chair nearby. "Would you like a nice glass of tea? It'll help to calm your nerves."

"Oh yes, sir. That would be most kind of you," she replied between sniffles.

It was plain to see that she had been crying up a storm and by the looks of her garments she had been travelling all night in the rain and mud.

I made my way up and around the series of catwalks that Grarr had installed for my use in the kitchen, to the stove. There, I put the kettle on and started to prepare another pot of herb tea. "So what is it that you need?"

She stood up and then fell to her knees, bawling, her hands clasped in front of her as she trembled. "Please, kind sir. You must help me. My sister has been kidnapped by the evil necromancer, Calabac!"

CHAPTER - 3

PIPE DREAMS

"What was that?" I asked in disbelief. "Did you say *Calabac*?" I was shocked. This was the name from my dream conversation with the great Shiddumbuzzin!

She kneeled in the middle of the kitchen floor, droplets of water still running from her clothes and hair. Her rain-soaked, gossamer evening gown betrayed her shapely secrets. Her eyes were full of tears, and her voice was full of desperation.

"Oh, yes kind sir. He is the leader of the Scave cult. I believe he is responsible for abducting my sister."

I calmed her down and returned her to her chair while I poured her a glass of herb tea. Her Elfish charm was powerful to be sure. But she was quite sincere, and certainly not *trying* to affect me. I concluded that this effect was passive, and not hostile.

She took a few sips and wiped the tears out of her eyes. "Please kind sir. You have to help me. I went to the wizard next door to you, Novak, he is called, but his servant told me that he was indisposed and that I should come here to talk to a warrior named Grarr. Does he live here with you? Do you think he will help me?"

"I can't make any promises without talking to the boys, so you wait here, and I'll go and get them." The tea seemed to be having an adverse effect on her charm, and it was now becoming easier to resist. I took note of this. Perhaps it was only activated when the Elf was in danger.

Anyway, where was I?

Oh yeah…

I gave her a couple of cookies from the cookie jar and headed upstairs to the boys' rooms.

First I woke up Durik and told him to wake the others and then join me in the kitchen. He agreed without any complaints. Then I went back downstairs to check on the nice girl.

She was still sitting daintily, solemnly drinking her herb tea, but at least she had stopped crying. At that moment she was staring at her hand and apparently admiring the "colours" as she enjoyed her hot beverage and cookies.

"Okay, deary…so tell me, how much gold *do* you have to spend?" Business was business, and we had expenses.

"I only have five hundred coins, but I do have several large and precious gems that are surely worth more than that," she replied, hoping it would be sufficient.

She looked at me with those lovely, violet, almond shaped eyes, those firm well rounded… "Did you say five hundred?"

"Yes," she responded. "And seven gems each worth at least that."

Just then Durik came into the kitchen with Grarr and Beornag in tow.

The girl almost screamed in terror, but I caught her eye and signalled her to relax.

"Boys, this young lady needs to hire us for a job," I reported.

"Who are you?" Grarr asked, straight to business as he took a seat across the table from her. To this day I think he must have had at least one G'nomish ancestor.

She stood up and wavered slightly before she spoke. "My name is Lillia Illianus. I am the daughter of Turelion Illianus, and I need your help," she replied with a curtsy.

I had to admire her composure. She had just been locked inside a strange building with three terrifying monsters and a dirty old G'nome.

Grarr later informed me that Turelion Illianus was a wealthy Elf merchant, one of a few who chose to live among the Humans of the Empire.

He used to have a castle not far from Briarwood, but lost most of his estate many years before the boys arrived in the area. He later died, mysteriously. The local constabulary reported that it was a suicide brought on by depression caused by all of his losses.

Turelion was survived by two daughters who, reportedly, sold the remainder of his wealth and purchased a small cottage in the western forest where they sold herbal remedies and love potions to the locals in order to make ends meet.

I introduced myself and the boys and prepared several cups of tea. This looked like it might take awhile.

Durik and the Troll sat down at the table. The kid was still rubbing sleep out of his eyes as he began to raid the cookie jar.

Beornag then spoke. "So ... What seems t' be da problem, little lady?"

"My twin sister, Alaeth, has been kidnapped by the evil necromancer, Calabac. I need you to rescue her," she replied as her eyes began to well up with tears again.

Beornag gasped in shock and concern, shifting his chair a little closer to hers.

Lillia continued. "Alaeth was seeing, on a romantic level, a Human named William Worthy. William was working as a delivery boy for a strange religious cult known as the Scave. He wasn't involved with them—or at least that is what he said—but he picked up supplies from the market and delivered them to some temple deep in the forest near the mountain pass—"

"So, where does this Calabac fit into the picture, and what makes you think he is involved?" Grarr asked.

Lillia almost jumped when he interrupted her, but again, she composed herself and continued. "Last Monday Alaeth met with William in a secluded glade near our home. He had sent her a message ahead of time to meet him there. She thought he would propose to her.

"She came home that night and said that he did hint at marriage but did not actually ask. He had given her a beautiful, jewelled necklace, which she showed me. There was a monogram on the back of the centerpiece." Lillia wiped her tears again.

"I thought it strange that a mere delivery boy could afford such a thing and I studied it closely. I told my sister that I just wanted to make sure the clasps and fittings were strong so that she didn't lose any of the strange stones. I am a junior lapidary.

"The monogram did not fit William's name nor any other that came to mind. Two days later I came to town and visited the university library. I was searching for clues as to what the monogram might be from."

She looked up at us, struggling to keep her composure, and after a sip of her tea she continued.

"I found that there was a house of Humans who lived long ago as lords of these lands. They were wicked and cruel and as a result were dethroned by visiting heroes who set up Briarwood's first government. The monogram belonged to that very house." Again, she wiped eyes, and paused to compose herself.

She took a deep breath and carried on with her story, "The librarian, Conan was his name, told me that there was another person, who had visited the library and studied those same records only a few months ago and that this person had taken several of the books on loan, but had failed to return them. The person's name was Calabac."

She looked to Grarr, hope in her eyes, "He said that I should go to see a man named Aazh Stelark who owned a curios shop in the central market, so I did just that." She sipped her tea again, and shuddered.

Beornag, again shifted his chair a little closer to her. He was so huge that his body heat was enough to warm the area a few feet surrounding him and Lillia looked grateful as she continued.

"Mr. Stelark was a kind old gentleman of Elfish and Human stock. He told me that Calabac used to visit his shop on a regular, bi-monthly basis to purchase rare spell components.

"On one such occasion a spirit dragon that Mr. Stelark had for sale was sitting on a perch next to the cash box. Spirit dragons are not really dragons they just look like dragons but are only the size of a pigeon. They are highly prized by the very wealthy as pets because they can sense a person's motives and emotional state.

"This particular spirit dragon reacted very negatively toward Calabac, and Mr. Stelark concluded that Calabac was first a wizard, because of the nature of his regular purchases and second, malicious, because of the spirit dragon's reaction.

"Mr. Stelark said that was the last time he ever saw Calabac. He told me that rumor had it, Calabac had started a religious cult called the Scave near the mountain pass." She paused again to wipe her tears and then went on.

"I then decided to go to see William and ask him where he had acquired the necklace. I found his home to be empty and his neighbours said that he had mysteriously moved away, during the night, three years ago, and that they hadn't seen him since.

"I tried to gain entrance to his home, but the door was locked, so I peeked in one of the windows. The inside was covered with cobwebs and dust. I concluded that the neighbours had been speaking the truth.

"Not knowing what else to do at that point I decided to go

home and talk to Alaeth. When I returned the next morning, I found our house in disarray. There was evidence of a struggle, and forced entry in the upstairs bedroom window. My sister was gone!" The look on her face was sheer terror.

"You can imagine my distress as I desperately searched the surrounding forest. I was unable to find her or any sign of her." Her fists suddenly clenched with frustration.

"I returned to the house to find that whoever had broken in did not take any of our valuables. I can only conclude that this…Calabac has something to do with my sister's disappearance. She is my only family.

"Please … you must help me." She fell to her knees. "There are no others who will."

Well she was nothing if not convincing. She seemed to have it all, good looks, smarts, money. I almost proposed to her right there in the kitchen.

There was a moment of uncomfortable silence as everyone looked toward Grarr.

Finally he spoke. "It's going to cost you—a lot."

She explained how much she had with a very worried look on her face.

"We are the best at what we do. You will not find, within five hundred leagues in any direction, anyone better," he began. "We can make that much cash escorting a dignitary across three days of countryside and be home without so much as a scratch. If this Calabac is a necromancer, and he has some sort of religious cult following him, it could mean some heavy fighting and the possibility that one or more of us might be seriously injured or worse. If you want us to do this job for you, you're going to have to do better than that."

Beornag and Durik protested. I, too, joined in when I saw that Lillia was beginning to cry again. She was willing to give us everything she had!

"I'll tell you what I'll do," he finally broke, gesturing for us to sit down and listen. "Here's the deal..." he looked straight at her and said, "You pay us what you have, and also agree to work for us here at the winery doing cleaning, and cooking, and other such chores. You also agree to use any other skills that you might possess to service this company while you work here. The contract will be for ten years and will include room and board as well as a modest allowance which will be paid weekly. You will not be a slave. You will, however, be legally bound by written contract to fulfill these requirements."

She was about to protest, but he continued before she was able to speak, "If your sister is still alive, we will get her back. That I guarantee. If we are unsuccessful, we keep the cash and gems but you are free of the contract and not responsible for any damages that we might incur on this mission."

He placed his monocle in his left eye and added, "If you need references, we can supply hundreds of satisfied customers. We have never failed to complete a mission. You have my word. This is my only offer and it is not open for negotiation".

I actually thought that the gems and money were a good deal, but Grarr seemed to know what he was doing. Heck he and the boys built this company from the ground up. Who was I to question his methods? It wasn't like he was tossing her out into the street.

"It would seem that I have no choice in the matter," she said, sobbing.

"Then it's settled," Grarr said as he stood and downed his tea. "Beornag will show you to a guest room. In the morning we'll send someone to get your things from your home. It's not safe for you there right now. Tomorrow afternoon I'll take you to see our lawyer and we'll draw up the contract and do the monetary transaction."

"When will you start looking for my sister?" Lillia asked.

"We've already started," he said with a menacing smile. "Trust me."

With that Beornag took Lillia away to find her a guest room while Grarr sat down again and began to fill his pipe with Goblin brain cheese (something he always seemed to have in abundance).

He then lit his pipe and offered it to Durik who had just about made it to the bottom of the cookie jar.

Durik accepted the pipe, but not before he picked me up and gently placed me once again on the table.

I sat down on Lillia's upturned teacup and Durik took a big draw from the pipe and sat it close, where I could reach it.

I also enjoyed a big draw from the pipe and then pushed it across the table to Grarr.

"Pops," Grarr then spoke." Do you have anything in that book that might help you investigate a crime scene?"

I thought for a moment and then... "There's a hootspa that helps me see into the recent past. That might be helpful. There's also a hootspa that allows me to detect the essence of a person that has passed through a specific area within a given period of time. I can also commune with Holy Shiddumbuzzin, but the book says I should only use that one in dire emergencies."

The hootspa that I thought would do the trick was a really neat divination that allowed me to virtually be in the past without actually being there. From it I could tell what happened during any given period of time in a specific area. I could even hear conversations that had taken place in that area.

For instance: you, the reader, just read about how I can see into the past, right?

See? It works.

Grarr smiled again and passed the pipe to Durik. "That'll do just fine. I want you to go out to Lillia's house in the morning and use your hootspa to find out anything you can. Take Durik with you in case you run into any trouble."

He paused in thought for a moment. "What about locks? Can you pick locks without damaging them?"

"Oh yea, that one's easy," I confirmed. "I have a simple hootspa that will open all but the most magically protected locks."

"Then after you check out Lillia's house take a trip over to William Worthy's place and break in." He grinned again. "Don't let the local constabulary see you do it. Look around for any other clues that we can use."

"I have a question. Can we really make that much money by just escorting a dignitary?" If that was the case, I was thinking that we should be advertising.

"No," he said, shaking his head. "But the risks are as I said, and I will not put our lives on the line for chicken feed, especially with so little information to go on. For all we know Lillia could be an imposter sent to kill us or lead us into a trap. We have made a few enemies in this business.

"Tomorrow I'll check out her credentials, just in case. Besides, we could use a maid—and one that looks like that won't hurt. I'll also get Raz to do a recon of the mountain pass area with Eekadinosaur."

"Who's Raz, and what's that other thing you just said." I had been there almost four days and never heard either of those names.

"Raz is our other partner," Grarr explained. "He's a Gillian, a big lizard man. Eekadinosaur is his pet ultraopteryx, a really big, winged reptile. They live in the tower."

"We have a tower?" I hadn't had much opportunity to explore the winery thoroughly, but I *did* think that I had seen most of it.

"Pops, if you haven't been to the tower, you probably haven't see the upper three floors or the five sub-basements," he said as he refilled his pipe.

"Apparently not." I responded. "I'll get Durik to give me a thorough tour as soon as the opportunity arises."

"Anyway, sorry, Pops," Grarr apologized. "I guess we forgot to mention Raz. He was on a delivery when we met you. He gets back tomorrow morning. You'll like him. He's different."

"As opposed to what?" I asked. "Everything *about* you guys is *different*. This is the most *different* experience I have ever had."

"If there is a temple in the Briarwood Forest, Raz and Eekadinosaur will find it." He was ignoring my sarcasm.

"I'm going back to bed," I said. "Kid, could you give me a hand down?"

Durik picked me up and put me down onto the floor. "I vill vake you for morning Sabbath Poppa Szvirf," he offered.

"That will be fine, Durik." I then hit the sack and dreamed of Elvish women and whipping cream.

CHAPTER - 4

RATS!

The next morning, when I awoke, Grarr and Lillia had already gotten up early, gone to see the lawyers, and done all the money transfers. They were sitting in the kitchen when Durik and I entered.

"Morning Pops," Grarr said as he poured me a glass of tea.

Lillia stood and greeted us before she went to the stove and began to prepare breakfast for Durik and me.

"Pops, you're going to Lillia's house this morning with Durik," Grarr began. "Lillia's going with you so she can collect her things. On your way I want you to rent a horse and wagon and hire a stable hand at the livery to take it to Lillia's house. Get him to load her things and bring them here.

"Here's some cash to pay for it. After that you and Durik go to William's and see if you can dig up some clues," he added as he stood up and tossed ten gold coins onto the table. "Keep the change; you might need some pocket money."

Durik lifted me up, put me on the table and then placed my little dining table beside me. "Now you can eat vit us, Poppa Szvirf."

"That's nice, kid. Thanks," I said as I sat down on the little wooden box the boys had brought for me to use as a chair.

Grarr continued, "I have to go and meet up with Raz. I'm sending him out to do a recon of Lillia's and the surrounding area before he heads off to the mountain pass. I'll tell him, if he sees anything that looks like it might be a threat, to take it out, so you three won't have to deal with it," He put his overcoat on and began to leave, adding, "Dress warm. It looks like we might get rain and there's a bit of a cool wind coming in from the west." With that he was gone.

Lillia was busy at the stove cooking eggs and flapjacks. She was also brewing some kind of mulled wine. She looked a little less anxious than she had when she arrived the previous evening.

"Flapjacks Durik's favourite breakfast," the kid said, trying hard to appear friendly to Lillia. "Pretty lady not be afraid today. Durik be protector for her and Poppa Szvirf. Not let anysing harm."

"You can count on that, Lillia. Durik here is the best fighter I have ever seen," I added to Durik's attempt to seem harmless to her. "Why, he and the boys saved my life, fighting superior numbers. Durik, you fought four of them didn't you?"

"Eleven Dark Elf killers," he replied.

"Eleven! I guess I missed some of the action while I was being thrown into the bushes," I said in amazement.

"Durik be lady's friend. Not vorry," he said as Lillia put his breakfast on the table. "Lady Durik's friend?"

"I...I hope so," she replied nervously. He was terrifying. "Enjoy your breakfast," she said as she turned quickly back to the stove.

After we finished eating our breakfast Lillia cleaned up and asked when we'd be leaving.

"As soon as you're ready," I replied.

"Well, seeing as all of my clothes, except the ones on my back, are at home. I think I am ready now. I mean it's not like I have to get changed or anything," she said with a sad look on her face.

"Then let's go." I said.

Durik had already packed us for the trip. He'd even packed a lunch. That boy was always thinking of other people and putting them ahead of his own needs. He may have looked like a demonic monstrosity, but he acted like a saint.

We started by walking downtown.

Briarwood was always so alive during the day. There were people of all walks of life in the streets. We passed hawkers selling just about anything you could think of, and street performers dancing and singing and doing all sorts of entertaining things, as well. It wasn't like home at all. Back in Sensimilia everything was very organized. Performers did their shows in theatres only, and there were no street merchants to speak of. Every merchant had a shop to sell their wares from. Very orderly.

Yet, as much as I was enjoying the sights, I still had to find the livery, so Durik took us on a couple of shortcuts that eventually led us to a stable.

When we got there, we hired a couple of guys and a horse and cart to go to Lillia's house to get her things.

As we did not want the crime scene disturbed before we got a chance to look it over, we arranged for the movers to arrive about two hours after we'd be getting there.

We then made our way through town once again with Lillia in the lead this time. Durik carried me on his broad, armoured shoulders. This worked out well for me as he had numerous spikes up there to hold onto.

We weaved our way through main streets and back alleys until we got to the west gate. There Durik and Lillia presented the guard with their citizens' passes, claimed me as a visitor, and bid him good day.

The walk through the countryside was very pleasant despite the slight chill in the air. I got to see things that, up until the last few days, I had only read of in books about the surface world. There were birds, grass, clouds, and all sorts of other things that surface folks would consider to be quite mundane. I, on the other hand, was finding it all to be very exotic.

We passed numerous groups of people coming to and from the city. Most of them gave us a wide berth when they saw Durik. Some were whispering to each other under their breath. This seemed to bother the kid, and Lillia appeared to notice that he was feeling a bit alienated. She tried to make small talk, but it was plain to see that she didn't know what to say to him. He was terrifying.

This went on for quite some time, but she never gave up.

After a couple of hours we came to a road sign which pointed west saying: To Al'Lankmire; and south saying: Briar Way—no exit. This was the way to Lillia's house.

Once we turned south onto Briar Way we stopped seeing people on the road, and the kid began to relax a little.

The whole mood of the moment seemed to change as Lillia showed us places where she and her sister collected herbs and roots for their potion making. We passed over a small bridge where, she informed us, she fished for trout and gathered their drinking water. As we got closer to her home Lillia and Durik actually began to speak more than two words to each other. Lillia was truly a lady, always polite and courteous, and considerate of others' feelings.

At first, I thought she might just be humouring the kid, but as the morning dwindled by I could see that she was sincerely enjoying our company.

Durik explained to her that she would be safe living at the winery and that she would enjoy many holidays and employee benefits.

I explained that there were no other employees and that her presence would be a nice shift from the norm, and that she could have her sister come and live there too, as soon as we found her.

The winery needed a woman's touch, I thought. Besides, she seemed to be really smart, maybe we could get her to do the books or something like that.

The entire trip took us about three hours, but we finally arrived at Lillia's house just as the sun began to burn its way through the overcast of rain clouds. There were no other houses within five or six miles.

Her home was a quaint little two-story cottage nestled in a cozy little clearing in the forest. It was painted yellow and green and had beautiful little flowerbeds all around the outside. We stopped at a gazebo about ten yards from the front door.

"Lillia, I think you should wait here while we go inside and take a look around. If you need us for anything you yell." I needed her to stay outside because I didn't want her emotional state to interfere with one of my hootspas.

She agreed and Durik led the way. He made me wait at the bottom of the steps as he stealthily climbed them and went through the front door. After a couple of minutes he reappeared and signalled for me to join him.

I climbed up the stairs, no easy feat as each one was almost half as tall as I am. At the top there was a cute little welcome mat with pictures of blue birds on it.

Once I was inside Durik lifted me up on his shoulders again. He carried me around as I directed him to where I needed to go.

We checked out the downstairs first. It was quite nicely furnished with antique cabinets and shelves. It wasn't hard to tell that two girls lived here.

The curtains and rugs were spotless, as were the surfaces of all the fine wooden furniture. There were floral patterns on everything and plenty of little keepsakes and knick-knacks on the shelves.

There was also a painting of a distinguished looking Elf couple sitting next to a hearth, which I concluded was of her parents.

We checked out the parlour where we found modestly rich carpeting and comfortable looking seating for five or six Elf-sized visitors. There was a nice little fireplace as well.

The kitchen was small but functional. There were numerous jars and bottles on the shelves some empty some full of liquids of all colours, all carefully labelled.

Here there were pots and pans hanging from a rod suspended from the ceiling, and in other areas there were all sorts of wild herbs, roots, and mushrooms tied in bundles and hanging from hooks in the walls.

In the center of the floor stood an antique dining table and four chairs that looked as though they had gotten very little use. All was as it should have been, or at least it seemed that way. There was no sign that anyone had been there for days.

"Poppa Szvirf hootspa house now?" Durik asked.

"Not yet kid. I think we should check out the upstairs first," I suggested as I took a look up the narrow, carpeted staircase. There was something about that staircase that was giving me the heebee jeebees.

Durik slowly carried me up the stairs drawing some sort of weapon. (I can't really remember what it was. He had so many different ones it was hard to keep track.) He was perfectly silent, which was an amazing thing in itself. How he was able to move so quietly in all that spiky, pointy, painful looking armour was beyond my comprehension, but somehow he managed.

At the top of the stairs there was a door to the left and another to the right. Both were closed so I decided to go left as the sun would be shining on the right side of the house and the left side would be more comfortable if there were any big windows.

We approached the door and Durik put his ear against its polished surface. After a few seconds he stepped back and turned the knob.

When the door opened, we saw what was obviously a girl's bedroom. Everything was pink and powder blue. There was no sign of a struggle or forced entry in this room. The window was shut and locked.

We decided to take a look around the room for any hidden clues. Durik began checking under the bed and in the closet while I checked what turned out to be Lillia's dresser. I was in the middle of searching for clues in her underwear drawer when Durik interrupted.

"Nothing here Poppa Szvirf." He started to approach me.

"Better check that closet again kid. You never know what you might miss. It's better to be extra careful than to let something get past you," I suggested as I continued to route through her soft, silky, gossamer, skimpy, lacy—clues. Yeah—that's it. I was looking for clues. I didn't find any.

"Okay kid, let's try across the hall," I called to Durik who was deep inside the closet.

He crawled out, with a few of Lillia's clothes hanging from the spikes on his armour. I managed to get them off without damaging them and we put them back as best we could. He then picked me up and we went to the door on the east side of the stair.

After completing the same door opening routine as before we entered what I guessed must be Alaeth's room.

Now this was a crime scene! There were definitely signs of a struggle here. Some of the furniture was tipped over and the window was wide open.

This room was much different than Lillia's. There were few clues as to the gender of its occupant. The furniture was very neutral. The colours were forest greens and rich reddish browns.

"Take a look around kid. We're looking for blood stains, footprints, anything that might tell us what happened here." I decided to bypass Alaeth's underwear drawer and start with the obvious.

The bed was unmade, and the sheets were pulled out of the corners of the mattress.

"Look here Durik," I said as I gestured toward a spot on the blankets. "She must have been pulled right out of bed. You can see where she was holding onto the sheets and blankets really tight as someone or something dragged her out by force. From this we can conclude that whoever or whatever it was must have been stronger than she was."

"See vhat Durik finds, Poppa Szvirf." He held up an amber coloured piece of glass he had picked up from the floor next to the bed.

"Let me have a look at that, kid." I had seen this before! "That's a broken firestone...But they only come from deep in the earth. Deeper than any surface dweller ever ventures. I wonder if this is part of that necklace that Lillia told us about."

"How it get to surface from G'nome land, Poppa Szvirf?" Durik asked.

"That's a good question, my boy," I replied. "I think it's time for me to hootspa the house now."

I prepared myself mentally and emotionally for the experience and when I was ready, I turned to Durik.

"Now, kid, I'm going to fall into a trance-like state. It's going to look kind of strange but don't worry. I might be that way for ten minutes or more and I'll need you to keep an eye on me so I don't fall over or walk out the window or something like that."

"Is no problem, Poppa Szvirf, Durik vill protect you," he replied as he sheathed his—*sword*! It was a sword! Now I remember.

Anyway, where was I?

Oh yeah...

He sheathed his sword and sat down next to me as I spoke the magic words to the spell.

"*Reruns. Always with the reruns,*" I spoke the mantra over and over until I was in a deep trance.

The room began to blur as a milky haze of smoke curled around me. I concentrated as best I could and tried to imagine someone sleeping in the bed.

After a few minutes the smoke began to take shape in several parts of the room, changing it slightly. It began to look the way it did before recent events.

I continued to focus my hootspa, straining my mind to draw out the images through sheer strength of will.

Then the smoke was gone, and I could see, through the closed window, that it was night. I was in the room, and I was really stoned. There was someone sleeping in the bed. It looked like Lillia. She was mostly naked, and the bed sheets were half off. I found myself wishing for whipping cream.

Then the window began to slowly open. It was silent, slow, and eerie, almost ghostly. I waited to see what was coming in through the window but at first I only saw the stars in the sky outside.

Then...slowly...right there, in front of my eyes...they began to materialize.

"Rats!" I screamed. "Giant invisible rats! They're all around me!"

The only creatures from the surface world that, on a regular basis, ever made it as deep into the earth as Sensimilia were rats. For little eight to fifteen-inch-tall G'nomes rats are quite a danger. They developed an almost addictive taste for G'nome flesh and hunted us whenever they could. We even imported domestic cats and trained them to hunt and kill rats as a precaution. No G'nomish police officer would go on patrol without a trusty guard cat. Most G'nomes are terrified of rats, and I was no exception to the rule.

"Rats!" I continued to scream in panic. And then the hootspa broke.

When I came out of the trance it was to a scene of total chaos. Durik, hearing me scream about giant invisible rats, thought we were actually being attacked by giant invisible rats. He was in the process of killing every last one of them, wherever they might be in that room.

He had already hacked the bed into toothpicks, smashed the mirrors, cut several new windows into the wall panelling, and cleaved almost every piece of furniture in the room into unrecognizable kindling. He was presently doing battle with the antique oaken dresser, which, unfortunately, wasn't up to the challenge, and it too joined the ranks of fallen furniture in furniture heaven.

"Stop! Kid! Stop!" I yelled until I finally got him to calm down.

"But you say…" he protested, shreds of curtain and clothing hanging from his points and spikes.

"I know, I know what I said, but it was just a vision," I tried to explain. "The hootspa let me see into the past. I saw three giant rats, walking on their hind legs, wearing armour and swords, sneak into the room under an invisibility hootspa.

"They materialized next to the bed, dragged Alaeth out from under the covers, and then they threw that firestone onto the floor releasing a spell that teleported the rats and the girl to who knows where."

I paused for a moment to try and compose my thoughts. "Kid—those rats were as big as you."

"You not like rats, Poppa Szvirf?" he asked.

"Rats not like *me*!" I replied. "They love the taste of G'nome flesh. They scare the crap out of me."

"Don't vorry, Poppa Szvirf. Durik not let rats hurt you. Durik crush them. Durik *cleave* them! Durik *hack* them to little … Aaaaagh!" Off he went again, hacking the room to bits.

When I finally got him calm enough to talk again, I convinced him that there was nothing left to kill in the room. "We really should be getting back to Lillia," I suggested.

But before we exited the room, I hootspa'd again to see if I could get a clue as to what those rats wanted with Alaeth. The empathic impression I detected was—*fear*. Those giant rats were afraid of harming her. It wasn't that they cared about her. On the contrary, they resented her, but they were afraid of what would happen to them if they damaged her in anyway.

I helped Durik remove the undergarments and shreds of clothing and curtains from his armour. "Kid, let's not mention anything about trashing the bedroom, okay?"

"Okay Poppa Szvirf," he replied as he picked a chunk of bedpost off one of his spikes.

"Oh, and let's not say anything about checking the other bedroom either," I suggested. "Especially the part about me searching the dresser drawers, okay?" (Hey if you could have seen her you'd be digging in her underwear drawer too!)

We then left the house and joined Lillia at the gazebo. She had laid out a blanket that Durik had packed in his rucksack and was preparing our lunch. She looked up at us with hope in her eyes as we approached. "Did you learn anything?"

We both sat down beside her, and Durik began to eat the sandwiches he had made that morning.

"Yes, as a matter of fact, I did learn quite a bit," I responded as I stopped Durik from eating and began to fill my pipe. "But first let us give thanks to holy Shiddumbuzzin for this food we are about to enjoy."

"Sorry Poppa Szvirf. Durik forget," the kid apologized.

"That's okay my boy, no harm done," I replied, adding, "I'm soon going to run out of Sensimilia herb. We have to think of a way to get some more, but first things first."

I recited the prayer of thanks and we smoked my pipe.

Then we began our lunch as I informed Lillia of *almost* everything I had learned.

"… so, as far as I can tell, whoever it was that took your sister also did not want her harmed. We might conclude from this that she is probably still alive. I have a pretty good idea who took her, I just don't know, as of yet, why, and where they took her."

"Was it Calabac?" she asked.

"Not directly, but I believe it could have been his lackeys. I'm not about to rule out any possibilities," I answered. "We need more information, and that might be found at the home of this William Worthy person. Let's just wait here for the movers, for now. Shall we?"

"Look Poppa Szvirf," Durik interrupted, pointing to the sky. "Is Raz!"

I looked up to see an enormous reptile flying by, hundreds of feet in the sky over us. It was gigantic. Its leathery, bat-like wings were at least eighty feet across. It blocked out the sun at one point.

On its back sat a huge black and bright-orange lizard-man carrying a long, wicked looking trident. The great pterosaur gave out a blood curdling screech and then disappeared behind the western skyline.

"What *was* that?" Lillia asked, obviously terrified.

"Don't worry dear. That's just Raz and his pet dinosaur thing. They work for us. He's on his way to the mountain pass to see if he can locate this temple of the Scave you spoke about."

"Poppa Szvirf, Durik make special lunch for you," the kid said as he opened a package he had taken out of the rucksack.

My eyes began to water and a lump was forming in my throat as I looked at what he had made. There in front of me was a plate full of deep-fried potato sticks and a bowl of pungent cheese dip. It was all I could do to keep from tearing up; I was so touched.

"That was very thoughtful of you, my boy," I said through glossy eyes.

After I ate my lunch, I started to take a look around the outside of the house while Durik and Lillia exchanged stories, as he attempted to impress her with his muscles by lifting just about anything he could get his hands on.

I began to appreciate how young he really was. In Human terms he was a teen-aged boy, around fifteen to seventeen years old. Grarr had found him in time to make sure he did not grow to be a murderous animal and had rescued Durik from a life of torment and abuse.

Kids, ya had to see him. He was terrifying to encounter under *any* circumstances—yet, in only a few seconds of being in his presence, one could sense his virtues, his honor, and his pure heart.

Durik was constantly aware of his appearance, and as a result he was constantly trying to ensure that Lillia was not frightened in any way of him. Lillia, in turn, seemed to become quite taken with him.

I wondered how she, an Elf, and probably near a hundred years old at least, might interact in an intimate way with one of so few years. Just by looking at them together, however, I could easily see that, in Human terms, Lillia was around twenty-three years old, and Durik was mid-teens, and in love.

How could he not be? Her Elfish charms were active even when she was not trying.

Yet, I could also see that Lillia was actually enjoying his company and was no longer on edge. They made a nice couple, you know? So opposite that they worked.

Anyway, where was I?

Oh yeah…

As I made my way around to the east side of the house, I was relieved to see that the damage Durik had caused in the east bedroom was not noticeable from the outside. That's when I found another clue—footprints.

They were no ordinary footprints. These were the prints made by very heavy, very large, bipedal rats. Alongside of them were a set of smaller prints that were made by an average, Human sized, pair of well-worn boots.

These boots would have been relatively inexpensive yet finely crafted. I concluded, by the plainness of their design that they would also have been relatively common and, as they had rounded edges to the souls, were probably made for someone who did a lot of walking. The kind of boots a delivery boy might wear.

The prints came from the south east, but only the booted prints returned that way. The rat prints ended at the house, just under the bedroom window.

I then returned to the picnic area to find Durik lifting Lillia up over his shoulders. The two were laughing and getting along quite well.

As I approached, he put her down gently and asked, "Time for holy ceremony now Poppa Szvirf?"

"Not yet, kid," I replied. He was really getting into this. "First I want you to come with me. Lillia, I think it best if you remain here. Nothing to worry about, mind you. If you need us just yell."

I guided Durik around the house where I had seen the footprints. "Look at these." I pointed to the four sets of prints. "The booted ones lead that way. I think we should take a look."

He agreed and drew a really long two-handed sword.

We followed the tracks to the edge of the clearing and saw that they kept going.

Durik sheathed his great sword and opted for two smaller short swords instead. We entered the forest and soon lost the trail. Here he sheathed one of his swords and took out an evil looking serrated knife.

"Wait here a moment, kid. I'm going to try something." I used a combination of two hootspas. The first was the seeing into the past hootspa, or the *Audit,* and the second one was called *Nosey*

Parker. This one allowed me to follow a set path without actually moving. Sort of like being out of my body or having a floating eye, which I could see through and move by will.

I prepared the two hootspas and informed Durik of what I was about to do. Then I hootspa'd.

Once again the hazy smoke curled around me and I was virtually transported to the recent past. There was a young Human male walking away from me through the forest.

The *Nosey Parker* hootspa kicked in and I followed with my remote-control eye. He began to walk at a faster rate, and I thought I heard a woman scream in the distance behind me.

I tried to keep up, but he started to run and I soon lost him behind a pair of huge boulders. When I got to the rocks and moved around to see if I could catch a last glimpse of the young man, there was something else there instead.

It was about as tall as Durik and was naked. Its skin was olive green, and it had big, black eyes. It had been squatting down and was just getting up when I turned the corner.

Then it looked right at me and snarled. Its teeth were all one serrated ridge, all yellow and nasty looking. It began to move toward me and suddenly I was aware that it could see me, but how could that be?! I wasn't actually there in that place, or that time. These events had already happened—days ago!

Just as it started to reach its long-clawed fingers out toward me I broke the hootspa. "Holy Shiddumbuzzin, kid." I looked up at Durik who was kneeling beside me.

"Vhat vrong Poppa Szvirf?" He stood and quickly looked around. "More invisible rats!?" he questioned as he prepared for battle.

"No kid. No rats. Something else. Some kind of creature was here—or *there*—in the forest when the Human—"

I saw that he was getting quite confused so I explained what I had just done and how I was following the Human in the forest. "Then he was gone. There was some sort of creature there instead, and I don't know what had happened to the Human, but he was gone. In its place was that—thing—and it saw me!"

"How it see you Poppa Szvirf? You not really there," he asked, still rushing from adrenaline.

"I don't know, kid. But I am sure it saw me. It reached right out at me." I got up and led him back to the house.

"Vhat kind creature you see, Poppa Szvirf?" he asked on the way.

"That, I don't know either," I replied. "It was hairless—and skinny. It was greenish-grey skinned with big, round, black eyes. Its teeth were not teeth at all, but some sort of bony ridge. Does any of this sound familiar to you?"

"No. Durik kill lots different evil monsters but none look like d'at," he answered while he scratched his head in thought.

Just then we heard the tell-tale sounds of a horse and cart coming up the lane.

We met with the driver and instructed him and his helpers on what to pack and where to deliver it.

Durik made sure that they understood that he would be quite upset if anything was missing or damaged upon delivery.

I paid them with one gold coin and got eighteen silver coins in return. This was way too much weight for me to be carrying, so Durik volunteered to carry it for me.

I didn't want Lillia to see the damage Durik had caused to her home, or her half-emptied underwear drawer! "Lillia, maybe it's best if you don't go back in there. It'll just bring back painful memories." I was grasping at straws, but it seemed to work.

She agreed and we then headed back to town.

The journey home was quite uneventful, and the dampness of the morning's drizzle was all but dried from our cloaks by the time we reached the west gate.

We were planning to return via the south gate, but decided, instead, to stop at an alchemist's shop to pick up some things I needed for my hootspa-ing.

We entered the establishment and shortly after a clerk arrived to serve us. I'd been there for just a brief moment and had only had time to scan the immediate area, when low and behold—there, next to a box of mummified lizards, was a barrel with the words: *Product of Sensimilia*, branded on its side.

The shop owner, an elderly Dwarf alchemist by the name of Rex Awl, explained that he'd purchased the barrel some twenty years previously from a travelling salesman out of the far east, who had said that he'd acquired it from a couple of Dwarf miners down on their luck, who, in turn, got it from a group of subterranean merchants. He thought there would be a market for imported herbs, but no one seemed to be interested. He'd kept it in stock anyway, under a preservation enchantment, ever since.

"How much for the whole barrel?" I asked.

"Truly?" he seemed surprised. "It is quite expensive. The best I have ever sampled, by the way." He grinned slightly, knowingly. "Although I have no idea where it originally came from. You see here," he continued. directing my attention to the gold embossing on the wood, "the language written on the side is not familiar to me, nor have I been able to find anyone who can read it."

"It's written in ancient G'nomish," I offered, with a wink.

"That's impossible," he replied. "The G'nome civilization is just a legend."

I grinned again, "Then I guess I'm a living legend, because I'm G'nomish."

He looked at me, seeming only now to realize my (shall we say) physically diminutive stature. "Truly?" he asked, amazed. "A GUH-nome?" He emphasised his understanding of the difference between a Gnome and a G'nome.

"I never lie about my species. The words on the barrel are written in G'nomish and they say Product of Sensimilia," I added. "How much?"

Durik chimed in just then, with a terrifying smile. "Poppa Szvirf is great hootspa-ligist. Is good person. Not evil."

I caught Rex's eyes as he was about to react, "I know," I whispered under my breath. I winked at him, to let him know that I understood his reaction.

Durik—looked—evil. It was just that simple. There was no way around it, unless you were willing to get to know him. I had been in his company long enough to know he was much more than met the eye.

"Well, if that's the case, I will make you a deal," he then, replied (with a wink).

He reached his pudgy little hand under the counter, pulled out an old ledger, and began to flip through the dusty pages until he found the transcript he was looking for.

I joined Lillia and the kid, already curiously perusing Rex's wares, while we waited patiently. Lillia was quite interested in his alchemical, and botanical stock, and suggested that we purchase several different kinds of herbs and spices for the pantry at the winery, as well as a few small pots of pigment.

She was an accomplished artist and, as such, was dealing with her trauma by focusing her emotional energy. She wanted to paint the kitchen and her own room, next to Durik's, which was across from Grarr's.

Anyway, where was I?

Oh yeah…

Soon enough, Durik had found a basket and was well underway, assisting her in gathering herbs for all of the cooking duties that she was about to inherit.

To be fair, Durik had done almost all of the kitchen duties at the winery up until the moment when I took up residency. He was something of a savant at it, (I'm not even kidding you), and I gotta tell ya kids, I just ate whatever he put in front of me, and it was really good, every time. Just sayin'. I even helped with the dishes— *that's* how good it was.

I looked back to Rex, who was playing with an abacus, and talking to himself. I had suddenly realized that Rex, this guy in front of me, was the *first* Dwarf who I had ever met in my entire life. I had to smile. The novelty was quite enjoyable.

After some final calculations were completed in his head Rex finally replied. "Fifty gold coins should do it, as long as you are willing to return to my shop occasionally and tell me some stories of your homeland. You see, I am a bit of an amateur ethnologist and would be very pleased to write a text on your people." His hands clasped in front of him, pseudo-begging for my acceptance of his proposal.

"There are, to my knowledge," he continued, "no texts to be found anywhere on the surface world that are dedicated to the subject of G'nomes. I know of your culture through my own people's legends and myths only. There are references in our own history, of your people sir, but again these references speak of G'nomes as only legendary. I am honored to have met ye. This is quite exciting, quite indeed."

"Kid,"—I turned toward Durik and Lillia, who were now carrying several baskets of herbs, kitchen utensils, and (what looked to be) bags of mushrooms—"fifty gold? Does that sound like a good deal to you?" I was not yet familiar with the surface world's economy, or the business ethics of this land, and frankly speaking, Rex seemed all too friendly and willing to deal.

You know? I've been around the block, so to speak. I *am* a G'nome, after all.

"Is big barrel, Poppa Szvirf," he replied, coming over to our locale and placing several baskets on the counter. "Very much herbs. Last long time. You say you need more herb, and here is more herb. Shiddumbuzzin, provide for us, yes?" He smiled—no teeth.

I took a brief moment to appreciate how much he had been listening to me when I was speaking over our last few days together. I had been missing my homeland and my family very much, and had been inserting that sorrow into my sermons, (which he had been partaking of, and inputting into). I spoke about things my dad had said to me, actually quoting the old man now and then. (I really missed my dad, and my ma, even after only a few days away from home.)

Durik had been listening more than I had given him credit for, it would seem. He smiled, again—no teeth, and turned toward Rex.

"Dwarf!" he barked. It sounded like a monster, screaming down a long stone tunnel. "Poppa Szvirf is good person." He continued to smile, struggling to not show his teeth. "D'is, good deal. Ve s'ank you."

Then, I turned back to Mr. Awl and said, "Rex, my man, you have made yourself a deal. I don't usually carry that kind of *cash* on me, so can I make a down payment and return tomorrow with the balance? Of course, I will leave the herb with you until then." I could only hope that I was doing business with this guy properly. All I had to go on was my own peoples' traditional mercantilist business practices to call upon as example.

"That would be agreeable," Rex replied. "Perhaps you might take the time then to tell me a little about your people?" He smiled, and for a moment I thought that he might be coming onto me.

But, after a double take, I could see that he was actually sincere about his request, and as such I replied, "No problem, if I'm not too busy. I'm right in the middle of an investigation, at the moment, but I do promise to make good on our deal," I replied.

"Poppa Szvirf not lie." Durik added, his voice sounding like it originated from miles away, echoing and shaping through an endless tunnel.

Even then, the sound of it made my skin crawl. He was terrifying, and Rex was not blind to this fact.

I looked back to our host for a reply, and he readily responded to our proposal with a happy and anxious nod, so I gave him *most* of the gold and silver I had.

"Add these herbs and spices to the total, good sir." I gestured to the baskets of dried plant material on the counter.

Rex, agreed and bagged everything for us while I counted the coins, placing them neatly on the counter. I then got a receipt for the deposit, signed for it, and bid Mr. Rex Awl a fond farewell as we gathered up the cooking supplies that Lillia and Durik had collected and exited the shop.

Outside, I paused at the curb to look around at the city street. People were shuffling about, and the daily business of living was well underway in Briarwood.

These were people who had *roots* in this town. I could see it in the way they walked—how they interacted with each other. Briarwood was a good town, with good people, for the most part.

I could smell the cook fires of the many street-food venders, the aromas of wines and special oils

wafting down the boulevard, inviting passersby to stop for a snack, or to purchase something for the evening's meal.

There was music from several street performers drifting down the lane from blocks away, which, for me, was *quite* exotic. There were no street performers in Sensimilia. People just didn't do it back home. This sort of made me feel sad.

My companions were kind enough to allow me my brief moment, to inhale the culture and try to distract myself from how much I was missing my ma, my pa, my pal Murray—Schnipsie.

I shook my head, then, and decided to top the morning off with a special treat. I took the kids out for ice cream, which Durik liked a lot, and I had never heard of.

There are zero cows in Sensimilia.

Kids, that stuff is amazing. After trying it, I have to say, ice cream could have stopped countless wars if it had been given to tyrants when they were kids, before they grew up to be assholes.

Anyway, where was I?

Oh yeah...

We were having so much fun I suggested we go to see an armour smith where I used the remainder of my money to purchase a shiny new spike for Durik's armour. After that we returned to the winery to find Grarr in the great library, reading an ancient text.

"How did it go, Redeye?" he inquired without looking up from the pages.

I politely asked Lillia to go and make us all some tea and then waited for her to leave the room before I unfolded the tale of the giant invisible rats and Durik's battle with them. I left out the part about the undergarments drawer.

"Durik s'ink rats vere real. Did not vant Poppa Szvirf hurt," the kid added, a bit embarrassed.

"These were no ordinary rats, Grarr," I continued. "They were standing and walking on their hind legs. They were as big as the kid. They wore leather armour and carried weapons, and they must have been intelligent."

"Why do you say that?" he asked as he put his book back on the shelf.

"They wore armour and had weapons. This to me indicates some level of higher intelligence," I answered.

"Good point, he replied. "Just what *are* these *firestones?*" he asked as he began to run his clawed finger across the spines of several other books, searching for one in particular.

"You can only find them in the deepest depths of the underworld," I explained as I handed him the firestone fragment Durik had found.

"I used to have a job in Sensimilia collecting them from the tunnels. G'nomes use them to hold powerful enchantments that, for one thing, keep the great machine city powered, but they can be used by any hootspologist to hold any hootspa (or so I am told).

"The beauty of the firestone is that because of its naturally enchanted state it is very easy to store hootspa in them. I don't know how giant bipedal rats would be able to get their hands on them though."

I then explained that normal rats were the only surface creature to venture as deep in the earth as Sensimilia, and how they had been one of the only threats that the great machine city really had in thousands of years.

"Just how much of a wiz—sorry—hootspologist are you, Redeye?" he asked, shaking his head as he took a book off of the shelf, and then another.

"I'm not really sure. I don't have any reference to go by. Back home we have hootspologists but those folks study for centuries to be able to do what they do.

"I've been at it for, what, a few days, maybe? Beornag and I have been studying the book of Shiddumbuzzin every night but neither he nor I are very experienced with hootspa," I answered. "He can't read. You knew that right?" I added.

He nodded.

I continued, "Okay—I *do* have some kind of hootspa in there called a static discharge that shoots something called lightning and it seems pretty powerful, but I haven't the foggiest as to what *lightning* is. Grarr, I'm a geologist from thousands of miles below the surface of the planet. Ya gotta work with me buddy."

He nodded his understanding. "Lightning is a powerful blast of energy that comes out of the sky, or *appears* to come from the sky, during big storms," he offered, then added, "I'm pretty sure it comes from the ground though."

"What are storms?" I asked.

"Here," he handed me a big book with a sigh. "Read this."

"Oh gee, thanks, another book," I said, accepting the ancient tome, and falling under its massive weight.

Hey, I'm only just under twelve inches tall, and that was a pretty big book.

The cover read, in Humanese: *A Complete Encyclopedia of the World as We Know It.*

He then helped me up and brushed the dust off my cloths. "Sorry Redeye."

"No problem," I replied as I dragged the book over to a small table.

"Redeye, I'm going to set you up with an appointment to see a guy we did work for a few times in the past. He can help you out with the hootspology and such," he explained, as he returned several other tomes that were on the table to their proper spots on the shelves.

"Great! Can he help me lift this *freakin' book*, too?" I said straining to lift the thing onto the low table.

"No, but he might be able to show you just how much of a hootspologist you really are," he replied, ignoring my sarcasm.

"He's a pretty weird guy but he is an accomplished spell caster—or so he claims," he added (almost) under his breath as he retook his seat and began to fill his pipe. "He makes good potions, and we have used his services in the past. He owns that big green jewel that the Dark Elves had stolen when we found you in the Briars."

"*Holy Shiddumbuzzin*, that reminds me!" I interjected. "I need a fifty gold-coin advance on my allowance. I found a store in town that has a big barrel of Sensimilia herb—*actual* Sensimilia herb, Grarr—ACTUAL! I could smell it though the wooden barrel!"

I sighed. "But he only has one." Then I smiled again. "He said he'd hold it for me until tomorrow. I was hoping this would not be a problem." I looked at him with anticipation.

"What store?" he asked.

"It's called, Rex Awl's alchemy and supplies," I replied.

"I know it. I'll send somebody over tomorrow to get it for you," he offered.

"I have to go personally. I made him a promise that I'd tell him about myself. He wants to write a book about me or something," I countered.

"Alright then, Durik is going to be busy tomorrow, so I'll have to send the Injoke with you," he said as he passed his pipe to the kid. "A book? Really? How long have you been here, Pops? You're already a celebrity." He grinned.

"Vhat *Durik* do tomorrow, Grarr?" the kid asked.

"Raz didn't find a temple today, bud, but he did find a couple of Swamp Trolls that tried to give him a hard time when he asked if they had seen or heard of the Scave. You and I are going with him tomorrow to *speak* to those Swamp Trolls and get a little information out of them.

"For now, why don't you two take a walk over to William Worthy's and get a look around." Grarr suggested. "Show the Redeye a little of the town. He's never seen anything like it where he comes from."

Durik nodded in agreement. Grarr was his hero. There was no doubt. He'd do anything Grarr asked him to do.

Just as I started to get glossy-eyed, thinking about their relationship, Lillia came into the room announcing that she had brought us tea and crumpets.

I had no idea what a crumpet was, but I had been high all day and hadn't had anything to munch on since the ice cream, so I was all over the food thing, and ate around six of them.

After we had our snack, she asked if there was anything specific we would like for dinner.

"Do your people eat fish?" I asked.

"Fish it is," she replied. "If Mr. Grarr would be so kind as to give me some money I will go to the market and get some supplies. We should put all of those wonderful herbs and spices we got at the shop today to good use. The pantry is almost empty."

"So is my wallet." Grarr dug in his pocket, produced ten silver coins, and gave them to her.

Then, as she counted them out and placed them in her purse he continued. "Remember, you're cooking for five who eat like twenty-five. Spend all of it and hire a delivery man. Also, get some horse meat delivered from the stock yards—and all of the vegetable farmers' throwaways." Then when he saw her shock at his request for the market's waste, "Beornag eats plants—vegetables, fruit, that sort of thing. He's not fussy," he explained.

"Durik and I eat the same food as you do, and can appreciate good cooking. We just eat a lot more of it than most." He grinned, teeth and all.

Lillia physically shuddered, then gave him an apologetic look.

Seeing the awkwardness of the moment, I interjected, "What's with the horse meat?"

"It's Eekadinosaur's favourite," Grarr replied. "We're going to need about four hundred pounds...no, better make it a cool thousand pounds.

After a brief pause for thought, he corrected himself. "You know? Come to think of it, get as much of it as they have. Eek is going to be home for a while." He dug out another twenty silver coins and gave them to her. "Get the old, stringy carcasses the locals have lost to natural causes. It's cheaper than the poor horses these

Humans kill for their hides."

She thanked him with a respectful nod of understanding and left the library.

"Pops, here, I got you something." He walked over to the room's large central table and picked up a tiny little dart pistol and a quiver of thin darts. "The guy who sells these in town, said Pixies use these to subdue their enemies. Be careful, the darts are poisoned. Just one will drop a rhinoceros. In this business you need to pack some insurance."

It was made from blackened and polished metal, with a horn handle. The firing mechanism consisted of an extremely powerful spring that rewound by means of a very basic and simple enchantment. It had to have been created by someone with a clock-smith's dexterity.

The darts were perfectly balanced, with hollow tips that drew venom from a reservoir in the shaft. They were actually fletched with the wings of insects, no less.

I accepted his gift and thanked him. Then I left him to his studies and gathered Durik for our next mission.

CHAPTER - 5

THE UGLY *DURIK*LING

Before leaving we took the time to have Lillia draw a map to William's house, so we wouldn't need to take her along. She had been through enough already, and I saw no need to have her there if we ended up running into anything traumatizing.

Durik read the map while I rode on his shoulder, as he was familiar with the town's layout. The map took us to the docks district and for the first time in my life I got to see an ocean, up close.

I could not have imagined a body of water so big!

"What's *that*?" I asked, pointing out to sea.

"Is ocean, Poppa Szvirf." Durik responded in disbelief. "You not know vhat ocean is?"

"Well, I've read about it, but I never thought I'd ever see one. Is it the only one?" I gazed out across the vastness of it. Never before had I seen anything so big.

"Is more, but Durik not know how many. Durik not smart like Poppa Szvirf," he said as we left the docks, crossing a small ornate bridge and entering a residential district.

"Hey, hey, hey, kid. Do not confuse smart with educated," I protested. "I've known quite a few knowledgeable G'nomes in my time and some of them were as dumb as a bag of pickled rocks. Just because you haven't had the benefit of a good education does not mean that you are not smart."

He smiled just then. He needed to hear that. He had been told, for most of his life, that he was a terrible creature who was stupid and dirty.

Tonight, you and I are going to sit down at the kitchen table, and I am going to teach you to read and write G'nomish." This excited him. "That'll most likely make you one of only two people on the surface of the whole planet who are able to do that. I'm the other one. Heck…they might even hire you at the university to teach it."

"You s'ink Durik smart, Poppa Szvirf?" he asked as we turned a corner to go down a narrow alley, the sounds of the busy docks now fading behind us.

"I have no doubt in my mind that you are smart. I went to school for hundreds of years and I couldn't even recognize an ocean without your help," I responded, patting him on the shoulder.

There were many vessels I took to be merchant ships of all sizes moored at the many docks and jetties, while stevedores were moving cargo of all sorts on and off the ships.

I watched, amazed as gulls flew around everywhere with their shrill laughing calls. There were no birds in Sensimilia and these were just about the most exotic animals I had ever seen.

The sounds of officers giving orders mingled with the cries of the gulls and the creaking of the many ships' rigging. Merchants were haggling with ship captains, and each other, while carts and wagons were being loaded with an assortment of mundane commodities. It was a very exciting place! I must admit that I was enjoying all of the new sights and sounds of the surface world.

There were also what appeared to be war ships in dock. Dangerous looking vessels that were much larger than their civilian counterparts. They were tall with four masts and bristled with giant crossbows and catapults. The seafarers on board these ships were all busy cleaning the decks and tying knots in ropes and such.

As we moved along the dockside I stared out over the vast, deep blue surface of the water in amazement.

Soon we reached William's house, in the poorest part of Briarwood. This narrow street was lined with empty crates and barrels, obviously from the nearby docks. Children were playing here and there, various articles of laundry hung over the street on lines between the buildings, and people were going about their daily routines until they saw us.

As we passed by, the residents got a look at Durik and quickly retreated inside their homes, locking their doors. Those who were not terrified of him, looked at him with contempt and disdain. There was no love for Durik in there. He seemed all too aware of that fact and hung his head in shame.

Soon enough we arrived at the address Lillia had marked on the map. "This would be William's house," I said, pointing at the number painted on the door.

The tiny abode was nestled in a corner against the city's north wall. Many old and broken items were strewn about the immediate area. There was garbage in the street, and someone had even defecated in a short alleyway beside the house. The stink was permeating the area.

The neighbours were peeking through their windows at us until Durik looked at them, then they disappeared behind their curtains.

I could see that this bothered the kid, so I quickly got to work. "Good thing those people went indoors," I said. "We wouldn't want anyone to see what we're about to do." I winked.

"You vant Durik kick in door, Poppa Szvirf?" he asked lifting his big, armoured boot up and placing it firmly against the door.

He was obviously a little frustrated with the local denizens.

"No, no, kid. I got this one," I replied. "I do want you to be ready to draw a weapon and defend me if there's something inside though. For now, keep an eye out for the guards. This will just take a minute."

I geared up for another hootspa while Durik kept watch. The street was now totally empty of people and that made things all the easier for me to do what I had to do.

I spoke the incantations and after about three minutes heard an audible click of the lock opening.

"Okay, kid we're ready," I announced quietly.

Durik drew a weird looking mace-like instrument from his weapons belt and opened the door. He ducked under the low portal as he quickly entered and closed the door behind him.

I waited outside for about two minutes until he returned and signalled for me to enter. When I walked into the house, I immediately noticed the smell. Not the stink of poop from the alley outside. This was stale and rotten smelling, like garbage that had sat in a moist environment for a long time. I took out my hanky and used it to filter the reek.

It was dark inside as the only visible window was covered with dust and cobwebs. Finally, I was able to remove my shades and look around with my own eyes.

We immediately started to search for clues.

The downstairs consisted of a small kitchen with an attached parlour. The furnishings were makeshift from old crates and barrels like the ones we saw in the street. There were no carpets, just flagstones and dirt.

The kitchen was even more frugal. There was one small shelf on which only a couple of dishes and one tin cup sat. There was no dining table. A very small hearth was in one corner, and it looked like it had never been cleaned.

From a string that ran across the ceiling hung two small cooking pots and a warped pan, covered, like everything else, with a layer of dust.

"In my homeland, kid, nobody would be allowed to live like this," I said as I looked around in disbelief. "Every single G'nome is taken care of. No one goes without, and we *all* pitch in to make sure that's the way it stays." Seeing William's house made me a bit frustrated that anyone would be forced to live in such squalor. Durik nodded in agreement.

From the kitchen there was a short stairway leading to an open portal. We also found a door that had been sealed shut with a big padlock. We opted to check out the stairs first.

There were only four stairs to climb but Durik gently picked me up and carried me to the top. "Here you go, Poppa Szvirf."

Beyond the open portal was a bedroom. There were rotting blankets on the bed that had not been disturbed since the last time it had been made—which seemed like years ago. The curtains on the window were makeshift from some burlap sheets. Other than that, there wasn't much of anything else in the room.

A chest of drawers revealed that when William supposedly moved out, he didn't take much with him. The drawers were full of old clothes. Although of very poor quality, they were all in surprisingly good shape for being left for as long as they had been.

A small closet was also full of several old patched and tattered coats and a few pairs of trousers hanging from hooks. We checked the pockets, but they were empty. There were also a couple of pairs of old boots with soles that matched the prints near Lillia's house. I pointed them out to Durik who gave a quick nod of comprehension.

"Well, that's all that's in here," I said. "Let's get a look at that locked door."

"Look here, Poppa Szvirf. Durik find something." He gestured to a small piece of paper crumpled and hidden in the corner of one of the drawers in the chest.

I smoothed out the piece of paper and found a short note had been written on it.

Will, I came by today to drop off the hatchet that I borrowed. You weren't home. I'll put it in the basement with the other tools. I'll be back in town in a few weeks. Maybe we can get together then. I miss you, boy.

It was signed: *"Love, Dad."*

"This is a note to William from his father. It says he dropped off a tool that he had borrowed." I showed the note to Durik. "Kid, this note has been in that drawer for more than a year by the looks of things. Look—" I pointed to the floor. "No footprints anywhere in here. No one has been here for a long time. Let's check the basement."

Durik, once again picked me up and carried me downstairs to the kitchen. He put me down next to the basement door and I began to hootspa the lock. After a couple of minutes, it still wouldn't open.

"Vhat vrong Poppa Szvirf?" he asked, knowing, instinctively that something was not right.

"I don't know, kid. My hootspa won't work on this lock."

"Durik vill try," he offered. "Durik vill be quiet."

He put his huge, clawed hand around the padlock and began to twist.

"I dunno kid. I'm thinkin' it ain't gonna give to hootspa, so muscle ain't gonna matter." At first, I thought he had high hopes of breaking a lock that big, but he strained and grunted a little, and with the tendons in his neck at the verge of snapping, I heard a muffled cracking sound. I thought he'd broken one of his fingers, but he slowly removed the lock from the latch on the door.

"Dhere you go, Poppa Szvirf," he said nonchalantly.

"Holy Shiddumbuzzin kid, that was incredible!" The lock was the size of my head. I patted him on the back of his leg and suggested that he get ready in case there was something nasty beyond the door.

This is when I noticed the quality of the lock. "Kid, there's no way anyone who lived here could afford this kind of lock. I mean, why this lock here, while the rest of the doors have cheap locks? Better get ready for the worst," I added.

He put away his weird looking flail and drew out a hand axe. Durik liked variety.

Then he gently opened the door, squeaking on its rusty hinges. Beyond, filled with dust-covered cobwebs, was a mouldy and musty set of stairs that descended into darkness.

I stepped forward and used my superior G'nomish vision to see where the stairs might lead. They ended about ten feet down at a landing, but I couldn't see any further as they abruptly turned to the left.

"After you, kid." I gestured for Durik to take the lead.

He carefully walked down the creaking stairs with his axe ready for chopping anything that might have the misfortune of startling him. I followed about two feet behind. Durik had night vision as well. It wasn't as sensitive as mine, but it should serve the purpose in this case, so I opted out of hootspa-ing up some light.

Here the stench was mind numbing. It was as though we were descending into some kind of legendary land of garbage.

Just as Durik reached the bottom of the stairs and was trying to get a look at the room beyond, I heard a hissing noise and then the sound of something big moving across rubble very rapidly.

At the same time there was a weird sound as though a thick

liquid was being forced out of a small orifice.

"Look out Poppa Szvirf!" Durik screamed as he threw himself between me and a long worm like creature that exploded out of the darkness. It was a monster with several multi-faceted eyes and multiple tentacles sticking out of its boney head. The thing was enormous! It had to be fifty feet long with hundreds of little legs like a centipede.

I watched in horror as Durik managed to reach the creature just as it started to spit some kind of sticky, viscous slime at me.

His body blocked the stream of noxious stuff as it spewed all over him. His axe came down upon the monster's head with an audible crack and the sound of wet flesh being cleaved. Over and over again he hacked at the beast.

I screamed a warning to the kid as I saw, out of the corner of my eye, another of the foul creatures. It was already spitting its slime at him from across the room—and then there was another!

Three gigantic monsters were now falling upon Durik as he tried desperately to fend them off. He swung his axe at them over and over connecting each time but the wounds he was making seemed to immediately heal themselves as soon as he'd remove his weapon.

"Run, Poppa Szvirf!" he yelled as the putrid fiends covered him with their foul slime. "Run! Durik gets dizzy! Slime is poison!" I could sense his fear, even over my own.

I have to admit, I was just about to do as he said—and then it hit me. How could I just leave him there to die?

I knew that the little dart gun that Grarr had given me wouldn't do much good. These things were much bigger than a rhinoceros, whatever *that* was.

There had to be something I could do. The beasts were on top of him now and he was on his knees. He had dropped his axe and was desperately trying to force the creatures off with his claws, but I could see that the poison was taking affect and he was weakening fast.

Their long probing tentacles were wrapping around his arms and pinning them to his sides as they pulled him to the floor, spewing their filth all over him.

Suddenly desperation turned to rage as I stood, helpless, watching my new best friend get cocooned in giant worm slime.

"Hey!" I yelled.

One of the creatures now noticed me.

"Get off of him you filthy vermiculite!" I pointed a threatening finger at them.

What else did I have? I always got scared when my mom pointed her finger at me and yelled. Right then it was just instinct that was guiding my actions.

"You're all *Schmatzel*." I screamed at the top of my lungs, trying to get their attention. I thought that they might end up chasing me and leave Durik alone.

What was I thinking?!

Just then, the immediate area started to light up as my finger began to glow green. The creature that had initially noticed me was getting uncomfortably close when suddenly, a blast of energy left my finger in a beam of green and blue light!

It forked into three separate beams about two feet away from my finger and struck the creatures with a loud hissing! I could smell their putrid flesh burning as they let out blood curdling, squealing sounds.

All three then took notice of me and quickly started to charge, their bodies writhed in agony from the sizzling, smoking wounds that my hootspa had made in their wriggling ghostly pale flesh.

"*Schmatzel*." I yelled again. *Schmatzel* is a really good way of telling someone, in G'nomish, that they are the worst kind of asshole.

Sure enough another blast of energy leapt out from my finger and struck all three of the creatures. This knocked me on my butt, and I was momentarily distracted.

Luckily, two of the beasts died from the sheer force of the blast's impact.

However, the third continued its advance toward me, as I struggled to get up. I crawled a bit and managed to get to my feet once more. The creature was quite close to me at that point, so I turned and desperately climbed a few stairs. Again, I am very small. Those stairs were like a wall to me.

I struggled and the going was slow. When I stopped and looked back, I gasped in horror when I realized it was right on my heels. Its slimy tentacles began to wrap around my ankles and pull me back down into the basement as I screamed in terror.

"*Schmatzel!*" I yelled again, pointing my finger at the beast's head.

This time the blast came out at point blank range and, as there was only one of the things left, hit with full force, square between the monster's many eyes. I covered my face as the creature's head exploded in a shower of sizzling, putrid, white and purple flesh and bone.

Standing up I tried to shake off some of the rancid goo. I was covered from head to toe in the stuff. It was all I could do to keep from blowing chunks right there on the steps. Oy!

Then I remembered.

"*Durik!*"

I jumped down the stairs and rushed to his side, slipping in the worm guts. He was not breathing and was covered in the poison slime. I couldn't get to him without touching the sticky gunk and that would only end up killing me too.

I had to think fast. I had no idea how long he would last with that stuff covering him. I pulled out my pipe and quickly filled it. Then I lit it and took the deepest draw I had ever taken before. I blew the sweet-smelling smoke all over his incapacitated form and spoke.

"Holy Shiddumbuzzin, I really need a miracle right about now. This young boy just risked his life to save me. *Me*, the only Redeye you have! I beg you to help him now in this moment of desperation. He loves you."

I took another long draw from the pipe and once again blew the smoke all over Durik. "Don't you let him die!" I demanded. "Don't you dare let him die!"

I was desperate, stoned, and without a clue as to what to do next. I fell to my knees, my head hung low, and began to weep. I wept like a baby, begging the Mellow One to help. I kept puffing the pipe and blowing the smoke onto the kid's helpless frame.

Eventually, after a few minutes of continuous smoking, I had to sit down. My head was spinning from indulging so fast. Tears ran down my cheeks as I sat there, stoned out of my mind, helpless and frustrated. I wondered how I was supposed to explain this to the other boys. They were going to be heartbroken. I surely was.

Then, the frustration took me, and I stood up straight, almost falling over. I regained my balance and did something desperate. I shook my finger at the kid's lifeless form, covered in slimy venom. "You listen to me, Durik Thuckov Eechitendie! You get up off that filthy floor and clean that slime off of you right this very minute young man!"

I looked up and pointed my finger at the ceiling. Then, realizing what I was doing, I pointed my finger at the ground. "And you—you get your proverbial crap together and heal this boy right now or I am out of here! Do you hear me?! I will pack up and leave and the entire civilization of the deep G'nomes will never have known you ever existed!"

That's when I passed out . . .

Yup. Another dream.

YUK!

The following wildlife vignette is brought to you by:

Gershwin, Gershwin, and Garfunkle's Fine Herbs and Hashery

"We totally forgot our slogan...ask us later."

The mound crawler is a fearsome creature straight from a nightmare. A member of the giganticus vermiculae family, these vile worm-like monstrosities can reach lengths of three hundred and fifty feet; though such cases are extremely rare and only found near huge metropolises where garbage and graves to feed from are abundant.

The mound crawler is almost always found in small family colonies that share in the gathering and pre-digestion of their putrid and grizzly banquette.

The mound crawler is usually pale blue or white in colour, although several have been spotted in the far southeast that were rumoured to have been a pale orange.

The mound crawler has twelve long prehensile tentacles that

erupt from a chitinous, armored head. Two of the tentacles are shorter than the others and are used to spit a sticky, paralyzing contact venom that immobilizes their victims permanently, slowly shutting down the victim's bodily functions. Prey is later taken to the main nest where, provided it survives the venom, it suffers starvation and thirst while hanging to die. The dead are later encased in a cocoon where they predigest in an acidic bile that the crawler excretes.

Crawlers are hermaphroditic and individuals possess both sexual organs, yet still need a pair in order to procreate. Each pair can produce up to thirty offspring.

Mound Crawlers lay their eggs in the rotting carcasses of anything large enough to hold them, before burying the host corpse. There, the eggs gestate for nine weeks.

Once hatched, the young feed on the putrid corpse/host for several days and grow exponentially until they finally leave the nest in search of food and breeding partners.

For more information about the Giant Mound Crawler or for a copy of this wildlife vignette, contact the G'nomish Film Board Society, 66 Six-Packs Street, Allthewater, Sensimillia. 420420420

HOOTSPA!

I was walking through a forest of giant herb trees, smoking my pipe. My cousin Bernie was there, walking beside me, and he was talking. Good gawd, I hate that guy.

"Szvirrrrf." He sounded a lot like Shiddumbuzzin.

"What? What is it this time?" I was not yet aware that I was dreaming again and, as so often happens in the dream world, I had forgotten all about events in the waking world.

"You have been loyal and devout," he said.

"Thanks. Glad you approve," I replied.

"I have heard your prayers," he continued.

"Oh yea? What did they say?" I asked. "And by the way you should be minding your own business and not listening in on other people's prayers. Just 'cause your folks got money it doesn't give you the right to eavesdrop. You're not that special, Bernie."

As I said before I was still in the forgetful stage of dreaming.

"But I am Shiddumbuuuzzzzzin," he replied.

"Bernie, you really ought to be careful of who you try to impersonate. If you get an omnipotent being angry with you, even *your* rich folks won't be able to bail you out. Besides you could have at least worn a costume or something," I scolded him.

"You see me as another because you miss your family and friends back hooooooome," he replied.

"Well, you could have picked a better image for yourself. I mean, I like Bernie and all, but it's not like I'm about to drop to my knees and worship him or anything."

Then, "Wait a sec. Come to think of it; I *don't* like Bernie. He's a schmuk, and that makes things even more confusing."

"Duuuuuurik, your friend, is dyinnnnng," he replied.

That's when it all came back to me.

"Durik! Holy Shiddumbuzzin! You have to save him!" I pleaded as the image of Bernie faded to swirling clouds of intoxicating vapours and smoke.

"You don't have to threaten meeee. I heard your prayerrrrs and was getting to iiiiit. You caught me in the showerrrrr," he continued. *"I will never forsake you Szvirrrrf, but you can only call upon these kinds of favors verrrry few tiiiiimes. They cost me a fortuuuuunnnne."*

"I don't care if this is the last time you ever help me! You must help me though," I continued to plead.

"Durik is speciallllllll, Szvirrrrf." His voice had then taken on a more urgent tone as he took on the form of a shadow in the mists and smoke of my dream.

"I know he is. He is my friend. Please help him," I begged as I floated gently downward to eventually land on soft earth.

"His body is twiiiiisted by chaaaaaaosss but his soooooooul is G'nooomiiihhhsh, Szvirf," he tried to explain.

"What do you mean?" I asked.

"He is the favourrred of the great harrrvesst. He is the protectorrrr of the seeeeeeds of truuuuth. Neverrrr leave his siiiiide. He shall be your chammmmmmpion—and minnnnne. Go nowwww... Goooooo."

At that he drifted up into the canopy of the towering herb trees.

That's when I woke up and looked over at Durik who was covered not with slime but with coils of effervescent smoke; a blanket of drifting holiness, the smoke's tendrils embraced him like an ethereal mother holding her child. Tiny streams of holy smoke found their way into Durik's nostrils, reaching far into his body, repairing the damage caused by the fiendish venom.

I struggled to get up as I watched it all unfold before my eyes. Amber and green sparkling lights filled the area like a swarm of multicolored fireflies, while the smoky, ghostly figure gently placed the kid's body back onto the basement floor.

Imediately Durik began to breath as the smoke exited his nostrils. He drew in great breaths and coughed as he lay there.

I ran to his side as the smoke dissolved completely and the lights faded away. I tried to no avail to lift him to a sitting position. In all that armour with all those weapons hanging off him, he must have weighed four hundred pounds. What was I thinking?

Eventually his eyes opened, and he turned his head to look straight at me.

"Holy Shiddumbuzzin talk to Durik in dream, Poppa Szvirf," he said.

I began to weep with joy. I had never been a parent, but I imagined that this is what it must be like. I wrapped my little arms around the kid and gave him a big hug. "I thought I lost you, kid! I really thought I lost you." I held on to him as tight as I could.

"Durik not lost, Poppa Szvirf. Durik right here," he said rather confused. "Big vorms jump on Durik and Durik say, 'run Poppa Szvirf!' but you not run. You blast living *crap* out of *big* vorms vit *big* hootspa. D'hen Durik fall asleep and hear voice." He sat up and looked around. "All vorms dead, Poppa Szvirf?"

"Yea, kid, all the worms are dead." I sighed as I stood there staring at him in wonder.

"Zat vas *very* good fighting, Poppa Szvirf. Vhat d'at hootspa called?" he asked as he stood up.

I could only stand there and chuckle.

"Vhat so funny Poppa Szvirf?" He was looking around at what turned out to be an excavated cavern, for whatever was making me laugh.

"I'm just happy that you're alive, kid," I responded as I, too, stood up. "*That*, my boy, was called *Schmatzel*. It's a very nasty thing to say to someone and, apparently, a very nasty hootspa as well."

"Holy Shiddumbuzzin say Durik is holy varrior. He say Durik must vake up and help Poppa Szvirf. He say Durik must find Hackem. He not say who is Hackem. So Durik vake up." He was now rooting around the dead worm bodies. "Ve take dead vorm home for souvenir, Poppa Szvirf?"

"I don't think that will be a good idea, kid. The cops will want to know where we got the fifty-foot carnivorous, poisonous, tentacle-headed worm we're dragging through the streets, and then they'll find out we broke into this house and—well there'll be a lot of explaining to do. It could get ugly. Besides these things reek!" I explained. "What's this about Shiddumbuzzin talking to you in your dream?"

"He say, 'Duuuuurik, must help Szvirrrrf.' He say, 'Duuuuurik, isss holy varriorrrrrr, protector of Redeyyyye. Durik must find Haaaaaackemmmm. Now vake uuuuuup.' And d'at all he say. Okay?" He looked as though he was being punished for something he wasn't supposed to do.

"What makes you so sure it was Shiddumbuzzin?" I asked.

"He say, 'I am Hooooly Shiddumbuzzinnnnnn,'" he replied.

"Don't worry kid. You didn't do anything wrong. I just want to be sure of what just happened to us, that's all," I reassured him. "The Mellow One spoke to me also. He said that your body was of chaos but your soul was G'nomish. I'm not sure what that means, but it looks as though holy Shiddumbuzzin has taken an interest in you personally. You are supposed to become the first paladin of the faith, a holy protector of the followers of Shiddumbuzzin."

"D'is be good thing, Poppa Szvirf?" he asked, still a bit confused, as he took out his hanky and began to try and wipe off the worm guts that were all over me.

"Well, I suppose it depends on how you look at it. If you like the idea of being the chosen hero of a powerful deity then I would say—yes, it is a good thing," I replied.

"But, Durik, that road will not be an easy one," I warned. "There are many rules that you will have to obey if you want to be a holy warrior."

"Vhat rules, Poppa Szvirf?" he asked as he began to take a better look around the cavern.

I followed close behind, kind of forgetting where we were. "Well, first of all...there's...ah...um... You know what kid? I don't know of any to be honest with you. Normally you would learn those things from the head of the religious order to which you've pledged your services."

"D'at be you, Poppa Szvirf," he concluded.

"Well then—I guess I'll just make some rules up," I replied.

Then I remembered where we were.

It was huge! The floor sank in the middle of the cavern like a big shallow bowl. It was about three hundred feet across and obviously stretched out under the city walls.

I also noticed broken, stone foundations of what were once underground rooms. These differed in size, and the walls were all demolished.

Upon closer inspection we discovered piles of empty coffins and other items that are normally only found in graveyards and mortuaries.

I took a moment to get my bearings using my *schmauz* and came to the conclusion that we were under the city cemetery and had passed under the north wall.

Kids, the *schmauz* is a special power that G'nomes are born with. It's a sixth sense that tells us where we are underground. I'll talk about it more later in the story.

Now, where was I?

Oh yeah...

These broken foundations laid out before us were once mausoleums and grave sites. The earth had been cleared out around them and they'd been looted from underneath. No one above would have ever known what was happening under the burial ground.

Something else was also uncomfortably evident. There were no bodies to be found anywhere. The coffins and burial sarcophagi had all be forced open and emptied of any contents.

There were even several areas, against the walls to the north and west, where other burial chambers had been located and raided, but the grave-robbers decided they had gone far enough.

Again, using my *schmauz* I determined that the edge of the cemetery above would have lined up with the limit of digging that took place here. There was no way that one Human could have done this all by himself. I wondered where all the rubble must have gone. Digging a cavern this big would surely have created a lot of loose dirt and rock.

It looked as though someone had been using the place as a dump, too. There was litter and trash of all sorts scattered over the area and the stench was mind numbing.

"Can we get out of here now? This place stinks and there are probably more of those things around—and maybe rats, too." I was thinking that we should probably come back with Grarr and the Injoke for backup.

"Look Poppa Szvirf." Durik was pointing at a barely noticeable crack in the wall that formed the shape of a rectangle about the size of a door.

I took a better look and concluded that it must be a secret entrance. I hootspa'd the secret door and moments later it opened to reveal a hidden chamber. We lit a candle Durik produced from his satchel and entered the room. Durik's dark vision depends on heat signatures and leftover impressions left by the sun's energy during the day.

This place had not seen sunlight in years.

We quickly deduced it to be another mausoleum.

When we got close enough to make out details, we saw that there was a skeleton inside, dressed in rotten rags that used to be clothing. The body was completely covered in cobwebs and dust. Durik kneeled over the corpse and began to search it, while he spoke a prayer for the lost soul of this unfortunate person.

I could see that this was the corpse of a Human man. It looked as though he died in the chamber from either suffocation or starvation or both. Someone had locked the poor man up in that stone vault and left him there to rot.

"Look, Poppa Szvirf." Durik held up a ring that had fallen off the skeleton's finger ages ago and rolled under the broken coffin.

He brushed off the mould and dirt and on the inside surface there was an inscription written in high Elvish: "To James Worthy, my friend. Thank you for your help. T.I."

"I wonder if this could be William's father", I thought. "Or maybe it's William himself. But if that's the case, who or, what was courting Alaeth? And who is this T.I?

We searched the man's clothes, some of which had William's name embroidered on them. With this in mind we took a closer look at the skeleton's remains and saw the remnants of the same embroidered name on the shirt.

Worthy.

Then it hit me. "The note—" I voiced my thoughts. "Love Dad, remember? It was crumpled and tossed aside. What if this was

William's father, and the bad guys caught him here?"

Then another thought came to me.

"He was going to put the hatchet back in the basement! He said so in the note. Durik, he must have come down here and caught whoever dug this all out in the act of doing so. They probably threw the poor old guy in this mausoleum and locked him in to keep him quiet about the excavations. He's been in here for at least a year, and probably died within the first day from lack of air." I sighed.

"Durik find secret place again, Poppa Szvirf," he said as he ran his hands over the lower portion of the small chamber's walls.

I hootspa'd the area and uncovered a hidden alcove just slightly taller than I am.

Using my hootspa I was able to open the secret door, revealing a short tunnel on the other side that led into small vault. It was far too small for Durik to fit, so I opted to cautiously take a quick peek inside myself.

I entered the short tunnel and soon emerged into a small antechamber where I found a large sea chest among assorted brass vases and plates, and a menagerie of other items one would expect to be found in the grave of a wealthy merchant or landowner. This was a secret chamber to hold the earthly belongings of the mausoleum's former occupant.

I first attempted to move the chest but was unable to after several tries. Whatever was inside was very heavy, so I called out to the kid, "Durik, do you have any rope?"

"Yes, Poppa Szvirf, Durik has rope. Durik vill get," he replied, and soon he had slung a coil of good rope into the chamber.

I quickly attached the end to one of the handles of the chest and took the other end back to the kid, who was waiting patiently, still studying the engraved ring.

"Here, kid. Can you pull that chest out of that room?" I

handed him the rope and soon he had pulled the trunk completely out of the antechamber.

The padlock on the chest was magically enhanced, and soon I was asking Durik to crush it like he had done on the entrance to the basement.

He took the lock in his hand and began to twist it. With a resounding metallic crack he forced the lock and opened the lid.

Inside we found a fortune in platinum. "Holy Shiddumbuzzin, kid! We hit the jackpot!" Even I knew how precious platinum was. We were stinking rich if we could get it all back to the winery. Durik started filling his pockets, and I followed suit.

Upon a more thorough search of the chest, we found a highly polished and twisted little stick of exotic wood. This could not be just a mundane stick. It was valuable or it would not have been in that chest.

We also found another ring, the sort one might use for a wedding. However, just holding it in my hands was enough for me to sense that it was enchanted.

"Look here, Poppa Szvirf." Durik held up a beautifully crafted, wicked looking dagger in a jewelled scabbard.

The handle of the evil looking knife depicted four bronze snakes, intertwined. The tails of the serpents extending into the steel of the blade, while the four heads held, in their mouths, a huge ruby.

It looked wicked and as such I suggested that we allow Grarr to see it before we ventured ahead with its analysis. Some items are said to be possessed by terrible spirits who, in turn, give those items their magical-like powers. Enchanted items are nothing to treat whimsically. They can be very dangerous, just to hold and study.

Finally, we uncovered a pair of Human-sized metal gauntlets, of remarkably exquisite craftsmanship. They were crafted of several alloys, including a metal that I did not recognize at all. That is saying a lot, as I am quite versed in metallurgy and geology. My dad was a machinist in Sensimilia, remember. You pick up a few things and I had always thought there were no metallic substances that I wasn't familiar with or at least aware of.

The gauntlets themselves consisted of very supple, black leather gloves. These were encased within countless interlocking plates of the strange red metal.

Other precious and rare alloys were also included in their makeup as studs, rivets and the like, while the strange red metal was threaded right into the palms. The metal seemed to have swirls of gold and rich orange hues also, as though it were on fire from within.

Durik decided he liked them, and he tried to put them on.

"There's no way those are going to fit you, kid. Your hands are way to—" I was corrected. The gloves stretched to fit him like, well, a glove. "Those are definitely enchanted, kid."

"Give Durik hootspa?" he asked.

"Let's take them off for now. When we get home Beornag and I will take a look at them and see if we can find out what they do," I offered, and he complied.

When he removed them they returned to their normal size again.

"We'll wait to see what the other things are about as well," I suggested. "Do you think you can carry all this money?"

"Durik has magic bag, Poppa Szvirf. Birsday present from Grarr, last year," he smiled as he showed me a well-made leather pouch attached to his belt.

"When is your birthday, kid? How old are you anyway?" I asked.

"Ve not know, so Beornag share his vit Durik," he replied.

"Ah, I see. So, when is the Injoke's Birthday?" I continued to inquire.

"Ve not know d'at too. So Beornag share Raz's birsday," he explained as he put coin after coin into his magic pouch.

"Okay…I'll bite. When is Raz's birthday?" I expected it to be the same as Grarr's.

"Same as Grarr," he answered with a smile. "Is Tuesdays."

We then collected our prizes and decided to leave.

Soon we had made our way up and out of the basement and back to the quiet streets, just how we left them. I relocked the front door after we exited and just as we turned to head home, we heard a woman yelling for help from up the alleyway in the opposite direction.

Durik immediately rushed to her aid with me keeping up as best I could. Soon he had turned a bend and I was barely able to keep him in sight.

When I saw him reach the woman, I recognized her as one of the neighbours who had earlier fled into their homes when they saw Durik coming. I could clearly see that she was being mugged by four villainous ruffians. Her clothes were torn, and she was covered with dirt from the street as though she had fallen, or more probably, been pushed down.

Three of her attackers were Human and the other was a stocky Dwarf with a hook for a left hand. They were all armed with clubs and surrounding Durik, looking to teach him a lesson for sticking his nose where it shouldn't be.

One of the Humans was even taller than the kid, and heavier too. He snarled at Durik, calling him a freak.

"Kid!" I yelled as I got closer. "Do you need some help?"

But by the time I was finished yelling Durik had clobbered all four of them with his devastating unarmed combat skills.

The Dwarf was unconscious, on the ground next to two unconscious Humans, while the taller of the fiends was now moaning in agony about his shattered kneecap and broken clavicle.

The poor woman just stood there in shock, and watched as Durik was in the process of tying the culprits up.

I quickly cleaned myself off with a simple hootspa before I approached her and calmed her down. She then told me of how the muggers jumped out of another ally and chased her to that very spot. They then began to tear at her clothes.

"Just as they threw me to the ground, he came out of nowhere and proceeded to beat them up."

She began to thank me for helping her when I interrupted and pointed out that it was *Sir* Durik Thuckov Eechitendie, *Holy* warrior of the faith of Shiddumbuzzin, who saved her from the dastardly villains.

She cautiously approached Durik while he was still in the process of binding the hands and feet of the criminals.

"My lord, Sir Durik?" she began. "I am forever in your debt. Thank you so very much. You are a true gentleman and a hero."

Durik was completely beside himself. He stood and bowed to the woman. "Holy Shiddumbuzzin make Durik do it," he said proudly.

She turned to me at a loss for words.

"That's the name of our deity," I explained. "Shiddumbuzzin. Oh, and kid—" I continued over my shoulder. "That was one hundred percent *you*. God never *made* you do anything. (He's so modest).

"Where is your temple, my lords? I must go there and give thanks properly," she offered.

"I am the high holy man, Redeye Neblinski. We do not as of yet have a temple in Briarwood," I informed her.

"Well if ever you open a temple, I will frequent it as often as your deity permits," she offered. "You are good people, and I will speak of you in that way to others. Thank you again."

Just then the cops showed up and a crowd was gathering. So, while the constabulary were questioning the victim, Durik and I slipped away before they discovered what we had been up to.

CHAPTER - 6

PUT *THAT* IN YOUR PIPE AND SMOKE IT!

We arrived at the winery, treasures in tow, just as Beornag was getting home.

"Ah—Redeye Neblinski an' Durik, how was yooze's day?" he asked as we entered the main production hall.

"Let's retire to the library and we'll tell you all about it," I suggested.

He agreed and after Durik volunteered to find Grarr and Raz, the Injoke and I made our way to the great reading room.

In the library we found Lillia dusting and organizing the books. "These tomes were in an awful mess. I took the liberty of trying to organize them better," she reported. "They are now separated into two sections: fiction and nonfiction. Those are, respectfully, separated by content, and from there, alphabetical order starting from the top down. Some were very dusty, so I cleaned them as well. Would you gentlemen like some tea?"

We said yes, mentioned that Grarr, Raz, and Durik would be joining us, and asked for some snacks as well.

She left the room and we inspected her work.

"Not bad," I said as I noticed the detail in which she had organized the categories. "Very nice. What do you think, Injoke?"

"Ize is not sure. As Ize ain't versed in da science o' readin' and writin', Ize feelz d'at Ize is not in a position t' give a reasonable opinionization," he replied. "*Looks* bettuh, dough."

"I am going to be teaching Durik to read and write starting tonight, would you like to join us?" I asked as I began to fill my pipe.

"D'at would be most generous o' yooze, Redeye. Do yooze t'ink d'at Ize could do it?" he asked as he sat down in one of two giant monster-sized armchairs. The other I assumed, was for Raz. Every room in the winery had chairs and other furniture made to fit the varying sizes of the building's occupants.

"Well, you *speak* more than one language. There's no shortage of brain power. I think if you're capable of speaking more than one language you should be capable of reading and writing at *least* one," I replied while lighting my pipe.

"Well, Ize t'inks d'at Ize should warn ya, weeze Hill Trolls are famous for weeze's hind brain," he explained.

"What does that mean?" I asked.

"Hind brain means d'at yooze might teach Ize sump'n but Ize won't actually learn it till sometime layta." He crossed his enormous legs and sat back in his chair as Durik entered with Grarr.

Two steps behind them was a sight to behold.

As he walked into the room, Raz actually blocked the light from the chandelier. He was as tall as Beornag, but instead of fur, he was covered with natural black and bright orange armour in the form of bony plates and scales.

His back had a strip of bright blue spines that travelled the length of his body and tail, while his eyes were deep amber with oily black slits for pupils.

He waved a long, clawed talon at me and spoke. "Missster Neblinsssski, welcome. I am Rrrrrrazzzzzzsssssss."

By this point I thought nothing would phase me but he

certainly managed. "It is a pleasure to finally meet you, my boy." I stood and shook his finger, being careful not to impale myself on his terrible looking claws.

I later learned that while working for a local merchant, moving valuables across country to the next town, Grarr, Durik, and the Injoke were attacked by a large group of brigands on the road.

Once most of them were dispatched the boys followed the survivors to a hidden cave in the forest where they finished the job.

This is when they found Raz—just hatching from his egg. The brigands were probably going to sell him to a circus or something, but Grarr decided to adopt him into the family.

Raz, being just newly born, and having already imprinted on the boys, had been with them for almost a decade, and although he was only nine years old, he was enormous, and more emotionally mature than Durik, who was about eight years his senior.

Gillians mature very quickly. Their childhoods only last one or two years before they develop into adults.

It was about four years after he was adopted that, one Tuesday, the boys bought him Eekadinosaur as a birthday gift. Grarr explained that he had traded an enchanted sword and pair of very good horses for the unhatched egg of Eekadinosaur, knowing full well what he was getting.

Eek's species matured even faster than Gillians, and she was large even for her age. Eek was an adult after only a year.

Four years later she was as heavy as a pair of elephants and her wingspan was well over seventy feet. The city allowed Grarr to keep the beast inside the walls with the understanding that she and Raz would be willing to help defend the city should the need arise.

The winery already had a half-collapsed tower, so they reserved it as Eekadinosaur's roost, and there she had lived ever since.

With chairs and floors creaking under their massive, combined weight, the three joined Beornag and me as we exchanged brief pleasantries. Soon enough, however, Grarr brought us to the topic at hand—business as usual.

"Well Pops, what did you and Durik find out at William's house?" He began to fill his pipe with brain cheese.

"Rrrrrreminderrrrrrr," Raz interrupted. "Package from sssssssouth." He handed Grarr a small crate which Grarr then opened, taking a long sniff of the contents.

I could smell it from my chair. It was packed full of fresh brain cheese.

"Shall I begin?" I asked, not knowing if there were to be any more interruptions.

"Yessssss, sssssorry misssssssterrrrrr Neblinssssski," Raz apologized.

"No harm done, lad." I replied as I passed him a pipe full of sacred herb.

I then told everyone about our ordeal at William Worthy's house, but when I got to the part where Durik was falling over from toxic shock the kid butted in and continued with the story.

"Poppa Szvirf hootspa big vorms and blast crap out of d'em! Big light and fire!" He had stood up then and was being quite animated. "Durik struggle to stay avake but poison make Durik sleepy! D'en Durik see Poppa Szvirf hootspa again and again. He make big hootspa and kill big vorms. D'en Durik fall to sleep."

"You actually died, kid," I interrupted.

"Durik vas dead?!" he asked. "How Durik alive now, Poppa Szvirf?"

I explained about my prayer and how Shiddumbuzzin gave me the power to bring Durik back from the dead.

Then the kid interrupted again.

"Shiddumbuzzin talk to Durik too, Grarr! He say Durik is holy varrior of Shiddumbuzzin and Durik must find Hackem." He stood in front of the boys with a look on his face that pleaded for their belief in his story.

"He's telling the truth," I added. "Part of what the great Mellow One said to me was that Durik was destined to be his champion and that the kid would be my protector and that I should not leave his side."

For a moment they all just sat there speechless. Then the Troll spread his arms and spoke. "D'at's *amazin'*! Wow! Durik, yooze has finally found yooze's place in society. Imagine—our buddy Durik—a *paladin*. Ize nevuh woulda guessed".

"There's more," I continued. "Albeit, not as impressive as all of that, but more directly related to our reason for being in that house."

I told the rest of the story about finding the body and the ring.

"That reminds me … How do we deal with spoils of battle when it comes to sharing loot?" I asked, "We did find a small fortune and some interesting artifacts."

"Usually, we work it out so that whoever finds loot keeps it unless they want to share," Grarr replied as he locked his gaze on my left breast pocket. The same pocket where I kept my herb. His monocle refracted the red light from his right eye into a narrow beam that danced over the pocket surface.

I reached in and took out my stash bag and handed it to him. "Help yourself Grarzy."

"What exactaly did yooze find, Redeye? Is it stuff? Ize loves stuff," Beornag said with anticipation in his eyes.

"We found about a thousand platinum coins which I was going to share with you fellas with the understanding that I am no longer an employee but a full partner. I figure my share of that money should suffice as my investment into the company. Does that sound fair?" I asked.

"If there are no objections…" Grarr looked around to the other guys.

"Holy hootspa!" Beornag responded. "Da Redeye saved Durik's life! Ize would t'ink *d'at* would be enough t' prove d'at he's wert 'avin' as a full pawtna."

"Then it's settled," Grarr said as he handed me his pipe full of a combination of Sensimilia herb and brain cheese. "Welcome to the company, Pops."

Just then Lillia came in with snacks and tea. Apparently, she was already acquainted with Raz, because she wasn't screaming in terror.

"Lillia, please sit down," Grarr said after she poured our tea for us and passed around a plate of deep-fried potato sticks and cheese dip.

"I noticed that you and Durik liked these at the picnic," she said smiling.

"This is sacred food," I replied with a huge smile. "Thank you, Lillia."

Grarr then told her about everything we had learned so far.

She sat patiently as Durik and I interrupted on occasion to clarify certain details or add to the story. Neither Grarr, Durik, nor I said anything about the platinum. Then she looked to me and spoke.

"The ring that William was wearing—may I see it?" she asked.

"I don't see why not," I answered, taking the ring from my coat pocket and handing it to her.

She studied the inscription and then sat for a moment in thought.

"Do you have something you need to tell us, Lillia?" I asked as I passed the pipe for the umpteenth time.

She waved a cloud of smoke out of her face and replied. "*T.I.* ...Those are my father's initials." She paused again, gave the ring back, and then continued.

"I remember, as a child there was a man who was my father's friend. He used to come by the estate quite often and my father was always happy to see him," she explained. "This man was Human. I believe my sister and I used to call him—Mr. James. It makes me wonder if Mr. James might have been William Worthy's father."

"That would be a little too coincidental if that was the case," Grarr replied. "I mean, here we have a man who comes to visit Lillia's father on a regular basis. He seems to be her father's friend. Her father then passes away under slightly mysterious circumstances and then years later *he* dies, his son is replaced by an imposter who makes like he's sweet on Lillia's sister, and then guides some giant rats to her home to kidnap her. He then disappears and is replaced with, or perhaps turns into, some sort of creature."

"Ize t'inks," Beornag offered, "d'at da question at hand is— why? Why would anyone wanna kidnap Lillia's sista in da first place—let alone go troo all a da trouble wit' impersonatin' a family friend d'at da family probly wouldn't recognize anyway?"

"The plot thickens," Grarr added. "Do you have any idea why someone would want to go through all of this trouble to kidnap your sister?" he asked Lillia.

"Not off hand, no. My father was a good man who helped the people of Briarwood. He had no enemies that I know of."

"Did your father own anything that someone might want bad enough to take several years in order to obtain? It would be something rare, or extremely valuable," Grarr continued.

"I can't recall anything of that sort; at least he never mentioned it to me."

"Did your father ever confide in you, talk to you about his problems or trust you with family business?" He was pulling at straws now.

"No, but..." She paused for a moment.

"Yes?" Grarr pried.

"Well, Alaeth was always the one who was good with numbers and business. I was the one who was good with the arts and creative things. She was virtually void of any talent, whereas I was useless with important matters of money and things of that nature."

Grarr interjected, "And it was Alaeth who was kidnapped, and whoever, or whatever took her was concerned with getting her alive, unharmed, and all her knowledge intact." He was on to something.

"What are you suggesting?" she asked.

"I'd rather not make any premature assumptions at this point. There is more here than just a simple kidnapping. Something else is going on," he said. "It has been a long day and we could all use a hot meal right about now. Why don't you make supper and let me think on this some more?"

"Alright then. I trust you all," she said as she got up from her chair. Lillia looked so out of place standing there, all prim and proper, surrounded by giant monsters.

She turned to Durik and spoke. "I am so happy that you did not die, Durik. It must have been terrible. If there is anything I can do for you, please do not hesitate to ask. Maybe we can clean your room together after we eat this evening, and then we can speak more." With that she left the room.

Durik's blue face suddenly turned slightly purple as he blushed, looking around at the rest of us.

We, in turn all knew how uncomfortable he was feeling after Lillia showed so much concern for his happiness. Never in his life had a girl ever even looked at him without grimacing or fleeing in fear.

We continued to pass the pipes without commenting. We sat in silence, trying to put it all together for some ten minutes or more before I finally spoke.

"Boys, Durik and I also found some other things in William's basement."

"Oh boy, here comes da stuff!" Beornag said, sitting up straight in his chair. "Ize loves stuff, Redeye!"

"What else did you find?" Grarr asked.

I signalled for Durik to empty his magic pouch.

He pulled the dagger, stick, ring, and gauntlets out of his satchel and placed them on the big round coffee table.

"I'm pretty sure that those gauntlets are enchanted, but I haven't had an opportunity to get a good look at the other things," I said as Grarr picked up the gauntlets and looked at them.

"These are plated with adamantite," he said, his eyes all ablaze with wonder. "It is the rarest of metals and completely indestructible. Only the fire giants of Talot are said to know the secret of forging it. You can be sure that whatever enchantments are on these gauntlets will be powerful."

"Durik took a liking to them, and I took the liberty of telling him that he could keep them," I said. "He already tried them on and they magically formed to fit him perfectly."

"You found them, bud." He handed them to the kid. "They're yours to do with as you see fit." He winked.

"Durik like metal gloves. Make Durik feel good," he said accepting the gauntlets.

"Redeye, Novac across the street has a hootspa that allows him to know exactly what kind of enchantments are on any given object. He charges us one hundred gold coins for the service. If you had a similar hootspa we'd save a bundle." (Grarr, always the penny pincher.)

"Beornag and I will take a look in the book after supper," I said. "We'll check out William's ring too; you never know."

"Good idea. Let me know if you find anything." Grarr then got up and prepared to leave the room. "I have to get cleaned up for supper. I'll see you guys in a bit." With that he was gone.

Beornag and Raz insisted that Durik and I tell the story of our ordeal at William's house once again, so we complied as we waited for our supper to be prepared.

This second telling had much more descriptive richness (for dramatic effect), and the story took much longer to tell.

When we were finished both Raz and the Injoke applauded with enthusiasm and congratulated us on our victory. Durik insisted that it was *my* victory and not *ours*, so I countered by telling the boys how Durik saved the woman from the deviants in the alley. Both Beornag and Raz commented on how Durik was well on his way to becoming a fully-fledged holy paladin.

Their encouragement seemed to sit well with the kid. He seemed to have a new aura about him. He was definitely proud—but not *too* proud.

After a while Grarr returned wearing a green and violet floral pattern smoking jacket and silk pajamas. I wish you could have seen *that*.

He informed us that supper was being served so we all made our way to the dining room.

Lillia needed Durik's help to carry the massive amounts of food to the table, but it was all brought out in good time, and Durik was more than pleased to have been asked.

Before we started eating, Grarr invited Lillia to join us and she was happy to do so (Though I have to wonder if, after the fact, she didn't completely regret it).

Beornag and I shared the responsibility of giving thanks for the repast and when we were finished thanking Ulm and Shiddumbuzzin, all mayhem broke loose.

Those boys ate like a pack of wild dogs at a carcass. On several occasions I had to yell out that I was not on the menu, as one of them would accidentally pick me up from the table, mistaking me for part of the main course (I'm small but—geesh).

When it was over, I didn't have the heart to just get up and leave without offering to help Lillia with the clean-up. Durik, seeing this, opted to volunteer his time as well.

It took about an hour to pick up all of the bones and scraps of food that didn't make it into a fang filled maw. Then we washed the multitude of dishes it took to cook and serve the meal. I used several minor hootspas to assist in the epic task of cleaning up the huge mess and we managed to complete the task in just under two hours.

After we were done, I told Lillia that I would look into hiring a couple of assistants for her. (Or perhaps an army).

Durik and I then went to the library and called for Beornag and the boys to join us. I had already retrieved the book of Shiddumbuzzin from my room so we sat down and began to smoke our brains out while we flipped through the pages, looking for a hootspa that would let me read an enchantment in an object.

It didn't take long before I had found one. It was called *Eureka*, and Grarr was very pleased.

Beornag was quite amused with how much it sounded like urethra and could not help but break into a stand-up routine on the whole subject. This somehow actually seemed to help the whole process.

We laid out the objects that needed to be identified on the coffee table and I began to prepare to hootspa the lot.

There were several incantations and hand movements I had to make as well as deep concentration, but after about fifteen minutes I was ready.

I hootspa'd each object in turn starting with Durik's gauntlets.

Grarr had been right about the gauntlets. Not only did they create a field of protection around the wearer that nullified the effects of heat and fire, they also gave the wearer the strength of a fire giant and the ability to speak and understand the languages of all Giant kind.

After much debate we concluded that Durik was not as strong

as a Fire Giant, and the gauntlets really would benefit him more than any of us.

The dagger with the snakes was next. It had been enchanted to be extra light and perfectly balanced. It bestowed upon the user immunity from disease and blindness. Any wound caused by this dagger would bleed terribly and would have to be magically healed or the victim would eventually bleed to death.

It all sounded a bit morbid to me, so Durik and I opted to let Grarr have it, and he accepted graciously. "This is an excellent weapon, Pops, thanks—you too, bud," he added to Durik. "

The ring, on the other hand (if you'll excuse the expression), was a hootspologist's ring. It enabled the user to do a multitude of things just by willing it.

This ring provided some protection against the elements by covering the wearer with a protective aura of magical energy that would defend against physical damage.

Any spell caster wearing the ring could store hootspas in it so that they could be released without any preparation at a later time. I also found that there were many other powers in the ring that the Eureka hootspa was not even *able* to tell me. One particular fun fact was that the ring's full power had never before been discovered by any of its previous owners.

I was also able to detect that it was not malicious in any way. Everyone agreed that I should have it, but it was fit for a Human-sized being.

Durik reminded me how his gauntlets were the same until he tried them on, so I attempted to put the ring on my finger—which didn't work. It remained its original size, so Beornag suggested I try it on as a bracelet.

That *did* work! It took some pushing and grunting but I finally got it over my hand and on my wrist. Then I tried to see if I could do something. I looked up at a book on one of the top shelves and tried to will it to come to me. It didn't—but *I* started to levitate in the air and right over to that book!

We were all excited about that and after about five minutes I finally figured out how to slowly come back down again. I decided that I would have to practice using it in order to discover its other unknown properties.

Then there was the stick. It was beautifully polished and seemed very old. Other than that, it was just a stick. Nothing else to describe, really, but when I hootspa'd the thing I found out that it was not just a stick after all but a powerful weapon. It had been cursed by an evil enchantment to make it *look* like it was just a stick.

After some poking and prodding with the *Eureka* hootspa I was able to safely remove the curse but was almost killed in the process! The little stick suddenly grew into what amounted to me, to be the trunk of an entire tree with the branches all cut off. It was still very nicely polished and still had its crooked, twisted, gnarly shape to it, but it was now about twelve feet long and it weighed a freaking ton.

Beornag lifted it off me while I tried to regain my composure, and, after a moment, I continued to hootspa it.

Here was an ancient weapon designed for use against an ancient foe that no longer even existed in the world. It was a club that had the potential to knock down entire buildings or cast aside whole platoons of enemies. It was called the *Maul of the Mountain*.

I realized that I had actually heard of this object before. During my many hundreds of years in university I had taken a lot of different courses to get several masters degrees. One of those courses was ancient languages, and I remembered reading an old Dwarvish text on a war that was fought eons ago between the Dwarves, their allies, and a race called the Hedrons. These were giant humanoids that were believed to be distant relatives of the stone giants.

After I studied the surface of the maul for a few more minutes I was able to locate a short inscription in very ancient Dwarvish. It read:

> *Maul for battle*
> *Strike the ground*
> *Try to bring the mountain down*
> *Maul for victory*
> *Win the day*
> *Make their army go away.*

These were the words that would activate the weapon to be joined with its user. Once activated, however, the user would not be able to wield any other weapon. Failure to follow this requirement would result in great suffering for the user. Thankfully this only included melee weapons. Missiles like arrows or throwing stones didn't count.

I explained this to the boys while we decided where it should go.

Raz was not particularly impressed with it. (He liked cutting stabbing and hacking weapons mostly.)

Durik didn't like the idea of only being able to use one big club to pound his opponents with, so he passed.

We all agreed that no one else was even big enough to carry it without looking like a lumberjack, and Beornag didn't actually own a weapon anyway, so it became his.

I found myself wondering if there was such a thing as an enchanted rubber chicken.

The Troll was so happy that he gave us all a hug—all at the same time, that's how long his arms were.

I explained to him that he would have to be very cautious about how and when he used such a weapon. If he misused it, he could end up doing a lot of harm and damage to those around him, and a lot of innocent people could be hurt, or worse, as a result. I volunteered to try some of my other hootspas over the next few days to find out exactly what he could do with such a device. He agreed to exercise caution.

Lastly, I hootspa'd the ring that Durik had found next to William's body. There were no enchantments on it to speak of. It appeared to be an ordinary ring, albeit a valuable piece of jewelry. There were markings on it, apart from the inscription, that I concluded were decorative as they didn't appear to be any kind of language I recognized. Other than that, it was just a ring.

We all felt that since Durik found the ring, he should be the one who decided where it should go—and with that he gave it to Lillia as a gift. "D'is be Lillia's Poppa's ring. Durik give it back. Is Lillia's, now."

I then thought it important to explain to the boys how this Calabac had been mentioned to me by the disembodied voice of Shiddumbuzzin and how that voice had told me to seek out Calabac as there were answers to questions that could be learned.

"Then this—Hackem (?) that Shiddumbuzzin spoke of, probably has something to do with all of this as well," Grarr added. "Do you have any ideas as to what or who Hackem is, Redeye?"

"I never heard of it before. Durik mentioned it," I replied.

"Well, that's just one more mystery to be solved then." He wasn't used to all this deductive reasoning stuff; that was sure.

The boys, up until that time, were doing jobs that consisted of a clear goal. They'd choose a method of accomplishing said goal and execute it. No mystery to be solved, no clues to be uncovered, just do the job.

He did seem to enjoy the change of pace though.

We smoked a bit more and Raz told us about his trip to the mountains to get Grarr's box of brain-cheese. He recounted his joy at seeing the white cliffs of the mountain pass and how the Goblins were, as usual, respectful and accommodating.

The Goblins knew who Grarr was. I would later learn that he had had dealings with their kind for many years, far to the south, in the Ice Lands. It is why they treated Raz so overly respectfully. They knew that he worked for Grarr.

I had never even seen paintings of Goblins before so, Durik, after looking for several minutes, grabbed a book from the shelf and brought it to my side. He opened the tome and flipped by a few colorful pages until he reached a two-page spread about Goblins.

Kids, if you could package terror, these guys would be it. They looked filled with hate and malice, and were as tall as Dwarves, which is substantially taller than I am.

They had sharp teeth, their limbs were spindly, yet strong looking. Their hands ended with sharp claws, and they had beady little eyes, much like a rat.

Oy.

After a few more pipefuls of herb, Grarr and Raz decided to turn in. Durik, Beornag and I stayed up for a couple more hours and started the task of teaching the two how to read and write. We opted to start with Humanese, which on the surface world was called common speech. Those poor guys didn't have the first inkling of how to read so I started with the alphabet.

It took two full hours just to teach them how to get from A to Z. I hoped that they might remember at least some of it when morning came.

After Beornag thanked me profusely he retired to his bed leaving Durik and me alone in the library.

The two of us stayed up a little longer and conducted a holy ceremony together. We sat, solemnly, face to face on the floor as I prepared the evening Sabbath-time.

Reverantly I placed my herb pouch on the floor between us and opened it. Instantly the perfume-like aroma escaped, and we both reacted, visually elated.

We smoked of the scared herb, and I noticed how much calmer and focused Durik became while indulging with me. Even the blueness of his skin became richer and seemed brighter and more full of life's energy. I swear, he seemed less—scary.

As I smoked and watched him prepare the deep-fried potato stick offering to The Mellow One, I realized how alone he was in the world. All he had was Grarr and the boys—his only family.

I decided, at that point, to add a rule to the book of Shiddumbuzzin for conduct as a paladin of the faith.

"Kid, this is your first rule of being a paladin."

He perked up immediately.

"Never judge a book by its cover," I said as I scribed the words into the holy book

"Is good d'at you teach Durik to read d'en, Poppa Szvirf." Then he let out a big yawn and said he was getting very tired.

I helped him to bed (even though he carried me all the way) and told him a bedtime story about my homeland. Then I told him to help Lillia when she cleaned his room, as that was a virtue of a paladin—to aid the meek.

He confessed to me how taken he had become with her, and how he was hoping that she would be his friend always.

"She's a smart kid, Durik," I said. "Lillia can see past the cover."

"Like, in book, Poppa Szvirf," he asked as his eyes started to close.

"Exactly like that. Good night, my boy."

I gave him one last tuck in and left his disaster of a bedroom. Then I began the epic journey to reach my cubby-hole in the basement, two floors below.

After I changed into my pajamas, I poured a nightcap, and filled my pipe.

Sitting at my little desk made from an overturned fruit crate and a nice slab of exotic wood, I added the events of the day to the journal section of the book of Shiddumbuzzin and gave thanks to the Mellow One for being there when I needed him.

I then smoked one last time and climbed into bed. There I lay for awhile, thinking of home, my folks and friends and how much I missed them, until I finally fell to sleep.

The next morning, I was awakened by a knock at my bedroom door.

I got up, put on my housecoat and answered it.

It was Lillia with a nice cup of herb tea. "Good morning, Redeye. I let you sleep in as I knew you were up quite late last night. Would you like me to bring your breakfast down to you, here?"

I had to stand there in silence for a moment. I thought at any minute another Elvish dame was going to come out of nowhere with some whipping cream.

Then I realized that this was no dream and that I was wide awake and feeling quite ashamed of myself.

What a nice girl.

"No thank you, deary. I'll be up in a moment; as soon as I brush my teeth and have a shower," I replied with a smile. "By the way, what time is it?"

"It's near ten o'clock," she replied. "The Injoke is upstairs in the library waiting for you. He decided to hold off on breakfast until you could join him. Should I inform him that you will be joining him shortly then?"

"Yes, that would be fine. Thank you."

I then handed her my clothes, which were still partially covered in filth from William's basement and the worm fight, despite my cleaning hootspa.

"Would you be so kind as to have these cleaned? They're the only clothes I have."

She took the tiny bundle and smiled. "Of course I will, Redeye."

I thanked her again, closed my door and gathered my bathroom things.

Then I made my way to my private washroom. It used to be for cleaning wine bottles and jars and such so it had a nice deep sink near the floor. The carpenters Beornag had hired had built a set of stairs for me to reach the counter and they'd installed a smaller hand sink for a toilet. It wasn't like back home in Sensimilia but it was cozy enough.

After I had my shower and brushed my teeth I got dressed and performed the morning rituals, then I headed upstairs to a wonderful discovery.

Lillia had cooked cheese omelettes and rolled oats. The aroma permeated the air and was accompanied by the wonderful scent of herb tea steeping on the woodstove.

"Good mornin' t' yooze, Redeye." Beornag was sitting at the table just tucking a napkin into his collar. It appeared to be an old ship's sail. "Would yooze look at d'is extravagant repast d'at Lillia has prepared for weezes?"

He was always sort of overly dramatic about everything but that really was part of his charm. We ate breakfast and laughed as Beornag told a couple of morning jokes. Lillia had joined us and after we ate, we got ourselves ready for the day.

"Is there anything in particular you would like for supper tonight?" she asked, pen and paper in hand.

"Why don't you surprise us with something from your own people's culinary selection?" I suggested.

She agreed with a smile and a curtsy. "Durik left you something in a box on the coffee table in the library," she added. "He made me promise that I would not forget to tell you."

Beornag and I made our way to the reading room where I found a box full of one hundred platinum coins and a small pouch with a letter that read: 4 U PZ. D.

"Hey, d'at's one a d'ose magic pouches d'at lets ya carry lots a stuff wit' out it bein' heavy!" Beornag explained. "D'at's what

Durik was so worried about d'is mornin. He was all up in a jitta about gettin' t' da magic shop and pickin somp'n up before d'ey had t' leave."

I put the coins in the pouch and attached it to my belt. It really was almost weightless.

It took another hour for my clothes to be cleaned and I used a simple hootspa to dry and press them. Once I was dressed, the Injoke and I left the winery for a morning of exploration in the streets of Briarwood. As Grarr had left us with no instructions we thought we'd just bum around for awhile until we thought of something constructive to do.

We spent the rest of the morning shopping. I needed a few more changes of clothes, especially socks and underwear.

We ended up having to go to a tailor to get clothes made for me as no store in town carried anything that would fit.

Then we made our way to Rex Awl's Alchemy shop.

When we entered, he was very excited to see me.

"Mr. Neblinski, it is such a pleasure to see you again," he said walking around the counter to shake my hand. "And who, may I ask, is your distinguished companion?"

"Nice to see you too Rex, may I call you Rex?" I shook his hand.

"Of course, may I call you…?" He was waiting for me to tell him my first name.

"Redeye, Szvirf Neblinski, but Redeye will do," I replied. This gentleman is a good friend of mine and the local leader of the faith of Ulm. Injoke Beornag, this is Mr. Rex Awl, proprietor of this unique shop."

"Pleased t' make yooze's acquaintance," Beornag said as he offered a finger to shake, but was good enough not to fart when Rex took it.

"I have come for my herb and to spend an hour or so

answering your questions about my homeland," I informed him as I began to dig out five platinum coins.

"Of course, of course. Can I offer you both a cup of Dwarvish mushroom tea?" he asked as he began to set up a small stool next to a table in a clear spot near the back of the store.

We politely accepted his invitation, and after requesting we allow him a short moment to prepare for guests, he quickly disappeared into the back room. Soon he returned with a tray of tea and some light snacks. He placed the tray on the table and asked us to help ourselves while he looked for something. We poured ourselves tea, and after a short time Rex returned with a folding chair fit for a Troll-sized rump.

"This chair was once the property of a nobel lord of the stone giants," he explained as he unfolded it and set it next to my stool.

"He carried it with him when he went on extended hunts or other outings. It has been enchanted to hold the impressive girth and weight of a stone giant so I assume it should be comfortable for you, Injoke. I hope it will suffice."

"D'at's mighty kind o' yooze, tanks," Beornag said as he took his seat.

I was impressed as the chair remained silent and sturdy. Normally furniture creaked when the Injoke applied his weight, even gently.

Rex then went back behind the counter and gathered some paper and writing implements as well as a small ornate box. "I am very happy that you decided to take me up on my offer, Redeye Neblinski. I am quite excited about getting started on my book about your people. Imagine, the only text known to exist on the surface world about the lost civilization of the Deep G'nomes. My colleague over at the university, Conan, the librarian, no less, will be so envious. I cannot wait for the bragging rights alone."

He returned to the table, pulled up a seat and began to ask all

---

sorts of questions about the physiology of G'nomes.

I answered as best I could, being very careful not to give him any misconceptions or half-truths. This was, after all, for posterity's sake.

He explained that he first wanted to know scientific facts about G'nomes as biological life forms, so as to have an explanation of what a G'nome was exactly. Thus the questions about G'nome physiology. He then asked about architecture and art and music before going on to life expectancy and family structure.

Beornag was very patient, but after three hours I noticed he was starting to fidget in his seat.

"Not to seem rude, Rex, but the Injoke and I have a very busy schedule to keep. Would it be too much to ask if we could continue this at a later date?" I asked as I stood up.

He stood. "My apologies, Redeye. It would seem that I have been all too selfish in my quest for knowledge. I have taken up far more of your time than you generously offered." He bowed apologetically. "I would be happy to continue this conversation whenever it is convenient for you."

Then he returned to the counter, bidding us to follow him, and there he opened his ledger. "If you would be so kind as to sign here?" He pointed to a blank spot under the purchase record for the herb. "Don't forget to include your address."

"Why do you need that?" I asked.

"I keep detailed records of all sales and purchases," he explained. "The local authorities demand it for tax purposes."

Just then I had an idea.

"Did you ever have to deliver anything to a temple or religious organization called *The Scave*?" I asked.

"Perhaps. I'd have to look in my records," he replied as he rolled the barrel of herb around to the front of the counter.

"I would consider it a personal favour if you could do just that,"

I said with a smile as I signed his ledger and added the address of the winery. "I do understand that it may take some time, but it is of utmost importance that we know the address of this organization as soon as possible. Lives could be at risk"

"I will begin searching the moment you leave, Redeye." He closed the book and then brought my attention to the ornate box he had moved to the table earlier.

"I thought you might be interested in this as well." He chuckled as he put the box on the counter and opened it. "I picked it up on one of my own travels."

Inside the box was a small supple leather pouch with some kind of faded symbols embroidered in gold on its surface.

"Go ahead take a look," he insisted. "I am curious to see what you think of it."

I gently lifted the item out of the box and took a look at the symbols.

"This is G'nomish!" I cried, looking up at him to see his eyes alit with delight.

"I thought so!" he exclaimed. "I purchased this about five years ago from a Dwarf merchant who said that it contained great power for the right person and great misery for the wrong person. It was part of a package of items that he was selling, claiming bankruptcy and the need for fast money to gain passage back to his homeland.

"I thought, at the time, that the markings resembled those on the barrel," he said, gesturing to the cask of herb now sitting next to me.

"When I got the pouch home, I was ecstatic to see that they were very similar. I am curious as to what they mean." He rubbed his hands together with excitement.

"The symbols are G'nomish writings," I explained as I gently handled the antique pouch. "It says: The greatest of civilizations are free to grow with the planting of one idea."

He gasped. "I must be honest; I never had the courage to open the pouch, after what the merchant said. I actually forgot that I even had it until after you left the shop yesterday. It took me several hours to find it."

At this point he was almost pacing the floor.

"What do you think is inside?" he asked.

"I won't venture to guess, but it feels like a lot of tiny little things," I replied. "What do you want for it?"

"Seeing as it is a G'nomish artifact, and you are the only G'nome who I have ever met, well, I think that you need only reimburse me for my costs and it will be yours," he offered.

"Now that is with the understanding that whatever is in the pouch, there will be no refund. The risk, however, as I am sure you will understand, is both of ours. If there is something quite valuable in the pouch it will be my loss, while if there is nothing of value in the pouch it will be your loss."

"No matter what is in this pouch, just having something from home is worth it to me to have," I replied. "How much?"

He looked through his ledger again and after a moment he came to the entry. "Ah yes, here it is. It was purchased in the Dwarvish capital of Ironhold on the twentieth day of April, five years ago, from a merchant named Hare Riss."

"He was a strange chap as I recall, a bit of a shut-in. He had a shop near the Spring Garden quarter, in old Anvilhaus."

He scratched his head for a moment and then, "He owned some peculiar looking dogs too... Yes, I do remember him."

He read on and then continued. "He said that he preferred not to divulge his source as they wished to remain anonymous. It cost me three hundred gold."

"D'at's a lot of coin Mista," Beornag protested. "Specially for an old bag. I can get a beautiful young assistant for d'at much."

Rex and I stood looking at him in silence for a moment.

"Yooze knows…? Old bag…? Beautiful young assistant? Get it? Aaaaah?" He held out his hands and waited for us to laugh.

I pulled three platinum coins out of my pouch and placed them on the counter with the five for the barrel. "You've got a deal," I said.

He held out the box. "It doesn't seem right; letting it go without the box that the artifact has been kept safe in for so many years. I imagine it must also be from your homeland, good Redeye. Take it, as well—no charge," he winked. "Call it a gift between two friends."

I placed the pouch in the box, thanked him graciously, and closed the lid. It really felt like I had a piece of home in my arms as I cradled the fine wooden box. I sighed, and my eyes surely got glossy right then.

Smiling from ear to ear, I signed the ledger for the sale and asked the Injoke if he would be so kind as to carry the barrel of herb, as my hands were kind of full, with bags of clothing and the box with the pouch inside.

Besides, you could probably have fit three or four of me in that barrel, so I had absolutely no chance at all of carrying it, even if my hands had been free.

Beornag, on the other hand, picked it up in one hand as if it were nothing more than a big loaf of bread.

We thanked Rex, reminded him to check in his books for the Scave, and left.

As soon as the door closed behind us the Troll spoke. "Man, Ize is glad t' be outta d'ere. I had t' fart sump'n fierce," he announced as he lifted his left leg and released something akin to the pits of hell opening up. "Aaaaaaah. Now *d'at's* betta."

Luckily I was ahead, and upwind from him, and was spared the toxic tempest that was a Trollish fart.

"Where now, Redeye?" he asked as we strolled up the main street.

"I thought that we'd first take these things back to the winery and then pay a visit to a certain Mr. Stelark at the curios shop." Lillia had said that he was doing business with William before her sister was abducted."

Beornag agreed and we headed home.

Even though the Troll was probably the tallest person in Briarwood and was a scary sight to behold (to say the least), his manner was jovial and friendly. As a result he was known, and even liked, by many people in the city.

As we strolled down the main street numerous people of different races and walks of life waved and said hello to him, calling him *Pelvis*, which I assumed was some sort of nickname. He waved back to them all, professing his love to each one.

When we arrived at the winery Lillia asked us if we would like to have lunch. We accepted her offer and soon she had cooked us some soup and biscuits. After we finished, we asked her to draw us a map to Aazh Stelark's curios shop. As an artist she was very good at drawing maps, and she seemed to know the city quite well.

Map in hand, Beornag and I headed out to talk to the half-Elf merchant known as Azh Stellark. It was now early afternoon as we travelled through the town. There were even more people stopping to say hello to the Injoke, and he took the time to introduce me as his friend and colleague to every one of them.

After an hour of walking and talking to passersby (mostly talking) we finally made it to the curios shop (which was, in all actuality, only about twenty minute's walk from the winery).

The fine shop was in the high-end market district of the city centre near the governmental buildings.

Displayed in a very nice, large window overlooking the street, were several curious looking objects: a silver brooch that was made into the shape of a flower; an antique dagger with a jewel encrusted handle; a man sized shimmering blue cape; a small Dwarf-sized umbrella; and several old books.

We entered to find a shop full of exactly what it was supposed to be full of—things of curiosity and intrigue. We looked around for a few moments at some of the bizarre objects on the many shelves and in the many cabinets until an elderly half-Elfish man approached us.

"Good day, gentlemen. Is there something in particular you are looking for?" he asked.

"We would like to speak to the proprietor of this fine establishment if that is possible," I requested.

"Well, that would be me," he replied.

"You are Mr. Aazh Stelark then?"

"Yes that is my name. What can I do for you?" He was a little over five feet tall with greying hair and green eyes. His facial attributes were not very Elfish, but his ears were pointed, and he was slight of frame.

He wore a pair of very nicely crafted spectacles, was dressed in fine, silken (multi-coloured) merchant's clothing and carried himself in a noticeably feminine manner.

"If we could have a moment of your time we would like to ask you a few questions about one of your clients," I explained as Beornag continued to look around at the inventory.

"I see that your friend is Hill Trollish, but I do not recognize your kind. Could you be of the Gnomish persuasion?" he asked, scrutinizing my small stature.

"Why, yes. I am a G'nome," I replied. "We are related to Gnomes."

"Of course, please excuse me for asking. I haven't seen one of your people since I was travelling in the far southeast, and that would have been...oh...over one hundred years ago," he began. "Said his name was...oh, what was his name...?" He tapped the nail of his right index finger against his teeth.

"You have seen my kind before?" I asked with excitement. I had never heard of a G'nome ever travelling to the surface world before me.

"Oh yes. I am sure of it. He said that he was from deep underground and that he needed to trade with *me*. He wouldn't explain why it was so important for *me* to be the one that he traded with, but he did insist that I be that one. I recall him saying that it took him several months to track me down. I remember he had a strange, puffy head of orange hair and was a bit taller than you are.

"I was travelling on a requisition journey in the Dwarf lands when we met. I believe I was in a small town called Riverside. Yes, that's it; it was in Riverside. I am sorry I can't seem to recall his name. He did dress similar to you though."

"What did he trade?" I asked, hoping for another barrel of herb. (You can never have too much herb.)

"He had some curious looking precious jewels he called firestones. They were really quite remarkable." Mr. Stelark stared into nowhere as he continued. "They glowed with a soft amber light that he said was totally natural. He also said that they were excellent storage devices for holding magical spells and enchantments.

"I took the lot from him and in return I gave him a few gold coins and a map of the Dwarf lands with detailed city maps and a guidebook—the last one I had in stock. That was all he wanted, and I have never seen him since, nor have I ever seen another of your people until today."

"Do you have any of these firestones left?" I asked.

"Why, yes, as a matter of fact, I do," he replied, gesturing for me to follow him.

He took me deeper into the shop to a glass case filled with all sorts of jewellery and there on one of the lower shelves were six firestones!

"What would these firestones cost?" I inquired.

"I can let you have all six for one hundred and eighty gold coins or forty coins each. I used to have quite a few more but I sold some over the years to different folks and, just recently, to a group of monks that have an enclave a few days travel from Briarwood."

He opened the case and took one of the firestones out to show me. "As you can see, they are really quite lovely. The craftsman who cut them must have been a master. I really don't know what they are worth. I do think that they are worth more than I paid for them, and taking into account inflation, and the rarity of such pieces, I think that the price I am asking is more than fare."

"I agree," I replied. "I'll take the lot."

"Excellent, shall I gift wrap them?" he asked as he removed the rest of the stones from the case. "I can also recommend a good jeweller who can have them placed in a setting for you. They would make a beautiful necklace for a deserving lady of stature."

"I'll pass on the gift wrapping. Thanks anyway. I will take you up on the jeweller though." I was thinking the jeweller he was suggesting might be the same person who mounted the stones on the necklace that William's imposter gave to Alaeth.

"Very good sir, is there anything else I can help you with?" he asked as he made his way behind the counter and began packaging the firestones.

"Well there were the questions I was hoping to ask you about a recent client," I reminded him.

"Oh yes, of course. Ask away," he responded as he wrapped the stones in tissue paper.

"Have you ever heard of a man named Calabac? Or an organization called the Scave?" I asked.

"Hmm…the Scave…that does not sound familiar," he replied. "Calabac, however—now that name does ring a bell."

He thought for a moment. "Oh yes, I remember now: Friar

Calabac. He was the leader of the order of monks I mentioned earlier. The same ones who purchased the firestones I spoke of. Odd chap, a bit eccentric. He bought quite a few things from me. Let me check for you."

He took a ledger from under the counter and began to search its pages. "Ah, yes, here it is: Friar Calabac. He made several purchases starting just over three years ago. He used to come by personally but later hired a young man to do his shopping for him, it being such a journey to and from the order's enclave."

Mr. Stelark ran his fingers over the page and then continued. "He purchased a magical pick and shovel from the Dwarvish high mountains, a wand of fire, a ring of pest control, a rod of growth, and a box of magical stones from the Sylvain Forest that, when placed around a large object, would make even a castle become invisible. Mind you, as soon as someone stepped through the invisible barrier created by the stones, they would be able to see the affected castle or whatever was being made invisible. Very nice though."

"Might you know where I would be able to find the good friar?" I asked.

"I am sorry, I do not. I offered to have my own delivery person bring him his purchases, but he declined. It would seem that his young man had other supplies and sundries to purchase and deliver to the monastery as well so it was more convenient for the friar to use his own people," he said, closing the ledger and replacing it with another.

He opened this book to a page that was, in part, empty, turned the book so I was able to read it and asked, "Will there be anything else?" Obviously he wanted me to sign for the purchase I was about to make.

"I would like to see that umbrella in the window," I replied. That morning, while I was waiting for my clothes to be washed, I had looked up storms and lightning in the encyclopedia Grarr had given me to read. That was where I learned what rain actually is and saw a drawing of a man using an umbrella to keep dry.

Mr. Stelark moved to the window and removed the umbrella. Passing it to me, he said, "It was crafted by a Dwarvish mage around two hundred years ago."

He guided me on how to open it as he continued. "As the story goes, the maker was short in stature, even by Dwarvish standards. The device, along with its obvious uses, is enchanted to deflect arrows both magical and mundane. It will also save the user from a long and dangerous fall if opened during that fall. It is supposed to cause the falling user to slow down and continue his or her descent as though they were as light as a feather. The cost is three hundred fifty gold coins."

"It's definitely yooze, Redeye," Beornag commented. "Ize t'inks d'at yooze should get it."

"So do I," I responded as I opened it and tried it out. "It will also be good for shading the sun from my eyes. I'll take it. No need to package it Mr. Stelark, I'll carry it out." I handed him the coins to pay for the umbrella and the firestones, signed for the purchase and thanked him.

As we were leaving he stopped us at the door. "I just remembered, once I did have to deliver an antique alchemist's apparatus to another address for the friar. He had sent the payment through his young man with a note as to what he needed and an explanation. The note read that his young man would be indisposed for the day and that another individual would be delivering the apparatus to the monastery and asked if I would be so kind as to deliver it to *him*," Mr. Stelark said.

"The individual's name was Vladimir Eupiess. He has, or at least had, a grand estate about six miles down the west road. I believe it was recognizable by the fact that it was the first stone structure you would run into if you were travelling from the south gate on the west road.

I remember that I sent the package with my servant who reported that there was someone there to receive it and that they signed the delivery receipt."

We thanked him again and left.

"Ize t'inks d'at weeze should get back t' da winery and get sump'n t' eat before weeze goes t' Vladimir's house," Beornag said as we started walking in the general direction of home.

"I actually wasn't planning to go to Vladimir's house without first informing the others," I replied. "Do you think we should go anyway?"

"Why not? Grarr, Durik, and Raz won't be back till much layta t'night. Weeze might as well do sump'n constructive," he responded.

"I guess you're right," I decided to go with the Troll's instincts on this one.

This Vladimir Eupiess might be able to provide us with some more information. I began to formulate a plan while we walked home.

Once again people waved and said hello to Beornag. Luckily, this time he politely waved back and didn't stop to talk to anyone, and we were home in about twenty minutes.

As we arrived Beornag picked me up and carried me the last half block. "Redeye, no offense, but weeze gotta get yooze some sorta fasta way t' travel. D'em little legs o' yooze's is gonna make it hard t' keep up wit' da rest o' us especially if weeze gotta run fast."

He was right of course. I just took it for granted that everyone walked as fast, or slow as the case was, as I did.

"What if I were to be carried by one of you boys?" I recommended.

"I didn't wanna even suggest d'at. I was afraid Ize might offend yooze or somp'n," he replied as he put me down at the door.

"Don't be silly, my friend. You are all much taller than me, this is obvious. I have no problem with being carried as long as it is in a dignified manner," I explained. "I don't want to be stuffed in anyone's pocket or anything like that. Riding on your shoulder is agreeable to me if it is okay with you."

"Okay, but yooze needs t' be ready t' jump if Ize gets in a fight," he said as he opened the door and held it for me.

"Well, with my new ring I won't have a problem with that, as it will allow me to float to the ground as you charge into the fray."

"Plus d'at new umbrella o' yours will do d'at too," he added, with a big smile.

We closed the door behind us and hung up our coats taking notice of how wonderfully clean everything was. Lillia had dusted the main production hall and even mopped the floors. The poor girl was doing everything in her power to keep her mind off her sister's disappearance. Luckily for her there was plenty to do at the winery and she was in no danger of running out of tasks to keep her mind busy.

"We have got to find that poor girl some help, Injoke," I said as we made our way to the kitchen.

"I was thinking that perhaps we should hire four or five townsfolk to help her with the chores and work in the production hall as well. I have a feeling that we are going to start getting busier soon, and we're not going to have time to make wine and clean this enormous place."

"Weeze can talk t' Grarr t'night about d'at, f'now let's get some grub inta us," he said as we entered the kitchen, which was also spotless.

Lillia was there slaving over a hot stove and oy, something sure smelled good.

"Good afternoon gentlemen," she greeted us as we entered. "Any news about my sister?" she asked as she stirred something in a cauldron on the stove.

"We are getting closer to finding Calabac," I responded. "After supper the Injoke and I are going to see a man who might know where we can find him."

"I'm starting to get very worried...I mean...more worried than I was. Alaeth's been gone now for days." She was crying with her back toward us. I think she thought we didn't notice. "I can't imagine what she might be going through. I hope she's alright."

"Don't yooze worry toots, Weeze will find y' sista, and weeze will trash d'at nasty wizid, or Izes name ain't Beornag, Injoke o' Ulm," Beornag responded as we both went to her side to comfort her.

She cried in our arms for a moment before finally regaining her composure. "Thank you both, you're so kind to me." She went back to work then, stirring the cauldron and peeking in the oven.

"What's on the menu?" I asked as Beornag lifted my little table and me onto the main dining table.

"I made a soup that my people call wild harvest broth, and picked up a few geese from the market that are almost through roasting. I also made Elf bread, which is sweet and fluffier than the bread that you are probably accustomed to. I hope you like it." She opened the oven and started pulling out roasted geese, one by one.

"We're going to look into getting you a staff tomorrow. How many workers do you think you'll need?" I asked, trying to keep her mind off her missing sister.

"Oh...well, I think if we had five people initially, we could get caught up on the cleaning. After that I could use one or two strong workers to do heavy lifting and maybe one other to help with the regular chores."

She closed the oven and started carving the geese. Every now and then she would stir a milky yellow substance in a small pot on the back burner.

"Fear not, lovely damsel, weeze is on da case, and shall hire, for yooze, a full house staff. D'at way yooze can concentrate on preparing us d'ose lovely repasts d'at yooze has been cookin'," Beornag offered as he gazed in amazement at the tantalizing gastronomic wonders she was dishing out.

Durik was an excellent cook, but Lillia had more recipes to draw from, and she was actually better at it than the kid was. Her meals were among the finest I have ever tasted.

She served us our food (the yellow stuff was a nice sauce for the goose) and joined us at supper. Beornag and I gave thanks for the repast and then we dug in. This time there was less grunting, growling, and mayhem. The Injoke was much better mannered than at our previous suppers. It was probably because he was in competition for food from the rest of the pack on those earlier occasions. The bread and soup were very exotic and they tasted quite good, so we ate all that we were allowed.

After supper we helped Lillia clean up and got ready for the road. I suggested that Beornag bring his Maul of the Mountain just in case we ran into trouble. He agreed and we were off to Vladimir's estate.

We headed to the south gate, which was just a few blocks away, as even more people waved to the Injoke and said hello.

"You're a bit of a celebrity in this town I see," I observed. "Hopefully I will develop as many friends while I'm here."

"Ize t'inks it's 'cause o' Ize's time spent at da Gruel and Grog," he replied.

"What's the Gruel and Grog?" I asked as we approached the south gate guard post.

"Oh, it's a bar d'at's a few blocks from da winery. Ize likes it 'cause it's got nice peoples an' stuff d'at Ize can relate t', namely gruel and grog," he replied as he showed his citizen's pass to the guard.

Gulls were calling to our left as they returned from their daily fishing excursions out to sea. I could also hear the mooing of many cattle ahead of us, somewhere outside the city walls.

The guard looked at Beornag's pass card and returned it, bidding us a good day.

That's when it hit me.

"Injoke, can I see your pass?" I asked.

"Sure t'ing, Redeye. Weeze gotta get yooze one o' d'ose real soon," he replied, handing me a (Troll) palm-sized card, a freaking billboard for me.

I examined the card closely and saw that his name, occupation, and address were printed clearly on the surface.

"Beornag, I think I have a good idea," I said as we left the city and headed down the south road.

"What's d'at?"

"It's a personal opinion, belief, or thought to be presented as a suggested means to solving a problem, but that's really not what's important right at the moment," I responded. "What *is* important is that Calabac had visited Briarwood on several occasions."

"Soooooo?" he prodded.

"Well, don't you see? He would have had to present a citizen's pass unless he was a guest, no?" I asked.

"Not really, he mighta had a visituh's pass, or a guest pass but Ize do seez where yooze is goin wit' d'is," he said as he picked me up and put me on his shoulder. "If weeze can get access t' da city records hall, and Crabby Sack has a citizen's card in his name, weeze might be able t' get his address from da recuds."

So much for only possessing hind brain.

"Exactly," I responded. "It might be worth a try."

"Da city ain't exactly in da habit o' givin out people's personal info d'ere, Redeye." He was playing devil's advocate. "How does yooze propose d'at weeze convince d'em t' let us gawk at da records?"

"Let me think about it." We needed a plan to get those records, but first things first; we also needed a plan to deal with Vladimir if we found him.

We'd travelled down the road for another fifteen minutes or so before we came to a bridge. There we came upon three little Human boys sitting on the edge, fishing. When we came close enough to cast a shadow, one of them looked up and screamed.

"Monster!"

He and another one of his companions got up in a panic and ran as fast as they could away from us leaving the other sitting there, terrified out of his pants.

"Please, monster, don't kill me!" he pleaded.

That was when I noticed that he was disabled. Beside him lay a finely made crutch.

"It's okay, young man. We are not monsters. Well, okay, *he* is a monster, but he is a *nice* monster." I comforted the boy from twelve feet in the air. "My name is Poppa Szvirf and this is Beornag. He's a Hill Troll, and a very nice one at that."

By this time the boy's friends were completely out of sight. "You're really big mister Hill Troll." He was almost crying. "Are you sure that you won't kill me?" he asked as the Injoke sat next to him on the edge of the bridge.

The water burbled gently underneath us as Beornag began to comfort the young lad. "Have no fear my little friend. Ize is one a da good guys." He bent over the side to see the fish in the river just beneath the surface. "Havin' any luck?" he asked.

The boy began to calm down, but it was still easy to tell that he was a little nervous.

Heck, I knew the Troll pretty good, and he still made *me* a little nervous at times. He was just *soooo big*!

"No sir. We didn't get anything, not even a bite," he lamented.

"What's yooze usin f' bait?" the Injoke asked as he put me

down beside the lad.

"Just worms, sir." The boy held up a can of dirt.

"Oh, well, d'ere's y' problem." He stuck his finger in one of his huge nostrils and pulled out a booger as long as my arm.

"Oooo, yuk! That's *really* funny!" The boy broke out into hysterical laughter. "What are you gonna do with that?!" he asked between laughs.

"Here, gimme d'at hook." The Troll reached over and pulled the boy's line out of the water. "D'ere's nuttin' better f' fishin d'en a big ole Troll booga f' bait." He hooked the sticky, slimy green and brown snot gob onto the fishhook and dropped it into the water. "Watch d'is."

The boy and I watched intently as the booger wriggled in the slow-moving water. Not long after it had submerged just under the surface a big catfish came up and bit the hook.

"I got one!" the lad yelled, laughing up a storm.

"Pull it in!" Beornag instructed. "Easy now so it don't get away."

After much struggling on the boy's part, he finally landed the fish. It was a fourteen pounder if it was an ounce.

"Told ya. Nuttin better d'en Troll boogas." Beornag then took to picking several other giant sized snot gobs from his nostrils and put them in the boy's can. "Here, in case yooze wanna catch some more."

The young lad was still laughing his head off as the Injoke put me back on his shoulder and we continued on our way.

"Gee, thanks mister!" the lad yelled after us.

"No prob, kid!" Beornag yelled back.

"That was a really nice thing you did back there, Injoke," I said as we continued down the road.

"Aw, yooze knows, Pops. Gotta take care o' da leaders o' t'morra. Deys is gonna be takin care o' us evenchally. Sides, the mayas' son couldn't run wit' his friends and Ize just wanted t' make sure he didn't go home t'night wit' nightmares."

"Did you say the mayor's son?" I asked.

"Yea, why?" he replied.

"That was the mayor's son?" I asked again.

"Yea, Pops, whattaya gettin' at?"

"I think I know how we're going to get to see the city records," I replied.

"How?" The Troll was not stupid by a long shot, but he was, sometimes, very slow.

I waited a moment.

...

Then I waited a moment more.

...

Then one more moment and...

"Aha! Yooze is gonna see if da kid can help us!" he exclaimed after ten minutes or so of thought. This is what his people called hind brain.

"No, *you* are going to see if the kid can help us. I just need to come up with a way for you to approach the mayor's mansion without causing alarm. Leave it with me, I'll think about it." There was definitely a plan here I just had to formulate it.

CHAPTER - 7

SILENT BUT DEADLY

After about thirty more minutes we finally came upon a large stone estate on the side of the road. It was surrounded by tall flagstone walls with an ornate iron gate. It was nearly dark at this time, and we could see lights flickering in some of the windows.

"Pops, d'at Elf food ain't sittin' too good in Ize's gut. Ize t'inks Ize might blow chunks from bote ends." Beornag was beginning to look a little pale. The dinner Lillia had prepared for us turned out to be a bit too spicy for his stomach.

"Can you hold off until we're finished here?" I asked.

"Maybe. Ize means, Ize t'inks Ize can," he replied as his stomach began rumbling like a sleeping dragon. "If it weren't f' da cramps Ize'd be having fun right now."

"I think we should just walk up to the house and ask to see Mr. Eupiess," I suggested. "The direct approach seems to be our only choice in the matter. What with your stomach problems."

Beornag's gut continued to rumble. "Okay Pops, but let's try t' make it quick, okay?"

We approached the gate and saw that it was open, so we entered the property while the sun continued its descent on the horizon. The grounds of the estate were overgrown with brambles and vines. It was obvious that a gardener hadn't been there for quite some time. The grass was wild—taller than me—and the road was littered with debris and potholes.

"It looks as though the lord of this estate might be pinching his purse," I noted. "This place is a mess."

We made our way toward the front entrance of the mansion as a hound bayed in the distance and the sun set fully. Beornag's stomach was really growling at this point, and I could see by the expression on his face that he was very uncomfortable.

"This shouldn't take long my friend." I tried to assure him. "We can ask the owners if there is a toilet you can use."

"Holy muddy rivuhs, Ize sure could use d'at right now," he replied as we climbed the front stairs.

To either side of the entrance there were statues of menacing looking gargoyles that seemed to watch us as we approached. The front door was a huge, ornately decorated iron wall, with gargoyles and other terrible looking things in bas relief all over its surface.

I gestured for the Troll to knock on the door, as I could not reach the gigantic iron knockers. He complied and we could hear an ominous echo answering the sound from within the estate.

We waited for a few minutes and then Beornag tried again. After a few more minutes a smaller, hidden door within the larger ones opened and a pale, thin man peeked out and spoke.

"Yes? Vhat is it?" he said in a raspy voice. He spoke with an accent that was similar to the way Durik spoke.

"Good evening, sir," I began. "I am Szvirf Neblinski, and this is Beornag. We are gardeners and professional grounds keepers. We were just scouting the countryside for possible clientele when we noticed the condition of your front yard. We were wondering if the lord of the estate might be at home so we can offer our services," I lied.

"Hmmm," he replied. "I vill check to see if ze lord vill give you an audience. Vait here please." He then closed the door, and we waited.

After several more minutes the two larger doors opened revealing the gaunt figure of a thin, pale man carrying a lit candelabra. "Master Eupiess vill see you. Please, come in."

We entered the mansion and stood in a huge foyer. Here the room was circular with a stairway winding upwards along the wall. There were alcoves along that wall with various statues, and between them old paintings hung. Everything was covered in cobwebs and dust and a musty odor was thick in the air.

"If you vould follow me please?" the gaunt servant asked.

He took us down a corridor as the hound bayed again in the distance. The long hallway was also filled with statues and paintings, but here there were suits of armour and empty candelabras as well. We soon came to a door with a lock that the servant opened and gestured for us to enter.

"I was wondering if it would be too much to ask if my friend here could use your toilet facilities?" I asked before we entered.

"Of course, zis vay please," the pale servant replied.

"I will wait in here for you Beornag," I said as I entered the dimly lit room. There was no way I was joining him in a wash closet while he was taking a crap.

"Okay Pops," he replied as the servant lead him further down the hallway.

I entered the chamber to find it somewhat clean. There were various statues and paintings too, as in the other rooms. I noticed a large hearth with several dust covered logs lying in it. A huge bay window overlooked the west side of the back of the estate where I could see more overgrown brush and uncut grass.

Night had fallen by this time, and the last rays of twilight had crept away when I noticed it begin to get a little chilly in the room. So I opted to light the fire.

A simple hootspa did the trick and soon I had a cozy fire to warm my old bones. I pushed a small, cushioned chair closer to the hearth and climbed up into it to await Beornag's return, or the estate master's arrival.

As I sat there alone, I could hear the hound again, baying in the distance. The sound was getting so intense that I got down from my chair to see if I could spot where it might be coming from. I made my way to the window, hoping to see a dog, or something equally mundane.

I wiped some dust from one of the panes and then used my hanky to clean it fully so as to better see outside. On a hill not far from the estate I could make out the silhouettes of what could only be tombstones in the full moonlight, obviously the family cemetery. There was also a large mausoleum and some pretty twisted and spooky looking trees as well.

The hound kept baying, though I could make out no heat signatures of any living things with my dark vision. I still thought I could see Human-sized figures walking about and entering the mausoleum.

After some time the servant entered with Beornag, who was not looking any better than when he had left.

"Feeling better my friend?" I asked as the pale and gaunt butler left and closed the door behind him.

"Not really Pops. Ize got some nasty cramps, an Ize couldn't go," he replied as he sat down on a large, cushioned divan. "Ize t'inks Ize gots a real gut problem now," he said.

He looked terribly uncomfortable, holding his side, just above his hip.

"Do you think you will be able to continue with what we are doing here?" I asked.

"Weeze is here now Pops. Ize'll just have t' hold on. D'ere's no use in leavin' since weeze has got d'is fa," he said struggling to hide the pain he was obviously in.

Just then the door opened and in walked a tall Human dressed in black. A draft of cold night air invaded the room, and the fire intensified for a brief moment.

This man was obviously someone of importance. He wore a cape of black and a saber at his side. Beyond him the servant closed the door, and I heard an audible click of a lock engaging.

His face was hidden by a dark hood, all that was visible was his chin, which was pale like the servant's face. He stood in silence for a moment while he studied us and then finally spoke.

"It has been some time since ve have had visitors here at Castle Eupiess. Velcome to my home. Blah hahaha."

His voice was deep and had that strange accent—kind of like the way the kid talked.

He came closer and seemed to glide across the floor without stepping. "Please make yourselves—comfortable. Blah hahaha."

I thanked him and climbed back into the chair I had been sitting in earlier. "I am sorry if we have inconvenienced you my lord," I began. "We are gardeners and grounds keepers and have just recently arrived in the area and are seeking employment. "We noticed that your grounds have been, shall we say, slightly neglected."

"Yes, good help is so hard to find," Count Eupiess replied as he moved closer to the fire. He came to stand between the hearth and Beornag.

"Perhaps you vould like to stay z' night and take a closer look at z' surrounding gardens in z' morning? I am sure you vill find zat zey have been terribly neglected, and zen you can give me an accurate quote on z' cost of upkeep. Yes?"

He was buying the ruse, hook, line and sinker but we needed to get back to the winery to report so I opted to give him another offer.

"My apologies sire, but we really do need to return to

Briarwood to confer with our associates," I said. "You see, we are part of a larger group that does work at different estates. That way we are able to pool our income and make sure everyone is taken care of. The cost for our services, however, will not be affected by this. No matter how many of us come to work here we will only ask for one set monthly payment." I had no idea where I was going with this.

"Please, z' road can be dangerous in z' dark. I must insist zat you stay z' night." His voice began to take on a demanding tone.

Just then the Troll fell out of his chair on his hands and knees and began to moan in pain as the master of the estate removed his hood.

Count Vladimir Eupiess stood in front of the fire, gazing at us with blood red eyes, his grayish skin glistening as though it was covered in a cold sweat. He looked to be the corpse of a Human being.

He began to smile at us maniacally as his teeth transformed into fangs. "You vill not leave here zis evening. You vill never leave here. You vill become my servants and I vill drink of your living blood. Blah hahahahaha!"

He raised his arms up and to his sides as his cloak turned into leathery bat-like wings. Opening his fang filled mouth he exhaled the stench of death in a cloud of greenish haze as Beornag's moaning grew ever louder and intense.

I began preparing a *sSchmatzel* beam to unleash on the fiend, while he grew taller. Pitch darkness began to fill the room and once again the temperature dropped dramatically.

"I vill start vith you little vun. You vill make a fine aperitif, zen your large and incapacitated friend vill feed me for days." He laughed as he took a step forward.

My hands went up and I pointed my index finger at our villainous host, just as Beornag let out a loud and piteous moan. I could actually see the gas being released from his backside as a steamy cloud in the now freezing room.

The expulsion caused an audible whooshing sound like a strong wind through thick bush, as he let loose the gargantuan methane bubble that had been lodged in his monstrous bowel.

While the gas filled the air between us and Vladimir, the undead creature actually stopped and choked for a short moment (Yeah! No kidding! The undead choked!) as he moved deeper into the translucent cloud, and closer to us.

Oy!

Beornag then stood up and straightened his back, standing over everything. He drew his maul from his backpack, and held it out in front of him, defiantly. His shadow covered the whole room at that point, as he had grown to at least sixteen feet in height. Then he attempted to exorcise the menace before him.

He didn't get the chance.

The noxious cloud of Trollish bowel gas reached the fireplace and ignited in a thundering explosion.

Vladimir was thrown forward, his clothes aflame while Beornag's great weight kept him firmly in place.

It was shear instinct that made the Injoke swing his maul in a mighty arcing stroke that impacted with Vladimir's flying, burning body.

He knocked over pretty much every piece of furniture within twenty feet of his massive form and sent the Vampire hurling back into the hearth with such force that I could hear the numerous crunches and cracks of the fiend's bones shattering from the tremendous impact.

I yelled out, *"Schmatzel!"* as I pointed at the vile creature's burning frame within the roaring hearth.

Vladimir was still trying to get up when the green beam of energy from my hootspa shot forth and struck him, lifting his frame and sending him flying against the back wall of the huge fireplace once more.

I then noticed the mind-numbing stench that filled the room and desperately tried to find an escape from the horrendous reek.

I will not venture to describe it further in fear of traumatizing you, the reader. Suffice it to say that it was really bad.

Beornag was yelling out some joke about two skeletons procreating on a tin roof, I swear I thought I heard an audience, applauding and laughing each time he paused for effect.

I held my golden, sensie-leaf medallion out in front of me and spoke the holy words defiantly, "Into the embers I send you! Smoke and ash you shall become! You're barred from the planet! Black listed, and evicted!"

Just as I finished reciting the holy words the Injoke reached the peak of his story and delivered the punch line, accompanied by what sounded like a standing ovation from a theater full of people.

Vladimir screamed out in agony as the door burst open and the servant entered with three other ghoulish beings in tow.

They barged into the room to save their hellish master, bat-like wings growing from their backs, fangs protruding from their mouths.

Like a wall of stone, the holy verses that Beornag and I were just finishing confronted them, and they all exploded in clouds of dust.

The windows shattered outward while the hound in the distance continued to howl. Wind rushed all about the room, strong enough to pull paintings from the walls and tip over furnishings and any statues that Beornag hadn't already demolished when he had swung his maul. I held on desperately to the edge of a large table to keep from being picked up and thrown around the chamber by the raging storm.

I was trapped in the middle of a fart cyclone, kids. It was horrific!

I could see Beornag among the flying debris and vortex of flame and smoke. He held high the great maul, defiant against evil, appearing as some mighty Titan in the swirling chaos.

Within the hearth, a violent tempest of flame was swirling. It became brighter and brighter, and I was forced to look away. I instinctively opened my new umbrella and held it out to block the intense light coming from Vladimir's spinning, burning, exploding form.

At one point I peeked over the top, squinting in pain from the brightness of flames and could barely make out the Troll lifting the large divan and holding it out in front of him as a shield to block the force of the fiery tornado.

After what seemed an eternity, the flaming vortex, and monster within the hearth finally exploded, sending flames and debris flying outward with tremendous heat and force.

Then it was over.

The curtains were smouldering and so was the Troll's shaggy coat. He was on the floor rolling to put out the embers. I ran to his side and assisted him as best I could, and we soon had him fully extinguished.

"Did yooze see d'at?!" he exclaimed with a big grin, as he stood up. "D'at had t' be da biggest fart in da history of fartdom!"

"Yes, very impressive," I said as I brushed the vampire dust from my clothes. "What do we do now? Vladimir is dead and we didn't learn a thing. Aw crap! Look at my clothes. I just had them washed."

"Weeze could take a look around an' see if d'ere's any clues an' such in d'is place," he offered. "Maybe there's some more stuff. Ize loves stuff." He blew the dust off me and almost knocked me over.

"Seems we don't have any other options at this point," I agreed.

We left the room and began a thorough search of the castle. The first floor consisted of other sitting rooms, wash closets, and the dining hall as well as an empty pantry and an unused kitchen—though fully equipped with what appeared to me very fine cutlery and cookware, ceramic and stoneware, even silverware and kingly table settings. There were tools as well, from vegetable peelers to great mixing bowls and numerous utensils, too many to list. These were covered in dust, as though they had not been used in many years.

There was statuary in the halls, of what I assumed to be nobility or the like. At first, I thought them portrait statues of, perhaps, Vlad's ancestors, but one detail in the works eventually stood out. The statues were all Elves—save one. This odd one in the bunch was a portrait of what must have been a treasured family dog.

There were also paintings on the walls, some of them huge, all of them covered in a thick layer of dust. Old tapestries, in good condition, but again coated with dust, hung in many areas. These no doubt had depictions of hunts or wars or occasions of note, but we were unable to tell. Many were massive and would once have been worth a fortune in gold each.

Candelabras were everywhere, so we were able to get ten candles lit to allow the Injoke to see. He held the light up over his head, illuminating just about everything within any given room that we entered.

The ceilings in this place were all twenty feet high and the rooms all huge, for the most part. The tapestries were obviously there to insulate the building in times of cold weather, called winter—which I had read about in one of the books that Grarr had provided.

On the upper floors we found bedrooms, also dusty and unused, as well as one chamber that looked to be some sort of museum. There were ancient suits of rusted armour, flags and banners, stuffed animals of various species, some known to us, others mysterious. Various glass cases with sculpture and antique items within.

"Hey, Pops. Look here," Beornag called as I was examining a beautiful but tarnished, set of silver trays.

He had forced open a large wooden trunk and within it were several smaller boxes and chests.

"Stuff." He giggled with anticipation.

We removed the contents and began to search the smaller containers. The first one was full of receipts and small ledgers that Beornag agreed I should examine later.

"Days looks all borin' an' stuff, Pops. 'Sides weeze gots lots a' paper back home in da batroom," he said.

The second, a small metal box was locked, but with my hootspa I managed to open it. It was full to the brim with jewels of all sizes and colours.

"There's a king's ransom in gems here!" I exclaimed. "Probably enough to pay off the winery and buy a second one too! Maybe even a third and fourth!" I had to calm down, I was hyperventilating.

"Any stuff?" Beornag asked.

I shook my head, and then opened a third box. It was made of iron and it was full of silver and gold coins—a *lot* of them!

Again, I started breathing faster and was in danger of passing out, so I tried to calm down by smoking some herb.

Kids, I had never had that much money dropped in my lap in only two days. Give me a break.

"Any stuff in d'ere?" he asked again. "Yooze knows? Like food, or slippers for Grarr, or maybe some *pickles*, Pops. Yooze likes pickles, right? Any a' d'ose?"

Finally, I had caught my breath and was able to continue. I mean, again, I hit the lottery, kids—*twice*—in as many days!

The fourth contained a magnifying glass and a small, square

piece of blue velvet with arcane symbols embroidered in its surface. "This might be enchanted," I said.

"Oooo boy, stuff!" He smiled. Beornag had very little concept of money, but he did appreciate tangible, functional objects.

The fifth box was wooden, and I had to hootspa a pretty nice lock in order to open it. Inside was a finely detailed sculpture in obsidian which was in the form of a bat. Wrapped around it was a red ribbon with arcane runes painted on it in silvery ink.

"I better have a look at this one before we do anything with it, my friend. We'll study it closer when we get home, but it is most probably an enchanted item of sorts."

The last two were small chests. One had an assortment of rings and amulets inside while the other was full of maps and scrolls.

The Injoke, rather disappointed at not finding any slippers or pickles, put all the boxes and chests in his enormous rucksack and we left the room.

I considered just looting the whole place and filling the Troll's backpack with almost everything that we could grab. His backpack was enormous, and you could easily fit an entire king-sized bed in it, several in fact as it too was a bottomless sack.

However, we simply didn't have time to pack the contents of an entire castle. We needed to find some clues and get back to the winery to report to the guys.

When we returned to the bottom floor, we made a second search for a door that might lead to a dungeon, or cellar and with a bit of hootspa I was able to locate and open one in the library.

Using my dark-vision, I found a very faint breeze, different in temperature, leaking from between two of the books on the shelves.

The titles were, *Gate Keeper* and *Escape to Within*.

These two did not belong where they were. They stood out from the other books around them, organized in proper alphabetical order. Both were in the section of books starting with the letter *T*.

The idea came to mind straight outta the blue, probably inspired by Lillia's fine work back at the winery, as our company's official librarian.

I asked the Injoke to lift me to where I could reach the books, and I attempted to remove one.

Then, behind us, an entire wall of the room, all of which was a bookcase, creaked audibly as it slowly swung open. Cobwebs, laden with dust, fell to the floor as the air was filled with a haze in the candlelight.

We waited for a moment, coughing from the ordeal, and clearing our noses, and eventually it all settled enough that we could see what was on the other side.

Beyond the wall was a great spiral stair which we descended cautiously. Soon it began to get cooler again, and we could hear the trickling of water ahead. There were sconces on the outer wall, and Beornag opted to pause in order to retrieve one and light it before extinguishing his candelabra.

As we descended, he paused at each sconce to light the torch within, and though the oil on the torches was very old, it still lit with a little coaxing.

We descended this way, spiralling down about seventy feet beneath the main floor where the stairs then opened up into a huge natural cavern. Across the middle of the subterranean chamber was a chasm with a rope bridge spanning its width.

"I'm not sure that thing will hold your weight, Beornag," I observed. "How will we ever cross it?"

"Hmmmmm." Beornag strained to think of a solution and after a moment *I* had an idea.

I concentrated on the other side of the bridge, and my ring of hootspas as well, and soon began to levitate. I then moved myself up under the Troll's massive frame.

"Please tell me you are finished passing gas," I pleaded.

"Da bellows is empty Pops," he replied as I lifted him into the air.

I manoeuvred us across the bridge while he giggled with delight, and gently landed us on the other side next to the entrance of a tunnel.

"Now d'at was amazin', Pops! Yooze is as strong as Ize is wit' d'at levatatin' ring o' yours," he said scouting around the tunnel's entrance.

I soon noticed that this was no natural tunnel. It had flagstone floors and the walls held sconces for torches, like the stairs and castle above. We walked slowly down the corridor, weapons and hootspas ready for the unexpected. It curved slightly to the left and as we continued on, we could only see about fifty feet ahead at any given point.

After travelling about a hundred and fifty yards we came upon an iron, barred doorway. I hootspa'd the gate but was unable to open it.

"Injoke, this gate is magically sealed. I am unable to open it without knowing the name of whoever set the lock."

"Oooo, Ize knows d'is one! Can Ize try, Pops, can Ize, please?" He almost begged.

I decided to go along with his *game* and gestured for him to try. When I was clear he grabbed the bars of the gate and pulled with tremendous force until the hinges and lock snapped with a loud clinking sound. Next he lifted the gate away from its place and leaned it against the wall.

After commending him on his titanic strength and quick thinking, I hootspa'd the iron door and it opened. "Team work." I winked.

"Yooze knows it, Pops." he replied with his own wink.

I found myself thinking of Murray, my best buddy from back

home. He knew the value of teamwork. Great guy, Murray.

Behind the door was a curving, descending stairway that led another seventy feet deeper. At the bottom was a huge, round chamber filled with tables covered with hooks, clamps, cables, shackles, and various other torture equipment.

Beornag stopped in his tracks and I sensed that something terrible was wrong. I could hear his breathing growing faster.

"Ize knows d'is! Ize knowz what d'is stuff is!" His voice started to take on an angry tone. I had never heard him angry before, kids. It was terrifying!

"D'at's bad guys stuff. BAD GUYS!" He roared, slamming his fists on the ground, shaking the very foundations of the castle.

He burst into the room, roaring, and screaming like a legendary, prehistoric monster. Kids I almost crapped my pants. I had no idea that he could be so frightening. I stood, motionless, almost driven to panic by the sound of his rage.

Like a juggernaut, he immediately took to dismantling, by sheer physical force of strength and rage, the entire room full of torture machines. I watched in awe as he visibly wept, tearing the contraptions apart with his bare hands. He yelled things at the ceiling. In absolute rage he yelled them, and I almost wanted to cry.

"MEAT! STUPID!" I would discover later that those words were the names the slavers had given to his late parents. I stood back and allowed him his moment of privacy to deal with whatever demons might still be haunting him from his past.

After ten minutes or so, everything in the room was obliterated and he turned to me, wiping his eyes. "Sorry, Pops, bad mem'ries."

"My friend, there is no need for apologies." I approached him gingerly, my hand out in a gesture of peaceful intent. "Take whatever time you need. I am from a very long-lived people." I found myself wishing I had a good joke to tell him, but all the best ones that I knew I'd learned *from* him. Instead, I patted him on his ankle—which was as high as I was able to reach.

"T'anks Pops, but Ize is finished," he said as he wiped tears from his eyes and approached the door nearest the room's entrance.

There were several doors in this room. All looked sturdy and old. They were strapped in iron, four bars horizontally, and each had a small sliding door at what would be about Human eye level—or Elf, perhaps.

He grabbed the handle and as he pulled, the door gave way to his titanic strength and broke in splinters. He was still angry about his resurfacing memories though he tried hard to conceal it.

The splinters and shards of the cell door were swept aside as the Troll entered, me in close support. Inside—huddled against the back wall of the cold, wet, and filthy cell—were two Human children.

A girl about ten years of age and a boy not much younger, embraced, shivering in the dampness of the cell. They looked up at us, but it was obvious they could not see us in the darkness. The girl shushed the smaller boy, as she strained her eyes, trying make out who we were.

I moved forward and spoke, unfortunately startling the poor things. "Children, you are safe now. We have come to rescue you. My name is Mr. Neblinski and my friend who is with me is Beornag."

They shivered even more then, now more from fear than the cold and damp. I could see that Beornag was doing all he could to refrain from rushing into the room and grabbing up the helpless youngsters.

"I am going to make some light so you can see us, but you must make me a promise…" I waited for a reply.

The girl spoke first. "Okay…but, I'm scared."

Then the boy. "Me too. Please don't hurt us anymore."

"Don't yooze worry, little ones," Beornag interjected, his voice like a baritone blanket of comfort against the terror they were experiencing. "Weeze is da good guys," He sniffed back tears of sympathy. "And nut'in' is gonna hurt yoozes, cuz weeze is mighty heroes, come t' rescue yoozes."

His voice was shaky. I could see that he was now struggling with his emotions, so I spoke up, "Okay, children, listen closely. My friend and I are not Human like you are. I am very tiny and am called a G'nome, while my friend is a big hairy giant called a Hill Troll. We might look different and even maybe a *little* scary, but we are very friendly and only want to help you. Okay?" I said, trying to prepare them for what they were about to see.

"We are going to take you back to your homes or at least send for your folks to come and get you. The bad man and his monster friends are all gone."

They both replied in unison, "Okay."

I hootspa'd a small light from my new ring and the jail cell lit up with a soft warm yellow glow.

Immediately the children noticed the Injoke and began to panic.

"Aaaaw, it's okay little ones. Ize is just big. Ize ain't mean." Beornag squatted down on the floor. "Come 'ere and Ize will carry yooze t' safety." He held out his tree-sized arms and the boy ran right into them crying.

In shock, the girl stood up and tried to stop him, but she was not fast enough.

I ran to her side and spoke. "Deary, it's alright. No one will hurt you or the boy. Don't worry about anything. We are friends. We live in Briarwood and are going to take you home as soon as we check to see if there are more people down here who need help. Okay?"

She looked down at me and then before I could protest, she had picked me up and was hugging me and sobbing uncontrollably.

It took about fifteen minutes before we were able to calm them both down and give them a snack and a drink.

"Now listen closely," I began. "My friend and I are just going to step out into the other room to check the other cells for more hurt people. You two stay here and wait. You'll be safe as long as you stay in this room. If we find hurt people, we will send them here to be with you. Then we will come back and take everyone home. Do you understand?"

"Yes Mr. Neblinski, we will stay here," the girl replied and then gave me another hug.

She put her arm around her brother and moved to the back of the room as Beornag winked at them and smiled. Then we exited the room and approached the next door.

There were eleven cells in all; in each there were one, or two more children being held prisoner.

We ended up going through the same routine as we had with the first kids. Each time we calmed them down we took them to the first cell where they were, in turn, comforted by the first two children.

We were just about to gather them all and leave, when I noticed a trap door in the floor and brought it to the Troll's attention. "We can't leave that unopened."

He whole-heartedly agreed, and lifted the massive door open, as it was not locked. Beyond was a stairway going down into darkness. I could see no heat signatures, and there seemed to be a membrane of blurriness, coating everything. Like a residual effect from an unnatural darkness, sticking to everything like an oily film that eluded my dark vision and made it hard to focus.

This, I decided was something we needed to investigate. I was unwilling to leave anything unexplored. We were there for clues, and so far, other than possibly the ledgers and receipts offering some light on our investigation, we had found nothing.

I ran to the cell full of kids and explained that we would be right back, and that they should stay there and be very quiet. They complied without argument, and I returned to the Injoke's side.

We then descended the stairway thirty or so feet into the middle of a long rectangular chamber. My dark vision was now quite blurry. The strange dark residue was stronger there and I was unable to focus on anything, so I hootspa'd a dim light in the center of the chamber.

As a G'nome I am acutely aware of my location when underground. It is a natural ability. I sense, so to speak, like seeing, or hearing—my *schmauz*. I could tell that this room was directly below the cemetery I had seen from the parlour.

My hootspa lit the room up well enough to reveal a large chamber and in it were a host of clamouring shuffling undead creatures.

On the north wall was an arched exit with a great staircase that I deduced would lead to the graveyard on the surface. I remembered seeing figures moving about that graveyard, probably these very same zombies.

I was then even more startled by a horrifying sound that echoed throughout the chamber. The hound was baying even louder now, as though it was in the room with us.

Turning to face us the zombies shuffled forward slowly, many of them armed and armoured. A hoard of undead poured out of the arched exit from the surface above, and into the room, as the baying continued to grow louder and louder.

I noticed that many of them bore the mark of the empire and concluded that they were once imperial soldiers whose bodies must have been stolen and brought to this location to be animated by foul magics.

It was then that I remembered, William's house! The great excavated cavern! His house was built against the inside of the city walls while the imperial cemetery for fallen soldiers and their families was against the outside. Right next to the poor boy's home. They must have been digging up an army in William's basement! No wonder it had taken years.

Beornag stepped into the room defiantly and spoke loudly in his deep bellowing voice. "Yooze is in fer a real crap storm now!" He raised the maul into the air and then with a sweeping arc, only inches off the chamber's floor, he swung the mighty weapon, creating a massive wave of force that swept the undead army off its feet. Many of them fell to the floor with broken ankles, struggling to stand.

Moaning still, they continued to advance, albeit crawling toward us slowly, as the others drew weapons and shuffled forward. Behind them, silhouetted by moonlight streaming into the room from the exit where the zombies were entering, a large figure stood up slowly. It was almost as tall as the Troll and was covered with oily black, matted fur.

"What was that?" I asked sincerely confused. "You broke their feet? Why their feet?"

The Troll grinned and replied, "Ize wanted a captive audience, Pops." He grinned again and very loudly began to tell a joke about an Urk walking into a bar with a toad on his shoulder.

I covered my ears while this new enemy let out a long baying call, which seemed to rally the zombies to his banner. The undead were now even more determined to get us and they came at us with a whole new fury.

Beornag courageously moved forward to engage the writhing zombie hoard, stomping the ones crawling on the floor and demolishing the others with his great maul.

I, in turn, raised my hands and spoke the incantations of the lightning hootspa: "*Schpickle schpackle sparkle blits!*"

A bolt of super-heated energy, all blue and white, shot out of my hand. I was barely able to keep standing as my entire body shook violently from the awesome power I was channelling.

I watched in awe as my lightning bolt shot across the huge chamber and connected with the hound-beast. It screamed in agony, lifted clean off the floor by my hootspa, convulsing violently from the massive static discharge. The heat and fire from the hootspa even destroyed ten or twelve of the zombies who ventured too close to the bolt and the burning monster.

Soon the hootspa faded and the creature fell to the floor, its hide smoldering. It was not finished however, and it began to stand up again, as it snarled and roared.

Then it spoke: "G'nome, you will not succeed." It stood fully then, and began to stagger toward us, stepping over destroyed zombies and fallen armour and weapons. Its hide was still smouldering, and it periodically twitched and shook from the after-effects of my hootspa still rushing through its body.

The Injoke had pretty much destroyed all the zombies in the first few seconds. His joke and maul were simply too much for even a hoard of thirty or more to endure. But not the man beast. (I later found out it was a *Hundwere*—a vile type of shape shifter that changes from a hound to a homonid-like, speaking being. As opposed to dogs, Hundweres are without nobility, or honor. They are abominations bent upon doing evil.)

Beornag then stepped forward again and grabbed the convulsing beast by the throat. "What does yooze knows about da Scave!? Why was yooze hurtin' little kids!? Tell Ize why or Ize is gonna end YOOZE!?" He roared so loud I was tempted to cover my ears again.

Laughing and spitting blood bubbles, the fiend responded. "I know the Scave will be the death of you, stinking ape. Do you believe you can stand against my lord and his army? When the soul-stone is purified and the flesh is given to *him*, the god will rise from the depths of his prison to possess the body of the chosen one. Your pseudo-gods will all die."

It coughed up more blood, "Then, he will devour the world. He knows you are here, G'nome. He knows who you are."

He laughed again, "He knows how to defeat you. It has already begun. You are too late. Soon the countryside will fill with the Scave, the armies of the dead shall rise, the sky will turn black and the waters will run red with the blood of all. Even *your* people will die in the great cleansing, you foolish little speck of flesh."

Even as Beornag tightened his grip on the foul creature, it continued. "Only the Scave, and those loyal to the great lord and his god of doom will survive the apocalypse. Muahahahahah!"

"Maybe", Beornag said coldly, "But yooze won't." There was an audible crack as he pulled the fiend's head from its neck and threw it across the floor. He tossed the body across the room in the opposite direction and roared at it.

Then there was a moment of silence, where he shuddered almost uncontrollably, his back toward me. After wiping his eyes again, he turned back to me. The look on his face was indescribable. Anger? Fear? Familiarity? I still cannot say. Nothing much worried the Troll, but this whole place had been having a foul effect on him.

"Weeze needs t' check for more o' d'ose guys, Pops," he said, and then turned and walked toward the opposite end of the room where a portal opened into a smaller round room. This chamber's walls had long rectangular compartments with coffins inserted into them.

There were ten in all and five were open. We looked inside one and found nothing but silk lining. We then began to search the other caskets one by one. Several caskets contained ancient corpses, but no dangers to be found. Each body was thoroughly dead and long past the decomposition stage.

Those with no corpses had linings of blackest earth, and stains of blood on the edges. We accounted for Vlad and his three ghoulish vampire helpers, whom we had encountered in the parlour, and were about to leave when I noticed one last coffin under the stairway.

We approached it and saw that it, too, was opened, like the other three with dirt. This one had the fresh impression of a Human-sized body in the soil, and I soon found soil on the floor, where someone had left the coffin and walked away. The soil was scattered but led to the stairs back to the cells.

One vampire was still unaccounted for!

Just then we heard the children start to scream above. We rushed to the stairs and ascended them to the torture chamber. only to find what was obviously Vladimir's mistress standing in the doorway to the children's cell, her wings flapping as she screeched in a terrifying, wailing voice.

She turned and pointed her finger at Beornag, shooting a bolt of searing, white-hot energy at him. It was a lightning hootspa!

With a mighty crash, the Troll was thrown back twenty feet against the wall, with a black smoking circle of now-welded links in his silver chain shirt. He fell to the floor with a thud, unconscious and convulsing.

Oy! Again, I almost crapped my pants.

Luckily, she had not noticed me, as I am very tiny, so I concentrated on my ring and held out my hand, palm forward, toward her.

As she turned her attention towards the cell's occupants, I felt a tingling in my fingers and my hand started to glow. My ring became white hot but did not burn my wrist. Tendrils of energy began to squirm and writhe from the ring to my palm, building into a condensed ball of warm, yellow light.

Just as she was about to pounce on the children a ray of bright power shot forth from my palm. It was so bright that it temporarily blinded me, knocking me on my back and stunning me. It strongly reminded me of the first time I had seen sunlight. But this time the gelded cat had been silenced.

Not long after that I came to my senses with the children all around me. Talli, the first little girl we had rescued, was holding me in her arms and stroking my forehead. They were all quietly whimpering.

I quickly arose and ran to Beornag's side. He was injured, burned and bruised, so I administered first aid and filled my pipe. I lit it, spoke the healing prayer, and blew the smoke all over his unconscious form.

I was relieved when he soon awoke and asked what had happened.

It was not until this time that I thought to look for the vampire that I had just hootspa'd. She was still standing in the cell's doorway. She appeared to be turned to stone.

My magical ring had supplied me with a blast of sunlight so intense it had knocked me unconscious, and the undead mistress of Eupiess was smitten to damnation. Exhausted, I was not so sure I would be able to do that again anytime soon.

As Beornag thanked me and gathered the children together I examined what was left of the mistress of Castle Eupiess. She had been transformed entirely into a statue of what appeared to be compressed dust. When I touched her, she crumbled to the floor in a pile of rubble and dry dirt.

I then suggested that we all leave immediately before something else reared its ugly head. Beornag agreed and he took up the rear with me in the front and the children in the middle.

As we left the room, the Troll looked back and swung his maul to strike the ceiling. The torture chamber, cells, and all else beyond collapsed in his wake. Never again would those chambers be seen or used by anyone.

When we reached the rope bridge, I took the children across in single file and then returned for the Injoke, carrying him over with my levitation ring. We all then climbed the stairs to the main floor and left the castle. In the distance there was no baying hound to be heard.

The walk back to Briarwood was uneventful and the Injoke had to carry a few of the smaller children, as they were exhausted. I told them stories about my homeland to keep their minds off their predicament, and ensured them that their bellies would be filled with wonderful foods, and they would all have a warm dry place to sleep that night.

When we finally reached the gate, the guard asked us for a citizens' pass and Beornag showed his, then reported to the guard that castle Eupiess had been inhabited by vampires, and that we had rescued the children that were with us from said castle.

In turn, the guard suggested we report this to the local constabulary in the morning so that they could begin a search for the children's parents. "I'm just a working bloke, gov. They don't pay me to investigate. I just keep the gate secure."

"Well," the Troll spoke up. "Looks like weeze is stuck wit' deez kids f' da night." He smiled. Then, looking at the children, "Yooze guys is gonna have so much fun! Ize got a sand box, an' Ize don't even poop in it!"

"Let's take them back to the winery and in the morning we'll find their parents," I suggested. "Who wants flapjacks for breakfast?" I added and was acknowledged with much enthusiasm from the children and Beornag both.

When we arrived back at the winery I opted to go in and give the boys a heads up about our new, youthful guests, while Beornag stayed outside and warned the kids about their hosts.

After several hours we had taken them all inside one by one and introduced them to Lillia who was more than happy to take them in and give them food and shelter. She gave them rooms on the upper floors, away from the presently occupied chambers and she explained, as best she could, that the monsters in the winery were all friendly and would be their protectors until their parents could be found—even the scary one named Grarr. Finally, they were fed and off to bed, and as it was well past midnight, everyone else opted to do the same.

As I lay there in my little hideaway bed, thinking about home, I heard a deep, fluttering, rumbling sound from somewhere on the upper floors, and knowing that the Troll had had one last expulsion left in his seemingly endless bowel, I was thankful that I was sleeping in the basement!

CHAPTER - 8

ALL IN THE FAMILY

Early the next morning, after instructing Beornag on how to babysit the kids, (oy) Lillia and I set out to city hall to report our findings to the local constabulary.

The sun was up in full force, and it was going to be a clear and warm day, so I donned my shades and umbrella.

The streets were fairly quiet that early. A handful of merchants were on their way to their shops, but they were few and far between. With no crowds of people blocking my view, I got a good look at the ritzier areas of Briarwood.

In the distance I could hear ships' bells ringing and gulls laughing their shrill cries. Every once in a while a dog or cat would cross a street. But other than that, the city still slept.

We arrived at Briarwood's center where we climbed a great stone staircase that led to the grand entrance of city hall. They were just opening the doors for another day of bureaucracy when we arrived.

We entered the impressive hall and approached the information desk where behind sat sat a Human female.

"Good morning, madam," I began. "We are here to report some missing children."

She looked at Lillia, and then me for a moment in disbelief.

"No! No, not *our* children!" I explained. "We don't have children. I mean... We are not... I mean—"

"What the Holy Redeye is trying to say is that we have found some children who were lost, and we are trying to locate their parents," Lillia explained.

"Second floor, room 27," the clerk replied.

We then thanked her and made our way up the stairs to the second floor and to find the appropriate office. Inside was another Human, this one a man. He was scribbling intently on some pages in a ledger when we entered, and he took a moment to look up at us (or down in my case).

"Yes?" he asked.

We explained about the children, telling the whole story about the vampires and the torture chamber and everything else (except the loot that the Troll and I had found).

"Well," he replied. "This is not an orphanage. You can file a report and then look at the notice board downstairs to see if their parents left an address or a wanted poster, or something. We will have an officer drop by your residence this afternoon to get some more information and start an investigation. That is all I can offer you."

I had not thought of the possibility of having to house these kids for more than one night. I couldn't imagine what we were going to do. They couldn't stay at the winery, what with all the business and booze and monsters and such that were there. Then it hit me.

"Where might I find the department in charge of property tax and that sort of thing?" I asked.

"Down the hall, room 21-A," he replied.

We left him with the address to the winery and headed down the hall to the department of property development and land holdings. There we met a Dwarf named Al Stait. Al was a jolly gentleman with a long white beard. He obviously didn't get many visitors and was very happy to have a break from his paperwork. He offered us some tea and we accepted graciously.

We explained what had happened with the rescue of the children, and the vampires. Al was quite taken with our story, and that's when the books came out.

"There is no Eupiess on record with this office," Al explained after a few moments of searching the pages of a massive tome. "Are you sure that is what the lord of the manor called the place?"

"Absolutely sure," I replied. "If you have a map, I can show you the exact location of the estate."

Al rummaged through a cabinet and soon produced a large map showing Briarwood and the surrounding area. I pointed out the location of the estate to him and he cross-referenced that with some other papers he had dug out of a filing drawer.

"That estate has been abandoned for eighty-three years," he replied. "It once belonged to an Elf lord named Illianus."

Lillia's eyes lit up. "Did you say Illianus?" she asked.

"Yes, Illianus *was* the name. He was quite famous around these parts. He had a large estate up on the north road as well. Do you know the name?" Al asked.

"Was it Turelion Illianus?" she asked in disbelief.

"Yes, my dear. Why do you ask?" Al stood up and looked at her curiously.

"He was my father," she replied. "But I had no knowledge of him owning another estate," she added with excitement, "only the north location, where I grew up."

"Can you prove that you are the daughter of Turelion Illianus?" Al asked.

"Why yes, I can." She produced her citizen's pass which had her name and resident's permit number on it.

"Can you wait here for a few minutes?" Al asked.

"Sure," I replied, as Lillia looked to me for permission. (She was our employee, and I was her boss after all.)

We had tea and a few Dwarfish crumpets while we waited in silence. Lillia was obviously full of mixed emotions about all of this.

After some time, Al returned.

"I had the census director check the authenticity of your citizens' permit number and you will be happy to find that you have passed. Which means that you have inherited the estate—legally.

"Congratulations. I will file the appropriate reports. Can you return tomorrow to sign the property deed so I can transfer ownership to you?"

She stood in disbelief for a moment.

I responded for her as I took her hand and led her out of the office. "Yes. We will be here tomorrow morning. Thank you so much, Mr. Stait."

I had gone into the office to ask if the place would be going up for auction as the owner was a lord of the undead and had been slain in combat. I never dreamed that we'd be getting the place for free.

Just then Al came running out of his office. "Miss? Oh Miss?" he called.

We turned and Lillia replied. "Yes, sir?"

"There is one issue of unpaid property taxes," he said.

I knew there had to be a catch.

"Taxes?" she said, worry in her voice. She was, after all, broke. Grarr had soaked her for every last dime she owned. "What is the total?" She flinched, waiting for the bad news.

"Twenty-three thousand, four hundred thirty-two gold," he replied.

She looked like she would cry as Al continued.

"Now that we have an owner and an address, we will require full payment within thirty days. I am sorry for being the bearer of bad news," he said, before returning to his office.

"Oh well. For a moment I thought I might have something of my father. But, alas, I am destined to be a simple maid it would seem." Her head now hung low, as we departed the city hall.

The streets were then coming alive with people around us as we started to make our way home. I noticed a small café and offered to buy her some tea. She accepted and we entered, took a seat and waited for service.

It was a very cozy-feeling establishment. The tables and chairs were made from rich woods, and beautiful green leather. A hearth sat in the middle of the seating areas, burning coals within, and a musician played a stringed instrument, gently, while he wandered about.

Once we had ordered, and were given some nice Elvish tea and cookies, I had an epiphany. I had been drinking tea all morning and really needed to pee. I excused myself and visited the establishment's facilities where I gave the morning's events some serious thought.

It only took me a few minutes to decide what I was going to do next. So, I washed my hands, straightened my hat in the mirror, and said, "Szvirf, old boy—this is the *right* thing to do."

I left the rest room, hands clean and bladder gladder, and proceeded back to the table. As I approached, it again occurred to me that Lillia was no maid. She didn't, *couldn't* fit the roll even if she was doing a great job. She belonged in charge of a noble's estate.

I climbed up on the table, tipped a teacup over and sat on it. I offered her a cookie and asked. "Lillia, what would you think if I offered to pay the back taxes and the costs for renovations and clean up at your castle?"

She looked at me, pleasant surprise in her almond eyes. "You would do that?"

"Well, nothing is free, you understand," I replied. "I was thinking that we could share the place three ways:

"One: you would be the lady of the estate and in charge of it as the resident *noble*." I emphasized that title.

"Two: we would open one of the wings as an orphanage for lost children, hire staff and such to run the place and take care of the kids that the Injoke and I rescued.

"Three: we would renovate the estate's chapel to be a temple to Holy Shiddumbuzzin. I would, in return, cover all the expenses to make it livable and keep the temple operational as well as the orphanage."

I paused for a sip of tea, then continued, "We could ask for a tax break as the place would then become a house of worship, and we could also ask for an annual municipal grant to fund the orphanage. You would continue to work at the winery as our original deal dictates, but you would have the choice of living there or at the estate. What do you think?"

She sat in silence for a moment, then her eyes glazed over, and she jumped up, lifting me from my seat in a soft womanly embrace, and whispered. "Oh, Redeye, you *are* a holy man. I accept. Thank you so very much. I will be honoured to have the temple of such a charitable and kind deity as Shiddumbuzzin on my property."

She then placed me back on my seat and returned to her chair, smiling, and wiping away tears of joy.

"Now, mind you, I expect *never* to have to pay rent while the temple is there," I explained. "I will also have a few other small details to add to the contract. But I think you will find them quite reasonable."

She agreed readily and after we finished our lunch, we returned to the winery.

Beornag had gathered all the children into a spare room and

was telling them funny stories when we arrived.

Durik came running out of the kitchen to greet us.

"Poppa Szvirf! Durik happy to see you again!" he exclaimed, hugging me tightly, as though we had been apart for months.

"I'm happy to see you too, kid," I replied as I gasped for breath under his python-like embrace.

"Grarr very mad at you. He in library. Say he is not babysitter, and, d'is no place for kids," he whispered in my ear. "Maybe you not go in d'ere for some minutes or maybe hours," he suggested.

"That's okay kid. I have some news that'll cheer old Grarzy up," I replied. "We need to have a meeting as well, to hash out the details of what happened yesterday and to examine some findings that the Injoke and I discovered."

Lillia went straight to the kitchen after giving Durik a peck on the cheek and wishing him a good morning. Her mood had improved dramatically since I made my offer.

I went to see the Troll in his chambers and explained to him what had transpired at city hall. Then we joined Durik and Lillia in the kitchen where she was preparing lunch for everyone, the children included.

I asked her to make a job posting for nannies, butlers, cooks, maids and grounds keepers and to put it up at city hall as soon as possible. I also asked her to look into hiring some carpenters and such for the renovations and to put together a budget for the estate/temple/orphanage.

The Troll and Durik were quite excited to hear about the plans for the estate and Beornag asked if he, too, could have a temple there. We all agreed that it would be more than appropriate for Ulm to also be represented at the new temple.

Durik was ecstatic about now being a paladin of an *actual* temple with walls and everything. "Poppa Szvirf. We grow sacred herb at temple?"

"Of course," I replied enthusiastically. "You can have your own training area too. There's a huge kitchen, and many rooms and halls with lots of statues of what must be Lillia's ancestors. Wait till you see the place."

After working out all the details and actually putting some of it on paper, we decided it was time to face the music, so we made our way to the library.

Soon after we entered, the crap hit the fan.

"What do you mean, you adopted seventeen Human kids?!" Grarr grarr'd. He had the Troll and me cornered, while we tried to explain why we had to keep all of the children we had rescued the night before.

"Do you have any idea how much they will eat?" he continued. "Not to mention the cost of clothing. Do you know how fast those things can grow?"

"Wait—" I tried to explain.

"They smell bad and leave their mess everywhere!" he protested. "Once they get to puberty, they get all moody and make life a living hell."

"Poppa Szvirf and Beornag have plan, Grarr," Durik tried to explain.

"What were you thinking?! How in the nine hells do you propose to take care of seventeen kids?!" Grarr continued.

"Weeze is gonna—" the Troll tried to interrupt.

"We are Mercenaries, not babysitters!" Garr was livid. I though he might strike one of us.

"Now just a booguh pickin' minute d'ere, Grarr." Beornag was now losing patience and we all started talking at the same time, no one hearing anyone over their own loud voice.

Just then, however, another voice *did* rise above our own.

"Quiet, all of you!" It was Lillia. She had entered the library when she heard the commotion.

"Look at the four of you! You should all be ashamed of yourselves! You are all adults—you're supposed to be heroes, or so you claim, and you are acting like a bunch of school kids!"

"Well, technically, Durik *is* still a kid," the Troll replied.

"Durik not kid, Beornag!" the kid barked, embarrassed and blushing.

"Silence, all of you!" Her voice, though stern and assertive, was also calming, so we all fell silent and stared in shock at the normally quiet and demure Elvish damsel.

"Grarr. The children will be out of here soon, even if we cannot find their parents. We have a plan. If you would just sit and listen for a moment you will see that things will be back to normal soon," she offered.

"The Redeye has an idea that will help all involved, and even give this company a boost in reputation," She added.

Grarr looked to the Troll and me as Durik gestured for us all to sit down.

"Now, I am going back into the kitchen to finish my work," she said with a stern look on her face. "You four talk this through and come up with a reasonable decision as to how you are all going to deal with this small problem. I don't want to hear any more roaring and growling coming out of here while I am gone. So figure it out!" With a scornful nod, she exited the library.

I never thought I'd ever see Grarr back down, but he did. I mean, she had a point, and he seemed to know it.

Yet, it *still* took almost an hour to explain to Grarr what we had planned, before he finally agreed to let the kids stay for as long as necessary.

"Just how do you plan to finance this estate's renovations?" Grarr asked.

"That's the *good* news, Grarzy," I started to explain. "The Troll and I found a king's ransom in jewels and coins in that place—I know, right? We didn't say anything to Lillia about it as all that treasure was probably the property of the vampires anyway." I winked at Beornag.

"Uh…yeah…da vampire's stuff. Pretty sure it was all his, ya gotta hate d'ose wealthy vampires," the Troll agreed with his own wink.

"How much of a king's ransom did you find?" Grarr asked, somewhat confused as to why we were winking at each other.

That was when Beornag got up and left the room for a moment, to retrieve his rucksack from the great hall. He returned and emptied *some* of its contents on the huge center table.

After putting back a whole assortment of strange things that came out of the bag, including a short, fat Dwarf who was screaming profanities, and a giant bag of what smelled like crap, he placed the things that he and I had found on the table to view.

I opted to open the box full of jewels. As I was a bit of a gem specialist, I took out a large diamond and began.

"This here gem, Grarzy, will finance most, if not all, of the cleanup of the estate."

Then I removed a large ruby. "This will pay for the renovations," I said. "This," I continued, tossing him a huge sapphire, "this thing will buy this winery lock, stock, and barrel— *and* some. And you see that there are at least twenty more just like it as well as some smaller gems worth anywhere from one hundred to ten thousand gold each. We are all stinking rich." I grinned.

"The Injoke and I will have more than enough to cover the costs of all the estate business with our share of the loot."

"Durik too, Poppa Szvirf," the kid offered.

"There, you see? No problems. If you want, I'll even rent you an apartment in the ritzy quarter of town until we can deal with the problem of finding the children's parents or moving them into the orphanage," I added. "On me."

Grarr sat in solemn silence for a few moments and then spoke.

"Pops, I am sorry. You too guys..." He looked to the Injoke and Durik. "I seemed to have overreacted a bit. I just don't like having noisy, smelly, needy things around here while they eat everything in sight and make a mess."

"Yooze don't like Ize anymore?" Beornag asked, hurt in his voice.

We looked at each other in disbelief for a moment and then all broke out in laughter, while the Troll tried to figure out what he had said that was so funny.

Grarr had to explain to him that he was talking about the kids—and that he *still* liked the Troll very much—and eventually all was well.

Next I examined the cloth and magnifying glass we had found and hootspa'd it. I learned that it was a device for identifying magical items, and I wouldn't have to hootspa anything else, anymore—no longer draining my hootspa reserves. This would leave me with more hootspa to do other things.

Hootspa!

I then took out the obsidian bat talisman and, butter fingers me, I dropped the thing on the floor.

It shattered in a blaze of scintillating lights that momentarily blinded us, but when our vision returned a moment later there was a huge, dog-sized bat sitting on the floor where the talisman had broken.

Kids, I almost crapped my pants, as I mistook it for a rat at first. But once it moved, and looked directly at me, I was able to see that my fear was misplaced. It *seemed* friendly.

We all looked in wonder at the animal for a moment, then I heard a voice in my head. "Master, you have freed me from my prison. I am forever grateful. What is your command?"

It was the bat! It was speaking telepathically to me.

Without warning, Durik suddenly stood up and grabbed a chair and was just about to smash the thing when I stopped him. "Kid! No! He's friendly!" I explained what had just occurred and we all found it quite amazing.

I later learned that the bat's name was Nikodemius, and that he had linked to me in spirit and mind. He had become my lifelong companion and would never leave my side—with the exception of doing my bidding or maybe taking a crap, that sort of thing.

Great, another mouth to feed. I could see those gems being worn away even as I calculated what my other expenses were going to come to.

What had I been thinking? Why was I suddenly starting to feel so generous and sympathetic? Back home it was—take care of your own, pay your taxes, do your job, the rest will work itself out. Taxes took care of the needy. Not that there were any truly needy G'nomes.

Here, on the surface world I was driven by an uncontrollable need to be nice. I chalked it up to the possibility of topside air affecting my judgment and decided that since I was going to be on the surface for a while I might as well just play it by ear. Little did I know that by doing this I was actually just doing what I was thinking of complaining about—I think.

Later that evening we all gathered in the library to report, and correlate what we had learned so far. Lillia had prepared snacks for us as usual, and by the time they arrived we had already forgotten we had conducted Sabbath four times and were refilling several pipes again. The great reading hall was now looking like the Briarwood docks on a foggy morning.

"Durik and I found the Swamp Troll caves near the mountain pass yesterday," Grarr began. "After we kicked the crap outta their toughest guy they were more than happy to speak with us.

"Their spokesman said that a powerful sorcerer approached

them and asked them to scare anyone coming into that part of the forest and to keep all trespassers away. In return the sorcerer would supply them with meat and items of power." Grarr puffed the pipe, and got it really smoking intensely, as he purred like some great jungle cat. "The latter turned out to be some very minor magical items that gave off light, or located underground water sources, and that sort of thing."

He continued, while emptying the now spent contents of the pipe. "We asked where the sorcerer was, and they said they didn't know, but he always came from within the mountain pass. Durik scouted that area but didn't find anything of interest. I am assuming that this powerful sorcerer is Calabac," he said, reaming out the bowl of his pipe and refilling it with even more brain cheese.

Raz spoke next. "Raz issss looking to the mountainssss and Raz findssss wagonssss and horsssessss up therrrre. Dirik isss farrr behind, and farrr below. Raz shhhhowssss you all when we returnssss." His head bobbed up and down with excitement.

Then I began to tell of our encounter the previous evening. "Beornag and I learned that there was an estate on the south road where a shipment was delivered by a mister Aazh Stelark, a curios shop owner here in town. That shipment was ordered by Calabac, but he was unable to get his delivery boy to pick it up, so he had it sent there and was supposed to have it forwarded from that estate."

I accepted the pipe that Grarr was handing me, dragging it across the table, closer to my seat.

"The Troll and I went to this estate and encountered a nest of vampires *which* we dispatched."

Beornag and I enjoyed a high-five, and then I continued. "We also managed to gather a lot of paperwork from a strong box. I am thinking that it probably contains a clue or two but haven't had a chance to look it over as of yet.

I lit my pipe again and continued, "Then we slew a beast-man who informed us that his lord was preparing to summon a god that would lead an army bent on the destruction of everything his lord deemed not of his liking." I looked to Grarr, "You caught that, right? *A god?*"

He nodded, a concerned look on his face.

I explained that I had been all day taking care of the business of the *former* vampire estate and making sure that the renovators and such would start work immediately. Lillia's taxes were paid with a single gem from the loot the Troll and I had acquired from the estate, and we even got change back. Within the month we would be moving all the children there along with our new hired help.

I looked to Grarr, again.

"Okay Pops, I want you on those documents as soon as possible. We need to find out what connection that place had with this Calabac," he suggested.

I nodded, then remembered something. "Oh, and one other thing," I added. "Mister Stelark said he had sold some magic devices to Calabac that could make a castle vanish. I have a hootspa that can detect those objects if I can get to within a couple hundred feet of them."

I passed the pipe to Durik who accepted it graciously, and reverently.

"How do you feel about flying, Pops?" Grarr asked.

"Well, I can levitate with my ring. Why do you ask?" I responded as I passed my stash bag to the Troll who was gesturing for it.

"I am gonna send you and Durik out with Raz tomorrow to recon that mountain pass and the local area where Raz found the wagons and horses. You will be flying on Eekadinosaur," he responded, a glint of malicious humour in his eye.

"Me? On that thing?" I replied in disbelief. "There's no way you are gonna get me on that thing."

He grinned mischievously. "Think about it for a moment, Pops. You will probably be the very first of your kind to travel not only on the surface of the world but *above* it. An historic event, I would think."

"Asides," the Troll interjected, "yooze got d'at ring d'at levitates ya. If yooze falls yooze'll stop just before yooze hits da ground. Not t' mention da umbrella. Ooooo, Ize likes d'at umbrella."

"I never thought of that." It was true, I didn't think of it until that moment.

This brought to light whole new possibilities. I could jump from cliffs, tall buildings, the back stairs even, and still not hit the ground. That ring was quickly becoming my favourite possession.

"Okay, I'll do it," I said as I accepted the pipe-full of brain cheese from Grarr.

With all of that settled we spent the remainder of the evening relaxing, something we had all neglected to do for the past week or so. It gave us an opportunity to play a couple board games, a hand or two of cards (Grarr won all of those) and get extremely intoxicated. Suffice it to say that both Shiddumbuzzin and Ulm were both given ample attention that evening.

Once everyone else had retired to their beds, and Durik was tucked in, I returned to the library to examine the paperwork that we'd recovered from the estate.

After several hours of examining all of the letters, postings, memos, receipts, invoices and references, I learned something quite interesting. There was a relic that Vladimir Eupiess had been searching for. Calabac wanted the thing really bad and had tied up all of his monetary wealth to search for it. All of the events that had transpired over the last five decades, leading up to present day, had been an ongoing attempt to acquire this relic.

Its name was never listed as far as I could tell, nor were there any descriptions of it. All I could uncover about it was that it had been found and sent to Calabac's laboratory, and that it was of utmost importance that this relic be controlled or destroyed as soon as possible, but not before its power could be drained and used to further Calabac's plans. Though there was no indication as to what those planes actually were.

I also found a couple of notes that seemed to indicate that someone else would be looking for this relic as well, but it didn't state who or whom.

I learned that the relic had been found in the sub-basement of the Eupiess (Illianus) estate, where the children had been kept. Then it was acquired and sent on its way to Calabac with an escort of something called *The Stealer,* whatever *that* was.

It appeared that Calabac had "acquired" the old Illianus estate, under a presumed name, after he had learned of the existence of the relic, which legend said was in the possession of the Illianus family. After taking control of the estate, he acquired William's apartment and was planning to build a tunnel system from the Illianus house to Briarwood. This would allow him and his minions secret passage into town for reasons never mentioned.

Poor William had been killed (I presumed) by the thing they referred to as the Stealer, and a duplicate of the boy was then created. But when local residents began to suspect something, and more guards had been assigned to the area of William's home, the digging and the comings and goings had to stop, so that is when Plan B went into effect. The passage had to be delayed.

Plan B was to kidnap Lillia and her sister and force the information needed from them. In the meantime Vlad would take up residence in the second, secret estate of Turelion Illianus, and keep searching for the relic—which was found. But there was something else that I was missing. Something important, and I had no idea what.

At that point it had become Sabbath time. I, being the head of the entire religion, *decided* that it was. I filled my ornate firestone pipe with sacred herb and began to commune.

When I finally woke up it was just before sunrise. I had passed out on the table with a roll of Vladimir's documents in my hand. Carefully, I gathered up all of the papers and stored them in the library desk. Then I climbed down from the table and made my way to my quarters. After some herb tea and a shower, I was refreshed enough to start thinking about what I had learned from the records the night before.

Calabac planned to use the power of a relic to, perhaps summon some kind of ancient and forgotten god to, presumably, conquer the local area as his own.

This, I deduced from the notes, would include Briarwood, and the surrounding farms, as well as every other village and town for three hundred leagues in every direction. The undead soldiers that the Troll and I destroyed were to be part of an occupation force for the countryside.

There were people from the west who were also involved, somehow with some other mention of supplies and mounts being brought from the far south.

The destruction of Vladimir's undead battalion would most certainly be noticed. We had now officially interfered with Calabac's plans, not to mention slaying his lieutenant Eupiess, and his Hundwere. From here on we would have to be extra cautious. Calabac would certainly know that we existed and would most probably be making plans to rid himself of our meddling in his schemes.

Such a stupendous undertaking would require an army, which I could only assume Calabac had planned for. The question was: how big an army, and an army of what, exactly?

After a couple of hours, sitting in the kitchen, thinking about everything, and getting rather *elevated*, I turned to see Lillia enter while tying her apron. No doubt to begin the titanic chore of preparing breakfast for the boys and me (mostly the boys, though). I took note of her determination to follow through with her part of our contract—her need to owe up to her *word*. In that moment she reminded me of my ma, back home, and from then on I would never have a dirty thought about her, ever again.

It was at that very moment, seeing her work to prepare food for us all, her dedication to her duties, that I became immune to her special genetic powers. I was becoming—*paternal*, and quite naturally, I might add.

I allowed her a few moments to begin before I made my presence known. Then, I assisted her with preparing the meal; remembering to ask her to make some more of the exotic Elfish soup and bread from two days before. I also instructed her to pack it away for travel, (it was tasty) as I would be making a road trip soon and would like to have some to take with me. She added that to her morning cooking duties, and we continued quietly cooking and brewing breakfast.

When it was almost ready, I took on the responsibility of waking the boys (which gave me a WHOLE NEW respect for her) and we all sat down to the morning meal, which consisted of me running as fast as I could around the table, grabbing what I needed before it all disappeared from the onslaught of several monstrous appetites, and then vacating the area before I became mistaken for a dinner role, or wedge of cheese.

Oy!

After the *horror* of breakfast was over, I gathered the boys in the library to report my findings on the records and paperwork that the Injoke and I had discovered.

"This is bigger than I thought," Grarr said as he ran his clawed hand over his tattooed scalp. "Relics and religions—things we don't understand—or have never seen before. This might prove to be more than we can handle so let's be extremely cautious from here on.

"Frackin' gods," he slipped in, under his breath.

Then, after he growled and grarred a bit, I was assigned to Durik and Raz for the day, while he and Beornag planned to travel by road to the western foothills. We would arrive well before they would, and were to prepare a base-camp from which we could scout the area for a hidden monastery.

We had come to the conclusion that there was an invisible temple or fort somewhere in those foothills, probably near the carts and wagons Raz had found. It was our job to locate this if possible and to formulate a plan so as to be ready when Grarr and Beornag arrived.

Grarr was counting on *me*. I knew it.

Eekadinosaur couldn't carry Beornag *and* Raz at the same time—as each one was a giant in his own right—and travelling alone was out of the question. Now that the enemy knew they were being hunted, they would be on their guard and the roads would be getting quite dangerous.

After our packs were full of what we needed for such a campaign, I was strapped to Durik's shoulder plate, and we ascended the tower, to Eek's nest.

Kids, the stink was insane. I'd smelled it before when I was outside and thought it was a backed-up sewer, but even then, it was defused by the wind and other city aromas. I never dreamed it was coming from the winery.

We followed the spiral stair though ankle deep dino-crap until we came to the tower top.

"Good gawd, kid. We really need to get someone up here to clean all this mess *up*. It's stinking up the entire town."

Durik chuckled here. "Is funny, yes?"

"We're gonna get a hefty fine from the mayor's office if he

finds out where the reek is coming from."

He then chuckled again. "Durik love Eek, Poppa Szvirf. She very awesome. You vill see."

Of course he thought she was awesome. He was seventeen!

But when we finally reached the top floor, I was forced to gasp with wonder. Eekadinosaur was far more impressive than I even imagined.

Here, the chamber had one wall missing, which acted as Raz and Eek's launching station. And there he was—six hundred pounds of reptilian muscle. Raz.

His fiery orange and red patches of scale, lit up by the morning sun, appeared as precious gems against a black velvet blanket. He wore what *had* to be *completely* customized armour plates that covered specific areas of his anatomy in a way much like the gladiators of the great arenas in the capitol must have worn. His right shoulder had a small plate to allow for easy manoeuvrability, while the left had substantially larger plates with long spikes for ample protection. His entire suit was coloured black with brass trim.

First he held his massive, clawed hand over his eyes to block the sun while he looked out into the morning sky. He then placed atop his head a mighty helmet that appeared to be more for protection from the elements than weapons. I later learned that it assisted with his breathing and had glass goggles to protect him from the wind.

He sat atop a monster among monsters—Eekadinosaur was the largest living thing I had ever seen up to that point in my life. She was the size of a very large wagon with a team of six horses, and she had wings that were too large to unfold on a city street. Her long, bony beak was filled with big, viciously razor-sharp teeth, and her claws were as long as scimitars.

Her scaly skin was pale sky blue on her belly and a dark, deep blue on her back. Along her spine ran a series of rich, purple spots ringed in fiery orange. Her eyes were the size of dinner plates and shone like massive yellow and orange jewels.

Strapped to her back was a black and gold saddle that had several clasps for an assortment of weapons: a long bow, a quiver of long arrows, an extremely long pike with a barbed tip and a flag that fluttered in the morning breeze.

Raz also had a trident, a halberd, a broadsword and shield, and a terrible looking long chain with several thinner chains at one end, each ending in vicious barbed hooks. This arsenal of weaponry was clasped snugly to the massive saddle just forward and to either side of where Raz sat on the Eekadinosaur's back. Each deadly weapon was within easy reach for the reptilian rider.

There were also three depressions in the great saddle for passengers—one to either side and one at the rear. These seats had protective hoods to shield against the rushing wind and other elements. I would learn in flight that the saddle was enchanted by a wizard from the capitol city to keep the mount, rider and passengers warm while ascending to extreme altitudes.

The whole package had cost the boys almost an entire year's earnings, but paid for itself within a month. Warped Speed Enterprises had, in Raz and Eekadinosaur, a wild card. Something extremely powerful that they usually kept for emergencies—when the two were not out on deliveries.

Grarr was, among other things, quite intelligent, and was always planning for the future.

Raz and Eek's services were acquired mostly to transport people around. Rich folks liked it because it saved travel time. The boys made a fortune every time Raz worked.

I gasped again as Durik climbed up onto the behemoth's back and strapped himself in. He drew his bone short bow and a small quiver of arrows and strapped them to the saddle within reach.

I was terrified, but determined to do my duty. I mean, somehow, Shiddumbuzzin was at work, right?

The Chronicles of the Great Neblinski

Durik and I would face the rear. It occurred to me that with me and the kid sitting in the rear in this fashion—hootspa and bow ready—and with Raz and his portable arsenal in the front, not to mention the sheer *size* of the animal we were sitting on, there was very little, I could think of, that could pose any kind of threat to us.

Then Raz turned and asked, "Rrrrready?"

EEK! A DINOSAUR!

The following wildlife vignette is brought to you by
Abe's Undies

The future of men's hosiery.

Join us for our grand opening this weekend and get a free underwear
consultation!

The **Ultraopteryx**, is a remarkable creature in many ways.

They are an evolutionary crossover stuck in the middle between reptiles and birds.

Hatched from an egg, (usually one of two to survive the eleven-year-long gestation period), they emerge as monsters in their own right, fully developed, smaller replicas of their parents.

Beginning life the size of a pony, hatchlings are reared by both parents while they eat their weight in fish and other marine life every day until they reach the size of a small elephant, with a wingspan of nearly thirty feet, only a year later.

Sub-adults, once weaned, are capable of hunting and feeding themselves quite effectively, and have few predators capable of challenging them. These yearlings travel alone for three to four years before they reach sexual maturity and their legendary size.

At over fifty feet in length, with wing spans of eighty to one hundred feet, the adult Ultraopteryx is an impressive creature to behold, able to challenge monsters the likes of dragons, and the mightiest Trolls. It knows no predators and is considered to be an apex ultravore—meaning nothing eats it and it eats whatever it wants.

One of the oldest species to exist unchanged from its first debut on the evolutionary stage, its legendary natural life span, and its ability to adapt to climatic and environmental change, lends it a secure future in the wild.

Ultraopteryx can reach ages of two hundred years, and rumours of two hundred and ten years and even older are common.

Adult ultraopteryx are covered in thousands of sharp, pointy, spine-like flat scales that they can raise somewhat like a porcupine, if threatened.

Both sexes use these scales to make a rattling sound to attract potential mates, and to make themselves look larger in displays of dominance during mating encounters.

Both genders possess a long shield-like growth that protrudes from the back of their head that they use to resonate sound, believed to be mating and territorial calls. Their voices can be heard from several miles away.

Ultraopteryx are deep sapphire to dark navy blue on their dorsal surface with a pale blue or white underbelly.

The females possess colourful spots on their sides that they use to signal their moods by changing their colour. These can be yellow to fiery orange, and rarely, emerald green.

For more information about the Ultraopteryx or for a copy of this wildlife vignette, contact the G'nomish Film Board Society, Sixty Six-Packs Sreet, Allthewater, Sensimillia. 420420420

CHAPTER - 9 PT2

THE MEAL WAS AWFUL, THE TURBULENCE WAS TERRIFYING, BUT THE MOVIE WAS GOOD.

A cool morning breeze came through the massive hole in the side of the tower. There was still half a roof to afford Eekadinosaur some shelter, and the floor was intact and covered with bones from assorted livestock.

This opening faced the south end of town, towering over most of the other buildings. Looking out, I could see the docks district and recognized the bridge that Durik and I had crossed to get to William's house.

I took a moment to notice how quaint and lovely the city looked in the morning, despite the shambled condition of the lower-class quarter, and the industrialized area near the docks. It had a certain hominess, like people had lived there always. It was almost familiar to me.

Briarwood was a city of thousands that managed to maintain a certain common architectural design which gave it a strong visual personality. The great dome of bureaucracy stood out on the highest hill near the center of town, like some half buried megalithic egg. Its stark white finish capturing the full effect of the rising sun. Even Briarwood's walls were created in the same white stone and beautiful grey wood.

I took a moment also to note that someone forgot to put aside money in the council budget for paved streets in all but the ritziest parts of town.

My thoughts were then interrupted when Eek turned around to face the opening in the wall. She let out a guttural squawk that was so loud as to loosen some of the dried guano hanging from the tower's broken ramparts. Of course, by that point the towns folk had all gotten used to her cry, but many of them still gazed up at the tower in wonder to see the magnificent spectacle that was Eekadinosaur erupting into flight. Eek had developed into somewhat of a mascot for Briarwood.

Though Raz rarely stepped foot outside of the winery while home, the citizens knew he lived there. At that point, everyone in town had already witnessed the mighty black and bright-orange reptilian titan on his blue, flying dinosaur, land on the old broken tower.

Indeed, the townsfolk had come to rely on Raz and Eek as a form of visual reminder that they were safe from any attackers. I mean, who would be stupid enough to threaten a place where those two were living? Right?

Still, few dared to enter the courtyard of the winery. Everyone knew what else lived there. Things more terrifying to look at than Raz and Eek.

There was a blue horror, and a mighty Urk in that place. Best to leave them alone, and not poke the dragon—so to speak.

The mighty Eekadinosaur perched on the edge of the tower, the sun glistening off the many brass buckles and clasps of her heavily armoured saddle and barding. Raz gave her reigns a gentle flick, and she spread her enormous wings.

"Hold tight, Poppa Szvirf," Durik warned me even as he reached up and secured my seat on his shoulder. I grasped two of his spikes and braced for whatever was next.

Using her powerful hind legs, Eek catapulted almost straight up. We were instantly in flight and if I had not been strapped onto Durik's armour I would most certainly have fallen due to the extreme inertial force created during takeoff.

I watched as the dust and small debris formed a cloud in the immediate area surrounding the winery while she flapped her wings, bigger than ship's sails. Looking back, over my shoulder I saw that Raz appeared to be unaffected. He was also strapped into the saddle, his toes gripping the stirrups.

We ascended high into the air in only seconds. Eek's wings sounded like thunder as she carried us ever higher. She clawed the air with them as I watched the rooftops of Briarwood getting smaller beneath me. At first, it felt as though she jumped and crawled through the air rather than flew. It was somewhat exhausting, having to fight the inertia, each time she "leapt" upward. She also spiralled, which only added to the struggle.

I managed all the same and when we reached a specific altitude her wings straightened out and she turned to the west, gliding effortlessly for hours before she even moved them again.

We even ate on the wing, although it was quite windy and inconvenient to do so, and I was unable to light my sacred pipe and partake of the sacred herb. No matter how much I protested, Raz insisted that we must stay on course and the sacred herb would have to wait until we had landed.

As he seemed to almost converse with Eek, and had way more experience flying than I did, I felt it wise to endure this minor inconvenience and make an attempt to enjoy the ride.

To our left and far below, I could see farms and small villages along the road. We were so high that the people looked smaller than ants. (We were also at an amazing altitude.) Either way they looked like ants. Good thing I had conducted an extra-long Sabbath that morning.

Once in a while Eek would flap her giant wings and gain altitude before settling again into a long, smooth, descending glide.

A couple of times we noticed something large, flying far toward the northwestern horizon, but as Raz didn't seem concerned, I decided it was nothing to worry about. I was sure that absolutely nothing would be stupid enough to threaten this saurian and his prehistoric steed.

After about an hour Durik fell fast asleep, his snoring making it impossible for anyone else to do so. I found myself so bored that I began to polish his armour, and the brass of the saddle, or at least what I was able to reach.

Luckily the weather remained pleasant. Perhaps a tad bright but at least it was relatively warm within the saddle's protective aura, and dry as well.

About three hours into our trip, we made a slight course alteration, turning more inland. We left the Imperial Highway behind us and made our way across river valleys and farmlands, patches of thickly forested wilderness, and vast fields of wild grasses.

Far to our right, across miles of wilderness, I could barely make out a chain of mountains that seemed to run north and east. After a total of about nineteen hours we intersected with those mountains and came to an area that Raz reported as being our landing zone.

He pointed to a road in the distance, about halfway up the slope of one of the mountains, explaining that it was there that he had seen the wagons and carts. We descended in a two-mile radius circle until he chose a clearing in the forest two or three miles from the slopes of the mountain.

He explained that we could climb the hills safely from that point, and that it was relatively close to where he had seen the wagons and horses.

"Trrrravel therrrrre." He pointed a long-clawed finger directly at the peak. "Grrrrrarr, comessss tomorrrrow, when ssssun issss high. We wait herrrrre."

He dismounted Eek and began to unpack her saddle bags. There were tents, pegs and poles, and several thick roles that I assumed were sleeping arrangements as they were of varying sizes. It was dark when we pitched camp.

The huge deciduous trees of the ancient forest seemed to almost lean in toward each other once we landed, as if to protect us from view. It was almost as though they *wanted* to protect us. And I wasn't the only one who felt this. The forest seemed—aware—as strange as that might sound.

Once camp was made Durik and I cooked up some food and Raz ate some of the local wildlife he found in a nearby burrow. The meal was simple and bland, and the fire was small and smokeless. We could not afford to let the enemy know we were coming.

That very spot had been used by the boys before as a campsite, so Grarr and the Troll knew where to meet us. They had camped there many times when they were crossing the mountains to reach Al'Lankmire, the capital city on the other side of the mountain chain.

Grarr had taken Beornag and Durik to the imperial capital in the past to do business and shop for rare items, like their bottomless pouches, Eek's saddle, and Raz's flight helmet, to name a few.

Soon after we ate, we decided unanimously that Raz should stay at camp in case we were discovered, and Durik and I would investigate the surrounding area, just to make sure we really were alone out there.

Durik left most of his arsenal at camp and only brought three weapons: a dagger, a steel headed mace, and a short sword with a small shield. The forest was no place for large weapons; the trees were too close together. For someone as tiny as I am, this was an advantage, but for a six-foot-tall monster it was limiting to say the least.

I reached into my pocket and took out my statuette of a bat and tossed it to the ground. It shattered and the dust-like glass particles reformed into Nikodemius. I then commanded him to stay with Raz. That would give me a link to our camp while we were away. He complied and Durik and I began a circling pattern around the camp.

We stuck close to each other, or I should say I followed as best as I could, as Durik silently made his way through bramble and bush, always aware of his surroundings, his mace and dagger gripped tightly in his hands.

We moved this way, circling the camp in larger and larger arcs for two or three hours, until we were a substantial distance from the base. Then Durik suggested we pause for Sabbath. I agreed and we sat down under a massive oak tree.

The forest was now coming to life with the songs of insects and choruses of night frogs. Small areas of the forest floor, and patches on trees began to light up with phosphorescent fungi, just now awakening in the darkness and casting soft glowing auras here and there among the foliage.

As I spoke the words of prayer and Durik held the pipe high into the air, we heard a rustle in the bushes nearby. In a split-second Durik had covered us with his leather cloak and hid the glowing embers of the pipe.

I peeked out from under the hem and saw the heat signatures of four tiny humanoid creatures. They were almost as small as I am.

I watched as they shuddered with fear. Obviously frightened, they were trying to hide. Eyes suddenly agape with shock, one looked over at us and yelled a warning to his friends in the strangest dialect of *G'nomish* I had ever encountered. I had never before heard G'nomish spoken with such a strange accent. It was broken and slurred as though allowed to degenerate into some sort of wild G'nome tongue.

As the four tiny people stood up to run, they found themselves trapped between Durik and me (still under the cloak and well hidden, although not from them), and a large humanoid creature that stood over them and seemed to simply appear from nowhere.

It was mutating right before our eyes, continually shifting its appearance, growing features and melting them away again. Among those features I noticed a ridge of serrated bone in its mouth, like a single tooth, and two large, saucer shaped black eyes.

"Kid! Kill that big thing!" I shouted as I rolled out from under his cloak, trying to gain the attention of the little folk.

The creature looked straight at me, and I swear there was recognition in its eyes.

I almost crapped my pants right there!

Durik exploded from under his cloak, his eyes glowing green in the dark of the deep forest. He leapt over the bushes where the small folk were, roaring his disturbingly insane battle scream.

The sound of his voice echoed through the forest as small animals and birds suddenly burst from their nightly shelters to escape the area.

Gasping with astonishment, the little people watched Durik fly over them. Then, with both the kid and the creature behind them, and only me in front of them they wisely opted to run toward me.

I signalled for them to follow just as the creature attacked, striking Durik and sending him flying against a tree with such force I was sure he must have broken bones.

He slid down the trunk for a split second, landed on his feet and immediately leapt again at the creature. This time when the thing swung at him, he was ready. He sucked in his gut, the claw barely missing his stomach, and came down on it with both armoured fists. The pommels of his weapons contacted the creature's head, and bone could be heard crushing under the force.

Durik screamed his war cry over and over as the little folk rushed past me. I could see his silhouette ripping chunks from the creature's body and throwing them over his shoulders. He had lost all awareness of his surroundings and was in full blood frenzy.

After this had gone on for several moments, I began to suspect something was wrong. I had gathered the little people and told them to hide behind a large rock about forty feet from the battle. Durik was tearing at the creature. Blood and flesh, bone and organ, had been ripped from it in that time, but it still struggled and screached.

I made my way closer to the monster to better see what was happening. Its front was mutilated. Its internal organs were exposed and missing, as well as many of its bones. Its face and throat were torn apart almost beyond recognition, but it still struggled.

The many chunks ripped from its body were turning to goo and oozing through the underbrush, making their way back to the creature's main form.

With horrified awareness I noticed its hair began to grow. It was growing one stiff ridge down the center of its scalp from the forehead back, and I knew what this shape-shifter was now becoming.

Its skin started to change colour to a deep, stormy blue. Stripes of velvety black were crawling over its surface and its shape was becoming hominid.

It was becoming Durik!

"Kid we really need to kill this thing fast!" I shouted.

"Durik trying, Poppa Szvirf!" he responded. "Creature keep growing back!"

Regeneration! The thing was able to alter shape and size. That meant it could add or subtract from its own mass at will! I had to think fast. This thing had to have a weakness.

That's when it hit me. Fire! If I could totally engulf the thing in fire and make sure it burned completely, there would only be ashes left. It was only a theory, but it was something to work with.

Durik was wearing his giant gauntlets and was protected from fire as well, so there was no danger of me hurting him in the process.

"Kid! Get away from it! I'm gonna hootspa it into next month," I yelled.

I was forced to repeat myself several times before it finally registered to Durik what I had planned. He rolled to one side, got up and quick to think, shielded his face with his forearm. The fire would not hurt him, but the concussion of the blast could be substantial.

Gurgling and squealing the creature stood as tall as the kid, while flesh, hair, and even a facsimile of Durik's armour began to generate in front of my eyes. It made hideous sounds like air squeezing through a hole in a particularly infected lung, bubbling and spurting while it wheezed.

"*Klakghal matza schmikle*," I yelled as I pointed my open palm at the beast. "*Shming'gul Latzkha!*" My hand began to glow as the beast noticed me again.

It lifted its left hand, and a dagger grew out of its morphing flesh. Trying to maintain my concentration, I continued to prepare the hootspa while the fiend raised its weapon in the air and prepared to throw it at me.

A blur of shining steel in the defused moonlight betrayed Durik's position as he brought his short sword down across the villain's skull, splitting the creature from top to midsection, and ruining its aim.

I dodged as the dagger flew past my head a few inches to the right.

Still bubbling and sizzling, the monster stood there for a moment, both sides of its body trying to pull itself back together. Then as it began to regenerate again, Durik picked it up with both hands and roared, "Hootspa now Poppa Szvirf!" while he threw the best into the air.

"*Pyric Schlemeki!*" I hootspa'd, and a ball of white-hot molten energy flew from my palm. It zigzagged through the trees and hit the foul thing as sparks flew through the air.

It all happened in a flash as though carefully practised. The ball of molten energy hit the creature and engulfed it in blinding heat. Its silhouette glowed white and lit up much of the surrounding forest as it descended. Nearby trees caught fire, and stones actually began to glow slightly. The heat was more than I could have expected.

I made a mental note to go and see Novak, Grarr's wizard neighbour buddy. I was supposed to do so earlier in the week but forgot entirely. Now here I was winging it with powers I did not fully understand.

In a matter of two or three seconds, the light went out and all that remained of the creature was a grey cloud that cascaded down over Durik's frame. With a grunt, the kid came running to my side with his sword and shield drawn, a cloud of ash descending to the ground behind him.

In the dappling moonlight he appeared to be some kind of ghostly crusader of justice.

"Any more, Poppa Szvirf?" His eyes darting around in all directions searching for more enemies.

"That was the only one, kid. Come, let's check on those tiny folk," I suggested, then extinguished the small fires I had started, and cleaned him up with a simple hootspa.

We made our way to the rock that the small folk were hiding behind and as I came to face them, they all dropped to their knees in a worshipping posture.

One of them spoke. "Cloud Walker—come you have."

"Cut that out," I said as I grabbed him by the arm and helped him to stand. "I am not a king or god, and I don't know what you mean by a cloud walker. I have never walked on clouds." I was speaking in modern G'nomish, but they seemed to understand me. "Who are you people?

"Weeze beez the unda-tings," one replied. "Weeze beez the escapers from the man house in the old points."

As I got a little closer to the rest, I could see that they were very similar to my own people. A little taller and greyer skinned, but the features, especially the noses and the large pointed ears were very close to being G'nomish.

I suddenly realized—these were *Gnomes*!

"Yooze is the Cloud Walker. Weeze sees yooze on flyer in sky. Weeze is escaping the man house and weeze comes to place of prophecy." They had a look on their faces that was part terror, part desperation and part elation, if you can imagine such a look.

"What prophecy are you talking about?" I asked as I gathered them closer.

I was surprised that they were not affected by Durik's presence at all. They paid him no more attention than if he were my G'nomish accountant, tagging along to tally the expedition's cost.

"You say you are *unda-tings*? What is that? You look like Gnomes to me," I said.

"We lives unda-tings sos we be unda-tings. Unda- rocks, unda-hills, unda-mountains. Many big years we be slaves to manhouse baddies, Cloud Walker.

"Old unda-ting says there be big magic joojoo and hero comes. Magic joojoo be there." He pointed to a star in the sky. It was sparkling yellow.

"Never we see big joojoo until now. Old unda-ting say Cloud

Walker have army of titans and all unda-tings be safe when cuminz they do, savin' all us.

He smiled again, "Old unda-ting says hero be dressed black, colour of sky at dark times, and yellow star be on his heart." He pointed at the golden Sensi-leaf amulet that hung from its golden chain against my chest. The symbol of Shiddumbuzzin.

I thought to myself—"very funny". As if I didn't have enough to worry about. Now I had to fulfill yet another prophecy or some such thing. *Mind if I finish one before you give me any more?* I mentally cussed.

"Stand up, and stop grovelling," I demanded. "I am not someone to worship. I am a G'nome just like you are. My name is Szvirf Neblinski. You say your people are slaves to the man house?"

"Yups. Sayzin that does me. Weeze bein' waitin' fer Cloud Walker to come for savin' us," he replied.

"Yooze is hero of old tells," another added. "Yooze has titans." He gestured toward Durik as he approached the kid without any fear. In fact, there was genuine adoration in his gaze—in all of their gazes.

The Gnome glowed with reverence as he stopped in front of the colossal giant that was Durik and ran his tiny hand over the metal of Durik's boot. "Holy titan, weeze beez unda-tings. Weeze wait fer yooze many big years."

"Poppa Szvirf?" The kid spoke, his voice quivering as he looked to me for guidance. "Gnome peoples—d'ey not be scared of Durik."

I swear he smiled gently, and as impossible as that might seem, he actually looked harmless for a very brief moment. "Durik like Gnomes." He squatted so as to seem even less threatening.

The rest of the Gnomes then approached him as well, reverently touching him and making sounds of spiritual fulfillment.

"So, you say there are more of your kind being held in this man house?" I interrupted.

"Many be us in that place," the first one replied.

On those words Durik began to growl menacingly. "Show us. Poppa Szvirf and Durik vill save d'em."

I gestured for him to calm down, and for once it seemed to work.

"What are the old points you mentioned?" I asked the first Gnome.

"They be the tall rocks older than all others, they be," he answered, smiling and pointing in the direction of the mountains.

Just then we heard a terrible screeching sound. Raz was calling out from deep in the forest.

I looked to Durik who produced a small horn from his bottomless pouch. "Is Raz, Poppa Szvirf. He vorried for us. Durik send message, now." He blew the horn and no sound at all could be heard. He then put the instrument away. Grinning like a shark, he added, "Only people Durik vant hear, can hear Durik's horn. Raz hear Durik fighting and yell to see if ve need help. Durik say no vith horn."

"Excellent work, kid," I commended him as the Gnomes continued to look to us for guidance.

At this point the evening air was beginning to chill somewhat and I suggested we all retire back to camp. These little folks were wearing burlap clothes that were torn and tattered. A warm meal and a cozy fire was what they needed.

When we arrived, I was amazed at their reaction to Raz and Eek. They gazed upon the reptilian monsters with admiration and reverence. Raz in turn was not bothered by them once he was introduced, and with some stern warning the Gnomes agreed not to wander too close to Eekadinosaur—for their own safety.

We expanded our camp to hold four more Gnomes, fed our new guests and set watches for the rest of the evening. We reported to Raz the encounter with the monster in the forest, and as I described the creature, one of the Gnomes spoke up.

"That thing, bein' it is, the Stealer." The others all whispered under their breath at the mention of the creature. "It be big evil joojoo monster. Stealin' faces and bein' like others, makin' fools of peoples."

"So you are saying it can change its shape into anything it wants? I asked.

"Things it's bein' touchin', is all," the Gnome replied. His name was Dinkle, and he was one of the older of those being held prisoner by what he referred to as the manhouse baddies.

Somehow the Gnomes had noticed the yellow star in the sky and knew that this event heralded the coming of the hero in their prophecy. They also knew they would have to do whatever they could to meet the hero before he found the manhouse, so as to warn him of what was to come and show him the way through the complex system of tunnels and caverns once inside.

He went on to explained how he saw the dagger, that the Stealer had tossed at me, turn to a black liquid and disappear into the bushes, moving toward the mountains. He was paralyzed with fear at that point and was unable to stop it or call out to warn us that it was escaping.

"Now, crawlin' back, it does. Make new self from old. Grown' back." He looked worried.

Soon they would know we were there, and they would come in force to dispatch us before we had a chance to act.

That evening I thought hard as to what we should do. I was no tactician or strategist. That was Grarr's department. Durik and Raz were in all actuality just teenagers and hadn't the experience to form an attack plan, other than breaking down the front door and killing everything that moved.

I introduced the Gnomes to the holy power of Shiddumbuzzin, and explained that he was the god of all G'nome kind, and that we had been denied his wisdom by an evil force that I had been commanded to erase.

With gasps of astonishment and wonder the Gnomes were quite responsive to the idea that they had a god of their own. It would seem that for many, many, centuries they had lived as a *lesser* race, worshipping an assortment of gods from other civilizations, with no known heritage of their own.

Now, this idea of having such a rich culture and religion that they might rediscover was enough to make them ecstatic. They trusted me without question.

At first I found this to be a little unnerving, but once I realized the extent of their imprisonment I came to accept that I had symbolized the hero in their prophecy and they had mistaken me for some kind of saviour.

I mean you gotta admit—the comparisons and similarities between me and the boys and the promised deliverer and his titans were quite remarkable!

After much thought I decided that the idea of the Stealer returning to its master and reporting our arrival was too much to risk. Someone had to try and find the hidden lair of Calabac, infiltrate the defenses, and try to rescue Lillia's sister—and as many Gnomes as possible—before they got wind of us and attacked the camp, or ambushed the boys on the road.

I decided that Raz should try and meet up with Beornag and Grarr on the road, to warn them to hurry. Once they all showed up the three of them would follow Nikodemius to my location, as he was able to locate me at will, and could act as a guide straight to my side.

The Gnomes would all stay at the camp and await the boys' return. Grarr would know what to do then.

Everyone agreed, except Dinkle.

He demanded that his part in the prophecy was important, and that we would never find our way past the maze of traps and corridors that awaited us in the manhouse. Plus, Durik and I would need a guide, or we could become hopelessly lost.

He went on to explain that, as mechanically inclined beings, his people were forced to make those corridors and design the traps that were placed there—and that he was one of the chief assemblers of those traps.

I couldn't argue with his credentials, so I decided that he could come with us. The last thing we needed was for the kid and me to become hopelessly lost inside the enemy's stronghold.

A couple of hours before daybreak we gathered all that we thought we would need and started out toward the mountains.

It was all uphill from there. The forest was thick in the foothills and the walking was difficult to say the least. We constantly had to climb over rocks and fallen trees, but it was better than taking the path that, although easier, was probably patrolled by the enemy.

Once in a while we would stop and I would attempt a hootspa to find invisible stuff, but always I came up with nothing.

At one point we came to a bit of a cliff, about sixty feet high. Durik placed Dinkle and me on his shoulders and climbed the sheer surface with ease. At the top he placed us down on what appeared to be a path or narrow road. I quickly gestured for all of us to get into cover.

We waited a moment to listen and heard only birds and the rustle of leaves on trees. We then continued, climbing further up a steep slope where we found a massive boulder jutting out almost directly over the road. It had a relatively flat top that sloped up and out slightly, and once we were suitably hidden atop and behind it, I began to hootspa again.

This time I detected a large energy source about one hundred feet away.

"Okay fellas. This is it. I found what I think is the lair of

Calabac. It is invisible and is just up ahead on that path," I explained.

"Weeze be movin' to there, no way," Dinkle said. "Weeze secret way goin'."

"There is a secret way?" I asked.

"Yup, yup, yup. I unda-ting who finds it many years gone. Escapin' past it and findin' Cloud Walker, we does." He hopped up and down with excitement as he gestured for us to follow him.

"Wait just a bud pickin' minute," I interrupted. "Why didn't you say something about this before?

"Movin' we are toward it for big hours. Thinkin', is Dinkle, knowin' it too, you do. Dinkle stays shutups," he answered, worry all over his face at my stern tone of voice.

"Okay, from now on if there is anything else you want to share with us about the enemy, please do so," I suggested.

"Manbaddy boss has dragons," he replied. "Ratty-monsters too—and rats."

"Rats!?" I cried. "Did you say rats?"

"Yup,yup,yup. Little rats like pools of dark water on ground runnin', medium rats walkin' like mannys, and big rats, titan-like, havin' sharpies and pointies-a-many for fightin' and Undating-beatin'," he replied proudly.

"Many face maggot thingies—invisible bein' those too sometimes. Also, stinky cheesy monster people who moan and fall apart."

"Cheese monster?" I asked, confused.

"Yup yuppers. Smellin' like cheese, fallin' apart. Manny boss have many, like stars in sky many."

He scratched his head in thought for a second. "Manny boss have evil mannys too. Evil mannys comin' all from way-away.

"So many... many as stars bein', too, those. Manny boss have magic joojoo baddies who make blackness where scaredy cat makers come from."

"Okay, maybe we should go back and wait for the others," I suggested as my brow began to sweat and my hands started shaking. "It's bad enough we will have to deal with armies of bad men and cheese men and maggots and blackness makers...whatever any of that is—but rats?!"

I looked to Durik. "Rats, kid. I don't like rats. They scare the crap outta me at the best of times."

Just then we heard the sound of someone approaching so we all ducked behind the large boulder that was on top of the rise. Once in place, we watched and waited.

After only a few moments, "Poppa Szvirf," Durik suddenly whispered, crouching behind us.

"What is it kid?"

"Durik must pee now," he said desperately.

"What is it with you guys and the bodily functions anyway?" I knew that if he started shaking his knees his armour would be like a school bell going off. They'd detect us for sure.

I listened to the sound of a caravan approaching from further down the path. As long as we could remain silent, they would go right past us.

So, immediately I went into action and whispered a quick silence hootspa on Durik.

Good thing too. He *really* had to go bad.

He unhooked his cod piece just as the caravan made the bend.

In the lead was a tall Human on a black horse. He was dressed in black leather armour and was armed to the teeth. A long pike attached to the saddle of his mount held a banner that fluttered in the breeze. I would later learn it was the flag of a nation of murderous villains living far to the south in a land of ice. He also had a whip at his belt and a great brass bugle.

Behind the lead rider were three armoured wagons. We were

high enough on the slope that we were able to see through their barred windows.

The first wagon was full of crates and barrels. Two armed Human guards were following close on foot. Behind them, the second wagon had many small prisoners all crouching down and huddling with each other. I concluded that these were more Gnomes to be used as slaves. The last wagon was also a prisoner transport. However, it contained only one prisoner.

This occupant was small, three or four feet tall perhaps. I could barely make out its heat signature. It appeared to be wearing a thick coat or blanket and was curled up in a fetal position in a corner. I was barely able to make out a small trail of blood coming from the figure.

For a moment I hoped for the impossibly coincidental to occur. Could that be Alaeth, Lillia's sister?

I quickly turned to face Durik as he unzipped his fly and let her rip.

A stream of steaming tannic acid spewed out of him, splashing and spraying all over the rocks. Good thing he was facing away from us. Still, I needed to warn him about the approaching caravan, but couldn't make any sound as the hootspa was silencing everything within ten feet.

I began to attempt a mental contact with him using my ring (hey, you never know), as the stream of urine began to creep down the slope toward the procession of carts.

This is when I made a mental note: ring does not let me telepathically communicate.

The smell was extremely strong. Durik's anatomy was such that he urinated once every other day. His body retained water and used it very efficiently. The result unfortunately, was that Durik peed something akin to pure ammonia.

Without warning, the head of the Caravan held his hand up

and signalled the wagons to stop. He turned his horse so his shield was facing the slope and with his right hand he lifted the visor of his helmet. He was definitely Human—and living—but different. He began to sniff the night air, scowling and signalling for the others to be on guard.

I watched with disappointment as he slowly reached for his sword.

We had been detected.

I discontinued the silence hootspa as the enemy drew his blade.

He turned to face the trickling rivulet of ammonia that came creeping toward him down the slope. His gaze followed it up the mountainside thirty feet where he squinted to get a better look in the moonlight.

In a flash, Durik passed us as he ran up the shallow slope of the boulder we were hiding behind. This time he didn't scream his war cry. Instead, he tossed his mace to the side of the boulder he'd been peeing on, distracting the enemy's attention further to that spot.

When he reached the end of the boulder, he drew a pair of serrated scimitars. (The very same ones he used to dispatch the evil Dark Elves when we had first met. Ah...nostalgia.)

He leapt from the boulder and fell thirty feet to the enemy below. Silently, like a bird of prey, he descended, his blades pointing downward like the fangs of some great serpent.

He hit the dark rider with such force I could hear the man's spine crack as the two of them fell from the horse. The mount fell to the ground, struggling to get up while Durik rolled with the momentum to end up on his feet, facing the enemies.

Once recovered, the horse turned and ran back toward the direction it had come while the two guards drew their weapons, readying themselves for battle. As it passed, the animal crashed into one of the enemy, sending him falling off the cliff, fumbling for his sword.

Lucky for us he almost immediately struck his head on a sharp rock and was silenced before he could scream. His body disappeared under the forest canopy below.

To my dismay the other guard had spotted Dinkle peeking from behind the rock and was now drawing a long bow. He notched an arrow while I slowly descended behind him, umbrella open and pistol drawn.

As the villain took aim, I shot him in the back of the neck. He swatted at what he thought was an insect and lost the arrow. But proceeded to draw a second arrow and aim it at Dinkle, who hadn't noticed him. The Gnome, grinning and laughing, had been watching Durik in battle.

I later found out that he was watching more out of humour than wonder. Durik, in his crazed blood fury, forgot to stuff his...ahem...manhood back into his pants. As such, being extremely well endowed, he had leapt into the fray with his dork swinging uncontrollably about. He had managed to accidentally pummel the guard in the face with it just before he landed on the armoured horseman, killing him.

Dinkle would describe how Durik's *schlong* smacked the dark knight right in the face, slaying him instantly, and how the enemy actually saw Durik falling on him but was so shocked at Durik's giant *mamba* that he was paralyzed with disbelief, unable to parry the *phallusious* attack.

Well, that was how he tells it and that is how it is written in more than one holy book...but I digress.

Dinkle was laughing up a storm as Durik turned to face the final threat. At the same time the archer turned and took aim at *him.*

The kid was still disorientated from the thirty foot or more fall he'd taken, and as yet had not noticed what the scoundrel was up to.

Then, just as I was about to toss away the dart gun as a fraud, the guard simply let go of the arrow, missing wildly, and collapsed to the ground.

I could still hear the Gnome laughing from behind the boulder as Durik came rushing to my side.

"Aaaah!" I screamed. "Put that thing away, will ya?! Someone could lose an eye!" It was longer than I am! I still have nightmares about it!

"Oh, sorry Poppa Szvirf. He sheathed his weapons.

"Not those! *That!*" I complained.

"Oh. Sorry Poppa Szvirf." He took a moment to shake, return the *titanboa* to its domain, and buckle up his cod piece.

Just then Dinkle came hopping down the slope and joined us. He looked at the caravan and the smile was gone in an instant. In its place was a look of terrible recognition. "Slaver wagons," he said softly. "Baddies catchin unda-tings left over. Maybe some livin' still, maybe." He pointed at the middle wagon.

Durik nodded at him and moved to the back of the mobile jail. I grabbed Dinkle's arm and we followed as fast as we could.

I asked the kid to lift Dinkle to the window and he did so gently.

Looking through the bars, Dinkle spoke, "Hey unda-tings, bein' Dinkle, I is. Knowin' Dinkle bein' you?" he asked.

From inside I could hear a weak voice. "Dinkle? Lopey, bein' I is. Catchin' us, dinkle. Man-baddies. Beatin' and cagin' unda-tings, do they. Havin' you gotz long ago knowins of Lopey, Dinkle?"

"Yep," Dinkle replied. "Remembrin' Lopey, is Dinkle." He looked down at me hopefully. "I gots remembrins of Lopey an' long ago knowins of his leavin' the old points, escapin' the baddies. Lots long times past and ago." He sounded amazed.

"Durik," I spoke up. "Can you open the doors?" I gestured for Dinkle to step back with me.

"Watch, Dinkle. Durik is a mighty hero. Our holy creator sent him here to save your people."

The Gnome began shedding tears of joy as he held my hand.

"Dinkle feels lovin' feels, Cloud Walker. Saviour, titan is bein'. Big tellins, this is makin' when times is gone past." I understood that he was referring to this moment being told as a story, many years from now, and was inspired by his elation.

His people's prophesy was true, as far as he was now concerned. I could see this in his eyes.

I almost wept with him.

Durik grabbed both handles, one in each hand and gave one great tug. He managed to pull the cart backward a few feet, against the horse's will, before the hinges and lock gave way.

The sound of metal tearing and ripping heralded the end of yet another set of so-called reinforced prison doors. The gauntlets of the Fire Giants had made him even stronger than he was originally. There was no lock that he could not break now.

He threw the bent and twisted panels over the cliff and then lifted Dinkle and me up onto the wagon.

Inside were two hundred and sixty-three frightened Gnomes of varying ages and genders imprisoned like livestock. They were chained together in small cages, at varying levels on shelving, like chickens in a giant mobile chicken coop. Entire families huddled together in terror, chained up in boxes one atop the other.

The heat inside was stifling and the poor souls had no water to speak of.

This was a disaster!

We were within one hundred meters of the enemy's fortress and had just liberated a horde of slaves on the main road, all while trying to maintain stealth. We still had to remove their bindings! How we had not been discovered by then was a miracle.

Then it hit me—the other wagon. Could it be that we came all this way only to stumble upon Lillia's sister in a slave train?

I turned to Dinkle. "Dinkle, can you ask them who is in the other wagon?"

He was busy trying to remove their locks and shackles. "I will do that." I interrupted his efforts, "Ask them the question," I said sternly.

"Listen up unda-tings. Cloud Walker, this bein'. Titan, there." He gestured toward Durik.

"Freedom-comin' now, is here. Great joojoo sky-showin' an' Dinkle eyes Cloud Walking, him," he said, pointing at me, then quickly, "Shhhh," he continued as he placed his finger on his lips. "Cloud Walker needin' knowins of inside unda-tings box, there." He pointed at the third wagon.

"Musky, bein' there, Dinkle," Lopey responded. "He be baddie slave too. Membrin's got you, of Musky? Musky freedomnappin' unda-tings, goin'free long pasts and ago. Bein' Musky, like guards but friend-bein', too. Livin' with unda-tings in new, an' secret place.

"Then, baddies come. Findin' Unda-tings us. Baddies hurtin' Musky. Crack, crack, crack. Friend-bein', Musky is, Cloud Walker. Please to free him," he begged. "Musky is hero. Lopey says so, and pleases to you, sendin' is Lopey."

I turned to Durik. "Kid, take Dinkle to the other wagon and free the other prisoner. I will hootspa the chains off of these people."

The kid wasted no time. He picked up Dinkle and moved to the back of the caravan.

"Listen to me good Gnomes. You are not unda-tings. You are Gnomes. I know this and I am wiser than your captors." I looked about and they began to sit up and pay closer attention. "I have been sent to rescue you. I was sent by the god of all Gnomes, Holy Shiddumbuzzin." I moved deeper into the barge-like mobile prison.

"I will show you that I am true. I will call the power of Shiddumbuzzin and release you from your bonds. I will need several moments of silence please." If there was one thing these

Gnomes were good at, it was being quiet.

The prisoners were all hypnotized by my speech (that's an expression, they weren't really hypnotized) and remained silent as I committed the image to memory.

Once I was sure I had a perfect image of the scene in my mind's eye, I imagined their locks all opening, and spoke the unlock hootspa.

"Schmendle heim heim levekki clecky." The locks simultaneously opened and fell to the floor, while the chains and shackles followed suite not long after.

I opened my eyes and placed my finger to my lips. "Shhhhhhh."

I gestured for them all to climb out of the boxes and follow me, which they did without protest or the hint of a sound otherwise. Within minutes all of the Gnomes were standing together between the caravan wagons and the slope. Gnomes of all ages huddled together for warmth, terror in their eyes. These were better dressed than Dinkle. Obviously, they had acquired better clothing after they were liberated by this Musky person who Lopey had mentioned.

I had climbed back aboard the wagon to make sure they had all disembarked, when Dinkle returned.

"Titan say good-guy needin' Poppa Szvirf, Cloud Walker," he added with a giggle and a stupid grin. "Good guy dying is. Good guy for unda-tings long past an agos. A little unda-ting, Dinkle is then, an' keeps remembrins of Lopey and the big run away-from. Good guy, unda-ting knowins. Unda-ting knowins of Musky. Hero, like you, Cloud Walker."

"I will save this good guy, but you must do a great deed for me and for all your people. Are you ready for this, Dinkle?" I asked.

"Dinkle finder of Cloud Walker, is bein'. Talkin' to'er of first Cloud Walker meets. Dinkle's famous will be in long agos not yet said." He grinned. "Good is Dinkle wantin' when long agos not yet tells the remembrins."

I smiled at him then, and he seemed to like that. "Good. I want you to take these people back through the paths you took when you escaped to find me." I tried to explain. "Take them back to the other titan, Raz. You understand? Raz? The—"

He interrupted me. "Stupid isn't, Dinkle. Gnome god hero, Dinkle is, for *Shit I'm Buzzin!*" he said proudly.

"Ummmm…Okay. Close enough. Take them back to Raz quietly. Good guy will help us get into the baddie manhouse now." I placed my hand on his shoulder and added, "*Heghklesmeln, aklehilm shmiff nihklem.*"

The blessing of Shiddumbuzzin. This was one of the few miracles I had memorized. It gave a sort of aura of good fortune to the recipient, allowing them an all-around better chance to succeed at any given task within a four hour period. It was great for playing the lottery.

Dinkle then silently gathered his people and passed the word to be quiet and follow. In only a couple minutes the Gnomes had disappeared down the path and into the shadows.

I then made my way to the back of the last wagon and called out to Durik. "Psssst! Durik. I need a lift, kid."

Durik came from out of the shadows his heat signature glowing brightly as the adrenaline from the battle was still pumping in his veins. He put up his hand and spoke. "Poppa Szvirf. Vait. D'is prisoner is…um…different. Durik sink Poppa Szvirf be not happy to see."

"What are you talking about, kid? Is it that thing we tried to kill in the forest?" I asked.

"Nope. Is not monster d'at grow back. Durik thinking scarier, maybe." He looked worried. "Durik say Musky is okay, and Durik is Paladin of Shiddumbuzzin. Okay, Poppa Szvirf?"

"Kid, if *you* say this person is okay, *I* say they're okay. Get me up there so I can help." I had no idea what he was up to, but time was not something we had in abundance at that point. The occupants of the fortress would notice the caravan on the road soon enough, the prisoner was dying, and Durik was acting like he had to protect someone from *me*.

He reached down and lifted me up onto the wagon. "Vhy you not use ring and fly up?" he asked.

I paused and gave him a dirty look. He had a point, and I was getting old. "Don't be a wise guy kid. Paladin rule number two. Never make fun of the Redeye," I said as I turned to the prisoner curled up in the far corner.

"Durik just sayin'," he replied.

"Go and search the first wagon. See if you can find some better clothes for this person. I will heal her." I scolded him, gently. Teenagers…

"Not her. *Him*." Durik corrected. Then he disappeared.

I had maintained hope that this prisoner was actually Lillia's sister, Alaeth. That would have been too easy, and in retrospect, I believe we still would have attempted to enter the fortress to exact justice upon Calabac and his minions anyway, even though he had an army of rats.

There was no way that Durik was simply going to walk away from this. He now knew that there were innocent people being enslaved inside the enemy stronghold, and that was not acceptable—not at all.

I wished Grarr and Beornag would somehow suddenly show up with Raz and save the day. I had no idea what I was doing.

I breathed deeply a couple of times and approached the prisoner, noticing its lithe form. It was smaller than a Dwarf but taller than a Gnome. It was wearing a brown fur coat with a belt hanging undone.

There was very little heat emanating from it, probably due to blood loss. I reached out to the shivering form gently, so as not to alarm the poor soul.

"I am Szvirf Neblinski," I said. "I have the power to release you from pain and injury and heal you, but I will need your assistance after. Once you have repaid your debt to me for saving your life, I will free you from all responsibilities. Do we have a contract?"

I needed every hand I could get to continue with whatever we were going to do next, and this prisoner was as good an addition to our cause as any.

He responded in a dialect I did not recognize, but it was roughly common Human.

"Ya mun. I is t'inkin' d'is 'ere offer is better d'en sittin' 'ere in dees chains. What you be wantin' I t' be doin'?" He turned to face me, holding out his furry hand in greeting. "Musky's I name, mun."

This is when I realized what he was. His body was roughly rodent-like with a slightly longer torso. His arms were long and sinewy, and his legs were once strong and made for speed. His body was covered with brown, oily fur, and he was unclothed save for a huge, bulbous, rainbow coloured hat, and, a colourful short-sleeved shirt with the symbol of SHIDDUMBUZZIN (!) emblazoned on the front.

The belt was not a belt at all but a long naked scaly tail.

Oy.

He smiled as the moonlight glinted off a gem in one of his long, yellowish, chisel-like, two front teeth. One silver earring in his left ear peeked out from under the thick braids of hair that seemed to be trying to escape the confinements of the hat. His whiskers twitched as he wiggled his nose and grinned at me.

The last thing I remembered was his voice.

"Hey, Mista *Slurpin' Whiskey*, you okay, mun?"

CHAPTER - 10

OY! I NEED BREAK!

Okay—I think I need a short break to freshen up for the next part of the story. Who wants a turn? You?

Over there! You! Dead guy! You're the guy who...Aha! I remember you now.

Okay, I trapped your soul here on this plane of existence—in a little crystal—eternally. Right?

Don't jump up and down; it's demeaning to you and embarrassing to us all.

Now listen up. If you want me to release you from an eternity of solitary limbo and forgive you for being such a nasty bad person, you gotta tell these nice reader people what happened to you, just before you became a ghost.

Now do a good job and transport them back to that last moment.

When I return, if they are still reading, I will let you go and allow you to seek forgiveness from the great golden leaf. Blah, blah, blah...

As for you boys and girls, humour an old G'nome while he attends to old people stuff. This dead guy is gonna tell some of the story for a bit.

Don't worry. I'll be back. Enjoy your intermission. It's about Raz and the boys meeting up on the road.

CHAPTER - 11

INTERMISSION

I am the spirit of a fool. I come to you, reader, to lament my wasted life. To speak of my end as a lesson for those who would follow in my path.

Pride and overconfidence are my downfalls; greed and cruelty my chamber maids. They were the accomplices to my untimely demise. The criminals I nurtured for so many wasted years.

But even death cannot erase the images that my immortal soul relives in memory, over and over again.

I invite you now to witness my final moments in hopes that I will be allowed to let go of them and continue on my way to the other side.

I beg of you to witness these events so that I, in some way, can be free of the terror that was my last experience.

After this...I will bother you no longer.

CHAPTER - 12

BUMP IN THE NIGHT...OR AT LEAST REALLY EARLY IN THE MORNING.

A drop of dew falls from a leaf, the only movement in false dawn's light. This leaf hangs from a mighty tree, that has stood in its place beside the road for almost a hundred years.

This is an imperial highway, the far southwestern portion of the great road to the capital, Al'Lankmire.

It is gravelled this far away from the closest city. Briarwood keeps the roads in good repair, if not paved, but here nature has been allowed to reclaim the curving fairway to some degree.

Tufts of grass encroach upon the edges of the path, while the branches of ancient trees now hang only feet from the surface of the road. In this area there is little civilization other than family orchards and the odd patrol out of Briarwood.

This early in the morning the road is completely void of activity. But something is different on this morning. Something approaches from the southwest.

Two voices—Humanese. They are riders, on horseback, moving slowly along the quiet highway. The sound of hooves on the gravelled road, softened by the absence of any form of horseshoes, is still enough to startle small animals and birds, who scurry off.

The soft chink-chink-chink of their chain armour is almost completely muffled by the supple leathers surrounding each link.

The animals seem to move strangely, though, as they toss their heads. Their stepping is not quite right. Their proportions are— subtly different.

Their *hooves* are—subtly un-equine.

The saddles and tack are black as pitch, with weapons of many descriptions placed strategically here and there. These are the tools of professionals.

Quality stuff.

Expensive stuff.

They have no idea they are being watched.

Most of the local animals don't even notice another creature in the great tree hanging over, far above the road. It could be nothing more than the sound of a breeze and a bush, or perhaps a branch that grew from the tree overnight, or the smell of a new fungus bursting from the mossy covering.

This is a great orange tree. Its fruit is covered in dew and ready to glisten in the morning sun. Each globe hangs heavy with juices. Bright orange on bright orange, they lie against the monster's skin as it lies in wait, high in the canopy.

The now fading darkness of evening seems to cling to the creature as though the predator could command them to stay in the face of the morning sun, the beast's blacker than black patchwork along its heavily plated skin.

This creature has been waiting for two hours, silent and as motionless as a stone. So still, even songbirds land on it to pluck parasites from its scaly skin.

This creature emits no odour. It barely shows a heat signature for those natural arboreal denizens who are able to see in that spectrum.

It is a monster born knowing how to kill, and now it is almost six hundred pounds of muscle, sinew, and iron hard bones, covered with an almost impenetrable hide.

Its mouth, more of a maw, is filled with needle sharp fangs that all curve back toward the throat.

The very last teeth, the ones just before the entrance to the cavernous esophagus, begin to unfold from their protective fleshy covering. These are hypodermic needles the length of a man's middle finger.

The tree is among several in this region that have been protected and maintained by the greatest orchard masters in all the empire. Its lower limbs are thicker than the trunks of most other trees. It endures the monster's weight easily.

Searching the sides of the road as they pass, the two men on horse do not see the creature on the tree above and just ahead.

Clad in dark grey plates of metal, and pitch-black leather covered rings, these men are veterans of battle, hired mercenaries, from the far southern wastes of a wintry realm. Weathered and tested against a hundred enemies.

They are heartless slavers and murderers of women and children, and they have been busy for many years. The high quality of their equipment speaks of their culture's penchant for war and pillaging.

False dawn has already arrived as the eastern sky begins to illuminate. Soon the sun will rise.

Confident that there is nothing on the road that could threaten them, the riders continue speaking to each other as they come closer to the great tree.

Now the dew begins to run over the fruit and leaves, pitter-pattering onto the road. Heavy droplets fall so frequently from the tree, it is as though actual rain is falling from its branches above.

This part of the road is very old; older even than Briarwood itself.

Mighty roots from the great trees in the many orchards along the road long ago forced their way through the modest stone walls that line either side of the fairway.

Twisting and burrowing into the now broken and crushed remnants of what had been a cobblestone road, first built by a civilization forgotten thousands of years past, now covered with white gravel taken from the mountains to the southwest.

Although well maintained in this way, the road is so encroached by the great roots of so many arboreal giants it winds and twists almost violently now. Wide enough for merchants' caravans, but little more.

The men continue on, Oblivious to the presence of the creature high in the tree ahead.

Their conversation is heard clearly now in the false dawn. They speak of a prisoner, a creature—a black and orange-skinned reptilian. They are seeking the accomplices of this monster as well.

They also mention an extra bonus should they capture the little one in black alive.

The beast in the tree becomes agitated at these words, but still it is silent and motionless even while something akin to rage begins to build in it. The glands in its lower jaws begin to swell with a terrible fluid, a mixture of organic super acid, and a cocktail of several powerful neurotoxins. Patiently, it waits, its mouth beginning to fill with chemical death.

The larger of the two is about six feet tall and looks quite strong for a Human. "Once Calabac is finished with him, I am going to skin him and make my boots out of his pretty scaled hide. It will match my cape so nicely."

The two laugh quietly as they discuss how they will add the prisoner's head to their collection back at their home in the Icelands, far to the south.

These men are Talotians, a culture of murderers and thieves.

They serve anyone who pays them and are known for being merciless, vile—evil.

Little do they know, aside from the monster in the tree just ahead, another enemy is hiding silently in the forest. This other enemy is a monster from their legends, and he knows what they are. He has killed *this* kind before, by the hundreds—*thousands* even— long ago.

He is infamous among them.

His glowing red eyes and greenish-black skin are the stuff of nightmares among the ice people, and he has been waiting for these men to arrive too.

This new enemy hates these men. He hates their people, their culture, everything about them. It is a hatred so deep that it resonates from him, and even the insects buzzing around his still form dare not land on him.

"Grarrrrrr," he purrs in anticipation as he waits for the signal from the monster in the tree.

Then…

The thing in among the branches finally moves, ever so slightly. Its cheeks are now swollen with caustic mucus. The scent of the chemical cocktail begins to permeate the area. Like vinegar and sulphur.

The two suddenly stop. "You smell that?" The first speaks again, sniffing the air.

"Smells like vinegar—*burning*," the other responds.

They begin to notice there are no songbirds singing, no insects buzzing anymore. Now the road is silent.

Meanwhile, the sun is rising to the east, warming the air while the titanic reptile begins to feel its adrenaline build.

"Let's make it to that hillock over there and get a better vantage point," the larger rider suggests, gesturing toward a small rise atop a nearby ridge. "*It* will have needed a fire in the night. Lizards don't like the cold," he adds. "I'm gonna guess we catch it off guard."

"I'm telling ya, that smell is familiar," the smaller of the two replies and begins to feel for his weapon.

"Quit worrying and come on," the larger one commands. "I'm getting tired of—"

He is interrupted as a massive branch overhead creaks with the weight of a titanic monster. It stretches as it rises to strike from above. It is far more dangerous than what these Humans were told.

"It's a trap!" the smaller barks as he begins to draw his blade.

His hand no sooner touches the supple doeskin that holds his long sword in its sheath, when the sun peaks over the mountains. Hot rays of energy cut through the openings in the twisting branches of the ancient fruit tree.

The orange and black monster above now stands completely on the massive limb, taking a great breath through its nostrils, filling its body with hot air and swelling to look twice its already titanic size.

Its skin, a natural bony plating, creaks under a suit of armour as it moves.

It is covered with patches of fiery orange on pitch black, its scales rattle like the tail of a massive viper, and it speaks. "I am Rrrrrraaaazzzsssss."

Quickly, the larger of the two horsemen draws a short bow, and begins to notch an arrow, seeking a target among the branches.

This would prove to be a terrible mistake. He should have run while he had the chance.

From the tree above he hears the spewing sound of thick liquid being forced out of a tiny hole, under great pressure.

He looks up, arrow drawn—a *slayer arrow*. He has been saving this arrow for exactly this monster. One shot, anywhere on the great reptile's body, would kill it—dead. Powerful enchantments have guaranteed this.

He is overconfident as he aims at the creature's left eye, a burning amber orb twice the size of the oranges hanging in the great tree.

Too late!

He is not fast enough, and the bowstring disintegrates as steaming acrid slime sprays all over the man and his horse.

He falls backward as his mount rears and throws him from the saddle. The animal then races off into the forest, screaming in terror and pain. A sound no horse has ever made. A splattering of venomous acid, bubbling on its skin and barding, leaves a trail of noxious vapours in its path. Even as it is galloping off, the acid eats through the straps and buckles, causing the saddle to fall to the road and drag behind.

Before he hits the ground, the archer's cheek is already turning to bubbling jelly. The leather of his expensive armor begins to smolder and dissolve. His eyes burn and shrivel like raisins from the caustic vapours, while he chokes on the sizzling insides of his own lungs.

The enchanted arrow falls, undamaged, to the ground.

The other Talotian kicks his horse into a charge and heads straight for the great mound of moving reddish-brown hair, what he had thought was only a small hillock on the ridge. Sword drawn he charges toward this new enemy as it rises taller, like some mountain being born before his eyes. But while he pushes his mount into a full gallop, he feels the steed almost trip as the ground suddenly shakes.

The creature in the tree has descended in a single leap from at least thirty feet above the road to land merely a few feet from the mount's rear end.

From the forest, and just over a rise, the screaming of the other mount can be heard yet again. It is a strange sound. Unnatural and terrifying.

Soon the screaming from the injured mount is joined by the terrible roar of some *other* titanic creature that had been silently lurking deep within the woods.

Even from hundreds of feet away, through the thick forest, the sound of bones can be heard snapping and in a split second the mount's bizarre screams end.

As the horseman charges forward, ready to cut the behemoth ahead down, the would-be hillock turns and rises to its full height.

This is no hillock.

It is yet another monster covered in a chain blanket with a great belt, two feet broad around its colossal girth. It is at least sixteen feet in height, standing straight, swinging a tree over its head.

A terrible grin is on its face, as it crosses its eyes and sticks out a three-foot-long tongue. In an almost subsonic, deep baritone it sings: "Nyaaaa, nyaaaa. Nya-nyaaa, nya!"

Now in a fit of rage, the horseman kicks his steed forward. He has slain monsters before. This is a snow-ape, from his homeland. It is considered a life's achievement to meet and battle with one of these creatures. His people call them *Klughast*.

Next, the tell-tale sound of a sling shot being fired. He hears it even over the hooves of his charging mount, before a tall, greenish nightmare steps from the cover of the forest.

With a gasp of primal fear and realization, the rider looks in the monster's direction, terror filling his very soul.

Him.

In that instant the assassin knows, with a cold certainty, that he cannot win. This green and black monster is the *Blood Baron*, the nightmare of Talot.

A legendary creature, the stuff of legends. His image hangs in the halls of the mightiest warriors as a reminder of why the Talotians uphold their military traditions so strongly. Why they must never allow themselves to be weak in the face of their enemies

Hordes of Goblins had ravaged their land under the leadership of the Blood Baron. His war cry, *GRRRAAAARRRRRRRRR*, was a wall of terrible sound that heralded the coming of the Goblin hordes.

City after city fell to the Baron's relentless campaign of genocide against the Talotian empire. No one knew why he hated them so. But the memory of that terrible red beam of light that was said to pierce a man's eternal soul was woven into the common knowledge of their culture.

A tiny stone strikes the horseman on the side of his head, and he hears a voice in his mind.

"Uh, uh, *uh*. You shoulda stayed home. Heimle-Shnikle Moishmackle!" The voice echoes all around like it is coming from all directions and inside at once.

Time stands still for the assassin, and then he sees chaos for only a moment, followed by a confusing menagerie of colour and sound and texture, swirling around him in a nauseating vortex.

Shocked, he now notices he is looking through a faceted purple crystal wall. He sees the great hairy mound in chain armour, and as it comes closer it grows to mountainous proportions. Its nose is massive.

The Klughast.

He realizes he is trapped inside a soul gem. He is a veteran and is experienced enough to know he will spend eternity in the thing until released by the caster of the powerful magic—the Blood Baron.

The Klughast is joined by the legendary nightmare, gazing at their new prisoner through purple facets.

These horrifying giants are then joined by the great orange and black Gillian named Raz. The cold-blooded monster tastes the air with a bright blue forked tongue, as it looks deep into the stone at him and grins.

The horseman realizes this was his quarry. The Gillian he was supposed to kill. The other two were not even mentioned by his lord and employer.

Then, the Klughast speaks, "D'is guy might be da *only* guy t' evuh *not* like gettin' stoned wit'-us."

The Baron chuckles slowly.

Confused, the horseman swears he hears, in the distance, the sound of a snare drum and cymbal. *Tada-tchshhh.*

A shadow then falls over the trio and their prisoner. Even larger than the great Klughast or Gillian.

This is a dragon to be sure, or something akin.

His quarry, the Gillian, then leaps effortlessly atop the titanic dragon-like creature, letting out a command in some reptilian language. With a deafening roar the winged monster jumps into the sky and soon the Gillian and his mount are gone.

"So..." The Baron speaks as he gazes into the stone, tapping it with his claw. "Now that I have you, the Redeye didn't explain what I should do with you."

He grins as the sun on his back peeks over his shoulder, refracting into a sharp beam, through a monocle covering his left eye. It pierces the gem where the horseman is trapped, and dances over his lifeless heart.

Worse than death, is an eternal existence inside a soul gem with nothing else. This is a prison where one is conscious in a never-ending nothingness. Trapped alone inside the artifact, where madness is sure to take over.

"Oooo. Can weeze take it back home and get d'at jeweller guy t' make a ring outta it?" The Troll asks.

"D'en weeze can come back and look for d'is guys friends...Oooo! Ize got it! Even betta! Weeze could take da ring back t' d'is guy's homeland and punch his mudduh in da face wit' it for raisin such a BAD...NASTY...GUY!"

These last three words spoken as the Klughast puts its face close to the jewel. His voice is like thunder in the horseman's ears.

The giant then turns toward the Baron and asks, "Do yooze t'ink, if weeze timed it right, and Ize farted at a bad guy *just* as yooze hit him wit' one a d'ose tings, d'at da stink o' da fart, and all its farty essence, would be sucked inta da eternal prison forever, t' ass-fix-i-ate da prisonuh?"

CHAPTER - 13

OOOOOO, THIRTEEN. OOOOOOO I'M SO SCARED. WHOOPDY DO.

Okay, I'm back.

Wooohooo! Let that air out a bit before anyone goes in there, okay? I gotta cut down on the garlic cheese dip and the refried potato wedges in onion butter. My eyes are burning.

Anyway, where was I?

Oh yeah...

Did everybody have fun? Did ya learn something new and mysterious about Grarr?

Was the nasty bad dead guy entertaining? Did he tell a good story? Hmmmm?

Okay everyone, listen up. If the dead guy told a good story, and made himself out like the bad guy, and you all had a good time hearing about how he and his buddy got smoked by the boys, turn the page.

If, on the other hand, you thought the story lacked substance, heroic elements, suspense, drama, humour, and general effort, don't turn the page, and I will commit this loser to eternal boredom at the bottom of our bottomless pit in the sub-, sub-, sub-basement back at the winery. Okay?

Oh yeah, and by the way. Those horses that Eekadinosaur ate, in that guy's story? Those were *not* horses but evil genetic experiments, created by *you know who*. So don't call PETA.

CHAPTER - 14
RATSTAFARIANS!?

I awoke to find myself lying on Durik's cloak. It took a moment for me to find my bearings, but once I did, I began to feel the terror building inside myself.

You must understand that rats were absolutely *the* most terrifying thing a G'nome could face. Scarier even than the Troll or *any* of the boys. The stories about what they did to us were the stuff of nightmares come true.

I shuddered as I noticed the damp coldness of predawn creep into my clothes. How long had I been out? Where was Durik?

More importantly—where was that…that…*thing*?

I noticed the sound of voices, and as I listened they got closer and I recognized Durik explaining to someone that he would have to make sure I was safe from the sun.

Then I heard *it*. "So…you be sayin' t' I, d'is bein' da symbol o' yer god, d'at god o' d'em *Ga*nomes, and now d'em Gnomes too?"

He laughed. "He-he-he, mun. Musky's people been knowin' d'is 'ere fer a long time, runnin'. D'is spirit come t' us too, bruh."

Then he added, "Oh and by da way, I really t'ought you said Slurpin' Whiskey, not Szvirf Neblinski. I mean what kinda name d'at be anyway? Don't sound like no name I be ever 'earin'."

"What was it saying", I thought, rage building in me. It was trying to trick Durik. My anger was overtaking my fear. I began to prepare a plan of surprise attack.

"'Ow we gonna make 'im know I is not a t'reat, eh?"

He was *smooth*, that's for sure.

That's when Durik came to my defence—in a manner of speaking.

"Poppa Szvirf say, '*Durik. You not see cover of book. You open and read. D'en you see vhat book is really'*. Poppa Szvirf, very vize. Is great hootspa-ologist. Poppa Szvirf hear great leaf spirit, Shiddumbuzzin. Great leaf spirit say Durik is holy guardian of faith. Poppa Szvirf is holy Redeye. Holy Redeye make sings okay for you too. You vill see. Vait here. Durik get's him."

I heard the kid approach, and I sat up. I noticed he had hidden me atop the boulder again for some reason. He gestured for me to remain low as he came around the top of the huge stone. "Poppa Szvirf, you okay now?" he asked.

I noticed he was covered in blood and pieces of—bloody—stuff. "I am okay kid. What happened to you?!" I stood up to get a closer look at him. I wanted to see if it was him that was bleeding. "Are you hurt? Good gawd what happened? Did I faint?"

"Durik is fine," he replied. "Poppa Szvirf pass out in vagon. Musky call Durik. Vhen Durik come he break Musky's chain. Musky carry Poppa Szvirf to rock, here. Many bad men come, Poppa Szvirf. D'ey make crazy sound and attack Durik. Durik say, 'Durik Paladin of Holy Shiddumbuzzin!' really loud, Poppa Szvirf, but d'ey still hit Durik." He looked enraged.

"Durik get angry, Poppa Szvirf. Durik destroy d'em. Durik chase d'em to castle in vall." He gestured toward the no-longer invisible fortress built into the side of the mountain.

"Durik destroy little, glowing boxes and make explosion. D'en fort appear to all. Durik kill many evil men, Poppa Szvirf. But ve are too late, Poppa Szvirf. Many Gnomes die on road. Durik is sorry." Here he looked ashamed.

I moved past him and walked to the top and outer edge of the boulder where I could see predawn getting dangerously close. The eastern sky was stained with the kind of reddish glow that heralds the coming of heavy rain. Smoke filled the air along the road, pools and rivulets of blood were scattered here and there, each belying the presence of death's recent visit.

While I was unconscious (most of the morning I was told), we had been attacked by an assault force from the fortress ahead. Durik faced them single-handed. Thirty-one soldiers lay dismembered and mutilated on the road. The rat man was now dragging body parts to the cliff and tossing them over the edge. Gore was everywhere and vultures were beginning to gather in the morning sky.

Only one caravan wagon remained. It was the supply wagon. It had been tipped over and was riddled with arrows and crossbow bolts on the side facing the fort.

There was also a fire ahead on the road. I later found out it was from Durik's retaliation. He actually stormed the fortress alone, passed through the barrier, and located one of the mass invisibility devices. After destroying it he was forced to retreat, but in his wake the enemy was revealed.

The road took on an even more terrifying façade closer to the fortress. It was lined on either side with javelins sticking straight up from the ground. Each pike had a Gnome impaled on it. There were also a couple other species, but the vast majority of the hundreds dead were Gnomes.

Crows and vultures were already landing and beginning their gruesome task as nature's sanitary engineers. Not long after they would be joined by gulls. I could see clouds of shadow dance around the elevated corpses and realized with horror these were millions of flies.

The side of the mountain had changed to reveal a multi-levelled city cut into the face of the rocky cliff. In the many openings and windows high above the ground I could see movement just inside and within the shadows.

Thousands upon thousands of entities seemed to be watching us just beyond the edge of light. They had a name that I later used to describe them. This was the Scave.

Not a religious cult at all. *This* was an army. An army of hundreds of thousands. A seemingly endless flood of rats of all sizes, and all levels of intelligence.

It was an army of diseased infested monsters with a single intent—to destroy everything and make garbage. Lots of garbage. They thrived on filth and grime. They were impervious to all diseases and were carriers of many.

These details, of course were unknown to me at that time. To me the fact that they were all in some way rats was enough to scare the k'schvipits out of me.

Even so, what was foremost in my thoughts at that moment was my homeland. If this plague were to find its way there, we would not be able to withstand its sheer mass. The entire civilization of the G'nomes would be destroyed forever.

I backed away from the scene of carnage, terror beginning to overtake me again. The end of Sensimilia. The end of everything I held dear. Mom…Dad…Abe…Bernie.

Okay not so much Bernie, but the others. Wiped out. Never to be seen again.

I dropped to my knees. Shock began to settle in. This was beyond nightmarish. The horror of it was too much for me. Oy!

Then, like a beacon in the fog, I heard the kid's voice. "Poppa Szvirf. Durik fight evil now. Ve go to var!" He turned and walked down the slope; a dark cloud seemed to hang over him.

"Wh-wh-what? War? *War?*" How had all of this come to be? I

was just a foreman. A working shmoe. I had no business being in a place like that. This was evil like I had not thought possible.

I thought of the suffering of those Gnomes, the plague of vermin awaiting the coming of night so they could fall upon us like a shadow of pestilence, and the carnage that would surely take place.

As powerful as Durik was, he could not face an army. What did he think he was doing? Even all the boys combined could not hope to defeat the sheer mass of the force behind those shadowy windows and crevasses.

Durik! I came to my senses, suddenly, and just then realized how my own dad must've felt when I was about to do something stupid.

Durik was being lured into a false sense of security. That thing had been down there with him long enough to twist his mind and make him act without thinking. It was the only explanation that I could think of for why he was planning to attack a well defended fortress virtually alone.

I checked my pockets to see what that thing had stolen from me. Nothing seemed to be missing, but still I thought it could be a trick.

I drew my dart gun and quietly cast a hootspa of invisibility on myself. Then, making my way down the slope toward the creature, I prepared a *Schmatzel*. I was fixing to kill the filthy beast where it stood.

As I reached the road, I overheard the two in conversation. "Is d'at last vun?" Durik asked.

"Ya, mun. D'at was a task, what?" The thing approached him.

"Soon Raz come. Nikodemius too. He is Poppa Szvirf pet bat. D'ey have special link in minds. Maybe help Poppa Szvirf." He handed the rat creature a rag and it began to clean the blood from its paws while he continued. "After D'at come Grarr, and Beornag. D'en enemy is very sorry. D'en...for D'em...much pain." He snarled.

I slowly approached the creature from behind, pistol drawn and loaded, while Durik turned to face the fortress only a third of a mile or so down the road.

A haze of smoke and the coming rainclouds from the east defused the morning light turning the sky blood red. He walked forward defiantly. Holding his shield and broad sword up, he roared. The sound filled the valley below and echoed off the face of the cliff. The shadows within actually receded momentarily.

I continued to prepare to kill the verminous creature. My surprise attack would be the last chapter in the foul beast's life. "Only a little closer", I thought.

Durik roared again. "Durik is herrrre! Power of holy light, comes now! Durik is death for evil! Death! You vill not live after d'is day! Hear Durik?! He is coming! Be afraid!" He pounded his chest with the hilt of his sword. "Aaaaaaaagh! I come for you!" He stepped up onto a boulder on the cliff face, hundreds of feet above the ravine below. "Durik brings doooooooom!"

"Inches away now", I thought, elated at the idea of ending the rat-thing's life. I remember thinking how satisfying it would be, to kill the filth with a mechanical thing as opposed to magic. Something tangible like—

Just then the kid turned to face the beast. "Durik sorry for your people Musky. Vee vill kill all evil creatures. D'en Poppa Szvirf vill help Ratsta peoples too. You vill see."

"Mun. I be plenty glad you're bein' on I side." He turned to face my direction as he spoke, and I remembered my rage at the creature's audacity. Trying to fool Durik.

I released my invisibility hootspa as I aimed my pistol at the foul beast. "Vermin!" I yelled!

It raised its arms to shield itself and spoke. "No, mun! Vermin is bein' I cousin! I be swearin' it!" He begged.

"Please don't be killin' I!" it almost sobbed. "I 'ave kids, mun!

Seventy four of 'em, mun! I not be seein' 'em in years, mun. Musky just tryin' t' get 'ome, mun."

He grovelled some more. "Oh please Mun! Not I! I is bein' on yer side, Mun! I can't be dyin' now. Ya just freed me from d'at Scave."

"Poppa Szvirf!" Durik yelled then. "Put veapon down!" He was aiming a slingshot at me. "You act not right!" He took a couple steps forward when I hesitated.

"Durik vill shoot you! Musky is friend. Durik not vant you harmed." He stepped closer as he seemed to struggle with his own actions.

Then, just as my finger began to twitch, the lights went out.

I woke up (again) to find that this time I had been tied and gagged.

I recognized the twine that was used in my bonds as Durik's dental floss from his travel bag. I was lying on the kid's cloak at the top of the boulder again, smelling minty fresh. I couldn't move. I heard a commotion in the distance. It sounded like a great battle. Then I remembered—*the rat-thing*.

I could hear Durik roaring over the sounds of screaming and the clashing of metal on metal. Helplessly, I listened to the sounds of horse's hooves and many sandalled feet moving fast along the road below.

I was startled when a blazing trumpet call from high above sliced through the morning air, calling for more soldiers to be sent to their deaths against Durik on the narrow path.

Eventually the sounds of many soldiers grew more intense, and I could hear Durik's voice being muffled as he called out in distress.

I struggled with my bonds but to no avail. Just when I thought it couldn't get any worse, the rat man came scurrying up the slope in its scurryingly ratty way—disgusting.

If I had had my hands free, I would have torn out its throat right there.

It ran right up to me and began speaking. "Mista Szvirf, I be not knowin' why ya hate poor old Musky so, but yer friend d'ere? Well, he be a good mun, and he be wantin' me t' save ya." He slung me over his shoulders like a sack of potatoes (well okay—a really tiny sack of potatoes) and I heard Durik screaming in the distance for me to run away.

If I could have spoken, I would have reduced the beast to ash. As it was, however, I was helpless to do anything but silently pray, as the creature scurried away from the battle, between the stones and through crevices in the mountainside.

I listened for Durik's voice, the sound of battle becoming distant very quickly as the beast moved silently, ever so speedily, further and further away from the kid. Then all fell silent, and even the creature's feet made no sound as it climbed the slope and made its way around to the northern side.

There was a point where I thought I heard Eekadinosaur screeching in the distance, but it was hard to be sure.

After several, exhausting hours I began to feel lightheaded. At first I thought the creature was casting a spell on me. It hadn't shut up for forty-five minutes. But finally it stopped and turned sharply as it entered a deep crack in the cliff face.

"We be safe in here, mun. D'em man tings can't climb up 'ere. Come nightfall d'ere's a bad wind gonna be blowin' up d' side o' d'is 'ere mountain though, mun.

"D'em Scave'll be wantin' t' kill us good. You and I need t' be seeing t'ings d'is 'ere same way if we're t' survive d'is and save yer friend. You 'earin' I?" He looked worried.

"Musky be knowin' 'ow t' be gettin' in d'ere, mun. Neva t'ought I be tryin' t' get *back* in." He pointed deeper into the cave. "D'at's w'ere yer friend is bein' mun. Now I be willin t' owe up t' I part o' d' contract. You rememberin' our contract, mun? I gonna tell ya about I, and d'en I gonna let ya free. After d'at we can see where d'is goes."

As he unravelled his story, I found myself mesmerized by the golden symbol emblazoned on the front of his colorful shirt. It had a pattern of vibrant rings that encircled each other: green, yellow, red, then green, yellow, red, again and again, just like his hat. Like a vortex of colour.

"I name's be Musky. Musky Ratlove, is I. I cousin be Vermin, mun, and I don't know what 'e done t' ya, but just so ya know, mun; Musky don't like 'im either.

"You got a good friend d'ere and we need t' be savin' 'im now d'at the Scave got 'im." He winked.

He sat me up against a rock and continued. "I be a Ratsta, mun. Not a rat." He sighed, "Okay, okay. I admit we be lookin' like rats, a bit. But we ain't d'em, mun. I mother kept a clean 'ouse and so do I six wives, mun."

He began to brush the dust and dirt from my clothes while he continued to speak. "Years ago, mun, I people were bein' taken from our islands an' brought 'ere across d'at sea. After a long time passin' I asks: 'Why d'is be happenin' at all, mun?' And ya know what? Not a soul could respond? Are ya believe d'at? Not a single Ratsta could tell I why we was bein' kidnapped all d'at time, mun. So bein' curious, I starts a search t' find I missin' people, mun."

He cleaned some dirt from a scratch on my cheek, with a hanky and some water from a nearby pool.

I found myself suddenly being able to relate to this guy. My head began to *clear*.

He continued. "Next t'ing I is knowin' d'ere be chains around I an' I be 'eadin fer d'at castle." He gestured behind him, toward the fortress somewhere in the distance.

"D'ey took I blood, mun. Right outta I arm. Kept I fed and kept takin' blood from I. Dose unda-tings was all bein' beaten bad by d'em Humans." He hung his head.

"All d'at time d'ey keep Musky, I be wantin' t' escape. D'en one day I gets I chance, mun. I sneaks past a sleepin' guard and brakes some unda-tings from d'eir cells too." He was quite animate in his description as my head continued to clear.

"I takes little Lopey and 'is people t' a place I knows, where all us t'ought d'em Humans wouldn't never be findin' us. We stays d'ere fer five years, mun. D'ose little ones and Musky. D'ose Gnomes 'ad families, mun. We made a village in d'at place, and 'omes, mun."

His eyes became glossed over as he continued. "D'ey killed so many, mun. I couldn't stop d'ey. I grabs up some babies and I runs. I runs into d'at night and hides, but d'ey find I, mun. D'ey beat I up real bad and ate d'em childrens. Musky screams when d'ey make I watch, mun.

"D'ose tings down d'ere ain't no Ratstafarian peoples, mun. "Ratstas not be eatin' flesh at all, mun. If it don't grow from da eart' we don't eat it.

"Dose tings down d'ere are what Calabac made from I blood, mun." He apologized. "Musky be swearin' it. D'em's monstas if d'ere eva was a ting, d'at's fer sure."

He then drew a dagger that I recognized as one of Durik's, and with a hopeful look in his eyes he reached out and cut my bonds.

I stood immediately, and for a moment was speechless. Okay, rats are scary things. But I am an educated G'nome. The way I felt and acted back at the boulder near the fortress now seemed somewhat insane. The extreme hate was now gone and replaced with reason.

I realized that this had very little to do with Musky's story, or Durik's predicament. Something unexplainable had happened back there at the fortress gates. Something altered my personality, or rather located, enhanced, amplified, and exploited my fear.

It occurred to me that this may be why Durik was screaming challenges at an entire army in front of their fortress, and why he did not retreat with Musky and me in tow.

I mean, the pair of us weighed about a hundred pounds combined, *with* equipment. He could easily have picked us up and run away, blowing his horn for Raz to come in the process. Why did he not call for Raz and Eek? There was very evil magic at work there. There could be no other explanation. Calabac was now much more of a danger than I had previously perceived.

"What will become of Durik?" I asked, my voice shaking with worry.

"First d'ey be takin' 'is tings, and chainin' 'im up. Maybe d'ey feed 'im t' d'at dragon d'ey got in d' chasm," he replied, an apologetic look on his face.

"Da boss in d'ere, 'im be wantin' t' know everytin'. 'Im talk t' everyone who come in d'at place. Iffin 'im don't like ya 'im feed ya, t' 'is dragon.

"Iffin 'im don't care, 'im trow ya in d'at slave pit t' work. Iffin 'im like ya, 'im let ya join 'im's cause.

"Iffin ya say no, 'im do tings to ya like what 'im do to Musky, mun. It ain't no nice tings, trust I."

"Musky…" I began.

"Where to start", I thought, as he waited patiently for me to continue.

Then I explained, "I want you to know that I am grateful that you saved my life. Back at the castle gates, my mind was being controlled, as was Durik's, I think. I am deeply sorry that I attempted to murder you. I am okay now and welcome your assistance graciously…and I have never met your cousin Vermin, and cannot formulate an opinion on him, as such."

"We be 'avin' a contract, mun, an' Musky never break 'is word." He placed his hand over his heart and smiled.

"I must admit, I am still in shock. At the moment all I can think of to do is have Sabbath." We sat for about thirty minutes together, in silence. Though it only took me half that long to realize just how much Musky was *not* like a rat. First impressions can be deceiving.

His face was pudgier, or at least I could tell it was supposed to be. He had been starving in that slave caravan.

We rested a moment and allowed the sacred herb to take effect. I was tempted to call upon absolute divine intervention from the great golden leaf, but I remembered I was to save that for absolute emergencies, when all else failed—if I even had the power left in me after what I had done in William's basement. This rest was just what I needed to compose myself and plan an offensive.

Then I suddenly realized that I had forgotten about something— *Nikodemius.*

CHAPTER - 15
THE FUN GUY WITH THE FUNGI.

There we were, sitting in that tiny crevasse in the cliff wondering what to do next. I was just finishing up preparations for some real nasty hootspas to toss at whatever ugliness we might encounter, while Musky was keeping an ear out for danger.

His hearing, I would soon learn, was extremely sensitive, especially toward rhythmic and repetitive sounds. In fact, it was astonishingly sensitive. He was able to hear things from a distance that I was unable to detect up close.

By now he and I both were well on our way to being stoned enough to function normally, and Musky was finishing up filling my firestone pipe with some of that nice Sensimilia herb for the third time.

For something that looked like the sum of all my greatest fears come true, I was beginning to really like this guy.

"Pops," Musky started. "I is t'inkin' d'at we git down d'is crack 'ere." He gestured deeper into the cave.

"D'em Scave be cumin' when da sun go down. D'ey're not like rats. D'ey not got d'ose good noses like all d'em rats do. We be okay if we git deeper where d'ey can't be seein' er smellin' us."

I agreed. "I tried to contact Nikodemius, my pet bat, through telepathy, but something is interfering with the mental connection," I explained as he lit the pipe.

"You say Calabac has a dragon? Well, we have a dragon too, and he rides on top of an even bigger dragon. We also have a giant, hairy Troll and a mighty Urk battle master, but the trick is getting a message to him and the boys so they know where to find us," I continued as I accepted the pipe and drew deeply.

"If I is right, d'is crack will be leadin' us t' d'em waterwerks in d'at slave level o' d' fortress...eventually...I t'inks.

"It be like a great smood road d'at have prisons on one side, in d'at place where d'at water is all bein' cleaned and made t' go places. Long it is, mun. Like almost a mile, I be t'inkin'. D'ere be unda-tings d'ere, and maybe d'ey be 'elpin' us t' find Durik if we be letting d'em all out a d'at jail." He winked.

"If not, I be tinkin' we still go in furder an' be plenty quiet like so we find 'im wit' luck only." He looked worried. "We don't want t' be messin' about in d'ere fer too long mun. D'ere be nastiness more d'at I ain't even been tellin' ya yet."

"Okay." I handed him back the pipe and he drew from its crystalline stem. "What can we expect inside the fortress?"

He exhaled and continued. "I know d'at he be practisin' dark doo-doo, mun. D'at whut Ratsta's be callin' evil magic, bruh," he began to explain.

"D'at Calabac got 'im an army o' d'em Scave, an' another one be all dead peoples too, mun." He waved his arms to show the importance of his words.

"Da Scave only be comin' out at night, mun. Da sun, it 'urts d'em t'ings and d'ose dead peoples too. I be t'inkin' bote d'ose be outside lookin' for us real soon, so we be safer in d'ere, d'en out 'ere." He winked again.

"We be needin' t' find Durik and d'en gettin' out before d'em all come back inside, mun. If we be 'ere when d'at 'appen we be caught fer real." He motioned as if cutting his own throat.

"D'ere be some big worms d'at eat garbage, but d'ose is only where da garbage be, 'an we don't be needin' t' be goin' d'at way." He started drawing a diagram in the sand to illustrate our route. "D'ere be a lot a d'em too.

"'Im got a t'ing d'at can become anyt'ing it want t' be. It can change shape, see?"

"'Im got a great dragon in d'at pit d'at 'im tro animals, and prisoners d'at 'im don't want t' be servin' 'im, into. D'en d'ere be da..."

The throbbing light of the innate energy within the firestone smoking instrument bathed the tiny crevasse in amber light; soft, and refracted in many beams and rays.

I was so stoned I completely missed everything Musky had said. I was mesmerized by the beauty of the orange illumination as it danced across the rough surface of the chamber walls, and thought of home, and my childhood, and...

"Ya know?" he asked.

"Know what?" I asked back.

"'Ow t' keep d'at zombie mucous from... 'ave you 'eard *anyt'ing* I just said, Mun?!" he protested.

"*Pfff.* Of course," I replied, a bit offended.

"Really?" he asked.

"Well...no. Not really. I am very intoxicated. I cannot stop thinking about cheese dip. What I wouldn't give for a bowl of Mom's best and a big plate of thick cut, golden fried, potato wedges. You, know? When the edges are so crispy, and brown, and the sides are golden, and the middle is tender and...oh served with a nice Sensimilia Red bud '63. Great year '63. You know the great house of Redhair produced a record crop of sticky bud that year. I was lucky enough to find two bottles in Gabe's Gulp Wines and Spirits. I saved one. It's back home in the wine cellar of my lower-level condo. That was also the year…"

"Pops," he interrupted.

"Yes?" I responded.

"Why don't we try an' concentrate on d'em problems we got now, d'en we be t'inkin' on how t' get ya d'ose tings you be askin' fer?"

"Good idea. You lead," I said.

About an hour (yeah, a good hour) later we came across an area where the cave widened substantially and had a small stream running through it. I was beginning to actually feel a bit nostalgic. Here the chamber was dimly lit with phosphorescent mushrooms I recognized as mycosis psychedelia, being quite common in the upper layers of my homeland.

I advised Musky to pick one to use as a lantern for his benefit. His night vision was excellent, but this was not night. It was pitch black—the blackness of underground—stone walls that had never seen the light of day.

This was *my* kind of place. Musky's vision, like Grarr's, and Durik's, depended upon residual energy left behind by the sunlight during the day—a sort of footprint left by the sun.

G'nomish visual acuity is dependent upon the density of the different items in our surroundings, as well as the subtle scents of the different minerals and subterranean flora, and even the variety of the white noise that total silence gives off. Even echoed *sound* is detectable by a G'nome's unique eyes. G'nomes have dark vision that cannot be matched by any other sentient race on or in the planet.

With the dim light of the mushroom in Musky's hand my sight would be reduced to what a Human would see in daylight. Musky would also see the same. This would limit my own visual sensitivity but at least Musky would not be travelling blind.

He did as I suggested. We paused at the stream and drank some of the water. He went over what we might expect to encounter inside the fortress labyrinth, and this time I did know what to do when the zombies spit diseases at us.

Musky then suggested that he scout ahead slightly while I rested by the stream. I was liking Musky even more at that point.

While he was gone, I enjoyed the chemical warmth produced by the glowing fungi. The trickle of the stream and the echo of my own breathing on the chamber walls also gave me a sense of familiarity and, to be honest, my feet were killing me, and I needed a rest.

After some time he returned and informed me we would be descending a deep chasm about three hundred yards ahead.

We paused when I handed him my firestone pipe filled with the sticky goodness of home. He lit it and continued with his report.

Musky had found the main chasm and had already climbed down about two hundred feet to locate the safest route for us to take. There, he had come upon a platform with a staircase leading down, deeper into the fortress. It was the place where the jailers tossed old, sick, or defiant unda-tings. At the bottom was the dragon pit, about five thousand feet into the dark smoking abyss.

The stairs would lead us to a long, wide hall, and from there we would be able to steal the keys and release all the unda-tings (or at least that was the plan).

He paused to clear the draw stem of debris and drew from the pipe again. Then he exhaled and continued. "What was I sayin' mun?" He handed me the still burning pipe.

I accepted it and replied, "About what?" I then took another draw from the holy device.

"What ya mean, '*About what!*'" He looked a bit offended. "I be talking away—*again*—and ya not but 'earin' noise instead of what I be sayin'?"

"Huh?" I had no idea what he was talking about. "I have no

idea what you are talking about."

"*What?*" he asked.

"*What,* what?" I replied. "Look—" I stumbled. "I need to sit down." Then I noticed we were already sitting, and after about ten minutes of complete silence...

"Oh yea! I be remembrin', mun!" he exclaimed.

"Remembering what?"

"About da crevasse...and d'en d'ere was d'at platform and d'en d'em stairs! D'ey be leadin' us t' d'at place w'ere d'ose unda-tings be prisoners an' w'ere d' water for d'is 'ere place runs!" he explained.

"Really?" I asked, truly fascinated.

"D'at's what I be telling ya, mun," he continued. "Afta d'at we be 'avin' t' sneak by d'em guards d'at d'ey 'ave d'ere. D'ose is not wut we be wantin' to meet up wit'—truly."

"Okay," I offered.

"Pops. Y'alright, mun?" he asked, concerned. "Ya been actin' all weird like since we entered d'is 'ere chamber."

"It might be the spores from the glowing psychedelic mushrooms," I said.

He looked around the chamber at the glowing fungi of all different growth stages. The air sparkled from the dust-like spores that were being pumped into the cavern.

"Dose d'ere mushrooms?" he asked.

"Yea," I replied. "You can make an amazing salad with these things," I continued as I picked a small one and began eating it.

"They're also good in a tea, or soup, but when they are in high season they kick up a pretty good dose of micro-spores that they release constantly into the air. That stuff is amazing for those after work TGIF parties at Abe's."

"An' you be sitting 'ere for 'ow long, breathin' all d'at in?" he asked.

"That would be correct," I pointed out, with an index finger and a wink.

This was also where I realized how glad I was to have Musky and his four or five brothers with us. If only they would stop all speaking at once, though.

"An' you was 'avin' us carry one along *wit'* us?"

Suddenly I realized my error. "You are exactly right, my fine, furry friend. Get a bag. The boys will want to try these. We'll take 'em *all*."

About an hour (or maybe it was only a few minutes or several days) later we were standing on the platform, overlooking an enormous hole.

Don't ask me how we got there.

Deep beneath us was an open pit where, presumably, the dragon lived.

I was so completely high on psychedelic mushroom spores at that stage I can only assume that the next few bits actually happened, so bear with me here.

The platform was cut out of the chasm wall, and far above us I could see the night sky. The stars twinkled like diamonds cast over a velvety, indigo blanket. Somewhere up there was a full moon—and Raz—I hoped.

The floor beneath me seemed to transform into gelatin each time I took my eyes off the obsidian surface. Again—the mushrooms.

Coming from beneath was a constant wave of dry heat that smelled of sulphur and various burning—and close to burning minerals—all ascending on a constant steamy cloud of noxious humidity. This was no chasm. It was a semi-dormant volcano!

Here the inner walls of the cone were littered with openings and balconies facing into the pit. The trickle of rain from days ago could be heard as the rivulets were still making their ways to the bottom, far below.

Countless years had allowed foliage to creep down from above. These were varying species of plant life that had adapted to the toxic fume that was the mountain's breath. Flora of many varieties, some even flowering, weaving their many tendrils of sinewy vines, intertwining into a vast netting of ample foot- and handholds for creatures of my and Musky's size.

Strange birds were nesting in the leafage covering the wall. These were the size of sparrows but had long, straight beaks that ended in points. They would periodically burst into flight if we startled them but left us alone otherwise.

Amphibians and reptiles of vibrant colors, and even some smaller mammals like voles and shrews were scurrying about the vast netting of life. An entire ecosystem had erupted from the sleeping mountain, and it was alive with movement.

Some of the many openings were natural and unattached to the fortress. These were the homes of the wildlife who had settled into the volcano's ecosystem. Many others were not natural, but balconies and windows, bridges and platforms created by hands.

It was incredible that the Gnomes had been enslaved long enough to create such a vast architectural marvel. It would have taken several hundred years, and an army of tens of thousands of slaves from labourers, to engineers and artists to make simple tunnels into grand halls and chambers like these.

The Gnomes, calling themselves unda-tings, must have been enslaved for eons, to have done so much excavation. Born into a life of hard labor, never having known what it was like to live as a free society. They would have had to spend many generations imprisoned inside the mountain to have been able to achieve such wonders of engineering.

I would later learn from Musky that we would find over ten thousand Gnomes imprisoned within the fortress. He explained that, when living among them, they told him ancient stories passed down for thousands of generations, of when their people numbered in the *hundreds* of thousands.

I looked out across a crater that was over a thousand feet wide, and in the moonlight I could make out movement inside some of those many cracks and crevasses in the volcano's inner surface. A motion that somehow was unnatural and terrifying to behold. I began to feel apprehension about continuing on.

I paused, considering if I should turn back or not. I was thinking that I had no place being there.

It was a miracle that I was still alive.

"A miracle", I thought.

I looked up at Musky, who was looking down at me, obviously wondering why I had stopped.

Then, "God is with us, my friend. I am coming." I took a deep breath and continued onward.

I must once again bring attention to the fact that, at that time, I suffered from a genetically imposed phobia towards rats and anything looking like them—Musky included. At that point, being extremely stoned on sacred herb and mushrooms was pretty much all that was keeping me moving forward. So don't knock the herb or the mushrooms.

Finally we reached a balcony where we were able to crawl onto a landing. Here the floor was flat and well cut from the natural stone. There were two exits from the landing—a stariway up and one down.

We began to descend the downward spiral stair as it wound its way through the solid rock. Torch sconces were on the wall, about six feet up and twenty feet apart, but no torches were present. Not that we needed torchlight.

It was evident that the area was not used or frequented much as there would normally be torches to light it. This allowed me some sense of comfort that we probably wouldn't be detected by anyone.

Far above us the ceiling was lost in darkness where even a G'nome could not see. I somehow sensed that it was a of darkness made from hate itself, as though hate were a physical substance. I had never felt anything like it before. It turned my stomach and made the air taste of mold and decay.

The stairway wound ninety degrees to the east and opened on its south side into a long wide hall with cell doors to either side. At one point we found a dried pool of blood, and the desiccated corpse of a Gnome.

D'is one be poisoned, mun, see?" He gestured to an arrow sticking from the person's back. "Maybe 'im be escapin' 'an d'ey shoot 'im. D'en he come 'ere an' 'im bleed out." He looked around the area quickly, and then reported. "No one be around 'ere fer a long time, mun. D'is fella be agreein'." He gestured to the corpse.

"Musky..." I paused, barely holding back tears. "This person died trying to find freedom. His people think that I am their saviour, promised to them in prophecies they have been retelling for eons."

He came closer as I continued. "I have to find some words for this poor soul." And then, in that very spot, I conducted my first funeral as the Redeye of Shiddumbuzzin.

I told a story about the Wazoos, back home. Those are the master crystal-smiths who manipulate the firestones into useful items like my pipe. I spoke of how the crystal comes from the earth, glowing and full of life, and how they must die, and be reborn in the hands of the Wazoos, to become greater things.

Honestly, it's all I was able to think of. My buddy Mort's brother, Jacob was the Grand Wazoo. *He* actually made my pipe.

Anyway, long story short...

It was the last really nice birthday gift I had gotten from anyone before I was sent to the surface world. I guess I was inspired by the story that he told when he gave me the pipe. Either way, I was saddened that this poor Gnome had died alone, and probably afraid and in pain. Plus, it was my job now. I was the Redeye.

We found another open portal at the end of the hall, leading to stairs. Here we descended another hundred feet or so and came to a crack in the outer wall, which Musky entered, and I followed. After several minutes of making our way through this natural fault in the stone, we came to an opening overlooking a massive subterranean vault, well over a mile long, and even more than that in width.

Far in the distance, at the end of the vault, (more like a great subterranean road) deep into the mountain's body, there were lanterns and torches flickering. I could see faint movement as something passed in front of the lights. Whatever was down there, it was big, and there were more than one of them too.

"Musky, what is at the end of this hall? What is there?" I asked, grasping his arm in my hand and gesturing toward the area where the torches were—where I detected the movement. I was suddenly sobered by the thought of the Scave coming after us across the long underground cavern.

"D'at be d'em jail keepas, mun. Da guards o' d'is 'ere prison. D'ose be terrible t'ings mun." He began to explain as he gestured for me to follow him along the east wall. "Peoples be callin' d'em d'ere, Anaga." He paused at the entrance to a jail cell.

"D'em be demons, mun. Creatures born from ter'ble places." We hid in the cell for a moment, and then continued along the left side of the megavault.

"Don't ya be lettin' d'em t'ings find ya, bruh. Ya not be wantin' t' see what d'em looks like." He guided me to the left wall, which was filled with prison cells.

We reached the first cell where he peeked in to make sure it was indeed empty, then guided me by the arm inside, and out of sight of the Anaga.

"D'em t'ings be big, wit' many faces, an' d'ey be lookin' like

big sweaty maggots, mun—but wit' many faces an' limbs an' t'ings."
He spat.

"I can make us both invisible, for a short period of time. About
fifteen minutes. Would that help?" I offered, as I looked around the
room.

I saw that the cell was clean and recently used. Someone was
living here on a regular basis but was not at home at that moment.

The bunks were stacked, three-tall and quite short. "They
are packed in here like livestock", I thought, my heart breaking.

Looking out again, I saw that both walls of the long
underground road had jail cells custom made to house entire
families of Gnomes. These were six floors high, with stairs and
catwalks connecting them to the floor.

Each level contained one hundred or more cells, all much like
the one we were in. The living conditions were appalling.

"This is where the Gnomes are being held when they are not
working," I thought out loud.

Musky, with a sympathetic glance, once again took my arm
and guided me out of the cell. This time we moved past three more
empty cells and then quickly into the next. We travelled one to
three cells at a time like this for a couple of hundred feet before we
stopped in a cell where there was only one bed.

It was a cell for a Human. Musky had no recollection of any
human being held in the prison when he was there. Though his
own cell was on the other side of the long chasm, he claimed to
have seen every last Gnome who had been a prisoner, and never was
there a Human among them.

I looked around the cell and in the surface of a very old and
used wooden table I found inscriptions.

Deeply scraped into the wood, were the words: *NOT Worthy*.
It made me think of William, the poor kid from Briarwood who
was being replaced by some sort of creature.

"Pops. Can ya be makin' only you invisible, longer d'en da bote of us?" He winked. "Musky not be gittin' were I is by d'ese good looks, mun. I can sneak past d'em d'ere Anaga. I dun it all before, mun. Maybe you can save power wit'out me usin' it all up on ya. No?"

"That's actually a good point," I agreed. "I can maintain the effect longer if I am only concentrating on one of us."

"I gonna go first, mun, d'en, after d'at, you be countin' t' five an' d'en you come followin' I to d'em steps down." He peeked around the corner toward the end of the long prison hall.

After he was satisfied that the Anaga had not detected our approach, he returned his attention to me and continued. "D'em steps be where d'ere be the great arrow and sign d'at be sayin': Down. You understandin' Musky, mun?"

"Gotchya," I replied as I made the silent hand motions that were the triggers used to manipulate the cosmic forces that was hootspa. "Big sign, arrow down, go downstairs. Find you."

I spoke the magical incantation—"*Schmoots*"—and vanished before his eyes.

Musky then moved like liquid around the corner and into the jail yard. He slithered into a shadow under a stone bench and disappeared. I counted to five, and then followed in the direction he was last seen travelling.

Eventually, the walls of the jail hall began to taper inward and in the distance, I was now able to see that they eventually met in a forty-five degree angle, exactly where I had earlier detected the movement among the light sources.

I was looking out over a sort of obsidian valley of black crystal and phosphorescent algae and lichens clinging to the sides of various stalagmites and stalactites. This stretched out between the prisons to either side.

The ceiling of the chamber was at least a hundred feet high, and the same impenetrable darkness lurked high into its vaults and fissures as it had earlier on the stairwell. At the bottom of this intersection of the two walls was a large opening, and above that opening about forty feet up, like a great window stretching seventy or more feet wide, was another opening, but this was natural.

It was a great underground cavern; a sort of giant, extremely deep, natural balcony in the face of an underground cliff above what looked like a grand entrance of sorts.

The Gnomes had burrowed out a vast network of tunnels and caverns many hundreds of feet beneath the great ledge, and under it as well. A modest lake had settled into the bowl-shaped floor of the upper cavern and streams trickled out over the ledge, creating waterfalls of extravagant beauty and majesty.

Vines and roots slithered and climbed over each other in a timeless frenzy to be the first to reach the phosphorescent lighting on the walls of the prison road.

Water from the overflow of the small lake, created a sort of sheet of falling water that fell into a long trough cut into the floor near the sign that indicated where the stairs went "Down."

This trough fed a chaotic looking system of small canals and reservoirs of varying sizes, and led eventually into a series of pipes that supplied the plumbing of the great mountain fortress. These pipes of all sizes, some massive, spread out in all directions and carried a constant trickle of fresh water.

They were concentrated mainly on the floor that the cells overlooked, and stretched out and all over the area from where Musky and I had first entered, all the way to the exit, where the lanterns and torches flickered—where I was trying to reach.

I moved as fast as I was able across a polished floor, cut right out of the obsidian cavern.

Wherever there was a pipe descending into the floor there was also an obsidian bridge over the mouth of the tube, and a strong steel grate covering the hole to prevent escape by those foolish enough to try and brave the darkness of the great drains and their murky unseen depths.

Each time I crossed one I could hear the roar of water many hundreds of feet under me as the great drains fed countless giant reservoirs far below.

Soon I found myself doing more uncontrollable sliding than any actual running. The floor, although cut to resemble tiling, was cut at odd angles to limit work time and the amount of material needed to be removed. It was crude yet quite efficient, obviously not intended to be used by pedestrians.

It was also covered with the mist and algae from the humid environment, making it extremely hazardous to traverse. Luckily, the sides of the great road, next to the prison walls, had walkways for the prisoners inhabiting the hundreds of cells. These were sidewalks of a sort, that afforded better footing, so I tried to stay on them instead of taking short cuts.

Soon after, I decided to activate my ring and levitate at my running speed toward the intersection of the two cavern walls where the sign indicated a way down.

I moved at a steady seven miles per hour this way about four feet from the floor, unseen. I passed small structures where pipes were converging together, as well as over and under several massive pipes that lay across the floor like some great sleeping serpents.

Shortly after, I approached the sign where there was a large staircase leading down and out of the cavern.

As I neared, the sidewalk I was following, and the one opposite, converged ahead where I found two large circular depressions in the obsidian floor. These were about twenty feet wide each and thirty feet apart. Inside of each was a lumpy, yellowy-brown, semi-liquid substance that seemed to move as though something was swimming just under its surface.

I gagged, as the stench was almost unbearable. It was something akin to vomit, various forms of fecal matter, urine, and roses all at once. It was putrid and sweet, and made me want to move faster than I was able.

A chill, unlike any natural cold, came over the very core of my life force, as though something could feel my soul with its own.

I felt my bowels shift into reverse, and my butt cheeks tightened up so hard I almost gave myself a sex change.

I looked to all directions but there were no people, or any other things there, that could have caused the flickering of the light that I interpreted as movement when I first looked into the great roadway. I had expected to find several adversaries that I would be forced to have to sneak by, but the way remained clear, and I saw nothing other than the empty chasm.

Those pools of vomit held a terrible presence though, and I could not get away from them fast enough. I could still feel something trying to touch my immortal soul—something vile and degenerate—something that derived sick pleasure from the most unspeakable of acts.

No, not an insurance company.

This was worse.

It knew I was there, could feel my living spirit, but it was not able to locate my exact position.

I hurried along at an even faster pace under the small waterfall that fed the waterworks of the mountain-fortress, and then passed through the arched portal in the foot of the two opposing cliff faces.

As I approached the exit, I came to a wide staircase that descended into torchlight beyond. When I reached the bottom of the stairs, about forty or so feet from the tall arched portal, I *felt* something become aware of me.

There I made my way down the wide stairs, struggling to go as fast as I was able.

Once again, I could *feel* those things looking for me, and my stomach turned sour. Whatever they were, they had stopped at the top of the staircase.

I was almost in a state of panic, as they had almost found me. I knew they were there, as though I could see them, but I could not. No more than they could see me.

They, too, must have had the power to become invisible. Though I could not see them, I could see their effects on the area around them. A cloud of dismal grey seemed to wash away the actual color of everything around the top of the steps.

I thought I heard people giggling maliciously— hundreds of people, yet so faint. I watched for a moment as small rivulets of the vomit begin to ooze down the steps ever so slowly in my direction. My heart raced. They were *right there*. Right at the top of the stairs and I was unable to see even a shadow.

Thankfully they were still unable to locate me, as well, and after a minute of searching the area, they seemed to lose interest. I waited quietly as they receded back into the cavern-prison. I stood at the bottom of the steps for a moment to make sure they were indeed gone and then continued onward, hoping to find Musky.

Ahead, there was a wide hall that led off to the right for about fifty feet to a dead end, and to the left on a curve around the hollow mountain core. This latter direction spiralled downward on a gentle slope and made its way deeper into the mountain.

To my right I noticed a massive sculpture of a giant pile of fornicating Humans—just sitting there at the end of the hall. It seemed kind of suspicious to me, so I gave it a good look over. After studying the erotic art thoroughly for clues, I caught sight of Musky hiding behind a huge urn against a wall further along the wide hallway. I took a second long look at the statue, just to be sure I hadn't missed anything important, and then I floated back toward the downward mega-hall.

This direction was a main thoroughfare connecting most of the fortress's infrastructure together. Every few hundred feet there was a long balcony on the right wall, facing out and over the hazy, smoking pit of the mountain core. To the left along the wall were various other statuary and bas relief dedicated to deviant and degenerate acts of debauchery and even murder. Between these were entrances to rooms and access-ways, (some larger than others) to various other levels of the fortress.

"How many Gnomes perished in its construction?" I thought, amazed at the sheer scale of it all.

I came to rest beside Musky and appeared long enough to let him know I was now with him again. Then I spoke the magical incantations once more, "Schmoots," and vanished for a second time.

Musky moved forward and down the slope at a remarkable speed, without a sound. I, of course, floated after him using my magic ring, silently and steadily behind, yet giving him room to scout ahead.

After we had travelled almost a mile along the continually descending parkway-like mega-hall, he led me to an area where there were several portals leading out of the main thoroughfare, all without doors. A main intersection of the mountain keep.

One of these halls was slightly larger than the others, obviously used to move livestock or horses, or maybe something even bigger. Just to the left of this door was a vent in the wall. It was covered in a steel grate that looked well maintained and was designed to look like part of the twisted décore.

Here I found him patiently waiting for me to arrive. I silently moved to his side and let him know I was there again. He whispered in my direction, "We be needin' t' get inside d'is 'ere vent. It not be opening cuz it be made not to. Musky slip troo da holes, kin ya do d'is too mun?"

I thought for a moment and replied, "I can make myself really small, and then I can." I prepared the proper hootspa, a silent one luckily enough, and became no larger than a grasshopper.

Musky squeezed through a larger hole, still not wide enough for me but somehow wide enough for him, even though he was three times my size. He seemed to have bones like rubber.

I activated the shrinking hootspa and passed through the open mouth of a horrible monster, as the grate was designed in bas relief to resemble many demonic creatures leaping from a hole in the stone wall. Even the inside of the duct works was tooled with remarkable skill.

Once inside the vent I returned to my normal size, and we proceeded through a maze of interconnecting ducts and shafts. It seemed like hours of descending and spiralling downward before Musky finally stopped and looked through a barred opening in the floor of the duct. He then reached through it and pulled a latch.

I came to his side and looked down to a site so terrifying, so completely frightening, I was momentarily driven to a state of silent and paralyzed fear.

"You be needin' t' be t'inkin' up a way t' drop wit' no sound t' da floor below, mun," he said as I stood there, my jaw hanging open and my eyes almost popping out of their sockets.

Below us was a vast chamber hundreds of feet wide on all sides. It was dark and in it stood thousands of soldiers. All of which gave off no heat signatures at all. This was an army of the dead. This was a force large enough to destroy Briarwood with the sheer numbers it possessed.

They stood on parade all swaying slightly, some moaning quietly, the sounds of teeth clattering at random intervals, and the ever-haunting shuffles in the distance as the odd zombie regained its balance from swaying too far.

They all wore various suits of armour from a multitude of

different armies, some of which had been long dead for hundreds or even thousands of years. Calabac must have been collecting the dead from every cemetery in the empire and perhaps beyond for decades to fill such an enormous underground chamber.

A sickly odor of dry decay, and the unsettled dust that fell from the now open grate, was so thick it caused a mirage as I tried to work out approximately how many death-soldiers there were down there.

"You're kidding me, right?" I finally spoke once I regained my composure. "There's gotta be an easier way."

"Ya mun, d'ere is. But d'at long tunnel be crawlin' wit' rats and Scave, an' I be t'inkin' you not be wantin' t' take d'at route." He waited for my response.

"How do you expect us to sneak past that army?" I asked. It's one thing sneaking past living things, even demons breathed and bled. But the undead I had read about, even the lowest and weakest of them, were able to sense life to some degree. Surely they would sense me trying to sneak between them. It was gonna get ugly.

"Musky 'ave no problems wit' d'em. Musky smell not like most peoples, mun. D'ose d'ere t'ings not be carin' about I. D'ey t'ink I is Scave." He seemed to be quite pleased with himself.

"Well that's all good for *you*. What about *me*?" I asked.

"D'em dead peoples not be waking till d'em be called on by Calabac, or iffin ya bump inta one," he replied. "Musky can climb on da pipes d'ere on the ceiling and all da way down t' da bottom. You follow right behind I and I gonna bring ya t' da door out."

He pointed in a westerly direction. At that distance we would be close to the outside crust of the mountain by only a quarter mile or so.

"I can't fly. I can only fall slowly, or float above a surface about ten feet," I informed him.

"Well d'en. You be *fallin'* till ya reach d'at ten feet d'en you be floatin' t' Musky. I be right ova d'ere mun, waitin' for ya t' come." He pointed toward what I was now able to see was a large, iron double door on the far west side of the chamber.

"Are you sure there is no other way?" I asked again. There's only *one* thing I fear more than rats. No, wait. There is nothing I fear more than rats. But still! *Thousands* of heavily armed zombies? I mean—*Really?*

"Like I be sayin' mun. Rats or da dead peoples. You pick. But Durik, he be in trouble and iffin ya wantin' t' be savin' 'im ya best be following I now." He was tapping his foot (silently I might add) impatiently awaiting my decision.

I couldn't leave Durik to his fate. He would not hesitate to face an army to protect me. He *had* already as a matter of fact. I had to try.

"Okay. I will try. But you wait for me. I can't move very fast while levitating." I took out my umbrella and prepared to jump.

What in the name of Shiddumbuzzin was I thinking? Had I completely lost my mind? Was I still high on mushrooms? Probably not, so I did what was necessary. "First we *gotta* have Sabbath."

Musky agreed, (he never seemed to have a problem stopping for Sabbath), and we smoked from the crystalline pipe.

After only a couple of draws, I noticed the effervescent wafts of smoke get caught up in a subtle, almost undetectable air current. At this point I was just happy to know the holy vapours were finding a way to escape this horrible place.

Moments later, as I inhaled the last of the Sabbath, I was relaxed and focused. I emptied my firestone pipe and gazed into the swirling fiery amber light of its core. There was a time when I could find firestones where others dared not venture. How else could I have ascended to legendary status as a firestone miner, to eventually become a foreman of a brand new claim? No G'nomish geologist before me had ever achieved what I had in so short a time.

"You ready, mun?" he asked.

"No, but go anyway cuz I am *never* gonna be ready for what we are about to do," I replied as I gestured for him to lead.

He was gone in the wink of an eye. Silent, and liquid-like, he flowed over the multitude of pipes along the ceiling until I lost sight of him.

I then said a very quick prayer to Shiddumbuzzin and jumped. I fell at first quite fast, butterflies in my stomach. I almost giggled out loud. Still, as I fell, I got a much better look at the vast chamber.

Using my umbrella to rotate my view as I descended into the pit of the living dead, I was able to see more of the *kinds* of things in Calabac's army. There were war machines here—mighty, steel contraptions for siege and mayhem, standing on legs as though they were able to move on their own.

I saw great prehistoric-looking, skeletal beasts wearing armoured houses on their backs. Each house carried a host of zombie and skeletal soldiers.

Other great machines that I was unable to recognise were also there, lined up and ready to be moved into action.

There were thousands of zombie soldiers, many with armoured war dogs, also undead and leashed, a cavalry of undead riders on horses that were nothing more than bones and leathery skin.

In the center was a circle of tall and well-armoured skeletal knights all wearing the same insignia. These held in front of them, black-bladed swords that were longer than the wielders were tall— the pommel of each sword, a silver skull, seemed to be weeping with sorrow, if you can imagine such a thing.

Their armour, though covered in dust, was black and white, with silver mail, and silver mail hoods. Their banner was that of a flower and bundle of wheat. Obviously, at one point these were some long-forgotten order of holy warriors. Once virtuous and charitable, they were now tainted and ruined by the dark forces of Calabac.

I looked upon many regiments of foot soldiers and a vast assortment of various other undead warriors from barbarians to imperial guardsman. This was only what I was able to discern clearly while falling, but there was much more in that chamber than I managed to see.

Soon I began slowing down when I reached about twenty feet from the zombie horde. At about ten feet I came to a full stop, far enough above the heads of the skeletal soldiers so as not to disturb the air or alert them to my presence with my scent or the sound of my beating heart—which, by the way, was beating like drum solo night at the Gruel and Grog.

I slowed my breathing and oriented myself to face the west side of the chamber. There I began to move slowly toward the spot where I assumed Musky was waiting for me in hiding. During the process of crossing the room I managed to avoid the taller parts of the army but on several occasions I had to zigzag between long lances and banners that some of the undead were holding.

Even then however, I was able to do so without touching any, or alerting them. This in itself was an amazing feat as I was so scared I had my eyes closed most of the distance. Finally I reached the west wall and Musky oozed from the shadows to slide up beside me.

"Okay, mun. You be needin' t' git small again sos we can slip unda d'is 'ere door." He began to squeeze his incredibly, flexible body under the doors, and soon was on the other side waiting for me.

I invoked the hootspa that shrunk me to a bug-sized G'nome, and crept under the giant metal barriers. On the other side there was a large hallway that led through an intersecting hall of the same width and height.

About fifty feet past the intersection was another set of great metal doors. These were heavily barred and had braces that held them against any would be attackers. Obviously this was the main entrance of the fortress. It was the place where Durik must have been brought in if he had been captured.

We moved slowly and quietly along the north face of the hall about thirty feet and paused at the intersection. Here there were great piles of crates and a plethora of various supplies and mundane sundries. Musky gestured for me to wait there in the shadows while he scouted ahead. I agreed and he was gone again, just like that.

The kid had a skill set!

I waited for five minutes…then five more…then ten more…then ten more again.

Soon I was running out of room to play solitary tic-tac-toe on the wall in my general surroundings, when I concluded that he was not coming back.

"Aw crap," I spoke aloud. I was lost in the enemy's stronghold with no idea where to look for Durik *or* Musky, or even knowing how I would escape.

I couldn't levitate back up to the vent in the Zombie cavern. That was way more than ten feet.

I certainly couldn't lift the many braces and barriers on the front gates, but I also couldn't just stand there waiting for someone to come along and discover me.

Just then I heard the sound of many armoured footfalls on stonework and as I peeked around the corner to the north, I saw an army of giant armoured bipedal rats marching in my direction, ten abreast, row after row, like a long and endless giant armoured bipedal rat caterpillar. If you can imagine such a thing.

I jumped back into the shadows—okay, okay—I fainted and rolled back into the shadows.

CHAPTER - 16

HOLY SHIDDUMBUZZIN!

"Szvirrrrrrf."

"Szvirrrrffffff."

"Szviiirrrrrrffffffff!"

I was dreaming again. "Hmm? Yes? What is it?" I was in a firestone cavern, lying on my back. Above me was a ceiling full of crystals. More firestones than I had ever seen before.

I sat up to get my bearings and there before me, sitting on a large mushroom was an ancient G'nome. He was far older than any I had known to ever exist. So old his skin was beginning to petrify, his hair was like roots and mycelium and it was full of lichens and mosses. His eyes were filled with the warming glow of the finest of firestones.

I wept with joy, though I could not understand why at that moment. All I knew was that I felt like I was home again, like I had never felt at home before. I quickly dried my eyes and cleared my nose, realizing that I was probably supposed to interact with him again.

Still, I was forced to look around at the other wonders that surrounded me. Phosphorescent fungi and minerals were glowing everywhere. A beautiful waterfall cascaded from a hundred feet up, dancing and jumping among rocks and outcrops of vegetation, filling a beautiful pool bordered by colorful flora. In the air the sweet fragrances of a multitude of herbal delights wafted throughout the cavern on clouds of pollen that tickled the senses.

The G'nome's beard and locks were like the ancient roots of the very first sacred herb forests. His presence, like the warmth of my mother's embrace.

Here and there, across the surface of his being, were rivulets of sticky resin lightly coated in the spores of a thousand varieties of hallucinogenic mushrooms. These wove their way across his form like a sparkling web of golden dust.

I knew then that this was indeed the great and ever slightly sedated—the holy and merciful to the laid back and devoted—the provider of herbal inspiration—the purveyor of proverbial cheese dip for the soul; the one, and only—Shiddumbuzzin.

I fell to my knees immediately.

Then I got up, wiped off my clothes, and wondered what I had just slipped in. Finding no animal droppings, or other reason for slipping and falling to my knees, I gave up the quest and paid more attention to the issue at hand.

Turning to face the Mellow One, I spoke. "Aw crap. I'm dead ain't I? Those rat…things…they ate me, didn't they?" I mean what else could it have been? Right?

"*Nooooooo.*"

I fell silent. The Mellow One had spoken.

I waited…nothing was happening.

"Nice chamber," I commented, looking around the familiar feeling subterranean canyon.

Again, the ceilings above were filled with firestones. Never had

I ever seen such a deposit of the sacred and precious crystals.

I took out my pad and pencil, and started making notes, so as to try and find the place at a later date. That way I could stake a claim as soon as I got home. Business is business.

I was hoping that this might be one of those *"vast riches beyond my comprehension"* parts of the story the Mellow One was telling me about when all this mess started.

"Mmm, yes it is," he said blandly, staring at me with an empty look on his face. Then he bit into a large sandwich.

I thought immediately of Beornag. "Gotta like the Troll, eh?"

"Mmhmhm. Yeah," he replied through glossy glowing eyes that seemed to stare through me. *"Thought you'd like him. I know his boss, by the way."* He seemed tired.

Then he tried to look at me more intensely, the same look Beornag and Durik would give me after about seven seconds of me trying to teach them to read.

"Hey!" I thought.

"Mmmhmmhmm," he chortled.

I felt confusion and really didn't know what was expected of me. "Is that it?" I asked.

"Is that what?" he replied, looking off into nowhere.

"Hey...You in there. It's me. Remember? The guy who works for you?" This was getting us nowhere.

"Hmmm? Ah...yes...no. That is not it," he said, sounding like he was struggling to remember.

"Well?" I moved closer to him and sat on a chair sized mushroom. "What *is* it?"

He handed me the golden stem of a hose that was attached to a wondrously, impossibly shaped crystalline smoking pipe. Don't ask me to describe it. I once did for a group of Swamp Trolls, and they fainted, lost three days, somehow traded personalities with each other, and woke up with the munchies. It isn't safe. Trust me.

He exhaled. *"Hhhhhhhave you figured it out yet?"*

"Have I figured what out?" I asked. Then I took a deep draw from the fantastical pipe.

"Why you are here?" He accepted the hose as I passed it back.

"Don't *you* know?" I asked. "Wait a sec...where *am* I?" I coughed.

"You are here," he replied.

"Where is here?" I asked.

"Here is home, Szvirf. Is this not where you want to be more than anything?" He passed me the stem again.

"Is this not where you pray to be every night? I thought you would be happy to be home again."

"You mean—?" I began.

"You just head north, one half day, and you will be home again, in Sensimilia. There is a false wall, there, in the east ridge. Look for the bright blue exit. That will be your safe way home." He started to chuckle again, but it seemed forced, and weak.

I added this new location information to my notes on the chamber. Then I remembered...

"But..." I demanded. "...but, what about, Durik?" My voice was suddenly quivering. I couldn't leave Durik to die at the hands of some asshole.

"What about Musky, and Lillia's sister, and all those Gnomes in those prisons?" Those people were counting on me!

"What about the Troll and his aspirations to be the imperial champion in the next pukeolympics at the Gruel and Grog?" Beornag was the funniest friend I had ever had.

"What about Grarr, and the children (but not necessarily at the same time and together, as Grarr doesn't like kids)?" I couldn't leave Grarr to take care of those kids all by himself!

"What about that gigantic barrel of sticky goodness I got stored at the winery. Hunh? What about all of them?" I was counting in my head.

Did I miss anyone? I wouldn't want anybody's feelings to get hurt—Raz! "What about Raz? What about him and his dinosaur? He's nice...*kinda*."

"*Yes. What* about *them? What about all...mmm...what were we talking about?*" Something was wrong. He was not acting right.

Then it hit me. Maybe he *was* acting right.

He was so completely mellow at this stage there was only one thing I *could* do. I joined him.

We sat there in the great firestone chamber for a long time in silence, passing the stem of the impossible pipe back and forth to each other.

Eventually, I began to worry about Durik again.

"Think, Szvirf, think," I thought out loud. "Only you can save them now. That army of super rats is gonna chew the boys to shreds, Eekadinosaur or no Eekadinosaur.

"After that, Calabac's army of the dead will be awakened, and will be made to march upon Briarwood. Behind it, the rat army will follow and who knows what else?

"Poor Lillia has no idea what is about to happen. There's *gotta* be a way." I racked my brains, even slapping myself a few times to try and invoke a response in the form of an idea.

I paced the floor in the immediate area, drawing from the mystical pipe, and desperately trying to keep my train of thought. A good five minutes later, I remembered what I was supposed to be doing. "I need to formulate a plan," I announced. "But first I need to find my way back to the mountain fortress."

I turned to the Mellow One and asked, "Oh great and miraculously sedated one, please...I ask of you to lend me a clue. A small hint—maybe a note on the back of a match book even. A sign that will guide me back to the path of righteousness and lead me not into temperamental giant rat armies, if you can at all help it, that would be extra-nice." I was trying to be dramatic, to show him I was taking this roll seriously.

"*I can send you to him.*" He smiled, his eyes suddenly alit with understanding and awareness.

"To who, your completely intoxicatedness?" I asked. The whole dramatic speech thing seemed to be getting through to him better than the direct approach.

It dawned on me just then. Perhaps he really was getting more coherent simply because I was worshipping him like a god—go figure.

"*The Phaladin.*"

"The *what?*" I asked. I couldn't even begin to allow myself to imagine what I thought he just said would look like.

"*Paladin! Sorry I had a seed in my tooth…had to get it out. Hate those. You know when you have a particularly succulent, yet crunchy dill, and the core is so fresh still it's like your drinking it, and a seed gets caught right under your dentures?*" he said as he slowly began looking through me again.

"You mean Durik? You can send me back to Durik?" I was beginning to gain hope now. Perhaps I was not alone after all. "Oh, enlightened One. Ember of ever glowing wisdom…I beseech thee…Send me to the Paladin."

I was going back, Wooohooo! I was going back to face the giant rat army! Heeehaw! I was—

What the heck was I thinking?! I was going *back?!* I almost crapped in several languages, if you can imagine such a thing.

"*Face your fear, Szvirf. Then you will know what to do. You will know how to find him. You will know.*" He smiled, and then blew a vast and thick cloud of smoke all over me. I was enveloped by it and couldn't see for several moments.

Then I felt dizzy.

"Aw crap," I said.

"*Exactly,*" he replied.

I almost hurled as the subterranean chamber began to spin all around me. I thought I was gonna spit chunks right there, when suddenly everything blacked out.

I woke up in a different place altogether. My head spinning and my eyes watering uncontrollably. I was out of breath and my sides were sore—but in a good way if you can imagine that—like I had been laughing for hours. I found myself craving a pickle.

"What the…?" I thought. "Ok*aaaay,*" I added softly to myself.

I checked my pockets to see if anything was missing but was relieved to find all my belongings still where they were supposed to be, including my money.

"What the…?" I said again.

The room I was in was small, and sort of cool. I reached into my vest pocket and took out my shades. This room was lit brighter than natural subterranean light. There were several rectangular glass fixtures on the ceiling that were magically lit. Being a hootspologist I knew what to look for. I'm good that way.

There was only one exit, and the bottom of that door was far enough off the tiled floor to allow me to walk right under without ducking.

Then, I began to back up as I suddenly detected someone just outside that door. After a few steps I was backed into a cool smooth structure. Turning around, I realized that I was in a bathroom stall. Just under the front lip of the toilet.

This toilet was big. Big enough for Humans. Hey—for me, that's pretty big!

I checked my bottomless pouch (which for me was a backpack) to see if the psychedelic mushrooms were still there. Yup. There they were. I was not hallucinating—at least not from them.

I peeked under the door and saw a tall, dark, armoured figure standing across the room, urinating into a wall-mounted, porcelain bathroom fixture.

I did not recognize his uniform or its markings and so decided to wait. I quietly climbed up onto the toilet seat and listened carefully for him to finish and leave.

"You just gonna sit in there all day, or are you coming out?" the man said as he finished up. He spoke in a strange dialect of common Humanese. Being a language specialist, I was able to decipher what he was saying. "For a little guy you sure stink up the place."

What could I do? He knew I was there. I climbed down and was just about to exit the stall when an answer came.

"Listen…I had to go bad, and I'm not finished. Wait outside. I won't be much longer," This second voice was sort of nasally and squeaky.

I was in a public washroom! All I could think of was, *do NOT touch anything.*

I peeked under the door and watched the huge Human in black armour exit the bathroom. Moments later another figure entered my vision without any stall doors opening. He was almost as short as I am and had walked under the door as I had thought to do myself.

As he stood in front of a mirrored wall adjusting his armour I noticed his—*TAIL!*

Holy crap! I almost filled my shorts at that very moment. The irony! In the can no less! You know? At my age keeping from having the crap scared outta me is a feat in itself. Gimme some credit here. Again, I cannot stress it enough; healthy diet and lots of fiber. Don't force it, let it happen, and pinch before wiping!

There it was—a talking bipedal rat-thing. It was wearing armour and a helmet, so I was not able to see its face at all. The only thing that gave away its identity was that long, scaly awful looking rat tail. It gave me shudders just to look at it.

I shivered as I imagined its whiskers twitching behind the face guard of its helmet. Its teeth were surely chattering there, razor sharp, G'nome-munchingly horrific.

Oh, the horror, the absolute afraidness of seeing it standing there before my very eyes, only a few feet away.

Afraidness—is that a word? Anyone? Okay, well it is now…

The absolute afraidness of it!

Yeah. See? That sounds okay.

The stuff of NIGHTMARES, even.

Oy!

It yelled so that the man outside could hear, and my sphincter almost blew an *O* ring.

"If you get to kill the blue one, I get to eat the little one…ahhh hahaha…when we catch him of course!" He chuckled.

"First I want to eat the blue one's brains right in front of that pesky little cave dwelling smokestack! Aaahhh hahahaha!" He chuckled again.

"I hate those little cheese eating, big nosed cave monkeys! Aaahhh hahaha!" He laughed aloud this time.

It was talking about me, and the 'blue one' had to be Durik. He was alive still! I dared to hope. They were talking about killing him as though it had not been done yet.

It moved toward the exit then suddenly turned toward the mirror and spoke again; this time to itself, in a different voice—a much more evil sounding voice.

"Once I eat the little one, I will know where to find the rest of his kind. Then I will finish the job my ancestors could not, and return to the surface with such power that all will bow to me. I will be lord of all the lands and never again will a G'nome walk the world—inside or out. All shall be mine."

It then turned to face the exit—and one extremely angry G'nome.

CHAPTER - 17

YOU DIRTY RAT! YOU KILLED MY BROTHER'S SECOND REMOVED COUSIN'S SISTER-IN-LAW'S GRANDUNCLE! (ON HER FATHER'S SIDE!)... *SEE?*

"You!" it exclaimed in a harsh whisper.

I expected it to start yelling for guards or its big Human buddy just outside the bathroom door. Instead I could see that it was purposefully trying not to alert anyone.

"That's right, bub. You picked the wrong G'nome when you started planning this one's demise." I had drawn my dart gun and was pointing it at his throat, the only spot beside his tail where he wasn't armoured.

"This here pistol is loaded with a dart that has been tipped with a lethal venom, perhaps not *the* lethal venom, but lethal all the same. One shot and you will die a horrible and painful death, so don't make a move!" He put his hands in the air as he looked nervously at the bathroom door.

I was doing it! I was facing a rat...thing! I was courageous, brave even. If only Bernie could see me now! In your face Bernie!

"Don't shoot, cheese monkey," he whispered. It was a *he*. I could tell from the pitch and tone of his voice. "I will call the guards if you do."

I cocked the firing mechanism of the pistol. "Go ahead. Call me cheese monkey—one—more—time. *Please.* I don't think you will call anyone. You'd be dead before they arrived anyway." I called his bluff.

He ground his teeth together and swallowed back more insults.

"Now, you are gonna help me out with some directions, or I am gonna make you wish you had. You follow?" This was my finest hour. I was actually talking bad ass right at him, and I was only *mostly* scared.

"I want to know where you are holding the blue one you spoke of. You are gonna tell me, and then I am gonna put you to sleep." Negotiations had commenced.

"If you don't cooperate, I am gonna let you meet whatever foul maker you pray to." I was being ruthless! Just like Grarr!

"You are a fool, G'nome." He used the actual name of my people. Not Gnome, but—G'nome. "You will never be able to reach him. You are small and frightened, and so you should be. The master is looking for you. His Stealer is looking for you. The Anaga are looking for you. The entire fortress is on alert and searching for *you*," he sneered.

"You can now begin to count your last moments in minutes if not seconds. Kill me if you will, but I will not tell you what you want to know."

Now *he* was calling *my* bluff.

This was a big mistake. Never call a G'nome's bluff. We seldom bluff, and only when we have a backup plan.

Okay, okay. We bluff all the time, but we *do* always have a backup plan, and, unfortunately for this guy, I had already formulated a brilliant one, right there in front of his very eyes.

"Last chance, vermin," I said as I took careful aim.

"Who told you my name?" he asked.

"Huh? I said.

"My name, how did you know my name?" he asked again.

"Your... name?" I repeated.

"My name—Vermin—how did you know it?" He seemed genuinely taken aback at the idea of me knowing his name.

"What are the odds?" I thought.

Then I decided to adjust my brilliant back up plan. "I know all about you," I said as I tried to recall what Musky had said about his cousin Vermin. If this was in fact *the* Vermin, I was beginning to realize why Musky wasn't fond of him.

Not being able to remember anything *else* about Musky's cousin, I opted to continue my bluff and take a few educated guesses. "I know how you betrayed your people and exposed them to this evil that is here in this very fortress. I know how your family disowned you for being so vile as to sell them out for your own selfish reasons." I was on a roll.

"I know that you plan to betray your new master in the long run, and how you plan to invade the underworld and steal the power of Sensimilia. I also know that you will not succeed. I have already warned the vast armies of Sensimilia of your vile devices," I lied.

"How? I have told no one? How could you possibly know all of that?"

Wow he was really in a panic now, and even more incredibly, I was actually guessing correctly. I found myself wishing I was somewhere near a lottery booth. If you can imagine such a thing.

"Don't even worry about it. I know, and that is all you have to know. Ya know?" I needed him to get scared, scared enough to tell me something that might help me find Durik, and now Musky as well.

"So...what will you do now?" he said as he looked at the exit again.

I then remembered there was a heavily armed Human fighter type outside waiting for this guy. Sooner or later that guy was gonna come back in to check on his buddy. "Take off your clothes, and drop your weapons, quietly," I commanded.

"My clothes? What are you, some kind of pervert?" he asked with disbelief in his tone.

"Just do it, or I shoot. You've got five seconds." I pointed the pistol even more aggressively at his throat.

Luckily this seemed to work, and he began disrobing quietly.

As he did so, I tossed a locking hootspa at the door, and a barrier of silence between the exit and myself, thus blocking the outside from the noise that was about to happen.

Once he was disrobed, I was able to see his face. He looked a bit like Musky, only much shorter, healthier, and better fed.

His eyes were different though. They seemed...distant and clouded over. His fur was not so oily and worn as my Ratstafarian friend's had been. It gave me a much better idea of how badly Musky was treated during his captivity.

It also gave me a new respect for Musky. Even in his emaciated state, he was willing to re-enter the fortress after being imprisoned there once (and almost delivered for a second internment), just to rescue Durik, whom he had only just met. Poor Musky, I wondered what had happened to him and hoped he was still alive.

For now, Vermin was standing in his tighty-whitey underwear in front of me shivering a little as I continued the interrogation.

"Where is the blue one?" I asked. "Tell me or I strip you of the rest of your clothes, and your fur too."

I was beginning to really develop a true hatred for this individual as his motives and means were becoming perfectly clear to me. "Speak now or I transport you to the G'nomish cat kennels and let the denizens there eat you alive."

He instantly perked up. His eyes were wide and full of terror.

"Cats!? But...how!? You're not supposed to still have cats!" he said in a panic. "Thukov would have eradicated them all in the *Descending*! There were none left. I was there!"

Thukov? Great Descending? What the hell was he talking about? "Yes, but he missed a few. They were later bred and had hundreds of kittens who all grew up learning to love the taste of— *you*." I continued to bluff.

"That FOOL! That blind over-confident fool! He was no better than his pathetic offspring being held in the ash pit—" Suddenly, his eyes lit up with the realized of what he had said.

He had spilled the beans and I was ready.

Ch-ting, went the sound of the dart pistol as the tiny projectile sank into his chest. My aim was a bit low but it mattered little. Almost instantly he fell to the floor.

I know what you are thinking. "Oh Poppa Szvirf, you murdered him in cold blood, an unarmed opponent!!! Waah wah wah."

Relax, in actuality I had not loaded a lethal dart and instead had loaded a sleeping dart. I dragged his limp form into a bathroom stall and prepared a mind-invasion hootspa. This guy was gonna tell me what he knew, one way or another.

I would be looking for the ash pits. He had also mentioned the name *Thukov*. That name sounded familiar for some reason.

I decided to cover all my bases. I disrobed, placed my own clothes into my bottomless pouch/backpack, and put on Vermin's uniform.

The things I have done for this company—Oy!

I then returned to Vermin, stuffed between the wall of the stall and the toilet, and prepared to enter his mind.

This hootspa, I had never attempted before. I could have practiced on any of the boys, but are you *kidding me*? Can you *imagine* what I might end up seeing inside one of *their* heads? No thanks. I'll stick to evil maniacs, demonic entities and that sort of thing; thank *you* very much.

There comes a time in one's life when one is faced with a realization, a conscious awareness of a truth so profound, that one is forever altered. Sometimes this sudden understanding can be wonderful and inspiring in ways that cannot be described.

Then there is the other kind.

The sudden awareness of something so horribly unjust, it could drive an ordinary being to places of insanity so purely manifested from rage that the being self-destructs.

That is what I became aware of almost as soon as I entered Vermin's deepest thoughts.

I was not alone in there—in his mind.

The Rastafarian named Vermin was only a prisoner of something far worse, something older than recorded time on this world.

A manifestation of terrible feelings and horrible sicknesses, a thing almost a god, yet denied by those who held the real power.

If it were not for my own super intellect, and ages old wisdom, I surely would have ended my own life, right there, in an act of desperate retreat from what I was exposed to next.

CHAPTER - 18

THE DESCENT

I fall, deep into the creature's memories, and I remember…

I am not alone. I am among *my* kind…no…*our* kind.

Its kind.

Darkness…

Foot falls…clearer now…*chink, chink, chink*…rough breathing.

I feel excited…hungry…

Chink, chink, chink…chain mail and scale. Spurs on boots. Buckles and toggles. *Chink, chink, chink*…

Dragging sounds…breathing…hot stinking breath…so sweet…decay and filth.

No…

I am not this thing…I am inside the mind…not my kind…

In a tunnel…There are many of them, and I am one of them. I am him, yet I cannot control myself.

Going ahead now…

I see…training…I am learning…no…he is…*it* is learning.

Tunnels.

I remember…

Learning to hate…

Learning to love…

Learning to love to hate.

So much…abuse…It is mine.

I…it…*he* learns to love this too.

Learning to master it and use it. To cause misery…misery…so much misery.

Joy from being…misery…joy erupting with satisfaction now…a satisfaction from power.

I own pain now…Pain belongs to me. I am powerful…I am pain.

The master made it happen. The master…

Going ahead now…

A gift, for me?

Despair…sweet despair, who grinds down and makes them want to cease being. Such beautiful, bleeding despair…Thank you master…Thank you for my suffering…I learn…

Going ahead now…

I am respected and feared…feared…*feared*…I am *respected*.

It is soon time…*chink…chink…chink*. We march.

I scream commands…I cannot understand the language I speak, but before my eyes, a great wall opens to reveal a vast underground chasm.

My armies listen, and they obey.

Still, the great walls open wide, as more of the seemingly endless underground mega-vault is revealed.

Moments pass as the colossal gap opens onto the amber glowing lights of the city below.

In its mile-high vaulted ceiling, clusters of giant firestones hang in great veins like rivers of crystal. Cables and tracks lining the walls, sculpture and art everywhere—loot for the victors.

I see now, a great lake, and a road of wondrous length and masterful construction. Finally the walls part, completely. Massive, megalithic doors crash to a halt and the enemy is laid bare before me. I stand on the edge of a massive plateau, the city of my victims beneath.

They have no army. They have no concept of what is happening. The people look up in terror at the open walls—the army of evil.

This is fear…This is the first fear…their last fear…They have never known fear like this before.

I answer to a great general—Thukov, the Cambion, half-demon, lord of the eleven hells. I am respected.

He is feared.

I am feared.

I am one of many, who command *still* even many more.

This is *my* time.

I was created for this. I am—a *monster*.

No! I am *not* this thing…

I will maintain myself. I will maintain myself. I know where I am…where *it* is.

Am I seeing what has happened? What will happen? What is happening? I will…will…I will maintain control.

I am *not* this creature!

Going forward…only days.

I am suicide's herald. I descend upon them.

I am filled with an ecstasy—euphoria from the blood—flowing pouring, spraying—warm raining blood…

G'nomes…G'nomes…delicious and slow. They scream—it is music.

Ahahahahahahaah! "Descend! Descend!" I command my armies to fall upon the enemy.

We descend on them…We descend by the tens of thousands…They are delicious…They scream for their lives…They bleed…They BLEED!

We capture them. Many, many, many, many, many…. ahhhhahahahahaa!

The general is powerful…powerful…He has the relic. Taken from their temple, it is brought to him.

Relic! Relic!?

I will maintain—sanity.

Going ahead now…ahead…

The city burns…all dead or captured…Rewards are sweet, and I am happy…The stone survives. The rest burns…burns.

I am returning home with slaves…breeding them soon…blood for the future…

I am old now…already so old…

Ahead now…Going ahead…

Something went wrong…The master is gone…There is no general…We are alone.

I fade from life. The thing I was is no more.

Then, I hear a voice. It calls to me. It draws me from the void. I answer. I arrive.

This…new flesh. Small, and weak. Foul thing…I am a foul thing.

What of my greatness? Why am I weak?

We turned upon them…Some of us leave…I remain with the many…we remain in the great hot hole…

Invaders…like me from the times before—Calabac…

Calabac is the master now…the *master* now…Cruelty and malice are his…despair is mine…He gives me a gift…He spits vile mucous on my back. I lick it and make it part of me.

Now pestilence, too, is mine…

Ahead…again…

A new master now.

The new fortress…almost finished…The slaves look different now…not the same as when they first came, many eons ago…Now we call them Gnomes.

They still taste the same. Succulent flesh, the babies are the tastiest. Mmm. I elate in their suffering, in their terror.

Calabac is the new master...I see his face...He loves the Stealer.

The Stealer returns...I hate him...Master loves him...I hate him...

I hate him...*them.*

We have the relic...Now the master will call upon the general. Through the seed of his demon, Calabac will condemn the world to his will.

Going ahead again...must maintain...more to see...

The mission is soon...stupid Humans. I have learned from my master...He has taught me well the arts of deception and manipulation.

He is a fool.

I will be master soon...First we capture the last G'nome, and I eat him. Then, I know what is to come...

You!...

I see no more...sleep...the rest has yet to happen...

CHAPTER - 19
YOU…DIRTY…RAT…
YOU…*DIRTY*…F*@#!^G …RAT!

Needless to say, when I awoke from the hootspa (which had in real time only taken less than one second to conduct) I was really put off. Big time! In a major sort of way even.

I'd just witnessed the creature's life go by in a split second and absorbed his deepest and most profound memories. This was not, after all, Musky's poor cousin, Vermin (whom no one seemed to like). It was in fact a demonic entity. A creature that was older than I was. Its personality filtered through a shadow of its hosts persona.

Of course Vermin was in there somewhere, but the thing that controlled his body was not a Ratstafarian, not by a long shot.

I took a look at the dart gun in my hand, and instantly had a new respect for pixies. In his mind I had just witnessed the total destruction of the G'nomish civilization. I had seen the end of what once was.

I had lived through an invasion of a G'nomish homeland that I was unaware even existed. I had witnessed the horrors that had taken place those many eons ago—the crimes committed by the forces of evil.

I had seen the *truth* before my own eyes—a history I was not taught in school. The unknown origins of the city of Sensimilia, the mysteries of G'nenesis (That's G'nomish for where something big started), and the decimation of paradise. I had watched the brutality of the invaders as they attempted to eradicate us.

Oooooo! That really got my shorts up in a bunch! I can tell you.

The atrocities I witnessed, the complete disregard for personal hygiene, and the horrors of the invasion were burned deep into my heart and my mind's eye.

Whole forests burning out of control! Buds of monumental proportions exploding, their pollen and resins mixing in the air, super heating and creating a flaming storm of destruction that devoured G'nomish village after G'nomish village.

The invaders were relentless!

Aaaah! *The G'nomility!*

Our great city, even greater back then than when I saw it last, being torn apart. Her gems and jewels looted from her while her people were slaughtered in her streets. The great cavernous chamber that held the heart of the empire was covered in soot and ash; the vaulted, firestone encrusted ceilings now black from the inferno below.

A murderous and thieving horde of chaos had looted the very heart of the G'nomish soul. This was the most heinous of all acts—the destruction of the sacred forests.

The G'nomes seemed to have had no army, no defenses to speak of. They would have gladly shared their wealth had the invaders attempted to do honest business.

I was beginning to realize the importance of this epic quest that the Mellow One had trusted to my abilities. My immediate thoughts were that the Gnomish empire must be preserved. Our great civilization that once was, must be restored to her former glory.

This creature was part of all that was poison to my people's existence. It revelled in the memory of it. This *villainous fiend* was one of the reasons Shiddumbuzzin was weak, and the once vast and peaceful empire of the G'nomes was reduced to only a few thousand souls.

We retreated to the deepest depths of the world. There we stayed hidden for a hundred thousand centuries—so few of us left. But when did we return to the old city and rebuild her to what she was now? Did we possess greater technology then, and simply forgot the uses of the mighty rods that protruded from the depths of the planet and supplied the great metropolis with heat and energy?

There were still so many unanswered questions.

I had to focus. The problem at hand was what to do with this murderous villain. He deserved no less than death—but also, my good reader. I have no heart for murder...

Wait lemme think a sec...

I'm checking. Gimme a sec...

Okaaaay. Yes. I do *not* have any murder in this story yet—so, no, I did not have the heart for murder.

That's when it came to me.

I prepared the shrinking hootspa. Cast it on the villain and shrunk him to the size of a bug, then tossed him in my bottomless pouch. I would deal with him later.

I proceeded quickly out of the stall, removed the barrier of silence and the lock on the door, cast a stinking cloud of noxious fumes, flushed one of the toilets, and dropped the visor of the helmet.

Then I invoked a simple illusion of a long, scaly, naked black tail. The disguise was complete.

As I was moving toward the exit of the bathroom the door swung inward and the Human was there.

"Whew!" He waved his hand in front of his face. "C'mon,

willya? We ain't got all day." He turned around and left.

I moved quickly to the closing door and slipped out just before it shut. There was movement everywhere. I saw armoured members of the rat-thing army grouped with Humans of differing uniforms, moving up and down a great intersection of six giant, vaulted hallways.

The rat-things obviously serving a different aspect of combat than the Humans, and ultimately the undead seemed to be controlled, in medium sized assault forces, by Human officers. At least this was my assessment of the situation.

These disgruntled pseudo-lords of the empire donned their hardly worn colours over their chain suits. Their numbers barely exceeding twenty or thirty men. However, these were seasoned fighters, and they would probably be in control of the rag-tag regiments of lost souls seeking adventure as fodder for Calabac's army.

We had certainly stumbled upon a whole lot more than we thought we were getting into, that night Lillia came knocking on the door. Good thing Grarr was on the ball for the negotiations. At the time I thought he was taking Lillia for everything she had. Now I could see that we *should* have asked for *more*.

The rag-tag fodder was not as numerous as the undead, but they would eventually mix with the horde and take cover therein. These were the Human riff-raff from local black marketers and organized crime rings that had been dismantled by imperial law enforcement in the past.

No threat to the imperial rule alone but bolstered by the addition of ten thousand armoured rat-things, a virtual plague of normal rats, and several battalions of undead creatures complete with war machines and unholy death knights. These small Human bands could act as elite strike forces, using the other units to distract the main defenses of their enemies. In any case, it appeared that Calabac had created a very efficient fighting force.

The main corridor was curved, and I could tell that it wrapped itself around the lower inside of the dormant volcano's core—similar to the one I had fainted in earlier; perhaps the same one.

I could also see that the volcano was only *almost* dormant—that's when it is dormant but ready to become not dormant, under the right circumstances.

Areas along the inside wall of the curving, road-like hallway were removed every twenty feet, for a stretch of about one hundred feet. Against the inside edge of these openings were short stone walls, like long balconies. Beyond these was a long drop to the bubbling, steaming mass of noxious super-heated muck—the volcano's core.

This was the lake that filled the mountain's crater; it was a mile across, consisting of the most dangerous stuff ever devised by Mother Nature—pyroclastic death, waiting to happen.

I breathed deeply. Aaaah. Good subterranean air. It's the little things you miss. You know?

I was grateful no one asked me anything as we moved forward. I tried to move like Musky and must have been convincing as even the Human in black did not suspect anything.

When no one was looking I reached into my bottomless pouch/backpack and grabbed a handful of psychedelic mushrooms. Looking around to make *sure* no one was watching I lifted the visor and stuffed them in my mouth—just enough, mind you, to calm me down and hopefully make me forget I was surrounded by rats and rat-things and, well, I assume you are following what I have been saying so far. Yes?

Good.

I followed the Human along the outside wall. We stopped a few times to allow the passing of a patrol or caravan of some sort. It was almost like an underground city street. Save that this was not a city. It was a fortress.

I deduced that its purpose was a staging point to attack Briarwood, block the mountain pass, and cut off trade to the northern reaches of the empire, driving the smaller settlements into chaos and unruly bankruptcy.

Its location was perfect for this.

It's always about location, isn't it?

Then, with the pass controlled, the capitol would be only days to the other side of the mountains, at the foot of long and gradual steppe lands. Al'Lankmire relied on Briarwood to defend this pass and hold it always against an invasion from the north.

With the fall of Briarwood, the capitol would be defenceless to the north. Of course no one really expected an attack from the north. The only real fighting force that existed in that area was the Elf colony of Silverwood, and they were trusted allies of the empire, albeit many weeks away to the northwest.

Briarwood's efforts to defend that pass were charitable at best. The empire was not prepared for an attack by an enemy that was already inside her borders. It did not expect a domestic threat to form.

From what I could see now Calabac could, in theory, attack the north, and use his forces so swiftly that imperial defenses would have no time to warn the capitol. If that happened, he could stage a second, *sneak* attack and sack the empire through the destruction of her capitol city *and* her emperor. But that would take two armies. So far, I had only seen one.

I mean, then again, what do I know, right? I'm no soldier or strategist. The question in my mind was why did he need Alaeth? This was getting weird.

Maybe it was the mushrooms again—maybe I was in shock—probably a bit of both, but I had to keep moving and hoping for a break.

Eventually we came to a massive staircase that went down very deep and into a gigantic hall with vaulted ceilings.

Again with the vaulted ceilings. Oy.

The vast chamber must have sat under the spine of the mountain chain. It looked like it may have once been a ballroom for the grandest of epic parties. This great hall was alive with horrific creatures, much like the boys—only foul—or at least foul*er*...or at least...

Forget it.

Anyway, where was I?

Oh yeah...

The chamber was alive with foul creatures all working at, around, or behind tables stacked with weapons and armour, and all sorts of strange things. Odds and ends of different suits of old and poorly kept protective wear, stacks of all sorts of mails, plates, spikes and bucklers, shields and gauntlets, and every piece of armour you could think of, only dirty and old and mostly ruined; all strewn about the tables and makeshift display stands.

Other unsavory characters were bartering and haggling over the tables. I even saw one of those purple guys with the octopus heads, like the stuffed one back at the winery.

I suddenly realized that this place was some sort of market for psychotics and horrific maniacs. I was surprised that the boys had not had a membership, or a preferred customer card, or something like that for the place. It would not have surprised me if I had run into any of them, right there, though.

That's how scary it was.

Luckily there were no rats or rat-things or Scaves or anything like that in the market—which was a good thing.

On the flip side, this *did* cause me to get a few stares from Cave Trolls, lesser Goblin merchants, pretty much every Human (and there were a lot of those) and everyone else.

My "partner-in-crime" remained calm and confidant, so I took his lead and did the same. Once we had passed through most of the action in the front and center of the Bazaar, my guide approached a lone merchant sorting through silver ingots and precious stones. Beside him was a golden harp and a blue cape.

His hair seemed strange. So perfectly boring I felt sleepy just looking at it. Lying on the table in front of him was an extremely gaudy looking golden, jewel encrusted scepter. I deduced that this Human was a much respected and dangerous person to be handling such wealth so openly and carelessly in such a place.

My guide paused a moment and spoke with another, larger Human, who was wearing the same armour as he was. It appeared that both these men worked for the one counting silver at the table.

"Could this be Calabac?" I thought.

I waited patiently and took the moment to glance around while I listened to their conversation. Looking back through the massive open portal fifty feet up, where we had just descended the great wide stairs into the market, I noticed some sort of a commotion beginning to take place.

Guards were running toward the great intersection. Many of them coming from the market itself. They took up huge nets and hooked poles. Some people (if you could call them people) were running away from the excitement while others were running toward it. Alarms sounded, and orders were being shouted out from all directions. The cacophony was enough to be heard from all the way across the market where we stood.

From back, up in the giant road-like hall, I heard the giant rat-things now screeching their screechy war-cries, and Cave Trolls harrumphing and groaning theirs. Then came the telltale sounds of wood and metal being torn apart, echoing through the fortress.

Either something had breached their defenses, or they had angered their master's dragon. At the time I could think of no other possibilities.

This of course meant that the mushrooms were wearing off…or starting to take effect.

Oy.

Suddenly there was a sound so loud and horrific, many of the soldiers and guards stopped dead in their tracks. It was almost too deep for humanoids to hear but gathered pitch and intensity as it came. It started as a thumping in their chests, then it shook their skeletons, and finally it rose in pitch to be just a bit deeper than a lion's roar.

This was unlike anything I had ever heard. Some of the merchants actually hid under their tables as would-be customers turned thieves ran off with a few select items. I watched in amazement as the subterranean buttresses actually shook enough to release century's old dust from between the joints in the stonework.

My evil compatriot turned to me and spoke. "We must get to the relic and protect it," he said, and moved off in the opposite direction of the commotion.

As I followed, I heard the great roar again. This time it was accompanied with a louder crash as guards and soldiers could be seen flying through the air, propelled by some powerful force. Bodies were being thrown through the great arch and down over the massive staircase. Some were actually striking a few merchant stalls nearer to the stairs.

Ahead of me the man in black made his way to the east wall, past merchant stalls and panicked onlookers, away from the commotion. We moved under one of two arched open portals about twenty feet tall and into a courtyard cut into the side of the mountain, where there was combat training equipment of all sorts.

I looked up to see the stars in the sky and hoped that Raz would suddenly appear on Eek's back to rescue me. My hopes were dashed, however when we crossed the ancient flagstone and approached an exit.

Here we left the courtyard through another arch, and our path began to descend, back into the mountain. As we travelled, the hall remained twelve feet square, and was perfectly cut straight into the rock.

Behind us in the distance I thought I heard voices screaming something about "shit," but my would-be guide didn't seem to care, and I made nothing more of it, so we continued on at a steady pace.

I noticed that the gradient of slope we were now descending was about four percent, so I used my *schmauz* to keep track of where I was under the mountain. I was thinking that if I needed to make a fast run for it, it would be nice to remember where the exit was.

Plus, I had just stuffed a handful of psychedelic mushrooms down my throat, so keeping notes seemed prudent.

At one point we passed by two huge loading doors, and what might have been a warehouse of sorts. Passing through the doors carrying a massive shipping crate, were two Cave Trolls almost as tall as the Injoke. They entered the warehouse as we passed, and beyond them I could just make out a couple more Trolls, stacking things atop one another.

I was unable to make out much of any more details about the warehouse as we were moving by so quickly, but I did get the distinct impression that it was probably just as massive as the vault full of undead monsters that I had passed through earlier.

Beside the doors, on what was obviously a loading dock, were several massive bins at various stages of emptiness, or fullness, (depending on your point of view). As with the many doors we had encountered along this corridor, we passed these as well, leaving the Trolls to their laborious duties.

We then descended deeper into the mountain, and closer to the core. With only thirty or so feet of stone between us and the boiling, mud-filled throat of the elemental behemoth, I could feel the mountain breathe. I could feel it digesting molten minerals and mixing them with water so saturated with ash and other ages old super-heated debris, the surface density was that of solid marble.

After a good ten minutes, at a very fast pace, I was just about to have an aneurysm when we came to a round chamber with half of its wall missing, overlooking a bubbling lake of liquid death. Here and there, were islands of stalagmites, surrounded by a boiling sea of ash and super-hot muck. Fumes of countless, chemical reactions taking place created mirages that made the walls of the mountain's throat seem to contract and expand. A dome-shaped magical barrier that covered the opening facing the lake, kept the gaseous poisons at bay. Here, there were three Human soldiers standing guard.

Holy crap, kids, that was a lot of running! I almost swallowed my dentures!

Trying desperately to catch my breath, I approached the edge of the barrier, looking out across the bubbling orange and amber lake of our *"mothers' blood."* The moment was not lost on me, as I thought of home.

I was able to look up through the mouth of the crater from there as well, and I thought I saw something block out the full moon, only for a second—then it was gone.

The dragon perhaps?

Could it be that the dragon was a captive, *not* a volunteer, and now it was free?

If only, right?

Oy.

Here the floor of the room was cut from an obsidian vein, just one of the mountain's many rich mineralogical treasures. In the center of the room there was another raised dais with a four-foot-tall railing that wrapped around the outside for most of the circumference of the platform.

He stepped up onto the dais through the break in the rail and looked to me. Not knowing what to do I joined him. He then spoke out loud and clear, "Ash Pit."

There was a tingling in my shorts, and I remember wanting to do that again. It was over all too soon as I materialized in a different place altogether.

I was still on a dais, but now I was in an intersection of hallways with the dais right in the center. Four guards in black armour snapped to attention and saluted us. I ignored them and followed the guy I was with as he made haste down a southwest hallway.

I followed him for another ten minutes and passed several closed iron doors, until finally reaching the end. He took out a ring of keys and fiddled with a couple of them before finding the correct fit.

Here the halls were lit with *evervinite*, a naturally occurring purple phosphorescent crystal that glows brighter the closer it is to an active volcano or geological fault. Although beautiful, it loses its light as soon as it is mined from its source. Much of the entire hall was covered in violet glowing veins of the stuff. The effect was staggeringly beautiful, and I was momentarily distracted by it all.

Finally, the clanking of locking mechanisms sounded, and I turned my attention back to the situation at hand just as the door swung open. Beyond the portal there was a laboratory of sorts. Alchemical devices of all kinds were set up on tables and apparatuses throughout the fifty-foot-wide circular chamber.

I soon noticed an individual sitting at a table. He was wearing a white laboratory coat, as well as a strange contraption of lenses and glass tubes that sat like a crown on his head.

He was Human and looked to be in his mid- to late-forties. He seemed somewhat familiar, but I was unable to put a name to his face. He stood, turning to us before he spoke, "It isn't ready."

"We must take you to the summoning chamber now." My guide moved closer to the alchemist. "Where is it?" he growled.

"My lord, if we open the case…he…will be drawn to it." He was now trembling with fear, his hands in a begging gesture. "The master gave specific orders for no one to open the case. Only the master is permitted."

He cowered before the man and fell to one knee. "What am I supposed to do?"

I noticed he was shackled to a chain from his right ankle, which led off into the dark recesses of the lab, behind some bookshelves and stacked crates.

With a sigh of frustration, the man in black removed his helmet, placed it on the table where the alchemist was working, and stepped closer to him. He was sweating, and looked now to be smiling diabolically, like a mad-man. He drew a jagged looking, evil feeling dagger and spoke, "What are you supposed to *do*? What are you supposed to *do* you ask?"

He was snickering maniacally at that point. There was something not quite right about him. A mercenary of this guy's obvious experience and ranking should not have been acting like he was on a bad batch of hallucinogenic cactus cores.

Don't ask—that's another whole book altogether.

I deduced that if the Vermin body could be possessed by a demonic force, then so could this guy, and perhaps he too was a demon in disguise. It would account for his behavior, and would make sense, seeing as his buddy was a demon possessing someone— or maybe he was just a psychopathic asshole. That was totally possible too.

I tried to think of a solution, something to get my would-be guide to back off. I needed to speak to the alchemist alone. There were questions that I needed answers to, and I wasn't gonna get any with my barbaric companion looking over my shoulder.

While the alchemist was pleading for his life, the man in black raised his weapon, ever so slowly, teasingly. He was enjoying the misery he was causing to this poor person.

At that point, I thought to myself, "What the hell." I was eventually gonna do it anyway.

Ch'ting, went the sound of my dart gun as a magical dissolving sleeper dart buried itself deeply into the back of the man's neck. He dropped almost immediately after he swatted at the *fly* that had just bitten him.

The alchemist stood in silent shock for a moment, then, "Wh-what have you done?" He was almost crying. "Calabac will take our souls!"

The man on the floor was in his early thirties, Human standards. He was large for a Human, and had some money, which he probably stole, so I took it to cover expenses at the orphanage. He had a couple nice rings too, and that dagger—yeah, I took that too.

The alchemist, who had not yet noticed that I was not who I was supposed to be, began to back away, when I again took notice of the shackle around his ankle, and the chain that was attached.

I looked again at the man's face. "Take off your apparatus," I commanded.

He quickly removed his array of spectacles, magnifiers, macrofiers and optical contraptionry from his head and as he did so, I removed my own and let go of the disguise hootspa.

Did you like that word? *Contraptionry*. I made it up. It means *all sorts of mechanical stuff.*

Anyway, where was I?

Oh yeah…

His face was familiar—somehow.

"What are you?" he asked as he calmed down and ceased his struggling with the shackles.

"Worthy," I said. I looked him in the face and said, "Your name is Worthy. Isn't it?"

"Whatever you are and however you found out my name, I cannot help you." He began to panic again. "Why would you even come to this place?"

"I am the Redeye, Poppa Szvirf Neblinski of the faith of Shiddumbuzzin I have come here to this perilous d'en of evil and impending doom, to free the slaves of this horrible pit of suffering, rescue the Elf damsel, find the holy relic, free the Paladin, reunite with the noble Ratstafarian guide, figure out who Hackem is, stop the army of chaos, prevent an active volcano from erupting and destroying at least twenty villages in the surrounding area, destroy the eons old sorcerer, lord of darkness and destruction, Calabac, and now…rescue you.

"What's yer name bud?" I offered him my hand.

He took a long look at me and finally spoke, shaking my hand with his finger. "My name is William, sir. William Worthy. I'm an alchemist and astronomer. I am also very good at finding out how things—*work*." He then gestured toward the shackles. "These, I cannot figure out." He shrugged in defeat, but it took me only a few seconds to hootspa the shackles off the man.

It was true; he did look remarkably similar to the William Worthy I had seen in the painting at the house in Briarwood. Lillia had also given me access to her surface memories so I could see the faces of those she thought were important to the investigation.

This man looked like William, but he was *older*.

"Did you have a son named William as well?" I asked.

"Wha—? No. I have no children. I am barely old enough to run the lab." He gestured around the room.

Again—he looked in his forties, perhaps even his early fifties.

"How old are you, William?" I asked, as I applied a simple healing to his raw and blistered ankle.

"Twenty-two, sir," he said as he smiled.

"How long have you been here in this mountain?" I asked him.

"Well...a year...I think. Maybe more...could be almost two years by now." He shook as he spoke. He was terrified. "I thought you were a Scave. I thought you were because of the tail."

"No worries, William. We are gonna get you out of here, and to safety," I comforted him.

Whatever they'd done to him he'd either lost track of how many years of his life had passed, or he had aged unnaturally. I was guessing the latter.

"William. Listen closely. As long as you stay in this room you will be safe. Keep working and act like you don't know what is happening, you just work here." I couldn't drag this guy all over the inside of the fortress.

"Where are you going?" he asked me, worry all over his face.

"I have to find the Paladin, and free him. Then he and I must find Hackem," I answered.

"You mean the relic?" he corrected.

"Hmmm?" I responded.

"The relic. It is named *Hackem*?" he asked.

"Do you know where it is?" I inquired.

"Yeah. It's right over there in that case." He pointed to where his chain disappeared into the shadowy darkness.

One single light hung from the peak of the domed ceiling on the end of a long chain. This sphere of illumination was only ten or fifteen feet across, and it was bright enough to diffuse the shadows even further into darker versions of themselves. Still, I am a G'nome, and was able to clearly discern details. Shadows were no barrier to my superior visual acuity.

He continued, "I wouldn't touch it though. It drains the life force from anyone who touches it." He stood and walked toward the shadowy area he was pointing to.

"Calabac was going to use it on the Cambion named Thuckov, who he has imprisoned in the Ash Pit. Its power needs to be harnessed in order to draw the life force from the Cambion's body, allowing the spirit of an ancient evil god to possess the creature and lead the forces of chaos on a rampage across the world."

He began pacing and wringing his hands. Calabac created a demon from the remains of another. A creature that existed many eons ago—a Cambion."

"What is this Cambion that you speak of?" I asked.

"It is an abomination—a creature that is the result of a coupling between a mortal, and a denizen of the nine hells." Again, he shuddered.

"They are almost always the favourite of some greater demon lord, or god of suffering, and are usually made into nobility in the realms of chaos and evil. Now, Calabac has imprisoned one, and is ready for the conjunction, when the stars of gold and red align with the *moonshadow*."

He brought my attention to some astronomical charts, accompanied by many old texts, and a few illustrations he had on a nearby table. "You see? The amber star has arrived." He pointed at an illustration. "Soon, the red will come, and the moon will be swallowed in shadow. The cosmic powers will align and feed the ritual."

Though he appeared to be obsessed and unstable, he seemed to have put a lot of work into all of his theories and discoveries. His charts and maps were beautifully drawn, and his notes and ledgers were all organized on shelves. I decided that I should listen to him, closely.

"Calabac is a powerful sorcerer, but he is no strategic commander. The demon is a manifestation of the very essence of war. Calabac has learned how to bind the god of evil and use *it* to conquer this whole world. His deity requires mortal flesh to manifest here in our world. The Cambion will be a vessel, to carry the soul of the evil god. He cannot be stopped. The conjunction has begun, and the pieces are set."

He moved toward a bookshelf that contained many strange objects, from a Goblin skull, to preserved insects, and of course, books. He took one small book from the shelf and opened it. From a small depression within the book's pages, he retrieved a key, and passed it to me. "Here. Take it. It will open the case. But don't say I didn't warn you. What difference will it make anyway?"

William moved away from me, his back against a large shelving unit, his table of experiments and open books between us.

"I don't know how it works or why it does what it does. Calabac would have executed me if he had known I was unable to analyze it. It's just as well you have it. Better that, than Calabac having it." He was desperate.

"Am I in any danger if I simply open the case and look at the relic? Can you at least tell me that?" I asked.

This relic named *Hackem* was important.

How? I had no idea, but I had to find out.

I realized I had not had Sabbath since the grate in the ceiling of the parade square chamber for the zombie army. I conducted a short ceremony and lit my crystal pipe. I offered the pipe to William who declined politely.

"I am sorry I cannot tell you anything else. All I did was open the case and look under the wrap. There is something terrible in there and it devoured a part of me that will never heal back." He was visibly trembling again.

Once I was suitably mellow, I approached the area where the case he spoke of was supposed to be. These shadows were cold and dark even to my eyes, but I sensed something ahead and in front of me, where the domed ceiling met the floor.

As I got closer, I could see the shapes of boxes and sacks, a storage area. Something was attempting to prevent me from seeing into those shadows. A dark magic was at work, but my will was stronger, and I was drawn ever closer to the stack of boxes.

Something was there among the crates, and it *wanted* me to find it. It was the weirdest feeling I had ever had. I swore at that point I heard Durik's voice. Very faint and calling out for me to help him.

I reached out toward the shadows and suddenly the crates were thrown aside by some invisible force. They smashed against the walls to either side of me, knocking over laboratory equipment and several jars and vials of chemicals and liquids.

In a flash, the area lit up suddenly in a warm, amber glow. I quickly raised my arm to block the light. When I lowered my arm, I was happy to find that the light was not so blinding as I had initially thought.

I gasped in astonishment as there, in front of me, only six or seven feet away, was a long, flat, red rectangular case spinning rapidly on one of its corners. I was frozen in place by a strange curiosity and uncontrollable fascination with this object.

Again, I heard Durik's voice, but it was so faint and so far away, I was still not sure I heard anything at all. I feared I was beginning to sober up, but I was actually quite inebriated still—otherwise I would have been escaping at the first chance I got.

Spinning slower and slower, the case finally settled on one of its ends in front of me. It looked a lot like a tall red leather door. There was a keyhole, and even a knob like a regular door, but it was positioned for someone of my height.

The surface was so shiny, so free of blemish or spots that it was as though I was looking at red glass.

I could see stars.

At that point I thought I heard loud drums and other instruments creating a slowly climbing crescendo that was a sort of background music for the moment. I also had a weird feeling that someone was considering suing me.

Anyway...

The key was now vibrating in my hand to the point where I was in danger of not being able to hold on to it. As I began to slip it into the keyhole it was, at the same time being *pulled* in. Some unknown force wanted the key to be inserted. I wondered if I was doing the right thing.

Too late!

It was in, and securely so. I was unable to control my need to see what was behind that door, and I turned the key clockwise.

At that moment it was as though all sound in the world was silenced. It felt as though, if a coin had fallen to the ground a mile away, I would have heard it. Like reality paused to take a breath of effervescent herb smoke and hold it in. It was *that* kind of silence.

The lock opened with an audible click that seemed to echo over and over again in my head. I opened the door while the light brightened, and inside was a gold silk curtain of the highest quality I had ever seen.

Those silkworms must have been eating lobster and taking milk baths, 'cause holy smokes that fabric was decadent!

As I reached for the sparkling, golden drapery, tears welled in my eyes. I was unable to control my absolute spiritual joy from what was happening to me.

I know it sounds like a cliché, but I started to hear a host of beautiful G'nomish voices reaching up gloriously in a resounding, klezmerizing choir of unimaginable beauty.

The scent of pungent cheese dip and golden fried potato sticks was thick in the air, accompanied by a swirling vortex of holy smoke rings. It was all such an olfactory bliss that I wept.

I touched the smooth fabric and it felt like it was not even there, it was so soft, like touching water that is exactly the same temperature as your skin—if you can imagine such a thing.

"If only they'd make underwear outta this stuff," I thought as I pulled my pants up.

I slowly drew back the covering, allowing bright, golden rays of light to burst from the portal. Gasping in shock, I was momentarily blinded—but in a good way, so don't worry. After a few seconds I opened my eyes slowly and gazed in wonder at what was there.

It was right then that I heard William run out the door, blabbering about losing his life's essence, or something. There was a great commotion outside and I could hear the sounds of guards moving in the hall.

This particular hall was a dead end with me *at* that end, I should have been worried that I was trapped, but all I could do was to stare in awe at the contents of the portal.

I didn't care. I was *klezmerized* by what I saw beyond the golden veil. My heart was lifted, and my soul rejoiced in the discovery that I had made.

There, inside, was an assortment of delicious mixed chocolates and a hot glass of tea.

Not really, I'm only kidding you.

CHAPTER - 20

THE *BONG*

I stepped through the portal, into a grand and delightful garden of sacred herb in a dark chamber about a hundred feet across. Not a forest of tall trees hundreds of feet high, mind you, but a groomed garden of small flowering herb bushes of many varying subspecies of sacred herb.

In the center was a small pond, about twenty feet across, with a strange fountain in the middle. It was made from multi-coloured glass—or at least appeared to be from where I stood, near the portal. It had a large bulbous bottom, with a long narrow trunk in the top which overflowed with cool, clean water that bubbled with the sweet smoke of smoldering herb.

Through the many colours of the fountain, multiple, ever swirling rays of light were casting tiny spots all over the inside of the place, and I could tell that I was inside a dome of sorts. To be honest it looked kind of tacky but who am I to judge? I wear a giant, golden herb leaf on a necklace.

Oy.

I approached the sparkling fountain and could hear the sound of guards coming closer behind me and down the hall outside the room. I gazed into the great smoking water fountain and wondered what it all could be.

Suddenly I was startled by the sound of a very deep bell resonating.

Why does everything have to be *suddenly*? If I was two hundred years older, I would be changing my shorts every forty minutes. Oy! Why can't I just once have a—*then, gradually*?

Bonnnnnng! It sounded, only once. Then there was silence.

"Bong?" I asked.

Immediately, I could see something materialize inside the tall crystal tube of—*The Bong*.

Yes, at that moment I decided to call this thing The Bong. It seemed to fit, and I am the leader of the faith, and that has a few perks. So, I am allowed.

I looked deeply into the crystalline depths of churning smoke and lances of multicoloured lights. As I approached The Bong, I could barely make out details—something, inside, beyond the smoke. It appeared to be a sword. A great sword, the likes Grarr would use, only slightly shorter and a bit wider. It resembled a sacred herb leaf with the central frond elongated as a great serrated blade.

I gazed through the glass in wonder—the serrations on the weapon seemed to be made of a sparkling, silvery-white metal I was not familiar with.

These *teeth* were separate parts from the rest of the golden blade. They were set in place one after the other and were attached to the blade on what appeared to be a track-like system. I deduced that they were designed to move rapidly along the edge and must be powered by pure hootspa.

Exciting right?

At the hilt, in the center of the blade was a relatively small grouping of contraptionry that must have been the engine for the weapon. Mounted in the middle of the contraptionry was a glowing stone as big as an egg.

It was in its raw form uncut and pure. It churned with veins of blue and amber light against a pitch-black surface, like the embers of coal in a smithy's forge—waves of light and sparks danced in its heart, while light and power boiled and swirled over the surface.

Its golden handle was long enough for one hand, but the pommel was a mushroom shaped firestone, six inches long and three inches across, and was situated so a second hand could theoretically be brought into play.

I didn't know enough about weapons to know what type of sword this was, but I concluded that it was created for Durik. I mean, who else, right? I ain't stupid, you know?

Suddenly...oy...suddenly, I heard footfalls behind me. So I turned and moved to the entrance of The Bong, where I found myself face to face with three armoured Scave, all about the size of Elves. They were chuckling, and obviously aware of the effect they would have on a such a tiny adversary as me.

I stood my ground, just inside the door to The Bong, suddenly aware that I was standing on holy ground, sacred to my faith—the same faith I was the supreme leader of.

Boy was *I* upset.

"Stop!" I commanded.

What the hell was I doing? I am only just under a foot tall!

"I am the carrier of your doom! Imbued with the power of holy righteousness. I am the sword of justice, and the hammer of judgement, and it is upon you, fiends! Fall to your knees! I command it!"

Holy crap I was scaring *myself!* I felt a force run through me from The Bong. It swelled up inside me as I immediately came to realize that the sword within The Bong was a sentient force and was using me as a vessel for its will.

I could not control it. Not that I wanted to. It felt great, like I was really, really super powerful. *This* after the joy ride through the tingly platform teleporter devise. I got an erection. Honestly.

Squealing piteously, the Scave fell to the floor, but one of them struggled to speak.

"You...w-will...not escape...the...m-master, little...m-morsel." It grunted and squeaked, trying to break the force that was pushing down upon it.

"You will never know either way *Scave*." I spat defiantly.

"We are going to...k-kill you, cheese...m-monkey." They continued to struggle and one actually almost got to his knees.

I held up my hand and splayed my fingers apart, again. I was not in control, but was fully aware. "Then you leave me no choice."

I made a sudden fist and their heads imploded into tiny raisins; helmets included. Their bodies followed immediately, and eventually they imploded so small they vanished completely.

Without a pause, and as though I was being controlled like a puppet, I walked out of the garden and back into the laboratory. Then I turned and closed the door, cast a shrinking hootspa on it, and put it into my bottomless pouch.

Without warning I was in control again, and I fell to my knees, the puppet's strings cut.

Holy Shiddumbuzzin! I had single-handedly defeated three guards, each five times my own size! I had wielded power I could not imagine. I suddenly realized what I really had in the box.

This was not only a relic. It was a *holy* relic, and it was created by and for the faith of Shiddumbuzzin and all G'nome kind. It was a weapon of holy power made specifically for something much larger than a G'nome, though; Durik, the secret weapon of the faith.

I loaded my dart gun, and conducted Sabbath, while preparing something I was looking forward to trying, a hootspa, supposedly, of great power called Sa'vem'yass.

I prayed to Shiddumbuzzin to guide my steps on the safest path, and to help me locate and rescue Durik. Somewhere down here was where they were keeping the kid and maybe poor Musky too. I was going to find them both if it was the last thing I did.

I prepared several other hootspas for combat and invisibility and stored the previous combat hootspas in my magic ring. Then I conducted Sabbath again, 'cause, you know.

I stood around for several minutes trying to remember what I was supposed to be doing next. Then...

I was off, and on my way down the hall toward the eight-way intersection to the dais where I materialized after the sex teleportation thing, or whatever the hell that was.

Boy I couldn't *wait* to try *that* thing again.

As I approached, completely invisible, I noticed William standing there, wringing his hands, and pacing nervously. I walked right up to him, levitated to eye level, and spoke.

"William." I materialized in front of his face, scaring the k'shvipits out of him. "You are going to tell me where the *blue one* is, where the vessel for Thuk—"

Holy crap I realized where I had heard that name before. Durik...*Thukov*...Eechitindie.

Was Durik then a demon as well? What was he? Why did he have the same name, and why were these infernal underpants riding up my butt crack? I should have paid the extra five bucks.

I then decided I didn't know enough about whatever it was I had just then forgotten about. William was looking at me, confused and waiting for me to speak.

"Thukov," I continued. "*You* should stay right here. When I return, we will leave this place. Now where is the blue one?"

"There, at the end." He pointed down the north hall.

I then became invisible again and floated down the north hall as fast as I was able. About halfway down I began to hear the sounds of an army moving above me. The marching of tens of thousands of soldiers and the movement of war machines rumbled through the fortress.

There was also an enormous thrumming like some great horn, heralding the start of the end, except it did that twice—so it wasn't really the start or the end the first time—or—whatever.

Even through many feet of solid rock and earth the sound of the military force's movement could be heard. The mountain literally shook under their mass and the great horn sounded a third time.

See? Told ya.

I tried to move faster and was able to pick up a bit more speed by doing a sort of breast stroke swimming through the air thing. After a minute more I reached the end, where there was a door that was barred and locked.

This was going to take some doing, kids because that was a prison door made to hold monsters.

Monsters like the boys.

Thinking back to Vlad's castle and the Troll made me wish Beornag was there with me to rip down the impressive barrier.

I began the tedious details of a lock picking hootspa, and hoped I still had time. After five minutes I broke the main lock, but there were three more to go and already the sounds of more guards could be heard back at the intersection.

They must not have found William, or they had and were locking him up again, or worse.

I continued my work as fast as I could and prayed in the process that the boys would somehow find us, and we would all be safe.

As I began to hootspa the last lock I heard them.

Behind me, coming up from the intersection, was the sound of a thousand bare feet on the polished evervinite.

Rats!

Calabac had unleashed my most feared nightmare with an overkill attitude. I stumbled—once—then again. I was forgetting the words.

I could *smell* their fur...

I was losing concentration! Durik! I had to keep going!

I lost it again! Behind me, the sounds were so terrible, so truly horrific, I nearly cried from sheer panic!

I had to start again! I had to hootspa the lock! Then I could take refuge inside the prison, where it would be safe!

Again, I fumbled.

With fatal realization I now understood my mistake. The final lock was magical! There was no way the picking hootspa was ever going to work. I needed to negate the magic already on the door.

Too late, they were almost upon me. What could I do? I needed time! They would kill me in seconds and eat me and gnaw my bones!

"Help me Shiddumbuzzin!" I screamed at the top of my lungs as I turned to face the moving pool of oily, scurrying, filthy...

"Musky?" He was standing about ten feet from me. There was a large group of Gnomes behind him.

"Who ya be *t'inkin'* it is, mun?!" he scolded me. I then realized that in my panic trying to hootspa the final lock, I had let go of my invisibility hootspa. Good thing it *was* Musky and not the horde that I had thought it was.

"I be telling ya t' wait fer I. D'en I come back, mun, and ya is nowhere t' be found!" He shook his finger at me and was obviously quite upset.

"Musky be crawlin' all over d'is 'ere place looking fer an invisible G'nome? Really, now? 'Ow you be t'inkin' I be gonna find ya, eh?" He put his hands on his hips and continued, "Of all da bone 'eaded t'ings ya could be doin'. 'Ere y' are, wandrin' d'em 'alls o' d'is 'ere jail, an' ya—"

I ran to him and wrapped my arms around his waist (he was taller than I was remember), and hugged him. "Musky, thank Shiddumbuzzin you are here, my friend." I stepped back.

"Well...d'en...seein' as you...um...be so glad t' see I, I is wonderin' what ya be doing down 'ere all by yerself mun?"

I now took better notice that the entire hall was filled with escaped slaves. William was with them. All were kneeling in silence (save William), and every set of eyes was on me. It was unnerving to say the least. My clothes were a mess.

"Musky," I began as I gestured toward the huge prison door. "I believe that Durik is being held prisoner—"

He interrupted me, "Behind d'is 'ere door, and ya not be able t' be gittin' past d'is last lock. Right?" He smiled, his fake jewel sparkling in his gold tooth.

"Why, yes, that's exactly right," I said.

"Step aside, mun. Let Musky show ya 'ow it's done." He cracked his fingers and approached the final lock. Then he literally bent backwards, and using only his ankles and feet, he dragged his body under the narrow gap between the door and the floor. His smiling face was the last we saw of him as his incredibly flexible body molded its way under the massive portal and disappeared.

It was almost as though he was made of a semi-stiff rubber.

After a few seconds the door opened, and he was standing there with a grin on his face. "Ya be looking at da limbo champion o' ma 'omeland mun. D'ere's no door d'at Musky c'not get t'rough."

I looked past his shoulder into a domed chamber. It was very dimly lit by one artificial light hanging in the center, much like William's laboratory, and so I was able to see quite well.

There was a big table in the middle of the fifty-foot-wide room. It was tilted slightly forward—and shackled to its surface was Durik.

I ran to the table taking flight in mid-stride. The kid appeared to be unconscious, so I began to examine him more closely to find the reason, or to tend to any wounds he may have suffered.

His ankles and wrists were bound to the steel table with very sturdy bands of iron. There appeared to be no locking mechanisms of any kind. He was alive but in some sort of stasis.

"It's alive! It's alive!" I shouted out with joy.

I looked around the room to make sure a lawyer wasn't watching me, but it was empty, save for the table, and a strange glyph painted on the floor in blue paint about ten feet from Durik's still form.

I looked back at the kid and as I suspected, he had a small wound on the left side of his throat. The blue paint was Durik's blood.

I conducted a healing miracle immediately.

"Musky not be findin' a way t' crack d'em d'ere locks mun. D'ere be no way but magic, I is t'inkin'," he apologized.

"Okay, get as many of us in here as you can. Everyone if that's possible. I am going to contact the Mellow One and use the holy power of Shiddumbuzzin to free Durik," I explained as I prepared for Sabbath.

Musky left the room, and with William's help, he began gathering up the escaped prisoners and sending them in. They entered in relative silence and knelt all around, facing the table where Durik was lying. Some could be heard whispering to themselves, almost worshipping Durik and me and even revering us as their saviors.

You know? What was I supposed to do? I'm sure you *must* be seeing the clues here, right? I really *was* the Cloud Walker. I was the salvation these people had been waiting generations for, to come and liberate them from their bonds of slavery. These were the children of Shiddumbuzzin, and the boys must be the titans in the stories that these Gnomes had been telling their children for who knows how long.

So I did what I figured I was supposed to do. *I put on the boots and made cheese.* That's an old G'nomish saying that means: I adapted to what I had to do—and did it.

Every Gnome in the hall made it inside the room. It was filled right to the edge of the table with Gnomes of all ages. Entire families looked up at us with hope in their glossy eyes. I conducted a Sabbath like no other Sabbath before. The entire room imbibed the scared herb. Many a puff was taken, and many a Gnome was mellowed.

"Now," I began. "I shall call upon the holy lord, creator of the G'nomes and the Gnomes too, apparently, to awaken the holy Paladin of our formerly-lost faith."

I walked around the edge of the table, being careful not to slip off and embarrass myself, as I prepared to contact the Mellow One.

"Uh…mun?" Musky waved a hand from the second row.

"Yes oh furry ally of our glorious faith? I gestured for him to stand.

"What gonna 'appen when him be wakin' up, mun? I mean he be 'avin' no weapons nor he gots any clothes sept 'is short pants and d'em gloves."

"Eureka!" I thought. The gauntlets! The gauntlets of super strength! Durik was still wearing them. But how could those help us? Durik would have escaped already if he was able. Unless he was unconscious when he was strapped down.

"William! Where is William?" I called out.

"Um, here sir." He stood up and waved from way in the back row.

"William, can you shed any light on how we should proceed? I want to wake up my friend here, and Musky wants to make sure my friend here will be able to defend us too…and…um…what was I saying?"

"Sir, if that guy is your friend, and the relic won't hurt you like it hurt me, maybe it is supposed to go to your friend," he replied.

"Oh reeeeally? You mean it? Of course there's no way I could have already figured that out myself." The nerve. Kids these days!

He looked slightly embarrassed, so I continued, "Do you know where Durik's equipment is? Do you know the best way to wake him up? Do you know how to release his bindings? Do you know a good tailor? My shorts are chafing my package and keep sliding down over my butt cheeks. It's a pain in the you know what!"

He moved through the crowd of Gnomes, to the table edge, where he examined Durik's still form. "He is drugged. A simple antidote will awaken him," William said.

"His equipment was all in those crates in my lab—cell. I was trying to figure out how some of it worked. The bindings are magical, and I do not believe you have the power to counter one of Calabac's enchantments; at least not this one," he replied apologetically. "No offense... And I don't know of any tailors in this place, but perhaps if we all manage to escape, I could provide you with one in Briarwood."

Around us the fortress was still rumbling with the movement of the great army, readying itself for war. Calabac employed mighty forces of Cave Trolls, and lesser Goblins on huge war steeds, gigantic undead monsters, and war massive machines.

My *schmauz* was telling me that the volcano was being affected by the unnatural seismic activity of such enormous weights moving around all at once, and I began to worry about an imminent eruption.

The volcano was only *almost dormant* in the first place. So, at that point I would say it had moved up to *slightly, almost* dormant. One more step up the spewing ladder and she would be *not* dormant but *somewhat groggy*, and then we all know where it goes after that.

Oy!

I was suddenly reminded of the sticky, resin coated buds all over the cute little bushes in The Bong's garden. Why it reminded me of this I do not know, but I got a brilliant idea, or a really stupid one brought on by copious amounts of herb, so I decided to do it anyway.

I reached into my endless pouch and pulled out a nice pickle, still cold from the cold cellar at the winery. It was so crunchy, and juicy...I also pulled out the door to The Bong's garden.

"Behold your salvation," I said to the Gnomes. "And yours too, William, if you want to avoid all the combat and war and stuff," I added in a whisper. He was now standing next to me, beside the table.

Floating to the floor just under the foot of the table, I placed the door to The Bong's garden down in front of me and cancelled the shrinking hootspa.

Spinning on one of its corners, it grew to full size in a matter of seconds. The Gnomes gasped, and *oooohed*, and *ahhed* at the wonder of it.

I walked around to the front and put the key into the lock, turning it clockwise. With an audible click it opened, revealing the mystical garden beyond. I then gestured for everyone to get inside. It took about ten minutes to get everyone in, and organized again, this time around The Bong.

I stood on the edge of the fountain about three feet above the gathered Gnomes, walking around The Bong as I spoke. "You must all wait here. I must free the Paladin, and then he will free the rest of us."

They were silent.

"Mun?" Musky called from outside the garden. "If ya not be mindin', I be taggin' along wit' you 'elping' Durik."

"I had hoped for as much my friend."

I floated down from the fountain wall and approached a

particularly oily and resinous bud covered bush. I had never seen resin like this before. The herb was definitely sacred Sensimilia but of a strain I was unfamiliar with. It surely was not one of the three commonly known species.

There, I gestured for Musky to wait, as I drew a few mundane items from my pouch. Then, shedding the Scave armour that I had been wearing, I put on my own clothes. Once dressed, I scraped a large amount of the resin from the buds onto a flat rock that I took from beside the fountain wall.

After assuring the Gnomes that all would be well, I joined Musky outside (William decided to wait this one out) and closed the door to The Bong's garden.

Next I cast a shrinking hootspa on the door, and put it in my bottomless pouch.

"Musky, I need you to guard Durik and keep him safe until I return. I must gather his things from William's laboratory." I then made my way back to the intersection and down the hall to the lab where William had been held.

The rumbling was now getting quite loud, and the mountain was actually trembling noticeably. Not much mind you, but for a G'nome who was sensitive to this sort of thing, it was spelling out eventual disaster.

I reached the lab and saw Durik's things scattered all over the floor. I had not noticed these were his things before when I was experiencing a religious epiphany, but there was his shoulder pad with the silver spike we got from the smith at the market in Briarwood. (He was a Dwarf named Hi Ho. The shop is called *Hi Ho Silver*. Check it out. Tell him Szvirf sent you and you might get a discount.)

Anyway, where was I?

Oh yeah…

I began searching the shelves for an antidote and finally found a jar labelled: Sleep Agent Antidote (go figure). I put it into my pack and gathered up as many of Durik's possessions as would fit through the opening of my pouch.

Afterward I made my way, this time invisible, back to the chamber with Durik and Musky. As I got closer, I could hear Musky speaking to someone. I approached slowly.

"...an' I be tellin' ya, 'im be comin' right back wit' d'at stuff 'im need t' be bringin' ya t' life again, mun." He was speaking to Durik but the kid was still out. "You done saved Musky, mun, er at least ya were tryin', so Musky now be savin' you, mun. I gonna burn d'is 'ere spliff in yer honor while I is waitin' for Mr. Neblinski."

I entered the room just as he was lighting a twist of scared herb leaves.

I became visible, then floated to Durik's side and landed next to the flat rock containing the resin-oil. I made my way to Durik's head and pushed with all my might to forcibly open his mouth. His jaw weighs almost as much as my whole body, remember.

"Musky, I need you to blow that smoke all over Durik's body and especially his head." I directed as I lifted the tiny decanter, a large bucket for me, to Durik's lips and administered a dose of the antidote, as instructed on the back of the bottle. William was a well-organized alchemist. I will give him that. I then spoke a humble prayer to Shiddumbuzzin and waited.

As promised by William, Durik's eyes opened, and he started to go into a frenzy right away. I jumped onto his chest and grabbed him by the cheeks. Looking him straight in the eyes I yelled, "Durik! Wake up, kid! Poppa Szvirf is here to save you! I am the High Redeye of the faith of Shiddumbuzzin!"

I pulled out my golden holy symbol and pressed it against his left temple. "I command you, to compose yourself! You are the paladin of Shiddumbuzzin, and I command you to obey the scriptures of the great book."

I then pulled out the holy book of Shiddumbuzzin, "Durik, son of Neblinski! You are the chosen one, Durik!" What the hell was I saying? I was making stuff up on the spot and pulling stuff outta my butt left, right and center, but it all seemed to make sense for some reason, and miraculously enough everything I was saying was right then appearing in a nice script on the pages of the open book!

I needed more mushrooms.

I pulled a handful from my pouch and ate them.

"Pops!" Musky yelled.

"What is it?"

"Durik be still freakin', mun. What ya doin'!?" His little arms were waving, and he was really panicking at this point.

"Give him a second, he'll calm down." I comforted Musky with a handful of mushrooms and we both made a game of seeing who could toss the most mushrooms into Durik's roaring mouth one at a time. We used potato sticks to keep score.

After about five minutes, yeah, a good five minutes, Musky won the contest: thirty-seven to twenty-nine. At last Durik finally spoke, which in itself was a miracle, considering he'd just eaten sixty-six psychedelic mushrooms.

"Where is Durik?" he growled. "Why so many sparkles?"

I jumped back onto his chest and looked him in the eye. (They were too far apart at that range for me to look into them both). "It's me, kid. Poppa Szvirf, I am here to save you."

He looked at me, and panic began to swell in his eyes. "Poppa Szvirf! Run! You must run! Too many for Durik—"

"Wait kid!" I grabbed his cheeks again. "You are shackled. Musky is here with me, and we are breaking you out, now straighten up or I will have to take away points for non-Palidinly conduct."

That got his attention. "Vhat you mean, Poppa Szvirf?"

"Look—kid—no time to explain. I am gonna smear this oil on your wrists and you are gonna slip outta those gauntlets. Then

Musky will put them on, and they will shrink to fit him, then he pulls them out and passes them back to you—and—why am I still explaining this?" Musky handed me the rock with the sticky thick grease-like resin.

I began to smear the slippery goo on Durik's wrists, and something occurred to me.

"Bear witness to this moment all who can," I spoke and realized only Musky was watching. But I had thought of something kind of profound and didn't want to forget it, so I went ahead and said it anyway.

"I taketh from the sacred herb of The Bong and anoint the body of our protector. See, oh holy One, oh mysteriously wise and perceptive One, see as the sacred oils of your creations seep into his being."

I looked to Musky. "Look on and remember, my Ratstafarian comrade, as I awaken the full power of Shiddumbuzzin."

I floated off the table to ten or so feet in front of Durik and landed on the floor. There I stared up at the great door to The Bong again, opened it and yelled in at the Gnomes and William.

I was secretly relieved that they were all still alive, because I gotta tell ya, right at that moment, I was not really all that sure they could even breath inside an artificial para-pocket dimension, let alone two of them.

I was relieved to see everyone stand and face me from within. Whew!

I stood in the portal momentarily, so that the Gnomes could see that I had returned, and then I floated up to about six feet off the ground and turned to face Durik.

"Durik…" I cleared my throat. "Durik Neblinski, adopted son of Szvirf Neblinski, divinely appointed high Redeye of the faith of Shiddumbuzzin, son of Ichghmaihl…"

I cleared my throat again. "Aka Iggi Neblinski, son of Ibram

Neblinski of Ibram and Stella's Discount Furniture (located at thirty-two seventy-one Upper East and Fifty-seventh Avenue South, open seven days a week, bring the kids and get a free soda), I command you to stand. Cast aside your bonds and stand."

Durik, right on cue, began to struggle to pull his hands out of the gauntlets. It took some time, and his wrists were pretty chaffed when he was done, but he managed to get both hands free.

After a moment of silence.

"Um...Poppa Szvirf?" Durik gently nudged.

"Yeah kid?"

"Durik's feet still stuck."

"Aw crap," I said.

"Just shrink 'im already an' get it done wit', will ya?" Musky offered.

"That was my very next choice, but thank you Musky." I hootspa'd the kid into a bug-sized Durik and placed him gently on the floor.

Musky and I laughed at him for a minute or two, then I cancelled the hootspa and Durik was free—naked—but free.

Does anyone have some tape, or maybe a coil of rope to bind the Paladin's pet mamba to his leg with?" I asked those inside, as I noticed women and children and even a few men cower at the sight of Durik's giant schlong.

"There is a roll or two in my lab," William offered from inside The Bong's garden."

"Thanks William. Oh, yeah—you wouldn't happen to have any clean screen filters in your lab for your chemistry stuff, would you?" I yelled back.

"Second drawer on your left, green cabinet with the skeleton lying next to it."

I looked back to Durik. "Kid, you have a choice here—"

"You vant *Durik* to be... Poppa Szvirf's *son*?" he interrupted.

"Poppa Szvirf is Durik's...*Fadher?*"

Just then I got this creepy deja vu and half expected him to cut off my right hand, for some completely unknown reason. I also got that *getting sued* feeling again as well.

"Well...not really, I'm a G'nome and you're...well...not a G'nome, but for all intents and purposes? Yeah. I am proud to call you son."

Can you imagine? Him? Coming out of a G'nome? The alternative is just as unlikely. "Now I have something you need to see. Come with me." I gestured for him to follow me through The Bong's portal and into the garden.

As soon as we entered, a resounding, and this time much louder *BONNNNG* echoed through the garden.

Durik followed me in through the throng of kneeling and whispering Gnomes. Not a single one seemed to be afraid, except for when his *schlong* swung around. Many of them reached out as we passed by, and touched my coat gently sighing.

Most of the buds on the multitude of herb bushes spit sparkling pollen into the air, making the whole moment that much more enchanting and intoxicating. Either one will work here.

The Bong began bubbling and spewing out copious amounts of thick sweet, smelling euphoria. As we reached the edge of the pool the fountain suddenly stopped functioning, and the water drained from the pool.

The Bong then slowly turned in a circle so that an opening near the bottom of the round base came around to face us. This hatch was located in the bottom of the lower section of The Bong. It was round and decorated opulently with gold hardware.

Beyond the hatch was a roiling, boiling, churning liquid I will not venture to describe further. Besides I was on mushrooms and the whole thing could have been a hallucination. Right?

Anyway...

The stuff in The Bong was really quite hypnotically strange. It seemed to be smoke of many colours, yet it was liquid as well. Some colours I could not even recognize.

We all fell to our knees and watched as Durik stepped over the short wall and into the now empty pool. He walked with purpose, looking back only once to me for approval, and smiling proudly I gave it, with a wink and a nod.

In front of the opening, he dropped to one knee and the circular hatch opened up. I expected the swirling stuff to pour out, but it remained inside.

The Gnomes were in awe, gasping and sighing with spiritual delight.

I watched, teary-eyed, as Durik reached up inside the open portal. As he did so he was taken—floating gently up and into the vapours of The Bong, where he and the mysterious weapon disappeared. The hatch then closed, and we waited in relative silence for him to return.

It was not long after when we heard guards coming. This time it really *was* the guards and not the rescue party.

We couldn't wait idly by. If they were allowed inside the door again, they would surely wipe out all of these Gnomes and eventually destroy The Bong too.

There was no way to be sure if I would be able to channel The Bong's power as effectively this time as I had done against only three Scave guards, or if it would even work again at all.

"Musky!" I signalled my Ratstafarian comrade. "You're with me!"

Then, "William!" I turned to the unnaturally aged alchemist. "If and when Durik comes out, explain to him what I had to do. I will try and look in to see if he returns later, but for now I have to try and protect you all!"

"I understand, sir! We all do! Go!" He gestured for me to hurry.

CHAPTER - 21

FAITH TO FAITH AT WATHT!

Musky and I exited The Bong's garden. I closed the door, shrunk it, and bagged it. I then turned Musky invisible, covered him with a force field of magical protection, and used my hootspas to make him stronger, and faster. Afterward, I hoospa'd myself invisible, and gave myself a minor protection aura.

Then I floated to the very top of the domed ceiling where the single light hung from a chain, and waited for Musky to make his move.

Through the doorway they poured into the room like a river of oily fur and armour.

The Scave.

They were like a living, five-foot thick, liquid blanket of armoured bipedal rats, and they reeked like a dump. They moved upright and on all fours, scurrying and scuffling into the room.

They sniffed the air and immediately picked up Musky's scent. Okay they smelled me, but Musky was hanging from the chain just underneath me, so it was probably a combination of the two.

There must have been thirty or more of them. Squeaking and scurrying all over the table and the room. Soon, they had caught on to our general location and were now congregating in the middle of the room, just below us.

Panic threatened to take me as they began to stand and boost each other up to get a lock on the scent of G'nome and Ratstafarian. They crawled on top of each other reaching up, grasping at the air. Some would boost others high, and those, in turn, would boost yet another, and another.

In mere seconds they would have us.

"Now!" I yelled.

Musky dropped and flipped in the air. He landed, still invisible, behind one of our assailants and thrust Durik's dagger, a short sword for him, into the nearest opponent.

I pointed both hands at the mob of murderous fiends and spoke loudly, "*V'shnicka, v'shnicka, v'shnicka, v'schnock!*"

Several white-hot balls of pure hootspa flowed from my hands and struck whatever I pointed at. Glowing orbs of energy exploded among them, splattering liquid fire all over them.

Musky had leapt toward the door a moment before the orbs exploded.

Behind him the Scave were screaming in pain, extinguishing their burning coats, and momentarily distracted.

Once again, he leapt among them, flipping and rolling, jumping and doing all sorts of acrobatic manoeuvres. Each time his feet touched the floor, wall or other surface, he thrust the dagger into another Scave, while launching himself at his next opponent.

Most died when he did this, some fell, mortally wounded, bleeding out. Between the mushrooms and the hootspas I had used to enhance his abilities, he had become almost unstoppable by his evil counterparts.

Ten Scave fell in mere seconds before they knew what was happening. We fought on, slaying them one after another. Their voices were maddening, screaming and squealing as they bled and burned and screeched.

Still, we fought on, but it was all for not.

Even as we were turning the tides in our favor, more guards were coming, far too many for Musky and me to deal with alone. Many more than the initial wave, and this time there were man-sized Scave among them, as tall as Durik. These were the most terrifying things I had ever seen in my life, yet still we fought on.

I tried desperately to formulate a plan of escape, but it wasn't long before Musky was overwhelmed by their numbers. Soon after, I was dragged to the floor even as I was slaying them with the last hootspas from my ring.

I was mobbed, belly down. I could see Musky struggling for freedom as they pinned him to the floor.

"Why aren't they killing us?" I thought. They were purposefully trying to capture us without injury, sacrificing themselves against our strength, slowly wearing us down.

Moments later Musky and I were too exhausted to struggle further. They had us, and there was little we could do. From my vantage point, face-down on the floor, I could now see the boots of a Human approaching. They were finely made, supple soft leather with brass buckles.

These were obviously very expensive boots. The kind a lord, or king, might wear. But there appeared to be dog crap all over them. In fact, I was now able to smell the foul odour of dog crap emanating from all of our assailants.

I struggled to look up at the man's face. He was younger than I expected. In fact, I had expected Calabac himself, but this was not him. I was sure of it. This man did not have the presence I would expect from a lord of an evil army of chaos.

This guy was too relaxed. His hair was a very light ivory color, his eyes were vibrant, icy blue, and he was extremely attractive for a Human man.

Not that I am attracted to Human men. It's just that... whatever.

Anyway, where was I?

Oh yeah...

His eyes were icy blue, and his skeletal structure was flawlessly symmetrical. It was as though he was—perfect—too perfect in fact.

"The Stealer," I thought. "It has to be the Stealer—but why the poop?"

He looked down at me and smiled. No one was that charming! It *had* to be the Stealer.

"Hello, little one. We meet again." His eyes sparkled. "My master wishes to have a word with you."

Then he turned to one of the man-sized Scave and ordered him to bind us. Soon we were tied and gagged, blindfolded and carried away, through hallways and tunnels, up ramps and stairways, until we paused, momentarily.

I had been lifted by the Stealer himself. I could tell by the smell of his cologne. This was no Scave carrying me, but that fact was of little comfort as I knew right then that if I didn't come up with a plan, Musky and I were gonna be dead as doornails by morning.

Using my *schmauz*, I was able to evaluate my position despite being blindfolded. I knew that we had been ascending through the fortress, and eventually, we had been carried back to the same level as the undead army storage vault.

"Crap!" I thought as I realized we weren't gonna use the sex teleporter thing again.

While we seemed to be standing around, waiting, I could hear many boots pass by us. Hundreds of soldiers were moving through the fortress, and with them the sounds of wheels, and the creaking of contraptionry. I was suddenly grateful that I had a bag over my head and was unable to see what was transpiring around me.

Once the sounds had passed and faded into the distance we continued on our way again. About thirty more minutes of being carried around the inside of the fortress, always ascending higher into the volcano, we finally came to a stop.

I heard the creaking of what must have been mighty doors opening ahead of me, and once the sound stopped, I was taken forward again. I could no longer hear the Scave as we passed through the doorway. All had become silent as soon as the doors began to open.

I was taken forward, now at a more relaxed pace, as the doors closed ominously behind. Only a short moment later, we stopped again, and I was placed on the floor, and forced to kneel.

There was no sound in the room, as though it was empty except for my breathing; the white noise from my *schmauz* telling me that I was in a large room, longer than it was wide, and twenty feet tall. My heart pounding in my chest.

After what felt like an eternity, when they finally removed my blindfold, I was comforted to find that I was beside Musky. At least he too was still alive.

Both of us were tied up, still gagged, and kneeling in front of a throne made from the bones of— GNOMES!

Sitting in the great seat of evil was a Human-sized being, not quite as tall as the Stealer who had brought me there. He was adorned in a rich purple cloak of which the hood covered most of his features in shadow. He gestured with an elegant, jewelled hand and the guards in the room turned away.

He then removed his hood.

His face was long and as expressionless as a doll. His almost perfect complexion was pale, and ghostly. He wore smoky eye makeup and his jet-black hair was slicked back into a braid that nearly touched the floor.

He looked at me from his throne of evil atop a circular dais, with eyes, black as pearls, cold and calculating.

This was Calabac. I knew it.

His clothing was overly rich and opulent, like that of a king or emperor. Rich burgundy, trimmed with decadent purples and blackest velvet. The collar was a strip of long, almost gossamer black fur that seemed animated by his slightest movements.

He wore rings on all his fingers that were encrusted with jewels.

I noticed that he was barefoot, and his toes too were adorned with rings and long pointed toenails.

His eyes were solid black and in their centers were two pinpoints of violet light.

He sat in silence and stared at us for what felt like forever, until finally he stood up and descended the dais gracefully.

The tension in the air was tangible.

He circled us, folding his arms as he studied us in silence, only the sound of his elongated toenails *clack-clack-clacking* on the stone floor.

At one point he drew from his robes a set of spectacles on a long telescopic stem, which he used to evaluate us with more scrutiny. It was unnerving to say the least.

Musky and I were still gagged, but he started to say something anyway, trying to curse at our captor. He then tried desperately to free himself, struggling at his bonds, and rolling on the floor.

Calabac backed away from us, and snapped his fingers, pointing at Musky.

There were several giant Scave here with their backs to us and one of them turned to face us. It took two steps and was right beside us where it picked Musky up by his bonds and slammed him down on the floor—hard—causing his hat to fall off. I watched as blood begin to seep from his nose while he lay there unconscious.

The *person*, who I was now pretty sure was Calabac, then continued to circle me several more times before he finally ascended the dais and sat down on his throne once again.

I took note how the Scave that assaulted Musky had turned away from his master, giving the impression that they were not allowed to look upon their master's face without permission.

I also took that moment to get a look around at as much of the place as I could. The chamber was one hundred feet long (give or take)—the throne at one end and a set of great bronze doors at the other. I saw two rows of massive obsidian pillars, twenty feet apart, that were lined up on either side of a long, red carpet that led back from the throne to the only exit.

The whole, massive, forty-foot-wide hall had been cut from a single geothermal vent that had, millions of years ago, filled with volcanic glass. It was a marvel of architectural engineering worthy of a G'nomish master builder.

I then noticed something behind the throne. A massive beast sat on the floor there, silent and terrifying. A mighty Cave Troll the likes of which I did not know could even exist. It was bigger than Beornag, and was wearing a suit of elaborate plate armour, decorated with etchings, filigree, and bristling with spikes.

Finally Calabac spoke. "Tho, fathe to fathe at watht. Thith mutht be the G'nome who hath been thabotawthing awe my pwanth? What thay you? Thpeak, you thwimey wittow inthect!"

CHAPTER - 22

WALK SOFTLY AND CARRY A BIG SHTICK

As luck would have it, the boys were well underway by the time the second scouting party passed the great orange tree.

These were not hardened veterans like the last unfortunate two, but were mere light riders. Fast moving scouts ready for quick retreats.

These riders had already passed the boys ten miles back along the road and didn't know it. They would ride all the way to Briarwood without seeing any sign of the bounty hunters *or* their targets.

Luckily the boys had decided to get off the road and travel through the forest; after ambushing the last two guys who crossed their paths. Grarr instinctively knew there would be more to come, and he insisted they move faster so as to reach Durik and me before the worst could happen.

There would be several scouting parties who would ride down that road, and much more to follow before all was said and done.

Raz had already filled them in on Durik's and my situation, as far as he knew. He had then gone on far ahead to make sure the woodlands were clear of enemies.

Grarr moved silently through the bushes—testament to his

experience with heavy armour and surprise tactics. He used his cloak, tightly wrapped around his body to muffle the sounds of his complex suit of plates, iron bands, and intricate rings.

Each time another scouting party came, he had already picked up their scent and informed Beornag. Then the two would wait for the enemy to come *too close.*

Fortunately, they were not forced to dispatch anyone else on that evening, and the riders passed by quickly on their strange horse-like creatures, unaware of the presence of monsters beyond the trees.

Beornag did not move like a Troll at all. His kind was made to move through thick forest despite their enormity. He had removed his chain armour and was now virtually invisible to the naked eye. His reddish-brown fur was highlighted with grays and reddish-browns, which made him almost undetectable among the autumn foliage.

He could stop on a silver coin, completely still, and become almost part of the surrounding woods and bushes. His camouflage was near legendary. Wait a sec...come to think of it, technically, it *was* legendary.

In some areas of the world, Hill Trolls were considered to be *only* legend.

In these mundane places, it was common for some people to follow the tracks of elusive Hill Trolls, casting their huge footprints in plaster, collecting odd tufts of fur, and reporting blurred and shaky encounters.

These intrepid adventurers would make up strange names for Hill Trolls and travel great distances to try and spot one. They would amass great heaps of slightly shady evidence and claim the creatures to be real. Of course they *were* real, but those few folks who believed in Hill Trolls, were considered to be crackpots and lunatics.

The Hill Trolls in turn found all of this to be hilarious and actually planted tufts of fur, stomped their feet (sometimes while doing elaborate dances), and made surprise appearances, simply to freak people out with a chance encounter and to preserve the legend.

Indeed, that whole area of the world became a sort of Hill Troll vacation spot, where Hill Trolls could go and play practical jokes on unsuspecting Humans.

Other Humans created an entire economy based on monster sighting tourism. People visiting the area might see Hill Trolls (or whatever name they might call them, and who, unbeknownst to those same tourists, were also on vacation), and have an amazing tale to tell afterward.

Meanwhile, the Trolls, who were not number savvy enough to cash in on the whole arrangement, found solace in the opportunity to have a great laugh at some schmuck trying to paint a picture of them really fast before they ran off into the forest.

While still others would tell horrific stories in the late evenings, around their fires and hearths. Stories about their own local forest ape, yeti, or whatever name they had given it. The stuff that makes children hurry home before dark.

No kidding.

By nightfall the boys had reached the camp and eaten the gory meal Raz had prepared, consisting of dead things—straight up. He had travelled back to the camp, ahead of Grarr and the Troll, to do just that.

Grarr at least cooked some of the meat, and Beornag collected some edible foliage and wild fruit. Raz ended up eating the rest, which was perfectly fine with him.

As they ate, Raz filled them in on what had happened before becoming separated from Durik and me. He spoke of the Stealer, and Durik's victory against it. "Little brrrother hurrrtssss it bad, he doessss. Sssendsss it runninnnng back to itssss massssterrr."

He mentioned the Gnomes, and how Durik and I had found them in the forest and brought them back to camp, and of how we had sent them ahead to Briarwood, leaving one of their group behind to guide Durik and me through the fortress inside the mountain.

He also mentioned how that same Gnome had returned several hours later with many of his kind following him, and how he reported that Durik and I were going on ahead, and that he and the boys should attempt to find us as soon as possible.

Raz had then sent the new Gnomes on the same path as the original few. They would sooner or later meet up and continue on to Briarwood, hopefully.

Grarr lit his stone pipe and handed it to Beornag. "So...altogether Durik and the Redeye have been missing for almost a day, right?"

"Yesssss. Give or take an hourrrrr orrrr twooo," Raz replied.

They were startled just then, when the blasts of a great horn sounded out in the distance. It echoed off the massive peaks to the southwest and throughout the forest. Again, and again it blared out and was joined by many others. Soon after, came the drums of war.

"Raz, get up there and see what that is. Come right back, we may need a hand before long," Grarr rasped before turning to Beornag.

As Grarr was speaking, Raz leapt across the glade, mounting Eekadinosaur, and the two climbed silently into the sky.

Grarr then turned to Beornag, "Bud, listen. I am sorry I got us into this. I should have followed my gut feeling and turned that Elf away that night she came a-sobbing." His palm moved across his tattooed scalp.

"Durik and the Redeye are probably dead. There is an army on the move toward Briarwood by the sound of it. *You* missed the target puking contest..."

"Grarzy, Grarzy, Grarzy, buddy. Yooze is like Ize's bestest friend on da whole planet. Maybe even da whole world? Yooze doesn't have t' say sorry t' Ize." He smiled showing his many huge, square, omnivore's incisors.

"'Sides…Ize is acshully havin' fun. Weeze ain't beat yet, Grarr. Durik's practicalitly indestructible, and da old guy's got some real powa up 'is sleeves. Ize seent 'im use it. It ain't no joke. D'ere's a good chance d'at d'ose guys is still kickin' bad guy butt somewhere out d'ere."

Grarr began extinguishing the small fire as he continued. "Depending on what Raz has to say when he returns, we may have to part ways in order to complete this mission." He began to check and double check his inventory. "Two veteran Talotians are one thing…"

"Um, Ize is pretty sure *d'at* is two t'ings d'ere Grarzy," he interrupted. "Ize been practicing numbuhs wit' da old guy, and he said Ize's mastered one t' five."

Grarr ignored him. "An army is something altogether different." He sighed, and then stood straight and tall, his great sword on his back, a large crossbow there as well. A very finely made belt pouch, probably bottomless, was at his left hip, and his new, terrible dagger was at his right.

His armour was black as night and did not shine. His black-green skin and the many blacker tattoos on his head added to the ominous, fearsome visage of the Urk battle master.

"We have worked way too hard to lose everything to a poncy sorcerer and his army of amateurs." He snarled as he paced, his red and black cape billowing and writhing like a living drop of blood in a glass of water.

Beornag had seen this before. Grarr's cape sometimes acted as though it were alive and would move on its own accord. It once leapt from Grarr's back to cover the Troll and hide him from an enemy, while Grarr dispatched the foe and saved the Injoke's life.

"I will not allow all we have worked for to go to waste because of some snivelling bookworm who hides behind his pathetic minions." He was building up a rage unlike any he had ever expressed before.

"Grarzy…yooze okay, bud?" the Troll asked real concern in his voice. "Weeze is gonna be okay. T'ink about it; Briarwood's got a decent awmy, and a navy too. Okay, it's an *old* navy, which means all da uniforms is prob'ly made in sweat shops and d'at sucks, but still—"

"We will know better when Raz returns. Gather your things we leave this place as soon as he reports back." His red, glowing eyes became even redder as he puffed on his stone pipe, releasing wisps of the sweet vapours from the Goblin head cheese in the calm evening air.

Beornag finished breaking camp. His backpack was huge and so had a larger opening than any bag the rest of us could carry. This allowed him to be able to fit large, folded tents and small livestock, and even the odd pile of corpses inside!

In fact, as you will soon read, there were and still are things in there that I dare not imagine, and even more that he has forgotten all about completely. That screaming Dwarf for instance. Remember, the one who was yelling profanities? I haven't seen him since he got stuffed back into that bag! I have to assume that he was a bad guy.

Not long after, a shadow passed over the moon, and Raz returned. He filled the Troll and Grarr in on what he had seen from on high: a large military force combing the mountainside and the road leading up a hidden pass four miles west and south. They were coming from a giant gate situated at the end of the mountain road.

He saw two caravan wagons broken to bits, a few hundred feet beneath the gates, at the bottom of a cliff face. There was no sign of

Durik or me, and the soldiers he had spotted were all of the giant rat variety.

"Only the rats?" Grarr asked, seemingly relieved.

"Yesssss, only ratssss," Raz replied, licking his lips. "Makesssss Raz verrrrry hungrrrrry."

"Don't worry big guy. You will get your chance to chow down on them soon enough." Grarr was still worried—really pissed off—but worried too.

The Troll knew him well enough to see that clearly, even through the Urk's almost impenetrable poker face.

"Raz , it's time to go to work, bud." Grarr announced.

"Oh, gooooody, good. Raz lovessss worrrrkinnnng. Say what Raz doessss, Grrrrarrrrr, pleasssse ssssayyyy." He was elated at the prospect of being trusted with something important.

"We need you to return to Briarwood," Grarr explained, "and warn them about this army of rat things being so close to the city. Tell them to recall the patrols and bring the locals all in behind the walls. We do not know their exact size but if they need bugles to signal with, they are at least as big as a battalion. Go as fast as Eek will carry you. Destroy any enemies along the way that you can identify. After that, come back here. We will either be right in this spot or we will be attempting to breach those gates."

He looked at them both and his voice softened. "Guys, we may very well be facing an army. With only three of us, we do not have much of a chance. We do not know our enemy's strengths or weaknesses, and they have either slain or captured almost half of our force with the Redeye and Durik."

He rubbed his eyes, "I won't lie and tell you I haven't considered cutting our losses and going back, but Durik is one of us, and so is the Redeye now, and we have to show this guy we are not to be trifled with." He snarled, showing his razor sharp, perfectly white teeth. "Time to bring on the hurt."

Raz once again mounted up and took flight on Eekadinosaur. Soon they were well out of sight.

"What now?" Beornag asked as Raz disappeared over the treetops. The drums were lowering in volume, which meant they were either moving away or there were less of them now.

"We find those gates," he replied.

Grarr began heading southwest, his cape wrapped tightly around him, while Beornag followed not *too* far behind. They kept within sight of each other, yet a good distance apart, should one be detected by the enemy the other could maintain surprise and counteract appropriately.

It took an hour or more before they came upon the first Scave.

"Da redeye wasn't kiddin'. Deez guys are all rat people and deys is all wearin' armour," the Troll observed.

"The trick here is to get by them and then past the gates," Grarr whispered, ignoring whatever the Troll was on about.

The two moved slower now and stayed still on several occasions so as not to be detected. They climbed over stones and gravel on their stomachs and hid in grassy areas. All the while the Scave were moving about, seemingly everywhere. It was a miracle that they were not detected simply because of their size.

Soon it was close to daybreak and they were now within sight of the massive gates. Here they found a good vantage point, on a massive boulder that jutted out and over the road leading to the fortress entrance. Once in position Grarr reported that just beneath them were the signs of battle.

Blood stained the ground, and the signs of large objects being pushed over the cliff were obvious. The smell of ammonia was thick in the air.

"Durik took a leak here," he said, the Troll agreeing with a nod.

From there they could see that beyond the great portcullis and iron doors was a large courtyard, and to either side, were many open windows that were now starting to fill with shadowy movement. The Scave were retreating from the impending sunlight and returning to their lookout vantages.

It was all Grarr could do to keep Beornag from rushing the gates in rage once he had seen the many pikes and lances lining the road ahead, each with a tiny victim impaled on the shaft.

Crows and other scavengers had gathered and feasted during the day. Even as they watched in horror (Grarr was hardly moved by such a site, so Beornag was the only one really horrified), several Human soldiers were exiting the gates with slaves in a caged wagon. These, they were obviously planning to impale and add to the collection along the roadway.

Their tiny voices could be heard whimpering and crying, begging for mercy. They were all old, sickly and injured Gnomes, with a few small children as well. It was obvious from their bruised and battered forms that they had been tortured and abused.

The Troll covered his eyes. "Tell me when it's ova, Grarzy. Ize can't bear t' watch."

"We're not going to watch," Grarr snarled. "We are going to save those people."

He took his crossbow from his back and loaded it with a painful looking bolt. He then lay prone on top of the rock and watched for a moment.

There were three Human guards. One guiding the mule pulling the wagon, one pushing another wagon full of long sharpened wooden poles, and the last was armed with a shield and long sword. This last one was the lookout and defender of the others.

As they moved toward an area where there weren't any impaled Gnomes, the armed one spat at the prisoners and mocked them.

"Talotians," Grarr growled. "What the hell are they doing so far north?" He hated them.

"Couldn't tell ya," Beornag spoke. "What's tallow shins anyway?

Does deys have waxy an' soft leg bones or sump'n?"

"Remember when we...wha—?" Grarr paused in mid-sentence. Then, "Never mind. Remember when we first met? You were being surrounded by all those guys with horns on their helmets, and they turned and started running when they saw me? Remember the way they treated you, and how they all freaked when they saw *me*?" he asked.

"Remember how cruel and purely evil they seemed by the way they acted—like it was all very natural to be that completely cruel and sadistic?"

"Yeah. D'ose was some real bad guys," Beornag said scratching his head. "But weeze fought d'ose guys and killed 'em...Oooo! Do yooze mean d'at d'ose d'ere guys are da undead forms a d'ose same..."

"No, no. Listen," Grarr interrupted. "These guys are the same species and nation as those guys in that bar—Talotians. They're cruel, mean, merciless cutthroats, every one of them. Talotians are so vile that even *my*—" He suddenly caught himself in the middle of saying something he was not willing to finish.

Glaring at his target, he spat again and took aim with the crossbow. "I want you to stay here and be quiet. I will draw them off, and when I do, you free those prisoners and get them to safety. We will meet up here, on this rock in an hour. Okay?"

"Got it," Beornag replied.

Schtoonk was the sound of the bolt as it pierced the Talotian guard's breast plate and skewered his evil heart. He fell over the side of the cliff, unable to make a sound, in shock, and a split second from his final breath.

Grarr was on the move as soon as the bolt was unleashed. He leapt over boulders while drawing his vicious crimson handled great sword. His cloak billowed out behind him as he took great leaps over stones and down the mountain side toward the Talotians.

In a matter of seconds he had descended the slope and in one final leap he was no more than fifty feet from his quarry.

"GRRRRRRAAAAAAARRRRRRRRR!!" No lion could make that sound. No bear, no wolf, no creature in the world.

To them, his name, when roared in fury, was itself a magical power. A weapon of fear and terror.

Even Beornag could feel a certain panic in his gut from the sound of Grarr unleashing his fury in such a way. The Troll had never heard Grarr make such a sound before. He felt as though he might be losing hold of who Grarr was. His friend really was a monster!

There was a blood rage within Grarr now, a force that had been summoned, a deep, buried hateful force, not unlike madness.

Grarr was still Grarr, but at the sight of the Talotians he was overwhelmed with what seemed like an insatiable hunger, to kill them all without mercy while causing terror in his victims.

If it were not for the knowledge that Grarr was doing all of this, storming a castle alone, risking his life and using himself as bait in order to rescue the poor defenceless Gnomes, Beornag would have thought his long-time friend and companion had actually become mad with fury, or worse—*evil*.

In truth, Beornag had seen Grarr in battle many times, and once against Talotian slave hunters, but Grarr had never screamed his name is such a way during any previous encounters. This was something different.

Meanwhile, the enemy stood paralyzed with abject terror. At first they were unable to move, but as he made that final leap and landed onto the gravel road, one of them let go of the mule's reins and ran for the gates.

Beornag wondered how this was all supposed to work. Grarr was supposed to lead them away from the gates, not chase them up *to* the gates. He watched, confused, but entertained.

The other guard who had been carrying some of the impaling

poles, dropped them to the ground in an attempt to also make a run for the safety of the fortress. They didn't even bother to try and fight. They ran like they recognized their own ghosts.

"GRRRRAAAAAAARRRRRRRR!" This time it was even more intense than the last.

To the Talotians, the sound his voice echoed off the mountain side and seemed to fill every nook and cranny of their being.

Grarr paused at the prison cart and glared at the contents, his first victim was just then smashing against the rocks, hundreds of feet below, with a crossbow bolt sticking from his chest.

With an ungodly screech, the mule pulling the cart took one look at this menacing new horror and collapsed to the ground, dead from a heart attack.

Beornag was certain Grarr was about to reach through the bars and grab a Gnome for a snack. Fear took over just then and he covered his eyes, not wanting to see what happened next.

The prisoners all cowered, clinging to one another, screaming and crying in terror. Some were desperately trying to open the lock and escape from the terrible menace that was Grarr in full battle lust.

His cloak billowed in the still air like it was a living creature, rearing up behind him, poised to attack anyone foolish enough to face this monster.

A long, red beam of needle thin light danced about, streaming from his monocled left eye as he snarled and roared. He reached down and grabbed one of the spears dropped by the would-be impaler, licked his thumb and held it high, then he closed one eye and focused on his target through his monocle.

The beam danced down the road and found a place between the man's shoulder blades. A short moment later he launched the makeshift spear into the air with a mighty grunt.

The heavy, sharpened, hardwood pole soared through the air at least sixty feet above the ground and was lost in the glare of the early morning sun.

Even as it was flying toward a place where no one, as of yet, had been, he drew his cross bow, loaded it, dropped to one knee and took aim.

Schtoonk.

The bolt flew past the impaler and struck the mule guide in the nape of the neck. It was instant death, and just in time for the impaler to witness his comrade's demise.

The mule guide fell forward into the gravel covered roadway. His teeth smashed against stone and his neck broken in several places as he bounced off his face, somersaulting forward down the road.

A split second after the crossbow victim hit the ground, the long wooden spear fell from the sky, and just as the iceman had turned his head to see if he was being pursued, it found its mark between the villain's shoulders. The pole went through his body and lodged in the ground; the man died, impaled on his own instrument of evil.

Grarr then went to the front of the wagon where the mule had died of cardiac arrest.

With one mighty sweep of his sword, Deathwind he disconnected the dead animal from the wagon and braced his left foot against the front axle. "Grrrrr." He snarled, straining against the weight of the cart.

"Graaaarrrr." He growled and with one slow but mighty push he sent the wagon moving down the gentle slope of the road.

Even as this was happening the denizens of the fortress were being alerted and the great doors were being unbarred, surely to let loose something terrible upon the Urk intruder.

"*GRRAAAAARRRRRR!!*" his mighty, two-handed sword, was quickly driven into the ground in front of him.

"*GRRRAAAARRRRRRRRR!!*" Twenty crossbow bolts lay within easy reach, and the weapon was reloaded.

"GRRRRAAAAAAARRRRRRRRRRRR!!" Five impaling poles were sticking from the ground at his left side.

"COME OUT AND DIE!" he screamed. "YOUR END IS HERE!" He roared at the top of his lungs in the Talotian tongue, heralding their doom.

"I AM *HIM*!! I HAVE YOUR KLUGHAST, DON'T YOU WANT HIM, YOU GUTLESS SWINE?!"

Beornag began to move down the opposite face of the great boulder in the road's bend. He knew it wasn't Goblin, Grarr was speaking. He had heard that before. It had lots more spitting and choking in it.

This was the language of the Injoke's oldest enemies. The ones who had enslaved him when he was much younger. The ones who murdered his parents. Their word for Beornag's people was Klughast.

Grarr was challenging them to battle in their drawling language, and he was speaking it flawlessly, like it was natural for him.

Rocks and gravel slid down the hill, as the Troll caused a minor landslide in his decent from the giant boulder, covering part of the road with debris.

"NOT A SINGLE ONE OF YOU WILL WALK AWAY!!" the fearsome Urk roared again. His voice carried like a lion across the forest canopy.

Birds took sudden flight and small animals ran in the opposite direction of the sound.

Then the gates opened and a large force of Talotians, in a phalanx formation, stood in the open threshold to the great hall beyond.

"YOU!" he roared in Humanese now. "YOU KNOW WHO I AM, DON'T YOU, TALOT SCUM!! I WILL END YOU THIS DAY! ALL OF YOU!

"GRRRAAAAAAAAAAAARRRRRRRRRRRRRRRRRR!!"

CHAPTER - 23

HOLY SHIT!

Beornag reached the base of the massive stone and reached out into the road with a long tree-like arm. As the wagon arrived at the bend, he grabbed it before it went over the edge, and pulled it quickly behind the boulder.

Grarr was yelling something else at the "tallow shins" and this was the Injoke's cue to rescue the slaves, or at least he assumed it was, since the original plan had gone to the toilet for some reason.

The Gnomes had *already* been terrified at the notion of being impaled. Then it was being eaten by an Urk, and *then* it was going over the side of the mountain. When they finally saw a giant reach out onto the road and drag their prison cart behind a massive outcrop of stone, many of them fainted, and one even had a heart attack right there in the cart!

Beornag then realized he was unable to speak Gnomish and tried something to calm the Gnomes within the jail cart. "Cheese," he smiled at them, speaking in common. "Really stinky cheese in Ize's boots!" He kept smiling and nodding, as though he knew exactly what he was doing.

They screamed even more.

"Pickle? Hows about *herb*?" He kept referencing things from

✳ 359 ✳

his experience with me, hoping something might work.

"Um…crap. No! Not crap! Um…hootspa!?" He struggled, trying desperately to calm them down. "Shorts! I gotta change my shorts?! Ooo, ooo, Money!? Um…Holy Shiddumbuzzin! No? Nothin'?"

They continued to scream and panic.

One of them however, an older male with a wooden stick for a left leg—who had just successfully conducted CPR on his comrade—spoke out and tried to help calm the others.

"Hey! Yooze! Little guy wit' da tootpick fer a leg! Yeah yooze!" he whispered loudly to the little Gnome who was now acknowledging *his* attempts to calm the group. "Can yooze undastands what Ize is sayin'?"

"Me is unda-ting. Titan of Cloud Walker be you?" he asked with piteous hope in his glossy eyes.

All of the other Gnomes now began to calm down. They looked back and forth from Beornag's giant face, which pretty much covered their entire field of view, to the elder Gnome speaking to him. There were several infants in the group, and they continued to bawl as those holding them attempted to calm the tiny things.

Beornag could not bring himself to disappoint these people. To him they were almost family. He too had been a slave once, a long time ago. He smiled at them, and they all seemed to have one last hope in their eyes.

Without even knowing what Titan of the Cloud Walker meant, he replied. "Sure, if d'at's what it takes t' git yooze all t' shut up an' listen, okay. Ize is from the sky jumpa—"

"Walker!" the Gnome corrected.

"Yeah. D'at's what Ize meant. Da sky walk—" he tried again.

Cloud!" the Gnome offered again.

"Cloud? Oh, cloud…Oh! *Cloud*! Cloud Walka. D'at's Ize," he lied.

"Nooo! You be Titan of Cloud Walker. Come to make Undatings all saved and happiness filled!" the Gnome half hoped and half demanded.

"Yeah!? Really? Ize means...yeah! Yooze tell em, little guy!" He turned to the rest of the Gnomes, still smiling and nodding, "What he just said. Plus Ize is da great and powerful Injoke, Beornag. Ize is gonna save all yooze guys. Would yooze like d'at? Hmmm?" he offered, hoping someone would make a decision so he could get on with the plan.

Finally, the elder spokesman turned to the others and spoke some language the Injoke could not understand. He then turned to the Troll and said, "Okay."

"Hang on little guys. Ize is gonna lift this whole cart and carry yooze off inta da sunset, t' freedomizations, and safetinesses." He took the wagon up, under his right arm.

Using his free arm and his legs he moved, not unlike a great ape, along the road and eventually over the edge and down the slope to the forest, hundreds of feet below. It took him only twenty minutes to reach the bottom, where he ripped the locked and barred doors off the wagon and freed the Gnomes.

He pointed in the direction of the campsite and said, "Yooze go d'at way until yooze finds where weeze camped last night. D'ere's gonna be lots a blood and fur bits and bones from Raz's suppa."

"Okay, Titan," the spokesman said. "I be Tinkletink."

He turned and spoke quickly to the group, and they all began to move slowly away, each looking reverently back over their shoulders at the Troll, one last time.

"Okay d'en. Yooze find a bush, or a rock maybe, t' tinkle tink behind though." He winked and waved goodbye to everyone until they were well underway, then he ascended the mountainside again—this time pausing to look out across the top of the forest canopy for any sign that the Gnomes might face resistance. When he was as sure as he could be that their path was safe, he continued upward.

Like some mythical, giant, great ape, he scaled the cliff, swinging and leaping from various stones, steadily upward. At one point he disturbed some of the cliff's denizens and spent twenty minutes being harassed by the many nesting birds in the cracks and crannies of the stone precipice. He swatted at them and roared as he ascended the mountain, half a sandwich in one hand.

Another half way up (as he describes it) he noticed a great dark storm cloud rolling over the mountain top. It quickly passed however, and he was glad that he was not going to get soaked.

Soon after, he reached the top and looked around for enemies, and when he found none, he made his way up the empty road, expecting to hear the sounds of battle ahead. Instead, there was dead silence. Even the flies and carrion birds had left for some reason.

He soon reached the tight bend in the road where the huge stone hung out over the wide path.

Mumbling a song about fur tufts and footprints, he climbed over the rockslide he had caused earlier, and made his way to the top of the slanted boulder, where he could get a better vantage point.

Here, he finished his song, adjusted his beanie, and took a quick look over the boulder's ledge to see if there were any clues as to what had become of Grarr.

"Gosh," he whispered, looking down at the road, eyes wide in shock, at a scene of carnage.

A large pile of Human corpses was now about fifty feet in front of where Grarr was last seen taunting the fortress and preparing for war. A bloody trail of other Talotian corpses led all the way to the portcullis of the gate house.

A tear formed in his eye then, Gnome bodies still lined the

road, impaled and in various degrees of decay. Hundreds of little people impaled on spears and javelins and long spikes of every description.

He growled under his breath, "Tallow shins." It was a deep rumble like an avalanche from afar. His small black eyes, close together under a huge unibrow, glossed over and filled with sorrow at what lay before him.

With a steady growl he moved back and put his wide posterior against the cold stone of the mountainside. There, he tried to think of something to make himself laugh but was unable. His fists clenched so tightly his knuckles creaked like the rigging of some huge sailing ship.

A tear escaped his left eye, and he sniffed back a three fluid ounce snot wad. Spitting it out, he thought of the annual target puking contest at the Gruel and Grog. It was happening that very night in only about sixty-eight hours, or maybe it was six to eight hours. The Troll had no concept of how to tell time, and mostly faked it.

What did it matter? He was missing it one way or another.

In fact, the Gruel and Grog was holding its eleventh annual Projectile Vomiting Pukolympics – starting that evening with the opening ceremonies where, Beornag, Injoke of Ulm, was supposed to conduct a sermon (for him a stand-up comic routine) and be the master of ceremonies. Beornag was also representing the entire Docks District as well as acting as *house puker*.

Oh, the pageantry, the prestige, the free beer and pretzels!

Another tear later and he came to realize that Grarr was late. It was not like Grarr, to be late. In fact, it was a real pet peeve of Grarr's to be late.

Something was wrong.

Beornag sat for some time longer wondering what he should do. Then it hit him. He should sit and try and think of what he should do next; so he did. He also had a snack and washed it down with some sour goat's milk.

Some time later, when he was picking his nose, and humming a song about old ladies wrestling in raspberry sauce (don't ask), he remembered he had forgotten to remember to do something he had earlier forgotten to do; all because he forgot to keep thinking about remembering to do it.

It was just that simple.

He stood up and descended the rockslide to the road. If Grarr was not coming back, he might be inside already.

"Just like d'at big gooba Ize just hocked out," he thought to himself. "Now Ize has gotta break all o' d'ose guys outta d'ere. T'ink, Beornag! T'ink o' sump'n. D'ere's gotta be a way." He scratched his brow.

"D'is place is just like a big nose fulla lots o' boogas, but Ize needs t' pick only da specificalized, (he paused to count on his fingers) t'ree boogas d'at Ize wants, an' Grarr, Durik, an' da Redeye, is d'ose very same gobs a semi-hardened snot." It was a revalation.

Just then something else occurred to him. He remembered that he was forgetting about the power he had so long pledged every part of his being to keep and use for the betterment of all.

Laughter and joy were his powers. Holy powers given to him by his own deity, Ulm the Freaking Hilarious; or so he was fond of claiming.

You see, only myself and the boys had ever witnessed him use the power of his all mighty deity. Most everyone else refused to believe him, or thought it was all just a comedy routine, which was, of course, all the better for him.

He dropped to one knee. Then he changed knees. Then he changed back again. Then again, and again a few more times. Then he tried two knees and decided finally that the first knee was the best one.

Then he changed knees one more time to be sure but finally changed back to his initial choice in the end, satisfied his decision was based on thorough research and good science.

Finally, he began to pray. "A Hill Troll walks inta a rat's nest and says, 'Hey! So d'is is where my mudduh-in-law goes t' get 'er hair done.'"

His prayer said, he stood, turned toward the ascending road of impaled Gnomes, and opened his eyes.

"Tallow shins," he grumbled, again.

Almost reluctantly, he moved forward, one step at a time.

In truth, he wanted to wait for Raz, but Grarr could be meeting a grizzly fate.

Actually, come to think of it...that would be impossible as Grizzly Fate wouldn't be able to climb a mountain road on account of a bum foot, and being a simple dish washer at the Grog, she would also have no place being in this fortress in the first place.

Grarr could however be in trouble, and it was time for Beornag to do what he did best.

With a deep breath and long exhale, he paused at the first impaled corpse and decided to take it down. Nodding—satisfied that his plan was brilliant—he decided to take the next few down as well. He moved forward this way for several minutes, until he had collected as many impaled Gnomes as he was able to carry in one hand—about forty-seven.

He did so solemnly, and with as much respect and reverence as he was able, apologizing to each one as he pulled them out of the ground—spike and all.

He then said a few prayers as he passed the others. "Aw, don't be a stick in da mud...Hang around. Ize'll come by layta t' see how yooze is doin'...Point taken...D'ey really stuck it t' yooze guys, eh?" All of this from lips, quivering with barely held back tears.

It is said that a Hill Troll's heart weighs seventy-three pounds, empty of blood; Beornag's had to be at least seventy-five.

He stopped at the great doors and waited a few minutes, the impaled Gnomes still in his hand like a giant, tree-like collection of morbid lollipops. No one seemed to notice he was standing there. This was amazing considering his size alone. He had walked right under the open portcullis and into the courtyard. None of the Scave in the alcoves and open windows had picked up his scent.

What the Troll was not realizing was that Grarr had already taken away the attention of most of the Talotians and only the Scave remained. Though sensitive, their sense of hearing was not very advanced, and their sense of smell was slightly less acute. The Scave relied mostly on their eyes, which were no better than the average Human. They simply could not smell Troll over what they were used to smelling, which was the reek of decaying and rotting Gnomes on sticks.

His collection of dead Gnomes was masking his own scent perfectly, and as such, Beornag was able to walk right past the wall of Scave guards hiding in their alcoves and windows. They remained in their places of sanctuary around the open portcullis, still blinded by the daylight.

Obviously, he was also under the divine influence of his deity, though it did not even occur to him that this was so. His prayers had conjured an aura of trust and charismatic appeal that had been acting like a buffer against the senses of his enemies, making him seem like an ally.

He now stood inside a great arch, between two empty guard houses, in front of a huge set of double doors, humming a song about sausages and some guy in a garbage can.

Finally he gave up and yelled, "Halloooooo! Anybody home in d'ere?! Ize is heeeere! Da enta*taaaain*ment!" He actually *did* have a plan.

Soon after a large door within the great doors opened, and two giant armoured rats came out wielding shields and terrible looking spiked maces. They ran up to him and he stepped forward startling them to a complete stop.

"Yooze!" He pointed at one of the guards and spoke in common Humanese, "It's about time! Does yooze knows how long yooze has made da great Pelvis Grizzly wait out here, while d'ere's brutes an' do goodas wanderin' da mountainside? Hmmm? Well? Does yooze?"

He then stepped even closer to one of them. "Yooze's masta pays a lotta gold t' have Ize come out here and entertain yooze loozuhs, yooze knows?"

He looked at the other one. "Well? Whatta yooze waitin' fuh? Lead Ize t'da mess hall, an' make a pit stop at da bat'room too—Ize been holding in da most giant turd f' hours."

He handed one of the impaled Gnomes to the first Scave, who actually accepted it. "Gnome on a stick?"

The second Scave then moved ahead, back to the small door within the larger two. He screeched an order and moments later the great doors were opened, and he was gesturing for Beornag to follow him.

Inside, there were many giant Scave, as well as a few Goblins, lots of Cave Trolls and other creatures the Injoke did not even recognize. They all gave way to the giant Scave who were leading him.

He followed close behind trying not to look *too* inconspicuous. He also decided to find out exactly what that word meant when all of this was over.

In the meantime, it meant waving his arms about in a flourishing manner; thanking his fans; blowing kisses and bowing as he passed through the two massive iron doors in the gatehouse and ascended a ramp into the fortress.

"T'ank yooze. T'ank yooze so much, Ize's loyal fans, Ize wants t' t'ank yooze all." He smiled as he walked between a platoon of Cave Trolls and a group of man-sized Scave in scale armour.

At one point he paused briefly to pick up a shiny stone he noticed on the ground. After placing the beautiful crystal in his pouch to give to Grarr for his slingshot, if he ever found him, he continued on his way, elated at the adoration of his fans.

"Gnome on a stick? How 'bout yooze? Like a nice Gnome on a stick?" He passed the impaled Gnomes out to the nearest non-Human guards, as if they were circus treats, and many accepted them graciously.

His ruse was working perfectly.

Understand, kids, that in the Injoke's heart and especially his mind, he believed that the impaled Gnomes were no longer needing their bodies (true enough) and that using them in such a morbidly hilarious way, and to rescue many more of their species on top of that, was actually a righteous and heroic thing by fooling all those guards and getting inside—sort of undetected.

I, as the new Gnomish religious leader, have decided that this was an acceptable use of the bodies of the dearly departed, and it was in fact a form of post-mortem vengeance upon their captors and murderers—sort of their way of helping out the cause, taking one for the team, that sort of thing.

He later explained to me that when he got the idea he had actually been digging through his backpack, searching for half of a sandwich he had put there a few months previous to meeting me, and couldn't remember where he had placed it within the pack.

Then it hit him. It would be the last place he would think to look, in front of his face. He had *already* been eating it and was distracted by all the fuss. It was in his hand the whole time. Therefore, he had decided to hide right in front of the enemy—and it was actually working.

He had only wished I had been there to make a few dead

Gnomes levitate, so he could tie long strings to their big toes and float them around.

He was adamant that one day there would be a way to float giant monsters high up above people's heads and use them as attractions in parades and festivals and such. Crazy right?

"Gnome on a stick? Here, buddy. Enjoy. D'ere's plenty more where d'at came from," he said to one particularly large Cave Troll. "Don't miss da show, eh? T'night in da mess hall. Bring a friend." He smiled and shook hands with many of them.

He made sure to look around, while stalling for time, and took notice of the short stone safety barrier and the balconies along the inner curved wall of the passageway he was in. He could see noxious steam and the flickering lights of massive gas fires deep below.

"Ooo! Nice volcano fellas! Ize bet da heatin' bills here is dirt cheap. Get it? Dirt?" He winked and pointed his index finger at them.

One Cave Troll actually asked for Beornag to sign an autograph. "Ummm. Peez makes it says…Ummm…Me had great time wiff Terdbreff. Love secret Casso. All me bess'. Peh'viss."

"Here ya go Terdbreff. Love da helmet. See yooze t'night."

Another lifelong fan made, they continued through the intersection where they took a right turn and made their way past another column of armoured Cave Trolls. Once beyond the formidable number of defenders at the gate and grand intersection as it were, he was led around a giant road-like hall, many feet wide and tall, with (go figure) vaulted ceilings.

He and his guides passed by a large troop of medium Scave wearing shoddy leather armour. These were marching in close formation in the opposite direction.

"Hi fellas! Don't miss t'night's show in da mess hall! D'ere's gonna be free food! Here, have a free Gnome on a stick." He passed out the last of his macabre novelty treats and continued on down the grand passage.

After only a few moments they came to a stop and one of the Scave pointed to a door in the wall. Beornag opened it and entered what was a bathroom facility (no it was not the same one that I had been in, but it *was* the very next one down the hall).

Imagine if it was the very same one. Maybe I should have lied and said it was. Oh well too late now.

Where was I?

Oh yeah…

He quickly opened his pack and took out his chain mail cuirass. These stalls were made for Cave Trolls, mostly, and were just a bit too small for him, so he hid behind a partition that separated the bidet from the urinals.

I know, I know. But believe me, Cave Trolls are surprisingly hygienic!

Once he had filled his thirst from the strange water fountain and his chain suit was on and properly adjusted, he took out his huge, leather girdle and wrapped it around his waist.

With a satisfied smile, he then farted.

It was a particularly long fart and he remembered to lift a leg and take a halfway sniff to test the vintage.

Afterwards he chuckled to himself a bit and continued preparing for battle, still farting for at least another minute or two. It was described as an epic fart, but not as epic as the Eupiess Anti-Vampire Undead-Destroyer Fart, (as the Troll liked to refer to that specific gaseous event).

Beornag was not taking any chances though. He took his maul from his backpack and whispered the command to make it grow into its full length. He remembered to hold it to his crotch and watch it grow in the mirror, while laughing quietly to himself.

Still smiling, he farted again. Only, this time it was quite loud, and actually *shook* the mirrors on the wall.

It was followed by him yelling toward the door. "Oooooh. Yeaaaaah ahaaaa. Man, d'at was a satisfyin' bowel movement!" He then flushed a toilet, farted again, only this time silently, and came to stand just inside the door.

"Hey, can one o' yooze guys give Ize a hand in here?" he yelled again. Then he hid behind the door and waited.

Soon enough it opened, and one of the giant Scave entered. As the door closed behind the fiend, it moved into the room, looking around for the Troll.

Beornag moved silently toward the enemy, while it waved the stench of three massive Troll farts from its face. Eventually it was forced to cover its mouth and nose with a piece of toilet paper it had pulled from an empty stall.

It actually gagged once. A freakin' rat gagged! Can you imagine such a thing? That should give you a better idea of the sulfuric and acrid potency of a Troll fart, and perhaps a bit more respect for yours truly. I have survived several—not sure if I'm proud of that or not.

Anyway…

At the last stall the Scave was unsuccessful at finding the Troll, and it paused, dumbfounded and confused. These giant Scave were not created for intellect, but for strength and savagery. As a result they were easily persuaded, especially if bribed with food.

This particular Scave was no different and it did not expect a thing. It stood, stupefied, with its back to the Troll as Beornag snuck up from behind. The Injoke quickly grabbed the creature from behind by the chin and the back of the head and twisted violently. There was an audible crunch, and the beast was dead. He caught it in mid-fall and put it quietly on the floor in one of the stalls.

He then recited a prayer as he retrieved his maul and moved to be right next to the exit, "D'ere once was a rat wit' a mace. His ugliest part was his face. But da door hit it square when da Troll kicked it d'ere. Now his blood is all ova da *PLACE!*"

He kicked the exit off its hinges and the Scave outside the door was struck with a four-hundred-pound oaken door, right in its face. Scave *and* door, together flew across the passageway and struck two Cave Trolls on the other side, slamming all three of them against the short balcony wall.

Roaring, the Cave Trolls fell over the top and down into the belly of the volcano. The Scave's neck broke instantly when the door struck him, and his back followed suit when he hit the edge of the wall.

Coincidentally one of his spikes punctured a major artery and when he came to a limp, broken mass on the floor, his blood spewed out and sprayed all over the place, even as far as halfway back across the hall toward the bathroom.

Beornag stepped out of the lavatory, maul in hand. "T'ank yooze! T'ank yooze very much! Ize is here til T'ursday! Don't f'get t' tip ya waita!"

He looked to the right and the passage was empty. He *could* run that way and be deeper in the fortress. But he had no idea where any of his friends were, or where to even start looking.

The *getting by the gate part* was where his plan ended. He was playing everything else by ear. "Ize is missin' improv hour at the Grog," he lamented.

Looking to his left he saw a group of Humans and Scave coming up the passage. They had noticed the stream of blood and the broken pieces of what was once the door to the Troll's lavatory, not to mention the giant mass of silver chain armour and reddish-brown fur wielding a twelve-foot-long tree trunk, filling almost half the passage.

Among the group were three Humans and two giant Scave, as well as at least ten of the Human-sized Scave in the black leather armour. They all wielded scimitars and small round shields.

He had been made, and the cat was outta the bag, as the enemy now headed straight at him.

After throwing the screaming feline at the host of assailants, actually startling them momentarily, Beornag sucked about nine cubic feet of air into his stomach and jumped in the air.

When he came down he opened his huge mouth and vomited a massive stream of what was once a five pound bag of onions, four whole loaves of sour dough bread (buttered), two pounds of wild leek, two pounds of wild blueberries, six pounds of cooked various small game, two pounds of wild aloe, two pounds of crayfish, fourteen pickled eggs, a whole smoked salmon, six pounds of baked beans, a whole wheel of cheese he found in a dumpster (that was only almost all moldy), and half of a seven-month-old ham and mayo hoagie, not to mention the two gallons of sour goat's milk and the keg of beer to wash it all down with—all over the three Humans as they came closer.

At twenty-eight feet away, it was a good hurl. Not a record, but more than enough to make the qualifying heat!

Instantly, the three men fell to the floor gagging and vomiting on each other. This only caused them to vomit even more, and as the Scave closed in they began to slip and slide around in the giant pool of puke.

The cat, unharmed, slinked away down the passage as fast as it could.

Beornag ran past the group, swinging his mighty maul in a great arc only feet from the floor.

All of the Scave were pulverized and sent flying back down the passage, bouncing off the walls, their bodies turned to twisted bags of crushed bone and hemorrhaged meat.

Meanwhile the three Humans were now completely incapacitated so he cracked them each on the head, knocking them out one by one.

Miraculously he avoided getting any of the rancid puke on himself.

Next he moved back toward the gates hoping to find a clue as to where Grarr, Durik or myself were.

"Wait a sec," he thought, stopping and counting on his fingers. "Me, Grarr, Durik, da Redeye...sump'n is wrong here. Ize is only s'posed t' be rescuin' t'ree people. Where'd da fourt' one come from?"

His mathematical revelation was interrupted when he heard another commotion coming from further back toward the gates, just around the curve of the huge passage. The guards had been alerted by the flying bodies of their comrades and the quickly travelling stench of fresh vomit. Now they were converging on the Troll's position, following a rivulet of bile, blood and half-digested nastiness.

There were a lot more enemies in this second wave and he was forced to fall back on a genetic inheritance, used to call potential mates across vast distances of hills and gullies. It came upon him suddenly and instinctively. He had never used it before, as he had always thought that he was the last of his kind, and there were no female Trolls, aka Trollops, left in the world.

He started by breathing in deeply and then slowly, he let out his breath over a series of larynx specific to his species.

So low was the sound at first, that when it hit the many crystalline veins that ran through the mountain, it resonated through most of the fortress as a slow pulsing thrum. As he continued, the pitch gradually rose, and the effect intensified.

In his immediate location, the walls began to crack, while ages old dust fell from seams between the monumental sized stones used in the construction of the great hallway.

Many of the nearby guards, the Scave especially, were now on their knees, holding their ears against the sonic assault.

Still the pitch rose until it sounded like a distorted tuba, only a thousand times louder.

While his foes were incapacitated, the Troll ran down the passage laying about him with his mighty tree of a weapon. As he hooted and hollered with glee, his enemies were bashed against the walls and broken into rag dolls with each advance. He stomped them and kicked them out of his way. Humans and Scave alike were getting the royal crap pounded out of them.

Soon even more guards were coming. Some were running into the passage from halls and open doors, searching for the cause of the alarm. One such open portal was huge, and it opened onto a great staircase going down into what looked like an indoor market.

"Ooo! Stuff!" Beornag roared as he tried to make his way in that direction. Arc after arc of his mighty weapon saw the enemy fall in groups, while others were catapulted through the air smashing against the walls.

He could now see down the corridor and past the gates at the big intersection where he entered the fortress. There, a group of eight Cave Trolls in scale armour, and wielding pole axes, were running toward him several hundred yards ahead. These were almost as big as the Injoke and looked like they meant business.

He roared again, and dust fell from the ceiling—this time accompanied by bits of mortar. The floor cracked and the enemies in the immediate area put their hands over their ears and fell to their knees.

Beornag almost passed out just then. He felt dizzy and would certainly not be able to do that again for some time. His natural subsonic *yodel* sapped a lot of his endurance and another one or two times, forcing that kind of sound out, could drain him enough to make him need real sleep.

Suddenly...oy...the last two Cave Trolls were charging up the passage, looking very angry. At forty feet away, Beornag, once again sucked in an enormous gut full of air and leapt toward them.

Chunky, off-white, foamy, sour, rancid smelling, slimy, steaming, semi-fluidic puke erupted from the Troll's gut and spewed forth from his gaping maw.

It was poetry in motion; athletic performance on a truly monumental scale, challenging the limits of regurgitation! It was the kind of hurl that could inspire generations of Pukolympic champions for years to come.

Forty-three feet two inches and some change.

Hooya!

The Cave Trolls, who were known for their strict hygienic practices, immediately took to puking inside their own helmets. Beornag's own vomit sprayed all over them and most of the passage, creating a pool almost fifteen feet across.

Desperately struggling to stand, they were slipping, falling to the floor, trapped in their own vicious circle of cause-and-effect vomiting. Soon they would drop from exhaustion after suffering agonizing minutes throwing up and then struggling with dry heaves.

He reached the top of the stairs that led down to the market, to see several Humans ascending them with nets and hooked poles.

Reaching into his belt pouch, (another bottomless pouch the size of a normal backpack), he pulled out a big bag of dog shit and threw it at the lead Talotian who was carrying a hooked pole.

Yes, that's what I said, a giant sack of shit!

There was about thirty pounds of dog crap in the huge paper bag, and it was all fresh when it went into the bottomless pouch.

I might have forgotten to mention that our bottomless pouches were also timeless and whatever went in was held in exactly the same state as *when* it went in. I would later suggest we market it as a kitchen appliance for keeping things fresh (but not *his* exact pouch, for reasons that are obvious—to us, anyway).

So, where was I?

Oh yeah…

The huge sack of fresh, mucky crap splattered all over these new guys climbing the stairs.

Screaming in terrified disgust, the man who was the actual target of the sack of crap's full impact was completely covered in fresh shit and falling backwards head over heels down the now shit covered stairs.

Several of the other men slipped and fell in the multicoloured mass of crap now flowing down the staircase. They began gagging from the stench, yelling things like: "It's in my mouth!" and, "My new boots! He ruined my new boots!"

"Boy is *yooze* guys in shit!" the Injoke yelled at them.

One of them had a weak gag reflex and he began to puke on his comrades. This triggered a six-man pukarama, as they fell over, rolling in the mixture and struggling to get their bearings on the slippery, ever increasing mass of vomit and shit, even as they themselves were vomiting on each other so as to create still another vicious circle of apocalyptic regurgitation.

Some of the men actually retreated, screaming in terror and dropping their capture equipment, while a couple stayed and attempted to navigate a way around the ever shifting and oozing shit/barf avalanche.

"He's gotta a bag of shit!" came a voice yelling from the market. Beornag took a quick glance in that direction to see merchants and patrons alike running frantically for the exits.

Guards dropped their weapons and shields and ran out of the massive hall. No one wanted to get splattered in shit. It was the perfect weapon.

Thankfully this was distraction enough for the Injoke to retrieve three more such giant paper bags full of crap and hurl them at anyone who moved. As soon as any guards entered the market and saw a bombardment of feces heading toward them, they ran off calling for reinforcements.

In total he tossed five thirty-pound bags, and seventeen eighty-pound sacks of shit at his enemies and he was never touched by a single assailant once.

After several minutes of throwing shit at people and laughing his head off at them, he descended the shit covered stairs into the empty shit covered market.

Shit was everywhere! He had covered the larger part of the market with the stuff and now you couldn't move without stepping in it. Yet *he* was experienced enough to avoid getting any on *him*, and that in itself was a miracle from Ulm.

He had virtually painted the market with shit, while some of the patrons and merchants added their own puke to the mixture. The mess was cataclysmic. The stairs were absolutely marinated in the worst smelling shit and puke imaginable.

The last two bags were full of waste taken straight from the sewers in Briarwood, just outside the front door to the winery! You cannot imagine the level of shit destruction he caused in that place.

Mercifully, the puke and shit covered guards, who were still puking and slipping in the pools of mingling shit and puke, were quickly dispatched and the merchants who witnessed the shit bombardment and *barfarama* had long since run away, forever traumatized by the whole event.

Beornag was victorious, and he managed to do so without getting a single drop of puke or shit on him anywhere.

He looked around at the empty shit and puke covered market and smiled, "Oh boy, stuff! Ize loves stuff!"

CHAPTER - 24

EXIT, STAGE LEFT

"You *know* who *I* am! GRAAAARRRRRR!" he screamed with rage, beating his chest. "I have come to kill you *all!*" His breath was visible in the cool morning air, like that of some great predator, burning hot with bloodlust.

A phalanx of twenty-five Talotian soldiers, standing with their shields held together like a wall, were sent to face him, but they were now hesitant to move.

This creature they knew from their childhood nightmares; he was the thing their parents warned them about. He was quite literally their *worst* nightmare. They were terrified of him, enough so that they were almost willing to defy their master's will—almost.

"GRRRAAAAARRRRRR!" he roared again and again, challenging the entire fortress to face him. "GRRRRAAAARRRRR RRRRRRR!"

Again, they hesitated. Their fear of this monster was instinctual.

He was surprised when they suddenly seemed to straighten up and once again begin to move. Something else was inside those gates and it was *making* them move.

At first they seemed to stumble a few times, as though there were still some who didn't want to leave the relative safety of the gatehouse.

He took several steps forward, as a few arrows flew past him, shot wide. "Cowards! I will feed on your children! I will erase you from this world!"

Realize, as in the case of Beornag Injoke of Ulm the Freaking Hilarious, evil was a relative term to be defined as the circumstances demanded.

Grarr was no more willing to murder and slay every last Talotian, than he was willing to let the Gnomes in the prison cart and his friend Beornag get caught, and he certainly didn't want to eat their babies. He simply wanted them terrified.

Grarr was very well trained by an extremely powerful being he is hard pressed to speak about. I can tell you that there was a time in Grarr's life when being evil was a natural thing for him, learned from the moment he tore his way into existence from a decaying corpse in the ground.

He was moulded and educated to be a master of war and torture. Created specifically for the purpose of tormenting and killing Talotians. There was some truth in what the Icemen said about him—his reputation and his legend. But that was long ago, and before he ever met the Troll or the rest of us.

Here, however, he remembered those times filled with the screaming and the blood of his victims.

He remembered the burning villages, and cities of Talot shuddering at the very notion of his advance. Back then he showed them no mercy, he showed *no* one *any* mercy.

Suffice it to say that his demon, that thing that haunted him for so many years before he finally cast it off, was beginning to crawl onto his back once more.

He was beginning to hear the drums in his ears.

He longed to feel the warmth of blood spraying all over his body, to once again see the rampant fires and wanton destruction caused by his wrath, to hear the music of his victim's lamentations, their screaming voices and their misery.

He remembered the hatred. He remembered the need to make them suffer, and his joy at doing so.

Back then, he was *mad*.

Closer they came, now fifty feet. They thought they were protected by their shields.

"Fools," he thought.

They moved a few steps closer, literally scuffing their sandals against the gravelled road.

He grinned, showing a maw full of clenched fangs, each a perfect, flat, razor sharp triangle, all white as snow. This was a bite designed to remove chunks with ease. His eyes shone like burning rubies in pools of blackest oil, even in the mid-morning sun.

They were now only thirty feet away.

The air was still.

The silence between his roars was deafening.

Even the flies had left the area. To this day we still have no explanation for that one, but what timing eh?

The soldiers shook suddenly, at the sound of his voice, "GRRRAAAAAARRRRRRRRRRRR!!"

Immediately, three of the soldiers broke ranks and ran for the safety of the fortress.

Grarr took one step back and reached for his great sword, drawing it from the ground where it was stuck. Leaping forward, he swept the spear tips aside with the mighty weapon. He then leapt over his enemies, his right foot landing firmly against the front most shield of the phalanx.

Even then the sound of spears being dropped and the cries of panic meant that three more of the formation had begun their retreat. He did not stop. He used the shield as a ramp and jumped over the group. He sprang off a nearby boulder to continue his momentum, gaining height over the five retreating soldiers.

He landed and rolled, instantly returning to his feet and swinging his great blade. The first of them was already on his way to the ground, his head bouncing down the road toward the others, when the next one stopped in his tracks and attempted to impale the great Urk on his spear.

Grarr turned aside and rolled down the shaft of the weapon, driving the tip of his sword through his assailant's chest. Then, letting go of his sword, he spun around once again.

As that enemy fell to the ground, sword still sticking out of his chest, the mighty battle master flipped the spear he had taken from the first victim to face the next attacker. In one, seemingly well-rehearsed, motion he squatted down and braced the back of the shaft into the gravel.

This Talotian had been running for his life and was not ready for this. He was unable to stop in time and was impaled upon the long spear by his own momentum.

Three were already dead in only seconds.

But then, without warning, *thunk* went the sound of a crossbow bolt piercing metal, flesh and bone. He was shot in the back of his left shoulder and went down from the sheer impact of the missile. The bolt was fired from a light ballista, a weapon designed to kill giants, and the force was enough to break his concentration and make him lose his balance.

As he fell he could see Beornag in the distance, running off with the prison cart under his left arm.

He hit the ground hard and was immediately assailed by the remaining two retreating men. Seeing their greatest nightmare fall with a bolt sticking out of his back, had bolstered their resolve and given them a new courage.

Terrible mistake.

"*GRRRAAAAAARRRRRRRRRR!*" He launched himself off the ground, drawing his vicious dagger and spinning rapidly in the air.

Like a mighty cat he landed in a squatting position as his next assailant's spear was thrust too high, missing its target as he ran past the monster.

Grarr's knife sank deep in the man's gut piercing his liver and severing a major artery. The force lifted the Talotian off the ground, and he slammed the Human's back against the hard gravel and stone.

The soldier lay on the ground leaking black fluid and blood from a vicious wound in his stomach, his back now broken and his skull cracked.

Again, imagine this: this guy is over seven feet tall; has really dark green skin that never seems to sweat. He's bald, and his head is covered in all sorts of tattoos. He weighs in excess of four hundred pounds and can bite a chunk of meat off a cow's leg the size of a big orange.

He has long sharp claws on the ends of fingers strong enough to puncture the average Human's skull, and he can scare the crap out of you just by roaring his own name.

On top of *that* he is wearing full battle plate armour, has glowing red eyes, can leap twelve feet in a straight line, is carrying a six-foot-long black sword, and hates you with a passion.

Get the picture? Scary right?

Then, in one fluid motion, he pulled the dagger from his victim, who fell to the ground, and threw it at the next man in line. As the knife struck *that* Talotian in the throat, Grarr had already grabbed his great sword and ripped it from the dead man, who had been wearing it through his chest.

He turned to face what was left of the phalanx, as another ballista bolt flew past his right ear.

Blood was now leaking into the left sleeve of his armour. His blood, a glowing green substance, slowly began to seep into his chain undercoat.

Unmercifully, the crossbow bolt was making its way deeper.

The pain was mind numbing. The bolt he was pierced with (unbeknownst to him), was actually *designed* to kill *him* specifically, and enchanted with evil magics. Such was the power of Grarr that his will alone prevented it from doing so instantly.

But Grarr had an enchanted weapon as well, and the man with the dagger in his throat was just then experiencing the terrible enchantments that were embedded into it. His blood was spewing everywhere from the mortal wound that the weapon had caused.

The Talotian grasped at the blade and his fingers too were cut, easily. The terrible weapon created wounds that bled more and more with each passing moment. He would bleed out before the fight was even over. His voice a burbling death cry, the man fell to his knees, a blanket of crimson now pulsing from his jugular vein and the multiple cuts on his hands and fingers.

Grarr then turned to face the shield formation, now covered with the blood of their comrades. Shuddering, the men stood paralyzed in terror as the great monster in front of them kicked the bleeding man over the cliff side, drew a slingshot and loaded it with a green-tinted crystal nugget.

Another soul-stone.

The bolt in his shoulder was now beginning to pierce through his shoulder blade. It would soon reach his left lung, but he had to give the Troll a head start.

Another bolt flew past his head. They were getting closer.

He took a quick glance toward the gatehouse, and then turned back to the phalanx.

He looked at them with death in his eyes. Then he turned to the fortress again, just as the Cave Troll wielding the ballista stood up from behind a short stone wall and was about to fire.

He didn't even flinch except to once again grin at his target. Then, simultaneously, he and the Troll fired their weapons at each other.

The two missiles almost hit each other in mid-flight.

Grarr stepped aside and returned to a crouching position, the bolt barely missing him.

The crystal struck the Troll, and in a flash of bright light the beast had vanished.

I had provided Grarr with two magic stones that I had managed to enchant (with much difficulty, I might add) that were enhanced with a hootspa that trapped any struck with them, in a pocket dimension, inside of the stone. The only escape from such prisons came in the form of the stone's creator nullifying the magic, or the destruction of the stone itself.

"GRRRAAAAAAAARRRRRRRRR!" he screamed as he stood and rushed the phalanx.

Again, a soldier broke ranks to escape. The remaining soldiers now had their spears positioned to repel the huge Urk. Seeing this, he once more used the long blade of his sword to brush aside the weapons and utilized the enemy's shields as a ramp to get to the other side.

He leapt over the phalanx and sprang off another shield on the far side, killing two of them with a stroke of his blade.

"You cannot run!" he roared.

"GRRRAAAAARRRRRRRR!"

He leapt again and landed just behind the now totally panicking Talotian in retreat, and cleaved the Human in half with his mighty weapon. The man fell in two pieces, his hardened leather armour sliced clean through.

Morally destroyed, the rest of the phalanx broke ranks and began to retreat. This was too much! The Urk lord could not be stopped!

"GRAAAAARRRRRRRRRRRR!" he roared as he dropped his sword to the ground and pulled a long, sharpened pole from the ground. He launched the makeshift javelin into the air, and before it struck, he had launched another and was reaching for a third. Six of the nine impaling poles he had earlier set up for throwing, struck home as the Talotians ran for their lives screaming in sheer terror.

Grarr was now roaring over and over. He was not even using words at this point, simply projecting his fury. It only took eleven of the twenty crossbow bolts he had prepared, to take down the remaining Talotians.

Then he screamed another challenge, "Is this the best you have?! Can you do no better?!" he taunted them over and over.

"I am here! Do you not want *me*?! Have you not dreamed of the day you would slay *me*?" He roared at the fortress. "What are you waiting for, cowards?! Swine! Filth! I am *here!*"

Finally, a shadow could be seen emerging from the sloping passage just beyond the great doors. At first he thought it was water, somehow climbing the slope and flowing out and into the courtyard. But, as it began to ooze out of the gatehouse and into the sunlight, he was able to discern what this was.

This was hate. Pure hate manifested into a magical cloud of blackness and shadow. A quazi-darkness elemental!

In its midst he could now make out a tall, thin man in dark robes. A sorcerer! He was *conjuring* the evil force. The sooty-black, gaseous substance clung to the ground and began to swirl around the new enemy.

Still in the safety of the fortress gatehouse, the spell caster was just outside of Grarr's crossbow range, or he would have been peppered with shots by then. He seemed familiar somehow, but the dark cloud soon hid his features, as he vanished all together.

Grarr's attention was then captured by something else. Behind the swirling black mass was a hoard of Talotians. More than he would be able to face alone—an army. Among them were a vast number of Scave, and every other spot was filled by a plague of rats.

He took notice that there were no Goblins around. This he had expected, despite the fact they they would have been an easy force for Calabac to employ. Grarr's battle cry is uniquely his, and among Goblin-kind Grarr is considered a sort of hero.

Once they heard his voice any Goblins that might have been in that place would have most probably left the area, or opted to join him. The lack of the latter could only have meant there was enough of a force within that fortress, to deter the Goblins from switching sides. By now they would be vacating the fortress from any exit they could find or make and heading back home.

He tried to reach the weapon that was sticking from his back, but could not. He was only causing more damage. Blood was now dripping from his hand and he could feel the warmth of it running down his left side and into his boot. He had to hold on. He had to give the Injoke a head start on these swine and vermin.

The black mass was swirling into a vortex around the area where the red robed figure had been. Grarr could hear him speaking evil incantations. His voice was gradually rising in intensity.

Hey—I said *gradually*. For once it wasn't *suddenly!!* Hootspa!

Where was I?

Oh yeah…

The red robed figure was now using his voice to coax the black mass into something terrible. This was a piece of *un*living night. A portion of the night, torn away and stolen from the other side of the world. Placed here, twisted and corrupted, to defy the sun and allow the movement of Calabac's evil army.

Suddenly…

Oy!

Suddenly the silouetted man was gone, as though he'd sunk into the ground in a fraction of a second. With that, the night quazi-elemental-thing then moved toward Grarr, and as it did it grew in size and mass.

Grarr was not a dummy by far. He grabbed up the bolts left sticking in the ground, sheathed his sword, and as the shadow was approaching him, he backed away. Like a blot of ink in a glass of water, the manifested entity of hate moved after him, forcing him to retreat in order to stay one step ahead of it.

Just inside the edge of the now pulsing, cloud-sized shadow, lurked hundreds of rats, Scave, and Talotians. The Talotians had been bolstered by Calabac's magic. (I am not calling his magic hootspa anymore. It would be a sacrilege to compare the two).

Their physical prowess, skill with their weapons, and even morale had been boosted, much the same way I had bolstered Musky's abilities. Their race, already stronger and tougher than normal Humans, had been made into super soldiers by the evil magic. The sorcerer obviously knew what he was facing in this unexpected assault from the Blood Baron.

Being an Urk, Grarr was not unknown among those who live long and were educated. His infamy in Talot was well known to Calabac. It is why the sorcerer hired the Talotians in the first place. They had jumped at a chance to have a powerful, magic practitioner to support them on a crusade, against an enemy that they would otherwise be hesitant to attack. They feared reminding Grarr that they even existed.

The Blood Baron once led an assault on Talot for ten years that resulted in the destruction of every village in the entire country. Only the four cities were left standing. Then the Urk war lord simply vanished, never to be heard from again for many generations—until now.

Calabac had known where Grarr was, in a general sense. He had sent envoys to find the Urk, but most of those never returned, and those who had returned had done so empty handed.

It had taken Calabac more than a century to eventually find Grarr. Finally, the sorcerer had gained the opportunity to watch the

Urk closely for several years, and from close by.

Now he needed Grarr dead.

Calabac knew all too well the danger involved with facing the Blood Baron, and so had never challenged him before. He had looked Grarr straight in the eyes, hoping that a mighty war master like him would prove to be useful.

But this, here and now would be the last time. It would have to be. Grarr could not be turned. Calabac had finally come to that conclusion.

An enemy like Grarr could not be allowed to exist. A strategic genius, the likes of Grarr was far too much of a threat to tolerate. Calabac needed this Urk dead and was pulling out a few wild cards to achieve just that end.

After several moments of cat and mouse, the cloud suddenly swelled in size and quickly moved forward. Grarr was barely able to avoid its cold embrace, or the sudden swarm of the Scave and their infestation of hundreds of vile rodents, bent on tasting his flesh.

As a group they moved, like an ebbing tide, reaching closer, then retreating, yet ever moving forward. These were not normal rats and were under the magical influence of Calabac. They would not break, nor would their Scave masters, or the sub-human soldiers who drove them forward. They had been stirred into a blood frenzy, yet unwilling to leave the cloud where they were far more dangerous.

"GRRRAAAARRRRRRRR!" the Urk roared, and the enemy paused momentarily, but still they came. This was the work of a powerful sorcerer, not an amateur at all. Their fear was no longer an option. Retreat was the *sound* maneuver at this juncture.

"GRRRAAAARRRRRRRR!" he roared as he moved down the road and past a landslide that the Troll had caused. Even in the state they were in, Grarr's battle cry was enough to make them pause for a second or two in their advance each time they heard it.

He was torn between facing this small army, or possibly leading it right down the road and into the Troll.

He eventually decided that the Injoke was not as stupid as he was agile and strong, and he could have descended the cliff easily with the wagon under his arm—he was counting on it.

So he lured the cloud away from the fortress.

Once over the landslide and back on the road, he loaded a crossbow bolt and fired it into the massive shadow. It struck a lesser Scave in the face, killing it instantly. Like zombies the others stepped over its limp form, eventually pushing it aside and over the cliff, before continuing on.

Grarr repeated this action several more times before coming to face the truth that he only had so many bolts, and it was folly to continue firing at a force of this size.

Grunting in pain, he kept moving away from the cloud and along the road. At this point he was running and moving at a good pace down the gentle slope, but his wound was bleeding rapidly. In mid-stride he drew bandages from his pouch and stuffed them under his armour, just behind his shoulder.

The road wrapped around a third of the mountain, and at its north face it sloped down into a copse of trees and eventually to the roads to both Al'Lankmire to the west, and Briarwood to the northeast.

Here he turned and descended the stony north face of the sleeping volcano. As agile and fast as he was...

Keep in mind we are speaking about Durik's combat instructor. This guy *has* written books on combat tactics and techniques. He is like so freakin' scary you cannot imagine. Are you following me here?

Good.

Now, where was I?

Oh yeah...

As agile and fast as Grarr was, this choice of action allowed the shadow to catch up to him somewhat. By the time he was at the bottom of the mountain and crossing the Imperial highway in the valley below, two hours had passed and the black cloud had come to be only a few hundred feet away from him.

Slowly but surely, it was catching up to him. The distance he had gained on the road was now halved and the cloud was still coming strong.

He paused for a few seconds to cough and catch his breath. The pain in his shoulder was now excruciating. He could feel his shoulder blade splintering and giving way to the point of the bolt, but he was unable to reach it with his armour still on.

Twice he faced single attackers whose courage allowed them a brief, yet fatal, reprieve from the darkness of the cloud.

He trudged on toward the east, through thin bushland, and hills. Ever downward toward the River Sylvania, hoping to lose them in the marshes. Looking down at his feet, he winced from pain and shook his head in frustration. He was now leaving a trail of blood that a clam with a lobotomy could follow.

He made his way across the valley, with each step the bolt coming closer to reaching his lung. Before he reached the marshes, he was beginning to feel cold. The sun was setting, and its rays were defused by the shadows of the mountains.

He thought he noticed movement among the reeds in the far distance to the northwest, but soon dismissed it as tricks of the setting sun, combined with his loss of blood and sheer exhaustion. His shadow stretched toward the east against golden marsh grasses now laid flat by the early autumn winds.

Eventually he managed to reach the river and walked the south shore until he found a shallow ford. This, too, gave the enemy a chance to gain ground. Several more times lone Talotians broke ranks in a frenzy and rushed him, only to fall to their deaths against him.

With a shudder he stepped into the freezing waters and struggled his way across the rapidly moving current.

Halfway across the river, Grarr was forced to stop so as to strangle a Talotian and drown him. His comrades, even in their state of insane frenzy, watching in horror from the south banks.

In some places the water was above his waist, and still he was able to maintain his footing and balance, but his legs were beginning to feel numb in the frigid rapids.

Pausing for short moment, he noticed his blood mingling with the swirling waters, and that of his latest victim. He was tempted to let go, to let the cold water carry him to the bottom of the river and out to the sea, but the thought of him not being, at the very least, a nuisance to the enemy in his last moments, was more than he was willing to tolerate.

Finally he reached the north bank and fell from exhaustion, his life's blood now streaming over his back and soaking into the cotton padding of his armour. He could feel the warm liquid leaking into a puncture in the backside of his left lung now.

On top of his sheer size and acrobatic ability, Grarr was also in extreme peak physical condition. Even so, he had just descended a mountain, over extremely treacherous terrain at full speed, and crossed a valley, only to wade across a cold mountain river with a barbed metal shaft making its way through his back. Give him a break. He's middle-aged for crying out loud!

"GRRRAAAAARRRRRR!" he roared defiantly and after only a couple seconds of rest he got to his feet and searched around the north bank of the river for a suitable place to make a last stand. He could see over his shoulder that the cloud was now on the south shore, preparing to cross.

Farther ahead, he noticed a small grassy knoll a few hundred feet from shore, that he had previously missed, and decided to make for it. At least he could gain some semblance of high ground.

He had never travelled this way before. He was in a wetland and wearing full plate armour, wallowing through tangles of marsh grass, dead brush and water holes with a bolt in his back, bleeding profusely and getting weaker by the minute.

He had a means to instantly heal himself, but the bolt had pierced metal, flesh, and his shoulder blade, and was now entering his lung. To heal the wound magically now would waste his elixir, as the bolt would still be inside of him, creating more wounds with every movement he made.

He had to remove the bolt.

It was absolutely incredible how he had been able to wield his weapon under such agonizing pain.

"GRRRAAAAAARRRRRRR!"

He moved toward the hillock, dragging his sword, his arm hanging limply at his side, his bright green blood leaking from him and dripping from his numb fingers. It sprayed over the dry swamp grasses with every breath he exhaled.

The sound of his rage was still the only thing that was slowing the cloud down. Soon, however, his voice would be completely gone as his lung filled with his own blood.

His thoughts turned to Durik, and me, and he was happy then, that I had come into their lives, and that Durik would have someone to take care of him after...

The cloud was halfway across the river now, sixty or seventy feet—and closing. He dragged his left leg, the pain now moving through his body, the bolt still cutting into him with his every step. He had to reach the hill so he could kill a few more of them. He needed that high ground, what little it was.

Blood was leaking from the many intricate joints of his armoured boots, and now his whole suit seemed to glow with it.

As he approached the grassy knoll, it wavered in front of his vision. He stumbled and climbed the hillock on his knees. Every slight breeze was a frigid, chilling reminder that he was now running out of blood.

Sooner than he had hoped, the cloud was across the river and well over the banks, only forty feet away.

In the west, the sun would be setting completely soon. Twilight had arrived.

His anger was building. He was preparing to fight his final battle.

At least he was going to make some good from it all. At least he would not be dying in vain. Beornag had escaped with the Gnomes.

Weakened beyond recovery he shivered violently, convulsing from a cold that should have killed him long ago; a cold deep inside his body. But even hypothermia and shock could not stop him, and he held on, still willing to kill a few more of them.

Alas, coughing violently, he fell to the ground on one knee at the top of the rise, convulsing from the cold.

Even then, the pitch-black cloud surrounded him. He saw the bright, glowing, green trail of his own blood through the cloud and across the marsh, like a river of light through the almost pitch-dark shadow that was still engulfing the knoll.

He rolled over to one side and cringed in pain as he snapped the end of the ballista bolt off.

The fact that he lived on went against all reality. "Aaaaaagh!" Blood sprayed from his mouth and nose as he reeled in pain.

The dark force ascended the hill as he desperately tried to reach the buckle for his shoulder plate and release it, blood rattling and bubbling in his lung with every breath.

His pain was beyond belief. He could hear the razor-sharp tip of the bolt scratching and tearing through sinew and ribcage. It was reverberating through his skeleton and echoing in his skull.

The effects were maddening.

He coughed out a splattering of blood and then choked up

more, as the things in the cloud were only ten feet away and reaching out into the failing sunlight to grasp at the air, only inches from his bleeding body.

"*Grr...rrraarr...rr!*" he tried to scream, one last time, blood spewing out of his mouth as he rose again to one knee defiantly.

This time the sound would not carry far.

The first to touch him was a rat that rushed ahead and attempted to jump out of the cloud and onto his chest.

He batted it away and back into the living shadow of evil.

Next was a Talotian, who was stupid enough to think he was worthy to touch the Blood Baron.

Grarr took hold of his assailant's arm and pulled him out of the shadow, breaking his wrist.

The man's eyes cleared for a split second as he left the magical effects of the cloud.

He was terrified and screamed out loud.

Then he was dying as the Baron tore out his throat with a single bite.

The Talotian fell to the ground, dead, with his blood spewing out all over the coming wave of evil.

However, here Grarr also fell. He now lay on his back, warm blood streaming down his throat as he drowned in the stuff.

He tried to shake his head while the world was getting darker. Cold shivering was now overtaking him as he looked up at the night sky, but the stars could not be found.

His ears were assaulted with the sounds of screeching, and the cries of the horde, as a multitude of hands and paws began pulling at his armour, his feet, his arms—pulling at him from all directions.

His armour was torn from him as he lay there near lifeless, his last life's blood draining from the bolt now sticking out from a hole in his chest. It had made its way through, and now he would die.

Screaming and squealing with lust and hunger, they were

dragging his body around like a broken rag doll. They laughed and snickered, one last insult to his honour, while prying at his armour and destroying it piece by piece. His dagger sheath was torn from his belt. His sword sheath ripped from his back. They stripped him of everything.

He knew they would take his body and display it to the rest of the army—and most probably parade it all the way back to their ice lands. Comanding the enemy was an officer of Talot, who took up the sword, Deathwind, for his own.

As each second passed he was swept further from what was happening. Now the sounds were getting faint, he didn't even notice that he was being pulled at from all sides anymore. A strange, terrifying peace was slipping over him like a thick blanket, pulled over his mouth and nose. Breathing had become so very difficult.

He looked up into the sky again and choked up more blood. They had paused in their revelry, and he was rolled over on his back again. He thought he saw stars, but this time his were eyes closed.

All fell silent.

He hadn't the strength to even open his eyelids. His heart beat one last time in his ears. He thought he smelled lavender and honeysuckle on the breeze, but that was impossible, as he was not breathing.

Then, once again, they were pulling at him, dragging him, as the black cloud of darkness closed in, and all was no more.

CHAPTER - 25

WHAT!? THAT'S IT?!

Of course that's not *it*. Did I not mention that I'm kinda smart? Hunh?

Well, I am. So don't worry kids, this story continues in another book. I didn't have enough jewels and gold and wealth left over to pay for having it published in one giant, gold-plated, red patent leather-bound, handwritten in calligraphy versions for everyone— so, for now anyway, these paper versions will have to do.

What do we know so far about the story, you ask? Well lets recap shall we?

Yours truly was captured by the evil sorcerer Calabac, along with my trusty companion and saviour, Musky.

About to be interrogated and worse, we were stripped of our weapons, bound and gagged, and with no means of escape in sight. No hootspa to cast, no poison dart to fire, and the key to the very survival of the future of the world was trapped inside of a pocket dimension, inside another pocket dimension, inside a pouch on my belt that the enemy had failed to search—as of yet.

Durik, once rescued by Musky and me, proceeded to enter The Bong where he melded with the swirling sparkling stuff inside, and vanished all together. A large group of Gnomes, surrounding the glass wonder, were also there, awaiting the return of the Paladin of Shiddumbuzzin.

Beornag, had infiltrated the enemy base and had dispatched many of their defenders while at the same time reducing the fortress entryway, and a large portion of the indoor market to a septic nightmare!

Raz had started a return trip to Briarwood, in order to warn the city of the army coming from the west, and had not been heard from since.

Grarr, our beloved leader and executive director, had fallen in battle against impossible numbers and magical forces.

He had sacrificed himself as bait to lure the fortress defenders away from the Troll and a large group of rescued Gnomes, who were attempting to escape down the side of the mountain.

Kids, the enemy had shown his quality to be the worst that evil could offer. His total purpose still a mystery to me, I had now only assumed that the mighty legions of the dead were a force with which to crush Briarwood.

I gotta tell ya right then and there, it didn't look so good for any of us.

Even the Troll, who was now inside the mighty fortress, and had been victorious in his siege and entry, was also right in the very *belly* of the beast, with no one to guide or advise him. Surely his luck would sooner or later run out and he too would be captured, or worse.

Now, like I said, I hate to leave you kids on a cliffhanger. This is just where one third of the story ended. It's as close to a perfect one third as I could get. Cut me some slack already. Oy.

However, there's still so much to tell, and so much to smoke. You cannot imagine how much...to smoke I mean...and to tell as well, I guess.

So, for now, be nice to each other and try smiling and laughing instead of frowning and cursing. Once I tally up my ultra-billions from book sales, I will publish the next installment of my story...

The Chronicles of the Great Neblinski

Book Two

MONSTERS!

AUTHOR BIO

Mark was born in Halifax, Nova Scotia, Canada, the youngest of 5 siblings.

He began his adult life as an artist carving stone and antler, painting, and any other medium of art he could get his hands on.

Later, in his thirties he began to write fantasy stories and included illustrations.

During his late forties he revisited his stories and began to write them into a manuscript.

The Chronicles of the Great Neblinski, a story of companionship, tolerance, loyalty, devotion to friendship, and healing.

Mark's author influences are Douglas Adams, J.R.R. Tolkien, Robert E. Howard, Michael Moorcock, and Frank Herbert, which inspired him to write The Chronicles of the Great Neblinski.

Today, Mark lives in Ontario, Canada, with his friend, their parrots, and a pair of giant wolfdogs, where he still makes art, composes music, and continues to write fantastical stories.